For Barbara Kelly,

I hope you enjoy the writing. I sure loved every minute of it. Thanks again for your support.

Carolyn

11/14/93

A TALE OF TWO TAPESTRIES

CAROLYN L. MARTIN, PH.D.

THE SILC FOUNDATION
PALM BEACH
FLORIDA

Published by:
THE SILC FOUNDATION, Inc.
2875 Ocean Avenue
Palm Beach, Florida 33480

Copyright 1988, 1990, 1993 by Carolyn
Martin, Ph.D., ISBN 0-9637148-0-5

Grateful acknowledgment is made for
permission to quote from the following:
"Sitting on the Dock of the Bay" and "I'm
Just Wild About Saffron."

Printed in the United States of America

Dedication:

To Goethe, whose 200th year anniversary
of his Italian Journey in 1987, led me to
retrace his steps through Italy and
Sicily where I discovered the clues
leading to this novel.

A TALE OF

TWO TAPESTRIES

PROLOGUE

Asia Minor, Maonia, Lydia (present day

Manisa, Turkey).

Circa 2000 B.C.

ARACHNE'S MYTH

"Cut her down," Idmon pleaded in anguish, unable to see through his blurring, rushing tears. He couldn't bear seeing the hanging form of his precious only child, Arachne, her thin lips darkening and her pale face bleeding profusely from the deep gashes and from the yarn that she'd wound into a noose around her neck. Idmon held onto her knees and felt a convulsive shudder rack through her delicate body, attesting to some last vestige of life.

Feeling as though his old heart would break, he threw himself on the ground, moaning in agony and begging for mercy from Athena, standing tall, her long, blond hair tucked tightly under her helmet and her regal, blue eyes showing no sign of pity. Her shuttle hung loosely in her hand, covered with Arachne's blood.

"For Zeus' sake, have mercy...please...stop this before it's too late." Idmon's voice quivered as he turned his bleary red eyes away, unable to look at his daughter's once perfect, beautiful face, unable to hold up under the unbearable agony of her pain which burned in him as though it were his own. "Take me instead. Oh...I beg you...take me...take me..." He moaned over and over.

The bright gazes of the fair Lydian nymphs dimmed. "Yes, please, Athena, be merciful," they cried in high pitched chorus. Gathered from the vineyards of Tmolus and the waters of Pactolus, they had come to witness the great spinning contest between the goddess and the mortal, but they had no idea that Arachne's exquisite, yet sensational masterpiece, would cost her this.

Finally, Athena coldly responded, staring expressionless at the hanging girl. "And why should I reverse her fate? It was she who challenged me to create a more perfect tapestry than human hands could spin. It was her hubris, her silly pride which denied my divine inspiration. I gave her her chance and she refused to admit her error. And just look at what she has created! You all say it is perfect. But no human should ever lay eyes on such a mortally harmful work. It is cursed, and it will doom the entire race if they gaze upon such a dastardly act. And to think she showed my own great father Zeus and all the other gods mating like common animals with your maidens." Athena cringed, her eyes greatly offended by the work's graphic depiction.

Zeus, as the great white swan, hovers over Leda's pale thighs. She throws back her raven hair, and her opal eyes widen in shock as he beats his broad feathered wings, his large black beak clasping the nape of her neck. Again, Arachne portrays Zeus as the great white bull. Europa's long slender legs straddle his broad back; her shiny, golden locks spread over her breasts as he kidnaps her and she tenaciously clings to the sharp horns. It springs over the waves, dampening her curls and spraying her delicate feet as she cries for help and looks longingly back at her distant shore which disappears in the mist.

Athena could stand no more. With fiery eyes, she glanced back at Arachne whose skin darkened to bruised blues and purples. "And why should I have mercy on someone so selfish that she has concern for no one but herself, someone who wanted fame more than life, someone who cared less for defiling her gods. She has taken no responsibility for her art and instead has used her greatest gift for her own self-serving ends. No, she has rightfully hung herself."

"Please forgive me, your goddess." Idmon lifted his suffering eyes and protected his face with his hands. "And do not strike me dead for saying so, but she hung herself to escape your torture. I of all people know of my daughter's ambition, of her headstrongness and her inability to answer to no one, but...look at her face." Idmon's voice broke; but determined, he tried to rise, an unbearable sadness burderning his heart. "Please, Athena, take her tapestry, finish destroying it, or hide it forever from human eyes, but, please, please let my daughter live."

A slow oozing breath, as though it were her last, escaped Arachne's lips. It sounded like daggers ripping through Idmon's chest.

But Athena resisted, shifted her austere gaze to her own majestic tapestry, and smiled approvingly at her recreation of the beginning of time. The great flood rushes into Middle Earth and fills the former Garden of Eden with the deep blue water of the Mediterranean Sea. Cecrops, the Mound of Mars, raises its red, rocky back and emerges from the azure sea. In its corners, "Danger" is woven in blood red rubies and hangs above the tortured faces of Antigone, moaning over the cold, stony face of Haemon and still paying for the tragic transgressions of her father Oedipus with his mother. Even the great King Cinyras, with his shining, suffering eyes as he begs for mercy on the cold temple steps, is not exempt, for he too must pay for his incestuous relationship with his daughter.

Even though it took only seconds for Athena's admiring eyes to scan her work, Idmon knew that his daughter had only a breath of life left in her fragile body. Growing more desperate than he even thought possible, he threw himself at the goddess' feet and tried to reason with her.

"You say my daughter has created an ill for the people to see - a bad example for them to follow, but look at your own tapestry, Athena. These tragic families

were forever split asunder because of
incest between these fathers and their
daughters. I know my daughter has
depicted a most detestable act, but
incest is no better example. Why not hide
them both forever? Here, take my urns,
these amphoras are my prize possessions;
I have used them for storing my phocis
purple dye that Arachne used for her
work, and they are perfect for protecting
the tapestries. They are water tight, air
tight, and their seal surpasses even
those used by the Egyptian embalmers for
their most revered pharoahs. Take them.
Hide the tapestries in the deepest,
darkest bowels of the earth, so that
human eyes will never again look upon
such heinous acts. But I beg you,
please, please let my daughter live."

"Yes, Yes, Athena, it is wise," the
nymphs cried in chorus. "Let Arachne
live. You, the perfect born from your
father's head. Let the people know you
are Zeus' true forgiving daughter. Let
the world remember you as a just
goddess."

For once, Athena listened. She saw
the wisdom of the nymphs, heard the
reasonableness of the old man, and even
felt a moment of mercy for the wayward
girl. With a quick slash of her powerful
weapon, she cut down the dying Arachne.

A low groan escaped from Idmon's
throat as he threw his body forward over
his daughter's limp form, protecting her
with his body, with his life. "My
Darling, my only child, my precious one,
breathe, oh please do not leave me. You
are all I have in this world. It's always

been just you and me. You are my soul, my heart, my being. I cannot live without you. If you die, I want to die with you."

Still there was no breath as Idmon continued moaning in Arachne's ear, whispering his love as his tears flowed all over her cheeks and her blood covered his face. But her body lay cold and quiet.

Again, he pressed his lips to her ear and begged her to respond, his heart pounding past its limits. "Don't die, my precious, sweet girl, don't die."

A second passed when suddenly a shutter racked through Arachne's body. Her chest rattled as she choked and gasped for breath.

Her eyes flew open, but all she could see was Athena's gold-sandaled feet firmly planted in front of her face. Without even looking up at her, her wild, tormented eyes bore the panic of an animal before being sacrificed. In one lurching, lunging moment, Arachne heaved her body to her knees and hands and tossed her suffering father aside. Making one last bold attempt to flee for her life, she tried to crawl away from the austere goddess.

But Athena had a definite purpose for the audacious girl. In her divine, unemotional mind, she knew the humans needed to be taught a hard lesson to prevent their extinction by forever burning in their memory an image of her laws forbidding sodomy and incest.

"Yes, live," she raised her deep voice as she reached under Medusa's breastplate and pulled out Hecate's black droppings, "so that you and your offspring will weave your venomous webs forever and remind all never to repeat these dastardly acts or they too will suffer similar, horrible deaths."

And as she sprinkled the deadly herbs, Arachne's body shrivelled and shrank until only her torso remained in tact. Her writhing screams ripped through the air and pierced the ears. They did not stop when her legs and arms were thin threads and her red hair singed black. As she continued screaming in horror beyond horror and feeling unbearable pain, her fingers extended into wiry legs on which she crawled away, only not as a human. Her movments appeared more like those of the spider, the arachnids who would eternally portray her fate.

Her brokenhearted father lay in a crumbled heap and never rose from Athena's foreboding shadow on the ground. He never saw the nymphs roll the tapestries, place them in the amphoras, seal them with the miraculous sealant, and load them onto Athena's chariot where she would take them to the most secret, sacred spot on earth and hide them away forever.

"Arachne's Myth," first recorded in Ovid's <u>Metamorphosis</u>, 8A.D., Book VI, and here reconstructed.

PART I: <u>ARACHNE'S TAPESTRY</u>
Chapter I: "This is no Myth"

Two Mafia publishers tracked down me and my dwarf sidekick. They trailed us like narcotic dogs, sniffing for my manuscript; from New York to San Francisco, they could smell the dirty scent of money that they knew the book would bring.

Clutching the precious work like a newborn, we entered the San Francisco office. We were certain that the work would be safe in the female publisher's hands, for we were sure we had outsmarted and lost the shrewd, calloused men.

"Yes, may I help you?" The middle-aged secretary asked in a strange voice.

"Yes, thank you, we called about your advertisement for new works. I'm Charla Morrow, the author, and he's...."

"Oh, of course, won't you wait in the inner office?" She said, directing us to the door behind her plexiglass window. The click of the lock sounded louder than life as the door closed behind us.

We heard the mumble of male voices before the door burst open and in walked the Mafia publishers.

"It's a set up!" I screamed, but the ominous clicking lock foretold our fate. It was too late to run.

The greasy, slicked back hair of the New York publisher darkened the door. Evil and death followed him and his equally dark yet smaller partner in crime who immediately attacked and began torturing my cohort.

Together, as I watched, their sharp, razor styled instrument skinned him alive. In horror, in absolute horror and disgust, as his writhing, pink jelliness and bloody, bloody mass of flesh slumped to the floor behind the desk, I witnessed his gory death.

Then, in shock and curdling silence, I realized that my torture was next. My eyes shifted from the bright red pool with the pink shining, fleshy ghastliness to the blackest pools of evil intent.

Right in front of my eyes, he held up the tool of torture - a file, a long, pointed file with deeply edged metal grooves that were ridged with sharp, razor like wedges. Closer and closer it came to my face. Until, in horror beyond horror, I felt the cold metal contact of the sharp file on my nose. With eyes opened incredibly wide, I saw the moving, scraping metal file away the flesh until it was a bloody stump.

"Oh, my God! Oh, my God, No, No!" I shrieked as I felt waves of darkness roll over.

I bolted upright in bed as cold shivers topped with goosebumps rippled my skin, ran up and down my spine and racked convulsively through every fiber in me. Squelching the nausea that swelled from the depths as I recalled the jellied flesh lying in the pool of blood, I realized that what had awakened me was the incessantly ringing doorbell. "Thank God," I said, thinking I might otherwise have died in my sleep; I grabbed my robe and rushed down the stairs to the front door.

It was Federal Express with the manuscript of my first novel. My heart fell as I signed; adrenalin shot through me at the thought of my dream being precognitive. Ripping the envelope open, I froze in shock at the publisher's words: "File it."

"Oh, shit!" I cried, sinking to my knees and clutching the letter in a tight ball. In shock, I didn't know whether to cry, collapse, curse, or try and ignore it until I could talk to Jane who was on her way over to walk with me to the office for our meeting.

I decided on the latter, since, upon looking at the clock, I realized that she'd be here any minute and I wasn't ready. No one was as prompt as my sister. From childhood, she had complained about my tardiness, telling me it was just so I could get attention.

"And this morning, I really need attention," I moaned, grabbing my clothes and running around like a wild woman. I needed Jane's expertise to tell me what the awful dream meant.

The doorbell was incessantly ringing again, and I could hear Jane yelling, "If you're late, I'm not waiting for you." I could also hear her heels descending the stairs.

"No, Jane, don't leave. This is important. Hold on." I screamed at the top of my lungs, snatched my briefcase off the table, jammed my arms into my jacket, and bolted for the door.

Stepping out into the sultry Key West air was like stepping into a steambath fully clothed. The blast of oven hot air hit me so hard that I reeled backwards, feeling a little lightheaded. Better slow down, I warned myself, forcing myself to concentrate on the ocean's bright turquoise color, but it calmed me only for a second. Jane was getting away.

"Jane!" I yelled again, scampering down the stairs and immediately starting to perspire. But she didn't even hear me. "Wait. You must wait. You have to listen to this horrible dream I just had. Jane?" Now I was desperate. I leaped the last steps with my heels wobbling as they hit the sidewalk running.

She never even turned around once to see me racing to catch her and looking as ridiculous as a teenager walking in high heels for the first time. As fast as most people jog, Jane moved gracefully along in heels much higher than mine. She crossed the street, stopping traffic as she usually did and ignoring it all as though she never even heard the howls and whistles - just scooted in front of a bicyclist, who'd stopped to stare at her, and kept moving.

Sweat immediately trickled into my eyes, causing them to sting and my mascara to run. "Damn!" I muttered, having to wait on the curb when not one bicycle slowed to let me cross. I ripped off my jacket, slung it over my shoulder and forced my way behind a rickshaw driver heading for Malory Square. "Jane, I'm going to tell the whole world this horrible dream if you don't wait for me, and you'll be ashamed of me. You'll...."

She plugged her ears which always made me furious. She'd just lightly press her fingers to her dainty earlobes which somehow shut out anything she didn't want to hear. "We'll discuss it after this meeting. Final. There is no time now," she calmly but firmly told me as I caught up with her after a few blocks when the old, uneven sidewalk threatened her fast, clicking heels. "And just who are we to thank for giving us such short notice? And just what is this emergency meeting?" She asked sarcastically and without any shortness of breath; she sped up again when the sidewalk smoothed out by the Hemingway House where his seven-toed cats stretched out lazily in the hot, morning sun atop the brick wall.

"You must listen to me now! Jane, you simply can't imagine how horrible this dream was." I demanded, grabbing her arm and forcing her to stop. I had to catch my breath and squelch the nausea I felt when I spilled the whole dream out to her. Chills again racked my body and sweat popped out on my forehead as I concluded with, "They were going to file me alive if I hadn't woke up, Jane, and with this razor sharp file with serrated groves that...."

She wiggled out of my grasp, lifted her right eyebrow, cast a sharp sidelong look at me with her piercing blue eyes, that cut right through me, then took off walking again at an even faster gait.

Now my hair was getting damp and my blouse was sticking to me, but I somehow managed to stay in step beside her. "Oh, my God, Jane. What...What if it's precognitive?" I blurted, horrified and aghast at the thought of the dream coming true, but experiencing a sinking feeling that warned me it might. My stomach always tells the truth, I thought, more desperate than ever to force Jane to help me. When I grabbed her arm this time, clenching it tightly, she knew I wasn't letting go.

"You are just determined, aren't you, to make us late," she complained, but she stopped and faced me head-on. "Okay, Charla. But you know that only time will tell. Look what you created in your novel, showing someone so self-destructive that she rolled from one abusive man's bed to another with only the mask changing on the same face. And you and I both know who "She" is. But, regardless, you know it's symbolic." Upon seeing my face turn sickly pale and ashen, she softened somewhat, saying. "Look, I realize you're upset, but this is <u>not</u> the time to discuss the same old childhood problem that you've had filed away," she half chuckled as only a psychiatrist could so knowingly do, "and probably filed alive for years."

"It's not funny," I protested in a small wounded voice, her words cutting deep as the images and dreams of men abusing me rolled quickly through my mind.

"No, silly, not funny, ironic. Lighten up. Besides, you know very well that something buried for that long is going to erupt at the most inconvenient times, so handle it. Where's your sense of humor?" She reminded me, but I didn't feel like laughing about anything. Without realizing it, Jane could easily intimidate me with her probing, insensitive words, especially when they hit home so squarely.

My face fell as I tried concealing my increasing pain over my horrendous nightmare and my disappointment in her not helping me with immediate release from the torturing grip it had on me.

"I'm not ignoring your dream, okay?" She said guiltily when my glumness looked like it could easily turn into tears. "But I don't understand why you insist on taking everything so personally. Your self-importance amazes me," she added which sure enough caused the tears to flow. I hung my head lower, hoping that she'd soften and not be so abrupt. It worked. Her voice lowered. "Sis, do you actually think you're alone in having this problem? Well, you're not! It's no myth that you're one of millions of women who've had a tyrant for a father, the worst possible example of an authority figure. And then they go on to choose the same kind of man to marry. Look at the bright side - you've survived that. And don't forget, he was my dad too. But I've already done my homework on Dad. All those awful things he said about us were really about him. Those were projections. Don't you get it? You must reprogram. When are you going to start? You're already 33." It didn't take long for Jane to revert back to her old confrontative self.

Her impersonal words made me to feel even smaller and more hurt. I braced myself, my eyes wincing with pain and resistance. But Jane surprised me. She reached out and hugged me so warmly that it made me start crying again.

"Come on, Sis. Give it up. Turn it around. You're already on your way. You're finally involved with someone who treats you like an equal, and he's a terrific guy. Don't blow it." She paused, waiting for me to get control of myself. Her mentioning Bill helped, and her giving me attention when I was acting so negative amazed me. "Good, now how about it?" She asked kindly, "Ready for this meeting?"

I slowly shook my head, forcing myself to listen. Then, with some reluctance, I shrugged as she pushed back my damp, hot hair that lay heavily on my back.

Upon seeing that I was fine, she took off swiftly walking again. "Good, now would you please tell me about this sudden meeting this morning? It'd better be of ultimate importance since we're half killing ourselves to get there. What time is it starting again?" She flicked away the tiny bead of perspiration that formed on her powder perfect forehead and shook out her long red hair that seemed to catch on fire in the intense sun. Despite my gnawing pain and irritability, I recalled all those times when we were kids and she'd be cool as a cucumber while I was so unladylike sweating away. And all those times when everyone would rave over how beautiful she was. And with brains!

I shoved my watch up in her face; and when she realized the meeting had already started, she broke into a run which soon caused even Jane's brow to shine. I smiled with some sort of smug satisfaction as we raced up to the entrance of the SILC Foundation. "And why so <u>secretive</u>?" She complained, breathing heavily as she paused to check out the tinted windows of our longest limo, parked in the circle drive. The car was running, and the chauffeur nervously waved, acting as though he were ready for a quick getaway. "What is this meeting about?" She questioned again as we exchanged concerned glances.

"I don't know," I half responded. I was in no mood for a meeting. Besides, I was burning up. My hair stuck to my face; small droplets were forming on my upper lip and smudging my lipstick. Plus, my wet aqua blouse had turned a sickly blue green. Regardless of what Jane had said, I couldn't think of anything but the writhing, skinned alive dwarf and his jelly pink flesh floating in the thick blood behind the publisher's desk. I felt like I was going to throw up. Jane shot me one of those get a grip on yourself looks. "Oh, yeah. Now I remember. Don said that a courier had hand delivered a letter. Something about a tapestry."

"A tapestry?" Jane looked back at me as though I'd lost my mind. We crossed under the sculptured driftwood caption, tresseled with brilliant yellow flowering vines and welcoming us with - "The

Science in Literature Communications Center."

I took a deep breath, inhaling the musky odor of the ancient ficus. The fern brushed our feet as we sped past the library and pool, past the cabanas and gazebo until we reached the grand old conch house, with its wrought iron balconies and haunting turrets.

"Hold on a second," I told Jane. "I know I look awful." I pulled out a mirror and examined myself, finding fault with my emotional filled eyes now changed to depressing dark green. My hair looked worse, totally out of control. Jane waited impatiently, with, of course, not one hair out of place. I slammed the compact mirror shut.

"A courier delivered letter?" Jane mocked, ignoring me as she opened the huge double doors and ran down the long hall to the conference room.

Rose announced in her most secretarial tone, "The meeting has already started. Tell Don that I've placed his call to *Signor* Morano in Rome."

"Rome!" We both gasped, then simultaneously smiled as we said good morning to the staff and pushed open the double doors to the ovaltable office.

Everyone looked up as we took our seats.

"*'This is no myth.'*"

The tall, extremely handsome courier paused from his reading to check us from head to toe and back up again as we sat down on either side of the long table. He grasped the official looking letter more tightly, creating a loud rustling in the quiet room.

No myth? the words screamed in my ears - Jane's exact words explaining my dream. Her lips formed into her old "I told you so" smile that drove me mad when we used to argue as kids. I always lost because I'd get so emotional and burst out either crying or yelling; then she'd always calmly tell me to not take myself so seriously. Now she ignored me as I glared at her, angry that she was probably right again. Just the thought of that horrible dream being indeed precognitive caused my face to contort and my right eye to nervously twitch.

And since she'd always impressed upon me that there was no such thing as coincidence, she'd probably also tell me why I was so attracted to this complete stranger. I tried to avoid returning his bold stare and instead forced myself to pay attention, hoping against hope that there was no connection between him, this letter, and my dream. Settling back stiffly in the plush chair in order to check him out when he wasn't looking, I was surprised to see him staring at Jane with such intensity that his eyes seemed to devour her whole.

He didn't even notice my well concealed reaction, for I'd long ago trained myself to remember that men had always been more attracted to Jane than me.

Finally, after a long, uncomfortale pause that made me start sweating again, he continued reading, his lips curving in obvious and pleased surprise.

"*'Arachne's Tapestry actually exists...'*"

"What?!" I gasped out loud, along with everyone else.

The courier paused as we recovered from our shock. Don Meldon, our president, was almost unable to introduce us. "Oh, excuse me. This is such incredible news! Uh...Doctors Jane and Charla Morrow...This is Dr. Norton Dudley; he's reading from a sealed letter, written to *Signor* Morano, the Curator of Italian Arts and Antiquities."

With my mouth open wide, I looked up to acknowledge our foreign visitor. But he was looking across the ovaltable at Bill Balfour, our documentary photographer, as though he were trying to figure out whether he belonged to Jane or me.

"Yes, this is shocking news! Please, please read on," Bill said persuasively, reaching under the table and squeezing my hand as though to indicate to Norton to keep his eyes to himself. Norton ignored him, pulling out a long, curved pipe from his inside coat pocket, locking his shifting eyes on me and then Jane, and firing the dark pipe. His smoke rose in gusting spirals around our heads.

"Oh! I almost forgot - your call is in, Don," I nervously whispered, attempting to keep my mind on the subject and off the audacious stranger with his tantalizing smile that smirked of a man who had always gotten every woman and every thing he'd ever wanted. Even his aristocratic, British accent attested to his smugness. Don broke the silence with,

"Yes, please, Norton, do go on. We can't
wait to hear how this ancient artifact
has survived."

> "'While I realize that
> this tapestry was never
> meant to be uncovered, I
> believe the world is
> desperately in need of
> this tragic, divine
> message. Since we are
> now faced with the danger
> of extinction, we can no
> longer keep it filed alive.'"

I felt like fainting. As a
mythologist, I was only too acutely aware
of the meaning of Arachne's Tapestry. The
thought of it being linked to my horrible
dream was unbearable. Jane eyed me with
concern. I could read her mind, asking me
just what the tapestry's message was. But
before I could lean over and whisper it
to her, Norton read on.

> "'But I uncover it amidst
> grave danger. Let me stress
> the value and pricelessness
> of this artifact. In all four
> corners of the tapestry, the
> most valuable precious stones -
> diamonds, rubies, emeralds,
> sapphires, onyz, topaz and
> more of the most rare gems in
> the world are woven into the
> threads, depicting DANGER in
> blinding brilliance.'"

Suddenly, I was all business. Our
clever writer had somehow managed to
communicate that Athena's Tapestry had
also been recovered because I knew that
"Danger" was her work's warning against

incest. I hardly heard Norton reading the next words.

> "*'Now you understand why I am forced to bring this tapestry out of hiding. With the rampant spread of A.I.D.S., we cannot wait another day to warn the world against sodomy. It has become an obsession, a collective sexual conflict.'*"

"SODOMY!" Everyone gasped, except me and Don. We exchanged glances of agreement. Yes, that was Arachne's message in her tapestry. However, I felt the "danger" applied to me directly. The news couldn't have been worse.

"'Scuse me ladies," Bill apologized in his deep voice. "Sodomy is having sex with animals as well as...." He stood, his tall muscular body matching Norton's.

"Exactly!" Don interrupted emphatically, seeing the tension between the two men. "Though most people refer to the, uh, sexual act that Arachne portrays in her tapestry as beastiality, it's the same as sodomy," he added carefully.

"Yeah," Jane laughed nervously, "The same type of information that also cost Freud his reputation when he published it! But wasn't the myth's message incest?"

I kicked her and with a stern glance attempted to tell her to be quiet. She indignantly raised her right eyebrow at me, shifted in the plushly cushioned chair, and was determined to speak. "Most people are painfully aware that Ovid was banished to die a lonely death on the

Black Sea for exposing this information
in the first place. And for Freud's
findings, he is to this day criticized
and labeled as no more than a sexologist.
Are we sure we want to hear more?"

"Whew!" I blew out, taking a deep
breath of relief that Jane had not given
away the hidden message in the letter.
She shot a sidelong glance at me as
though asking what the hell was going on
and daring me to kick her again.

"U-u-m!" Norton more persistently
cleared his throat, as though demanding
our attention. "Now may I continue?"

"Yes, of course, please read on," Don
said.

> "*'Now you understand the
> grave danger. It must
> be placed in the right hands.
> Ownership can be debated
> between the Turks, since it
> was created in Asia Minor
> and the Greeks, since it
> deals with their namesake,
> Athena. More importantly,
> given the recent disruptions
> on Cyprus and the old
> bloodbaths between these
> two archenemies, I must
> beg of you, for the tapestry's
> security, my safety, and the
> prevention of war between
> these countries, that you say
> nothing of this to the Italian
> government or to anyone.
> Instead, I request that you
> deliver this letter to the SILC
> Foundation in Key West,
> Florida; it is a well endowed*

> *organization with the highest*
> *ethical standards. You can*
> *trust that my old friend, Don*
> *Meldon, and his staff will do*
> *everything humanly possible to*
> *secure the tapestry.'"*

"Oh my, God," I blurted out, unable
to control myself any longer and wanting
to get up and run. Everyone stared at me,
except Norton. Not surprised at all, he
just lowered his eyes condescendingly and
finished the letter.

> "*'If you cannot personally*
> *deliver this letter to the*
> *Foundation, I would like to*
> *suggest Dr. Norton Dudley, a*
> *former student and colleague of*
> *mine from Oxford who now works*
> *and resides in Rome. His*
> *address and telephone number*
> *are enclosed. Needlesstosay,*
> *Signor Morano, we must take*
> *all due care in protecting*
> *ourselves and our most precious*
> *tapestry. Again, please*
> *utter no word of this to*
> *anyone, or you will place us in*
> *an extremely dangerous position*
> *that could cost us our lives -*
> *and, most of all, the most*
> *priceless treasure on earth.'"*
>
> *Your friend,*
> *Alexander Aliamo, Ph.D.*

I went into a zone, not even hearing
Jane when she asked, "If we get involved,
does that include <u>our</u> lives? And just who
might threaten <u>our</u> lives?"

Nor did I hear Don speak with
Norton, telling him how shocked he was to

discover that the letter was from Alexander, his old Oxford friend who'd disappeared over 10 years ago, and asking him if he knew of his whereabouts. Nor did I hear him thanking Norton for having delivered the letter, reassuring him that we'd be in touch with *Signor* Morano in Rome, and bidding him goodbye.

All I could hear was the loud roaring in my ears that left me speechless. Stunned beyond belief that I was about to undertake a journey that would probably cost me my life, I held my breath, afraid to even consider the pain and trauma stretching out in front of me like some vast plain that would roll and tumble me toward a black abyss containing the deepest, darkest secrets of the human mind that had been shoved in the cobwebbed depths for millenium.

CHAPTER II: "WAKE UP IN *ROMA*"

Jarred out of my repeated, horrible dream with the file pressed against my nose, I awoke to the sound of landing gear striking hard on the runway, to the sound of blasting, reversing jets with wind rushing against flaps, and the sound of "Welcome to Leonardo Da Vinci International Airport!" If I hadn't dreamed, I wouldn't have believed I'd slept at all on the long, overnight flight.

In a matter of minutes it seemed, the plane was pulling up to the gate. I scrambled to gather all my belongings, especially the leather briefcase containing three weeks worth of research. I tucked the precious work tightly under my arm, reminding myself of the urgency of getting it to *Signor* Morano as soon as possible. Don and I had uncovered Dr. Aliamo's findings which Jane said contained a new theory for psychology. She was hooked. She had to finish a children's dream seminar in Palm Beach and would be joining me soon.

So would Bill. Unfortunately, his grandfather died, so at the last moment he was delayed, and here I was all alone. A chill racked my already exhausted body. Just the thought of solely tackling this task and confronting Norton by myself caused another tremor. I was pushed out with the throngs of passengers and down the corridor to the customs' booths. As I waited in the long line, I recalled my last moments with Norton.

We were all to meet for lunch after the meeting, but somehow I had wound up at the Pier House with Norton by myself. His behavior during the meeting was tame in comparison. Dressed in an unbuttoned, turquoise and pink tropical shirt which exposed his blond, curly chest hairs, he had undressed me from head to toe with his steel blue eyes before he pulled down his dark shades and continued devouring my body with his greedy eyes, just as he'd done with Jane. His unmistakeable cologne engulfed me as the wind blew blond whisps of his thick hair on his forehead. He had the look women drooled over, and he knew he was gorgeous. I wondered how I could have been so attracted to him earlier.

Up close I realized how tall he was as I shook his extended hand which held onto mine and directed me to the chair beside him. As he pulled it out for me, he leaned far over so that I could feel his breath on my neck. "May I call you, Charla?" he asked, pressing his leg against mine as he pushed his glasses up on his head and looked confidently into my eyes without even a flutter of his long, curly lashes.

"Yes, Norton," I responded soberly to his seductive glance as he offered to pour me a glass of champagne.

"In celebration," he said, holding his glass for a toast. "Don tells me you've planned a vacation in Italy to...uh...what was it...celebrate the

200th anniversary of Goethe's journey? Well, whatever, I'm so delighted you're coming. You <u>will</u> allow me to escort you around *Roma*?" He said more than asked, clinking his glass to mine.

"Yes, Bill and I would love that!" I responded, suddenly put on the spot, but thinking any mention of my relationship with Bill would dissuade him. It didn't. I couldn't believe I didn't respond to his intense blue eyes that were firmly planted on me the entire time he sipped his champagne. I also couldn't believe I now found such a gorgeous man to be a turn off. In the past, I'd have been vulnerable to the persistence of such a playboy. I'd have found his teasing, pursed mouth and his muscular body very seductive. I wanted to laugh at my blood not boiling, at my libido not rising. I wondered if Jane were right about my getting past my old, almost obsessive compulsive attraction for such a potentially abusive man. In fact, instead of desire, I felt a bit repulsed.

"It would be a privilege to spend time with a truly intelligent woman," he said. "You can't believe how many beautiful females I meet who have no brains," he smiled, taking another sip of champagne and lightly rolling his tongue around the rim of the crystal. I well knew the old tongue routine and its obvious seductive reminder.

"Yes, I've had the same experience with men," I candidly retorted, trying to ignore his obviousness and feeling angrier and a little ill as I recalled all the times that I'd complimented men just to appeal to their ego. "Yes, intelligence is top priority for me as well."

As I spoke, he hung onto every word, as though there were ultimate importance attached to everything I had to say. I also knew this old trick; how many times I had turned my spotlight on the most handsome man in my midst, I didn't want to recall. I looked at the menu, trying to allay his intense attention. Suddenly, I didn't feel hungry at all; I feared I'd have to pay somehow for my past.

"You must try the Oysters Rockefeller," he suggested as he placed a shell on my plate and ate one himself. He drew in his breath and, at the same time, sucked gently on the oyster. With a sliding motion of his tongue and slight suction from his lips, he slowly slipped it into his mouth and swallowed it greedily, never taking his eyes off me.

"No...No thank you," I quickly refused, looking around to see where the others were and hoping Bill would hurry and rescue me.

No luck. Norton ate another oyster, and all I could think about was Jane's being right again about her explanation of the link between food and sex. I'd never before seen the relationship between the two depicted so graphically. I felt more ill. "Uh, I'm sorry, Norton, but will you excuse me? I suddenly don't feel very well." But he blocked my leaving, pressing his leg even harder against mine and trying to find out where I'd be staying in Rome. He did everything he could to seduce me, and all I could think about was how much worse he'd be if he ever truly got me alone. And with no Bill to rescue me.

I jumped when the agent asked me for my passport. Nervously, I jerked my head left and right searching everywhere for Norton. Outside customs, I scanned the crowd gathered behind the plexiglass window. Thank God, no Norton, I thought as I took a deep breath, blowing out the tension. Hopefully, I'd outwitted him since he'd never found out my arrival time or hotel. Avoiding the stares of the Italian men, I headed for the currency exchange line.

As I waited, one man after another approached me, propositioning me in Italian. Though Bill consistently complimented me by telling me how beautiful I was and how I didn't believe it because of my having been overshadowed by such a gorgeous older sister, now I wondered if he might be partially right. I hadn't considered their being so aggressive; even the cambio teller made some kind of remark. I filled my wallet with the colorful lira and tried to ignore them all.

Plus, I felt like a zombie. Pulling my castered luggage, I walked outside when, out of nowhere, a uniformed man approached me, asking, "*Roma*?" I feebly shook my head, unable to shake out the sticky webs as I looked around for the taxi stand. Before I could respond, he had grabbed my luggage, tossed it into the depths of the lower compartment so that I couldn't reach it, and jumped on the bus. I hesitantly stepped into the bus as he impatiently tapped his foot. "*Piazza del Popolo*?" I asked, filled with intimidation when all the tired passengers stared at me as though I were delaying them. The agitated driver shook his head then ignored me. The door slammed shut behind me, and he took off with a jerk.

"Oh, shit," I moaned as I fell into a seat. My aching body sank into the vinyl as the morning wind rushed through the open windows with a puff of hot, suffocating air and the distinct scent of oleander; it burst into full bloom along the road and blurred the land with all shades of red from the palest pink flush to the deepest, blood-red rose. It didn't even cheer me to see their colorful carpet, spread out as though welcoming me to Rome. I knew I was off to a terrible start and didn't know what to do.

I couldn't think, and I was so tired that the droning of the bus made my eyelids heavier by the minute. I barely caught sight of the Tiber, passing quietly beneath a bridge. My eyelids drooped lower as it cut a path through the rolling hills on the outskirts of Rome, serpentinely meandering across the undulating terrain. The spirals of morning mist seeped up from its frothy current. The hills relinquished its shining, fresh dew like an offering to the rising sun. Hoping I'd be no similar sacrifice, my eyes involuntarily clamped shut.

When I awoke, the mist had evaporated as the fringes of Rome appeared. My eyes

closed again as tall apartment buildings,
stacking family upon family in whole
complexes, one looking the same as the
next, passed monotonously by. I forced
them open to see the eerie, gaping
Colosseum defying gravity. Giant stone
blocks darkened the gates on the lower
level, and I could imagine all the
terrified people crammed in, waiting to
be killed. I shivered. A foul air seeped
from the Forum's subterranean ruins now
exposed to the harsh light. I
instinctively covered my nose and tried
to keep my eyes open. After a short
distance farther, the smell diminished as
the bus pulled up to a huge station and
everyone piled out and walked away.

"Hotel Valadier?" I yelled at the
driver who hopped down the stairs and
took off running. "Wait!" I grabbed my
briefcase and hurried to the door as he
vanished around the corner, "Where the
hell am I?" I asked, wearily climbing
down. A deep voice from behind the bus
startled me.

"Yes, may I help you." A handsome
Italian crossed the length of the bus in
a few strides. "Let me introduce myself.
I'm Michael Venturi with the Italian
Tourist Bureau." His ingratiating smile
brightened his dark face. His pressed
navy blue uniform appeared official with
a label reading "Michael" on his left
shoulder.

Wary of his feigned friendliness, I
stepped back, hugging the briefcase
tighter to my chest. But he wasn't headed
for me; he proceeded directly to the
luggage compartment, grabbed my bag, and

took off, saying, "I have the perfect hotel for you, located just a few blocks away."

"Hold on just one minute," I finally found my voice. "I already have reservations." But he had crossed the streetcar tracks and disappeared around the corner. "Damn it, stop!" I yelled, taking off after him. As I dodged to keep my heels out of the deep tracks, I looked up above the bus to see the "*Termini*" carved into the old buiding. "Oh, no, shit!   STOP!" I screamed, scurrying around the corner, not even caring about the stares from pedestrians who stopped to watch. But he was a block ahead and couldn't hear me. He ran by an outdoor restaurant, a small park, turned the next corner and again vanished from sight.

Exasperated, hot, exhausted, and fuming, I finally rounded the corner and saw above my head, the plaque - "Hotel *Roma*."

I peered inside, saw Michael signing the registrar, and burst through the double doors with my mouth ajar.

"You'll love it. Have a wonderful stay," Michael smilingly told me, cool as could be and acting as though nothing had happened; then he walked through an arched alcove, saying he'd send a porter to take up my bag.

I saw red as I stormed up to the desk where a kindly looking, old gentleman sat smiling at me. "Excuse me!" I tried controlling my voice. "Does Michael work here?"

He lowered his grey head and wouldn't look me in the eye, muttering guiltily under his breath, "No English, *prego, Signorina.*"

I was too tired and angry to resist. "Oh, okay, where's your phone?" I asked impatiently. When his face went blank, I placed my hand to my ear; he smiled sheepishly and pointed to the corner table.

Sulkily, I shuffled through my purse, shoving everything bruskly as I looked for the hotel's number. My hand shook as I picked up the phone, but I was baffled when I discovered that my reservations had been cancelled and that it was booked solid. Now I really felt hoodwinked and more confused than ever. A kind looking porter had loaded my bag in the elevator and waited patiently.

"*Buon giorno!*" he said as I stepped in and felt the exhaustion, confusion, and anger invade me from the toes up. I forced myself to take some deep breaths and count to ten as we made our way to the third floor and down the dark hallway. The young porter had so picked up on my negative energy that he quickly bade me, "*Chiao!*" as soon as he unloaded my bag. He didn't even wait for a tip.

I took another deep breath, resisting the red stinging in my eyes as I recalled that the area around the Termini was just where Norton had insisted I stay. While I realized that Michael's job at the hotel was to take advantage of naive tourists, I wondered what connections he might have to Norton.

I fought the tears, feeling like a little kid with no control over an awful situation. My mind fogged. I looked around, searching for any sign of comfort. At least it has a bidet, I considered, and a window. "Besides, you have no choice. You're alone in a foreign country. You don't know what else to do, so just accept it," I tried talking my way out of breaking down and crying my eyes out.

I could just hear Jane telling me to "lighten up"; she always threw it up at me just when I was most upset. Blocking out her words, I dragged my aching body to the bathroom, and as I sat there, I realized that Jane was wrong. It had nothing to do with my attitude. "It's jet lag!" I said aloud. Thank God, I wasn't losing my mind. I knew I'd never make it to *Signor* Morano's office, for I could barely crawl to bed, remove my clothes, and fall face down before my eyes closed as solid as rocks.

After an interminable time, the sound of screeching pulleys invaded my dream like the chill of a scraped blackboard just as the slimy publisher pressed the sharp grooved file on my nose. I sat straight up in bed and looked out into the courtyard nestled some stories below. I adjusted my eyes to see dozens of women staring at me as they cranked their pulleys and reeled in their clothes through their windows.

The afternoon sun lit up the bed. I grabbed the sheet and kicked the wooden shutter. It slammed with a jar as I wearily forced my body toward the shower. The cool splash of the water woke me up, but it didn't remove the crawling discomfort eating away at me. The symbolism of the "*Termini*" lingered in my mind. I knew what it meant. Termination. Zip. The end. But the loud growling in my stomach spoke louder than my mind. "Oh well, it's probably too late to go to *Signor* Morano's office anyway," I mumbled, resolving to go first thing in the morning.

I walked out of the bathroom and saw the pink rays of the setting sun, peeking through the shutters. Just the thought of venturing out on the streets at night terrified me. Then I remembered the small, outdoor restaurant a couple of blocks away that I'd seen when I was chasing Michael. I hurriedly finished drying off and rummaged through the suitcase which Bill had primarily packed for me since I was so busy with the research. I grabbed the first dress I saw, a red silk, one of his favorites, with the red heels packed next to it. I quickly pulled it over my head, stepped in the shoes, grabbed by briefcase, stuffed my red bag with my money, airline tickets, passport, and travelers' cheques, and headed for the door.

The wall mirror by the door caused me to stop and examine how brightly the red dress lit up my long, thick blond hair and made my tanned skin glow. My wide opened eyes traveled down my body. The dress clung to my hips and waist and rounded curvaceously around my breasts, making them appear even fuller than they were. "Oh, God," I realized. I'd always been so accustomed to being with Bill when I wore this dress that I'd never considered how other men might respond.

Now I did. For the first time, I saw myself as sexier than Jane, not as beautiful, but more voluptuous. "Oh, God," I repeated as my stomach growled so deeply, that it felt like it caved in. I locked the door securely behind me and peered down the long, dark hall; I took off walking for the wide marble staircase, descended to the lobby, and passed the clerk, who still couldn't look me in the eye, though I could feel his eyes undressing me from behind. Michael was nowhere in sight.

The shock of being truly alone in a foreign country struck just before I reached the outside door. The twilight wrapped a hazy purple ribbon around the city. The street was filled with men; and the moment I stepped outside, they headed for me. I hurried for the corner, having to dart around the men approaching me. Afraid Norton might be among them, I scanned their faces. I fought the panic that streaked through me. As I turned right at the corner, I suggested to myself, pay attention, look back, and don't forget where the hotel is.

I crossed the streetcar tracks, trying to shake the aggressive men. Carefully placing my red heels between the rails, I flashed on the time in Jerusalem when my ex-husband and I actually lost our hotel room. What the hell are you doing thinking of Nader? I caught myself; the darkness of the centuries old buildings, the clanging of cathedral bells, the flickering yellow street lights, and the men still chasing me caused me to flinch as the abuse I'd suffered in his hands poured in my mind. But I shoved back the awful images, determined to stay alert.

I passed the small park, my eyes darting down its dark paths where mounted police rode under the large trees and ousted the homeless, bedding down for the evening. "At least there's help if I scream," and I could almost imagine their large horses bearing down on the likes of a Michael, a Norton, or one of these determined Italian men.

Then I saw the restaurant up ahead, looking like an oasis; bright orange linen tablecloths over white ones covered its sidewalk tables, all elegantly set for dinner.

"Thank God, but how am I ever going to order my food?" I questioned, as deep purple rays darkened the sky. Remembering the trick of talking with the hands and the fact that I probably had tourist written all over my face made me a little more assured. An end table under some scaffolding caught my attention. A canopy of vines permanently attached themselves and added privacy from the street. It was perfect. But I wondered if the restaurant were open. My stomach rumbled demandingly as I walked past the empty tables and up to the lit up menu stand; it was under glass in between two large, open entrances. The men waited across the street and lecherously observed my every move.

I felt weaker by the minute. Inside the small restaurant, a bar was packed with men. They all looked up and stared, undressing me. Norton wasn't among them.

I glanced at the glassed counters containing breads and pastries and smelled the aromas of chicken cacciatore, veal parmagiano, and seafood fettucine, causing my mouth to water. Several of the men stood up, yelling something in Italian to the others. I panicked, wondering if I should run.

Suddenly from behind, a deep, sonorous voice in rhythmic, broken English shocked me so much that I spun on my heels. To my surprise, I looked into the deepest, darkest, and warmest brown eyes, framed by equally dark hair; it was short, thick, and perfectly parted. His eyes rounded wide with a smile and a magical spark. "Good evening, *Signorina*. For you, I have menu *tourismo*!" He extended his hand. "Let me be of service. My nama is Paulo Mosatello. Welcome to my restaurant."

Just his presence caused the tension to vanish. The men across the street walked away and the ones at the bar resumed their drinking. I was instantly spellbound, and as I reached to shake his hand to thank him, he kissed it instead, a feathery, light kiss with the softest, most sensual, full lips I'd ever felt. It was an obvious gentlemanly gesture, but I could feel it down to my toes.

"Charla Morrow," I said, smiling with relief from ear to ear.

"Ah, Charlotta! What a beautiful name for someone equally as beautiful. Come. You must sit!" He insisted, showing me to the corner end table I'd just admired.

"I'm...uh...not too early?" I politely questioned.

"*Prego*, sita...sita...!" He insisted as he pulled out my chair. He leaned over so close that I smelled his musk cologne. His long dark lashes fluttered as he smiled broadly, which lit up his handsome face and his perfect teeth made even whiter by his glowing bronze complexion. He offered his finest wine.

"*Si! Gracie*!" I answered, and as he turned to leave, I thought, "Now there's a potential friend." I knew I was going to need all the help I could get.

I quickly scanned the menu for chicken cacciatore.

I searched the dark corners of the street for any sign of movement. All was still. How could I trust a complete stranger? I questioned myself. Besides, I felt an obvious attraction for Paulo. His eyes were so sensitive and honest. He approached, smiling and carrying a crystal of sparkling wine.

"Yes, thank you!" I responded as he poured the wine; his musk smell overwhelmed me again. I questioned how I could possibly be attracted to someone else when I was so passionately involved with Bill.

"May I suggest *pollo alla cacciatore*!" He offered, glancing deep into my eyes and making me wonder if he could read my thoughts.

"Exactly what I wanted!" I exclaimed.

"Me *madre's* special for those most hungry! I take care of me madre and she take care of you!" He admitted proudly, heading for the kitchen before I could ask him to join me.

Trying to figure out why I would even consider inviting him to sit down with me, I sipped on the wine and observed him, flying out of the kitchen to refill my glass, or to serve me his special bread, minestrone, fresh green salad, more wine, *cassata, pollo alla cacciatore*, more wine, ice cream with fruit, more wine, and finally cappuccino.

He kept me so busy laughing, drinking and eating that I never had a chance to ask him any questions. Finally, after several hours, he joined me. Scooting his chair close to mine, he asked if I were married, then exlaimed in shock, "Why you no married?!"

"Well, I'm involved with someone named Bill Balfour who'll be here as soon as possible. He's...well, he's my best friend," I said. I couldn't tell him that I was too afraid to ever get married again after Nader.

"*Si*, I have best friend - but she no beautiful!" He interrupted, his brown eyes widening.

I thanked him for the compliment, and in the background, I could see a dark headed little woman in black whom I guessed was his mother. I wondered how much she affected his current relationship.

Regardless of his choice of women, oh, how he loved to flirt, to sensually tease and provoke candid responses which, I'm sure, was his way of figuring me out. And it worked! His warm, congenial manner caused me to relax, laugh, and share in a lighthearted way.

When the evening was over, I felt as though I'd truly found a trustworthy friend; after searching for just the right words, I asked, "Uh, Paulo, I was wondering if you could help me with something?" I grabbed my purse and briefcase in preparation to leave, hoping no one had overheard.

Paulo listened attentively, knowing it was important. "Yes?" He urged me when I paused too long.

He looked at me admiringly. His soft eyes expanded as they centered on every feature. "And you have most beautiful hair!"

Unlike the urgent conquest that I had sensed in Norton, Paulo's deep, yet sincere yearning, caused me to forget my attraction for him, and almost feel sorry for him. From what I could gather, he somehow had excluded having a relationship with a woman whom he truly admired and appreciated. "Thank you," I warmly responded, his deep brown eyes difficult to resist.

I stood up, hesitating when the men at the bar stood up as well.

Paulo again took my hand, pressing it with a feathery whisp of a kiss and saying with concern, "Don't say *buona notte*? Where you stay? You walk?"

"Well..." I hesitated again. "Actually, I'm only a few blocks away...and wondered...could you walk me there?" I asked, glancing down the dark, empty street. "Or call me a taxi...?"

"No problem," he excitedly volunteered, his face lighting up a huge smile. "Just one minute." And he ran in to tell his mother who acted like I was stealing her son. As we walked down the dimly lit street, I could hear the excited talk of the men and his mother saying something in Italian under her breath.

Only a few feet from Paulo's haven, we encountered a strange alienness as the bare bulbs cast yellow, lurid shadows. I couldn't see the tracks very well as we crossed over to the park. Paulo suspiciously watched two men who passed us; they turned around to stare a moment too long, and ran headlong into a parked car. We heard their deep grunts as they disappeared down the dark streets.

"Nothing to worry about there!" Paulo chuckled and pulled me close, causing flutters in my stomach. He sensed my uneasiness, wrapping his arm lightly around my waist as we turned the corner, walked through the empty hotel lobby and up the wide marble staircase.

On the last floor, I peered down the long, dark hallway before walking to my room, slowly opened the door, turned on the light, and stepped inside. Everything was as I had left it, but I felt a presence.

"No problem, Charlotta," Paulo announced as he emerged from the bathroom.

"Everything seems to be in tact, but I think someone's been here," I said, leaning against the door and taking a deep breath.

Within a flash, he stood beside me, his face close, his lips pursed. Then he was kissing me. At first, I tried resisting his full, sensual lips, pressed like urgent rose petals against mine. Tingles shot to my toes; throbbing pangs pierced my stomach. My knees grew weak, and I barely had the strength to pull my lips from his soft, sensual caress and push him away. My eyes fluttered, wanting to mist over and close.

I fought the urge. "Thank you so much, Paulo, you'll never know how much I appreciate your getting me back safely." It was almost a whisper.

"*Et domani*?" He persisted, not wanting to leave; but upon seeing my body stiffen and my arms fold, he said, "You come to see me tomorrow?"

"I'll do my best," I assured him, thanking him again, almost forcing him out the door, and locking it securely behind him. I leaned against it for support, my wobbly legs not allowing me to walk to the bed. "Wow!" I gasped. "Bill, you'd better get here as fast as you can!"

The silk dress rustled as it slid over my body still titillating from the press of Paulo's chest. I threw it across the bed and collapsed. After a moment, I shook off my shoes, and, overwhelmed with missing Bill and the intimacy we shared, I lapsed into fantasy, imagining Bill and me having sex. I even stroked my body, but it only frustrated me more, for I couldn't rid myself of Paulo's beautiful eyes. Resolved to shut him out of my mind, I rolled over and fell sound asleep.

What seemed like a short time later, I sat up, erect and attentive. The morning light poured in from the open window and reminded me that I had to get to *Signor* Morano's office as soon as possible. I staggered out of bed, still suffering from jet lag. "Coffee," I reminded myself, "Go get some coffee," and I remembered the porter telling me the dining room was just down the hall. In no time, I was dressed in some shorts and out the door. I stepped into the small room where lace covered tables sat under open windows. It was empty and safe looking. I sat down, trying not to think of the awful dream that had awakened me like some persistent warning.

The same sweet looking porter, now turned waiter, walked in from the kitchen. "*Buon giorno. Cafe?*"

"*Cafe latte?*" I responded, already tasting the frothy coffee.

Almost instantly, he was crossing the dark floors, with spirals of steam from silver pots trailing behind him as he set down the silver tray.

"*Grazie!*" I warmly thanked him.

"*Prego,*" he said and turned to the kitchen again.

I gulped down the delicious coffee; before the waiter returned with sweet smelling pastries and jams, I had finished the pot.

"I'm addicted!" I admitted, totally energized. I was so loaded on caffeine my eyes were shining. After I thanked the waiter again, I had to run to use the bathroom. As soon as I opened the door, I knew something was amiss. My eyes wildly searched the room for my briefcase. It was gone. "No!" I screamed, ran out of the room, and flew down the marble steps two at a time. The same old clerk saw me coming and, by the shocked look on my face, knew what had happened.

"*Signorina*!" He yelled excitedly, pressing his hand under his arm to indicate my briefcase, then ran to the door and pointed down the street. Almost knocking him down, I pushed through the large doors and rushed outside. At the corner, all I could see was a tall woman with incredibly long, platinum blond hair, running at full speed around the corner. I couldn't have bolted any faster, but in the few seconds that it took me to reach the corner, she had vanished.

Tears burst into my eyes. I didn't know what to do. If I called the police, they'd question me about the research and possibly cause the Italian government to get involved, which was just what Dr. Aliamo warned us against. "Shit!" I cried.

Not even noticing that I was attracting another hoard of men, I sadly turned, slowly walked back to the hotel, and ignored the men ganged around me. The desk clerk stood waiting, looking guilty as though he were somehow a part of my misery. The tears flooded out; I wearily climbed the stairs and stumbled down the hall. Nothing else was missing. Overwhelmed, I sat on the bed and sobbed.

Self pity struck deeply, causing the image of the writhing skinned alived dwarf to enter my consciousness. I could just hear Jane telling me about my indulgence. No, I stood up resolutely, determined to resist that dream ever coming true and to resist Jane being right. I realized that whoever stole my research was headed for Morano's right now and might impersonate me in order to get information about Dr. Aliamo's whereabouts. I jammed my red dress, shoes, and other articles back into the suitcase, snatched out a white suit, and quickly dressed.

Deciding to leave my luggage with Paulo, I headed for the lobby; there was no sign of Michael. Besides, I reminded myself, Michael wouldn't have wanted my briefcase. Norton would; he sent the blond and probably had my identification fabricated. As I checked out, the old clerk never looked me in the eye.

Stepping outside, I could feel someone watching me. To my relief, the street scene had transformed itself. All the shutters were open, displaying a variety of small shops and a bustle of movement.

I pulled my suitcase over the uneven sidewalk and headed for the corner. I saw no familiar faces, yet I felt someone's eyes on me the entire time as I headed across the tracks, past the homeless continuing to sleep soundly in the park, and towards Paulo's where his mother worked alone. I struggled with the suitcase through the wide entrance and up to Paulo's office, indicating for her to open the door. She reluctantly agreed, never raising her black scarved head, then getting back to work as I thanked her. *"Prego, Signorina, prego,"* she mumbled, disappearing into the kitchen.

Feeling sure that it was safe, I took off, lightened from the heavy load and very anxious to get to Morano's with all possible speed. I neared the *Termini*, quickly spotted the taxis, and within a moment, was in the backseat telling the driver to hurry. In no time, he was letting me out in front of a building that at first resembled all the darkened old buildings in Rome, but something was different. I walked up the steps toward the huge wooden doors. On the panel, I saw Morano's office; then I saw "The Goethe Museo." I couldn't believe it. For so long I'd dreamed of visiting his apartment.

Almost forgetting that I might have been followed and that I could be in a very dangerous situation, there was no resisting the temptation of ringing Goethe's bell. To my surprise, there was no answer. I pressed again and again, until I heard someone yelling into the street. "*Signorina, Signorina.*" I stepped out into the street to see a sweet, grey haired little painter, smiling and crossing his hands palm down as though to tell me that I couldn't come in. Suddenly his entire expression changed; his eyes grew wide. He screamed at me in Italian and pointed for me to look around.

I jerked my head to the right to see a car charging at me so fast that I barely leaped up the stairs and fell headlong into the great door with a crashing thud just as the door mysteriously opened, the buzzer ringing with a shrill pitch in my ear as I fell face first onto the corridor's marble floor. I scrambled to my feet and bolted toward a wrought iron gate which was locked. "Shit!" I moaned when the huge front door swung open behind me. My heart beat rapidly, and a scream rose in my throat; however, in shock I watched as a small old woman, holding a grocery bag and fumbling with a key, stared at me with concern.

Though I shook uncontrollably, I had to get her to let me in. "*Scusi, Signora,*" I said to which she nodded her head in polite acceptance. "*Parla en Englesa? Goethe Museo?*" I questioned as calmly as possible, wiped the smudges off my white jacket, smoothed my hair, and noticed her peering over the top of the leeks in her grocery bag in order to observe my scuffed knees and torn stockings. Her silver hair intensified her wise eyes which looked directly into mine.

Again, to my surprise, she exclaimed in English, "Oh, my dear! The Goethe Museo has been closed for over three months." Upon seeing my eyes turn red, she added, "I'm so sorry, but no one wanted to walk up the stairs." She pointed to the beautiful marble staircase.

"Come, my dear"; then she unlocked the gate, walked over to the black, lace-iron elevator and motioned for me to follow. Pushing the button, she said, "You see, our little elevator holds so few that they didn't want to wait. Finally, they stopped coming altogether. Now his place is being rented! I know -

it's a shame," she continued as we passed Goethe's apartment and reached the third floor.

Her calm, reassuring energy quieted my fears and insecurities. I said goodbye and forced myself to go that instant and confront Morano about Norton. I just couldn't accept that what I'd just experienced was an accident. I never felt so brave as I scrambled up the wide marble steps, cautiously opened the huge wooden door to his office, and stepped inside. My courage was immediately tested by a dark haired secretary. "*Parla en Englesa*?" I asked. Her dark, Mediterranean eyes quickly checked me up and down before somewhat suspiciously responding, "*Si*."

"Yes, uh, is *Signor* Morano in?" I asked, doing my best to control my voice which wanted to crack, for I could tell that somthing was amiss. I flashed my biggest smile and attempted to maintain eye contact while I checked out the desk for any possible clues. The office was so dimly lit that at first I didn't see the familiar looking handwriting on the envelope which lay opened on her desk - its contents strewn as though it had just been perused and restuffed hurriedly. I recognized the handwriting from the meeting at the SILC Foundation - it was Dr. Aliamo's. I tried to keep my eyes from giving my discovery away.

"Uh...no...*prego*, I'm sorry, uh, he's just stepped out. May I take a message?" She asked me nervously. I tried ignoring her strange behavior and grabbed the moment of opportunity. There it was. A stamp. A commemorative stamp of a female saint with the name Santa Rosalia printed under her sweet smiling image, but I couldn't read the blurred postmark. The secretary looked at me sharply and shoved the letter out of sight. Feeling danger, I backed out the door.

"No, no thank you. I'll check back later."

I didn't trust her at all, nor the situation. The blond who stole my briefcase had apparently gotten there before me, and I didn't know what her connection might be, but I suspicioned Norton had his filthy fingers involved in taking Dr. Aliamo's letter which probably gave his address. Terrified that I'd have to encounter Norton again and find out his true colors, I fled to the wrought iron gate and opened the great wooden doors with caution. I wasn't feeling so brave anymore; in fact, my old insecurites overcame me. I breathed a sigh of relief when no one was in sight. I grabbed a taxi and headed for Paulo's.

What I was going to do, I hadn't the clue. Then I remembered it - Goethe's description of the Santa Rosalia Cave Sanctuary, located deep within Mount Pellegrino in Palermo, Sicily. That's it, I thought. And I knew I'd have to get there as quickly as possible. But how would I get out of Rome without Norton catching me? The first place he'd look would be the airport. Then I recalled how Goethe headed for Naples and took a ferry over to Palermo; that's what I'd do, only I'd fly from Naples. Just the thought made me panic and want to get a plane home, to forget all about this dangerous mission, but something in me wouldn't let me turn back. A determination I'd never experienced swelled within. But it made me start shaking uncontrollably. No, I decided. I couldn't do it. I'd go get my bag from Paulo's and leave. But I knew what Jane would say. How she'd tell me I could do it, it was just my usual bad habit of projecting myself to fail. I didn't know what to do. I was so torn over whether to call Jane or not that I didn't even hear the driver asking for the fare. I was never so happy to see Paulo.

"Charlotta," he exclaimed, kissing my hand and telling me how beautiful I looked. I almost forgot about the danger of being followed as I gazed into his warm eyes and smelled his cologne. In fact, I almost forgot everything except his protective arms and the memory of his lips on mine.

"Uh," I distracted myself, "are we out of earshot, Paulo?"

"What earshot?!" He asked in amazement, then held up his finger to his head, pulled it back and forth as though it were a trigger, and, with deep concern in his eyes, stared at me, knowing I was in trouble. His uneasiness unnerved me, and I decided in that instant to call Jane, even though he assured me in his authoritative tone, "In my restaurant, no problem."

"Oh, thank you. I'm fine, I just wondered if I could use your phone to call my sister? I have an international card so...."

"*Prego*, Charlotta," he seemed to sense my nervousness; and from his shocked expression, I thought something awful was about to happen or that he might mind my using his phone. "You have a sister?!" He asked in wide-eyed disbelief. "Is she as beautiful as you? And does she have a Bill as well?"

I forgot everything, even the danger. Just the thought that he was already more attracted to Jane, and he'd never even met her made me mad and ready to walk out, but the determination to prove something to Jane overcame me. "Well, do you mind?" I asked with a sarcastic edge.

But he looked at me so expectantly, still waiting for me to answer his question, that I clenched my teeth and grimaced, "No, she's unattached."

"Impossible!" He gasped, stepping aside as his mother scooted around him and lifted the phone from the stacks of paper on his desk. He left, shaking his head in disbelief. I picked up the receiver with vigor and did my best to stay calm as I talked with the operator. Rose answered, saying it didn't sound like me and asking if everything was all right. I assured her and politely asked for Jane.

"God, am I glad to hear your voice!" Jane answered "Are you okay?

I tried to put my disappointment in Paulo aside, but I still felt angry toward her, remembering all the times in the past when she got the gorgeous men. "Yes, but I'm leaving for Palermo. I don't intend to handle this job by myself. If you and Bill aren't here pronto, I doubt very seriously if you'll find me in godforsaken Sicily. I'm outta here." My voice was curt and short. I couldn't believe my own words.

"Find you? Now, hold on just a minute. I know that tone of voice. It means rescue me. This trip is for your growth, remember? You're the authority here. And, yes, if you have to handle this job alone, you damn well can. Aren't you tired of having to rely on me or the Bills in your life?" She confronted me directly. I couldn't believe she knew. I didn't say a word for a few minutes. Neither did she. As defensive as I felt, I knew my safety was more important than my agelong feuding with her. I told her everything, and she listened intently.

"This is much more dangerous than we thought. Bill's on his way. I'll be there as soon as I can get out of Dodge, but how will I find you?"

"I don't know, Jane. I'm taking the next train to Naples and then flying to Palermo, and I have no idea where to stay. Maybe somewhere near the Public Gardens where Goethe visited. Remember, where he discovered his plant theory." I said, when Paulo knocked softly on the door and walked in, saying,

"*Scusi*, Charlotta. I couldn't help but overhear." I wondered just how much he had heard. "But I have a good friend in Palermo who has a wonderful hotel called "*Soderno*," near the *Giardino*, and when Jane comes to Rome, I will take her there," he concluded with certainty and quickly left to get the number.

"Who's that?" Jane questioned. "What a sexy voice."

I was mad all over again. "I figured you'd ask," I told her sarcastically. "He's Paulo Mosatello, who was _my_ friend." I paused not wanting her to detect my disappointment. "Yeah, I think coming to Sicily with Paulo is a good idea." Suddenly I felt almost smug over the fact that Paulo had no idea what he was in for with Jane. But I clenched my teeth even tighter over the fact that I'd have to once more take the backseat to her.

"So he's gorgeous, trustworthy and helpful?" She inquired. My silence answered her questions. "Yes, by all means, do give me his number."

As I gave her Paulo's number, he came back in, telling me the number to his friend's hotel in Palermo. "Got it," Jane responded, asking me to please be careful and that she'd get the message to Bill and see me soon. I almost hung up on her, impatient to get off the phone, but I carefully replaced the receiver.

Paulo never noticed how my face had fallen; he just grinned from ear to ear. Dragging my suitcase out to the sidewalk, he snapped back to reality and noticed me again, cautioning me to be careful and sensing that I might be in some danger.

I assured him that I was fine and headed for the _Termini_. But he was right. I wasn't two doors down when I saw Norton far at the other end of the block. I pushed the phone call out of my mind and tried to think fast. I couldn't go back to Paulo's; it would ruin everything if he found out that Paulo was involved. I panicked, unsure of what to do. I shook uncontrollably, especially my knees. I forced myself to think, shoving my suitcase out of sight under the end table of the restaurant. Then, unable to control the urge to flee, I took off running toward the hotel, hoping I could lose him or that the mounted police would still be around. He was much faster than I ever dreamed, catching me by the time I reached the park. "What's the big hurry?" He demanded, attempting to act wounded over my having avoided him.

"Well, hello, Norton," I casually responded, my knees trembling even harder and wanting to buckle as he lecherously looked me up and down.

"I see you got smart and left Bill at home," he said, pursing his thin lips in satisfaction as though he knew he had the upper hand and would have his way with me. "Why haven't you called as you promised?" He sneered, his entire appearance changed from our previous meeting.

"I was going to; just recovering from jet lag, you know." I played him along, feeling faint and leaning for support against the large pillar at the entrance to the park. He stepped closer, and I could smell his odd, unmistakable cologne. His eyes hardened and his fists clenched. I wanted to run with all my might or scream at the top of my lungs, but I hesitated, hoping I could get rid of him.

No way. He stepped even closer to me until I could feel his hot breath on my neck. Then he grabbed my hand and forced me to walk down an isolated path that led toward a dark clump of trees.

"You're hurting my hand. Please let go, or I'll scream."

"Go ahead. Get the police involved, and I'll tell them how you're here to steal their precious artifact; but you'll never have it, do you hear? It's mine," he threatened, his hand slipping around my waist and pulling me forcefully to him as the trees thickened, and we entered the dark, hidden area where the homeless slept. My hands shook violently and my heart pounded as he roughly thrust his hard chest against mine and forced his thin, cold kiss on my lips, pressing so hard that he almost made them bleed. I tried biting him, but it only made him more aggressive. Bewildered and overcome with panic that he was going to rape me, I forced myself to be calm, realizing I'd have to try a different tactic to get out of this one.

"Ummm," I sighed, "I'll bet your cock tastes like nectar from the gods." My mind raced wildly, grasping at anything as his hand slipped easily under my skirt, and his fingers forced their way inside my panties while the other hand held me bound against the tree.

"I love a woman who talks dirty to me," he moaned, his fingers roughly jamming inside me with such vigor that he lifted me off the ground.

"Oh, yes, yes," I moaned in return, then added in the next breath, "But, come on, Norton, this is tacky out here in the open. Let's go back to my hotel room where we can take off our clothes and do this right." Then he jammed his thumb in my anus with such a rush that I was pinned against the tree like a wiggling doll.

"Oh, a virgin! I'll teach you what getting involved with this tapestry means, and we'll just see if you want to stay involved," he growled. "I'm going to sodomize you."

My eyes hazed over with pain, and I thought I'd lose consciousness. But I fought for control, unzipping his pants, slipping them to his ankles, and inching out of his painful grip so that I could cover his gigantic penis with my mouth before he could resist. I gagged, wanting to throw up as he shoved his huge form farther down my throat. He grew more swollen by the moment, and I knew I had him where I wanted him, moaning and groaning as though he were dying. Just as his eyes rolled back in his head, I bit him so hard that I tasted blood in my mouth. Then I stood up so quickly and raised my knee with such force against his big, vulnerable balls, that he reeled backwards, shrieked in pain, and doubled to his knees.

In a flash, I was off, running at a speed that I didn't think I could possibly reach, grabbing my suitcase from under the table, and literally hauling it in the air down the street to the Termini. I never looked back for fear he was right behind me. Once in the station, I mingled behind the stacks of luggage and the throngs of passengers scurrying through the corridors.

Slowing as I neared the ticket windows, I noticed the line up of men starting to gather around me, hiding me from view. Sweat poured into my eyes, stinging and blinding me. Steering past one man after another and keeping a sharp lookout for Norton, I finally saw an available window and scooted to safety in front of a handsome, young ticket agent who peered out from behind the bars, his long lashed, dark brown eyes sparkling with interest. "*Parle en Englesa*?" I asked.

"*Prego*, no!" He apologized sympathetically.

"Uh...*Napoli? Per favore*?" I struggled, wiping my forehead.

He smiled and held up one finger to indicate the number traveling.

"*Si*," I responded when his long lashed eyes darkened; he held up one plus three fingers and pointed to his watch. "Pronto, *per favore*, pronto."

Followed by the barrage of men, I ran with all my strength to Gate 13, where the train was pulling out of the station. The cars were all full with people hanging out the windows and yelling goodbyes. Jamming the well wishers with my suitcase I finally saw a hand extended by a handsome man, leaning out the next door and motioning me to get on. I grabbed it as he swung up my luggage and pulled me into the rolling train. I thanked him profusely as he quickly moved back to his position by the window. I was stuffed like a sardine, squished against the back of the car and caught by the door between the cars that kept opening and exposing the tracks. Somehow wedging myself up on my suitcase, I sighed with deep relief, not believing that I had escaped by a hair's breath. As the door opened, the loud rumbling of the tracks beneath poured in as the floors between the cars shifted to and fro. I knew I was a sitting duck, especially if Norton had by some slim chance boarded. My insecurites grew greater with the clacking of the tracks.

I could take it no more. I bolted off the suitcase, determined to find a safer space, mumbling "*Scusi! Scusi!*" as I climbed past the people, crammed into the aisle like herded cattle, determined to hold firm with squatter's rights. Then I saw an unmarked door and slowly turned the knob. It was the pillow and blanket room. I grinned with relief as I quickly closed the door. The squatters groaned even louder when they saw me returning with my suitcase.

I locked the door securely and collapsed on the soft pile of pillows. Numb and exhausted, my eyelashes fluttered as the aqueducts lined up outside Rome. The thought of Norton caused me to shudder and re-examine my entire connection to the tapestries. But I was so tired that I was put to sleep by the droaning rhythm of the train. And as it lurched forward between the rising mountains, ploughed past fertile farms and small villages, disappeared through long, dark tunnels, and climbed its final mountain before the station, I slept.

What I did see was the razor sharp grooves on my nose, filing it to a bloody stump. I awoke, surrounded by a pool of sweat and knew that it was imperative to confront the dream and my own stored away, dark sexual conflict. Jane, I painfully admitted, was right, and I shuttered at the thought of having attracted Norton. But how I could prevent it happening again, I was at a loss to say.

The train slowed down, and the outskirts of Naples appeared in all its poverty and squalor. Finally, the train reached the station, and I trudged off down the long platform of again, Gate 13 which filled me with uneasiness.

I stopped to order some food and a litre bottle of water from the small restaurant in the terminal and almost drank the entire thing as I watched carefully to see if anyone were following me. "Oh, Bill, where are you when I need you the most?" I moaned, indulging in self pity.

Around the entrance, I saw the taxi line-up and headed for it, hoping that I'd get one to deliver me safe and sound to the airport. Instantly, I caught the dark eyes of an equally dark skinned taxi driver who opened his door and motioned me in with an authoritative sweep of his hand. With reluctance, given the sneer on his lips and the contempt in his eyes, but not wanting to hurt his feelings, I crawled in. He jumped in, and with a lurch forward, floored the accelerator, cursing under his breath, "American women."

"What?" I asked, but he completely ignored me, even when I told him, "The

airport." With his dark eyes filled with
hate, he stared at me maliciously in the
rear view mirror; he zoomed into high
speed and zigzagged recklessly in and out
of the rushing Neapolitan traffic.

"*Napoli* is a beautiful city!" He
growled.

"*Si*," I responded in a placating
tone, fearing he might go faster. It
didn't work; he shot out in front of a
bus, missing it by inches.

"Good! I give you tour!" He asserted
with even more loathing, filling the taxi
with his raw, dangerous tension.

"Uh, no *grazie*, the airport, *per
favore*," I repeated as carefully yet as
firmly as I could, causing the wild eyed
driver to floor it again.

So quickly did we get through Naples
that before I knew it he was zooming
through the gates to a dock, screeching
to a halt next to the end of a giant
ferry, and dumping me out with my
suitcase crashing beside me. He spat on
the ground and sped off, not even wanting
a fare. For a moment, I stood there
watching in shock as he disappeared into
the dingy distance.

"Oh, shit," I exclaimed, turning
around to look at the gigantic whale with
busses being loaded into its huge cargo
pit; black smoke oozed out across the
wharf where an even angrier, screaming
dockmaster eyed me with disgust.

"Oh, no, not another one," I thought,
trying to figure out what to do. There
wasn't a taxi in sight, and I wasn't sure
I wanted to get back in one. I decided to

check and see if I could get on the
ferry.

The dockmaster shouted angrily after
me as I disappeared into the crowd. I
rushed inside the terminal, purchased a
sleeping berth, and got in line to board.
I was beginning to feel put out by all
the foreign rudeness and grew uneasier
than ever as I trudged up the high
gangplank where two white clad stewards
stood at the top and directed me to store
my luggage. Wondering why I needed to
store my luggage at all, I told them,
"First class."

"No, *Signorina*, no. *Seconda* class,"
they both said with final firmness and
directed me to the luggage racks and up
the stairs. I reached my destination
four flights later, after pushing through
hoards of shoving passengers. I wondered
why some passengers had sleeping bags
laid out in rows on the deck. I soon
found out why when I worked my way
inside, shivered from the frigid air,
then discovered airplane seats that
didn't recline. I sat down, trying to
figure out some way of getting
comfortable, curling my feet up under me,
but the seat was too short.

Deciding to deal with the horrible
situation later and feeling certain that
there was no way Norton could have
followed the crazy taxi driver, I watched
the sky darken and the shadowy backdrop
of Mt. Vesuvius disappear in the purplish
black sky as we crossed the wide Bay of
Naples. I forced myself to try to sleep,
but I never got comfortable. Thoughts of
the scene with Norton haunted me.

The next time I awakened, the ship was making landfall. The sun was coming up, lighting up Mt. Pellegrino which rose high over the darkening water, shadowing the sleeping city in its valley below.

"*Cafe latte.*" I requested of the white clad waiter behind the bar which I drank greedily. Ahead, Mt. Pellegrino reflected in the blue water. Fear spread through me as I watched the people swarming about on the dark wharf far below; I got pushed and shoved down flights of stairs and out to the ramp.

Dark specks dotted my eyes as I stepped onto the narrow, dizzying, sharply angled gangplank. Not thinking I'd ever be able to face being in Palermo alone, much less just making it down, I wanted to panic, to turn and run back, but I forced myself forward down the steep plank.

Carefully observing the emptying wharf far below and not seeing a taxi left anywhere, I step by step made my way. About halfway down, my spirits fell lower and lower, when, as though in a dream, I heard my name called. The voice was unmistakable. It was Bill, standing at the bottom. Laughing and crying simultaneously, I ran headlong down the plank and leaped into his arms.

CHAPTER III: "FREE AS A RAVEN"

"Oh, Darling, oh, thank God you're here," I sobbed into his shoulder as he patted and comforted me, saying over and over,
"I'm so sorry. I'm so sorry. Jane said you've been through real hell. I know it's not my fault, but I feel so bad about all that's happened to you. I left the funeral as soon as I could," he said, hugging me so tightly I couldn't breathe. "God, I've missed you so much, and I'm here to protect you now; nothing else is going to happen to you." When I finally calmed down, he grabbed my luggage from the dock and supported me as we walked over to the only taxi left in the lot.
"It's all right. I'm sorry about your grandfather." I responded, getting control of myself. "But, Bill, how did you know I was coming in on the ferry?" I asked in amazement, looking back at the monstrous ship as the wind picked up. It blew in an intrigue that both repulsed and lured me toward the dreaming city, surrounded on the bay by a large, darkened green area of ancient trees. We loaded our suitcases into an even smaller taxi than the one in Naples.
"Process by elimination...and intuition. Since you weren't on any flight, I checked the ferry schedule. Don't forget, I've also studied Goethe's journey, and I know he arrived on a boat

as well," he said, grinning and stooping so far over to get into the small back seat and appearing so cramped, that it almost made me laugh to see how he dwarfed the car. I covered the huge smile with my hand when I caught the driver's serious stare in the rear view mirror; that is until Bill said in too much of a western drawl for me to keep a straight face, "*Parle en Englesa?*"

I didn't laugh long, for the driver looked even more somber as he sped off down the wharf and replied a bit too curtly, "A little."

"Uh, *Signor* Soderno's hotel?" I asked to which he quickly shook his head and zoomed off down the palm lined streets, swerving to avoid the heaps of garbage.

Bill cuddled me close under his arm; I lay my head on his shoulder and closed my eyes. No words were needed to express my relief and my love at not being so desperately alone. I wanted to tell him about how I'd fought being rescued and how afraid I'd been; but upon seeing the driver's contemptuous look again, I said nothing and decided to concentrate on the happiness I felt sitting next to Bill. But, for some reason, a pang of depression passed through me as I scanned the bay area. For years I'd looked forward to visiting the Public Gardens. Then I realized that we were driving directly in front of it. The old dank, familiar odor smelled like the Forum yet reeked of even older civilizations; it floated heavily through the windows. I peered past the gigantic trees into the dark, inner garden. "*Giardino?*" I quickly asked the driver who suspiciously eyed me in his rear view mirror before cutting sharply across the busy lanes of traffic then speeding up and driving as recklessly as the Naples driver.

"Stop," I told him too late, but not before, out of the corner of my eye, I caught a glimpse of Norton, leaning against one of the pillars surrounding the park and pretending to pour over a newspaper. I slouched down in my seat, overwhelmed by such nausea and blurred vision that I wasn't sure if he'd spotted me. Pain caused my face to twitch. I couldn't believe he'd traced me so easily. "Oh, shit!" I exclaimed, unable to utter his name, much less tell Bill. This made the driver eye me even more suspiciously and turn the car so sharply that he almost rammed into the city gate's pillar before coming to a screeching halt in front of an abandoned, vandalized building.

"What's the matter?" Bill asked, trying to ignore the crazy driver who slammed out of the car, threw our suitcase out amongst piles of debris, and acted as though he were going to throw us out next. He jerked open the door and stood there glaring at us with his hand out. I barely had time to dig in my purse and pay him before he jumped back in and took off so fast that he scattered dirt and debris all over us.

I screamed at him, "*Signor* Soderno's hotel?!" But he never heard me.

"Listen, Bill, I saw Norton back there at the garden." I blurted, spitting out the dirt in my mouth.

"Whaaat? Where?" He questioned, his mouth ajar. "Let's go back." And he ran off down the narrow street to find another taxi.

"Don't leave me," I screamed, peering inside the glass shattered, deserted area that oddly had an intercom mounted on one of the outside walls. Someone could easily have been lurking inside the debris strew lower entry were it not for a locked, giant iron gate that prevented any entry. As Bill turned to come back, I looked farther within the bars and spotted an iron caged elevator on the back wall, partially hidden by the empty paint cans and assorted containers.

Bill ran back to me, hugging me, telling me not to be afraid, and assuring me that he was there to protect me. We stood for a second when, from directly behind us, someone with a deep, masculine voice said very authoritatively,

"Yes, may I help you?"

It didn't sound like Norton, but it scared me so that I spun around and was eye to eye with a handsome, dark-eyed gentleman. I was totally relieved. He looked so composed, in an elderly, stately way, that I knew at once he was Paulo's friend. "*Signor* Soderno?" I asked, hoping my intuition was working.

"Yes! You must be the Americans Paulo called me about; I've been expecting you. Won't you come in?" He asked in perfect English, as he unlocked the giant outer gate and we waded through the debris and pushed past the cans. Then he unlocked another inner iron gate and finally the door to the iron caged elevator.

Bill stooped to get into the small elevator and crammed in the suitcases.

"You must excuse our entrance. Construction, you understand. Vandals have forced us to the upper floor, but you will find our small hotel very comfortable," *Signor* Soderno assured us.

We were silent as he pushed number three; and as we slowly made our way up, the awful image of Norton pinning me against the tree rushed into my mind. I stumbled on the oriental rug as I stepped into the lobby. I hardly saw the ornate bar, glistening with crystal cannisters of cognacs, whiskeys, and other liquers or the giant, gleaming brass coffee urn; all I could think about was Norton.

After Bill secured the key, we entered the long hallway to the rooms. He could tell something was bothering me, but he didn't push me. As we reached number eight, he simply swept me off my feet, holding me close to his chest, kissing me and assuring me that everything was going to be all right and that we'd take care of Norton and business - later. I melted; and as he carried me over the threshold and closed the door, he shut out all the problems I'd had and all the dangers I'd faced. The horrid images of Norton vanished out the open window as he placed me on a comfortable, large bed with crisp, white sheets, smothered me with kisses and started undressing me.

Only once, I glanced out the window into the courtyard and saw an adjacent terrace in close proximity to our window; the surrounding buildings were abandoned.

I ignored a faint nagging fear that told
me to close the shutters, for I was
immersed in Bill's urgent, passionate
kiss, in his muscular body that cradled
me back and forth as he pulled me onto
his lap. His lips slipped down to my
breasts with such tenderness that I
intertwined my fingers in his auburn
curls and pressed his head closer.

"Ohh, I've missed your soft touch,"
he moaned as his lips traveled farther,
and my hands grasped his hair more
tightly until I pulled his lips back to
mine; our bodies intertwined. We moved in
perfect harmony to the throb of the
emotions, pouring from deep within and
healing the aches of separation. Bill's
eyes shone with love, then misted over as
the driving energy quickened and demanded
outlet. Staring deeply into his hazy eyes
and feeling all the emotions rise to a
mounting peak, we hovered in between
realities. Then the tears of happiness
and pain flowed like a river, cleansing
and purifying. Bill clung to me with all
his might until slowly his muscles
relaxed, his embrace slackened, and his
body fell into deep exhausted sleep.
Savoring the feeling of ecstatic oneness
for a moment, I joined him, our slow,
rhythmic breathing attesting to our
peaceful, complete surrender to sleep.

The sun, shining directly into the
wide window and onto my bare back, awoke
me with its scorching, burning intensity
and an overwhelming urge to get up, go
find Dr. Aliamo, and rescue the
tapestries. I quickly rolled over,
sitting up on the edge of the bed and

looking directly at the maid who shook out her dust mop on the adjacent terrace. Leaping back, I jerked the sheet up and glanced down to see Bill completely exposed. I covered him and calmed myself. Without warning, the image of the bloody file pressed against my nose came pouring in on my mind.

"Oh, Bill," I nudged him. "I just had that horrible dream again. I've got to talk about this; it's driving me crazy." But he didn't budge. Frustrated, I leaned up. Glancing across the courtyard into an abandoned building. I couldn't believe my eyes. It was a file, an actual file laying on the construction strewn floor. Dumbstruck, I stared at it when the sun struck it in such a way that I could have sworn that it was covered with blood. "My God!" I gasped, nudging Bill again so hard he let out a yell and sat straight up in bed,

"Wh-what, Charla? You okay, Baby? You look like you've just seen a ghost!"

But I never answered him. I crawled out of bed, out of sight of the window, pulled some clothes out of the suitcase, repacked it, and started getting ready; my hands shook and my tears welled, ready to overflow. I'd had enough. I wanted to go home.

Bill crawled down on the floor beside me, took me in his arms, and held me until I could tell him about what I'd seen. He leaped back on the bed and stared across the courtyard as though daring anyone to invade our privacy. I slowly crawled back up beside him, peering out the window. He looked at me curiously, saying, "Honey, I don't see a damn thing!"

"Whaat!" I gasped, but Bill was right. It was not to be found in and amongst the empty paint cans and other debris. "Now I've really lost it, or my eyes are playing deadly tricks on me."

"I don't know, Charla, but I smell a rat. I understand that you're upset about having seen Norton, especially since that means he's following us. But we expected that to happen. Come on, Honey, you're no quitter. I already see some real growth in you, but something is eating away at you. Level with me. What's happened? Did you have an encounter with Norton?" He asked, but upon seeing my face contort with pain, he stopped and wrapped his arms around me; as I told him the grueling details, he held me tighter and tighter. He was quiet for some time, then whispered in my ear, "Don't worry about a damn thing. I'll take care of him."

His muscles tightened as he stood up and dressed with such speed that I barely had time to get ready, grab my purse and race out the door behind him. "In fact, I'm going to take care of him right now," he yelled. I'd forgotten how prompt Bill could be in taking care of matters related to me or how protective, overly protective, he became if anyone in any way threatened me. I quickly wondered if I'd made a mistake in telling him, and if so, I feared I'd just placed Bill's life in danger.

"Bill, hold on," I pleaded. "You don't realize how cold blooded Norton is... nor how dangerous; he's a true villain, who will do anything to get what he wants. And he wants the tapestry at any cost." But there was no stopping him. He sped down the dark hallway and swung open the door to the lobby.

Signor Soderno attentively waited behind the desk, our cold cups of coffee and rolls still sitting on the silver tray. He detained Bill by asking for the key and offering him the rolls which Bill politely took. As I entered the lobby, *Signor* Soderno's eyes widened. "Oh, you must be very, very careful with your purse; street crime is terrible in Palermo. Hold it securely under your arm, or they will rip it off your shoulder." Then he stared at Bill who leaned over the rolls like a bull ready to enter the ring. "Is everything all right? You are comfortable? Your accomodations are in order?"

"Yes, everything is great, thank you; we just need directions to the Public Gardens," Bill said, his words forced, his face flushed and his eyes intent.

"It's just a few blocks over; you can't miss it, but please be careful," he warned us again as Bill bolted for the elevator. There was no talking him out of confronting Norton.

Peering out from behind the elevator's bars at the trashed out, lower area and then at the abandoned, desolate looking street, I questioned our safety. I clutched my purse and grabbed Bill's hand when he took off in a fast stride down a street that quickly zigzagged and dead-ended. After a few more confusing turns, a taxi passed. I could have sworn it was the same driver as earlier. Even the small car was the same. "Bill, did you catch a glimpse of that driver?" I asked nervously, but he had been so preoccupied that he'd missed seeing him. "I think he's the one from the ferry, and I'll bet he's going to the Public Gardens. When I questioned him earlier, he was just too wierd." I thought about it for a second.

"Honey, I'm scared that Norton might have more people involved than we realize. I'm convinced that in Rome he hired a guy named Michael. We've got to be careful. This really is more dangerous than you think. We don't even have a gun. Why don't we just concentrate on finding Dr. Aliamo before Norton does," I reasoned with him, but to no avail. I tried to keep up with his quick pace as we turned along the bay. Up ahead, I could see the large, green park with its unusual diamond shape. So did Bill who took off running. "Come on," he yelled.

But I wouldn't give up. "Bill, slow down and listen to me. If that taxi driver has been hired by Norton, it's not safe to be on these streets, at least not without a car. Let's stop and call *Signor* Soderno, so he can order us one; then we can follow that driver." And I muttered under my breath, "If that's possible in this labyrinth of a town." We passed a newstand, and I spotted a phone. Somehow I got Bill to stop; but the entire time I talked, he tapped his foot and paced up and down. He barely heard me when I told him we couldn't get a car until the next morning; instead, he again grabbed my hand and hurried me across the street to the park, surrounded by an incredibly high, iron spiked fence with giant, sculptured pillars at every corner and fronted by an ornate gate that was covered with scaffolding.

Thank goodness, Norton was nowhere in sight. Nor was the taxi driver, but Bill wouldn't give up, insisting that we take a quick stroll through the Gardens just to see if Norton had ducked in out of sight. Even with Bill present, I couldn't bear the thought of another encounter with Norton, especially in a park. But I followed him, rushing through the side entrance. Off to the right, I was relieved to see a guardhouse and a group of men who sat in wooden chairs, chatting amicably but stopping to stare at us as we headed for the center of the Gardens.

They watched as we took off down the palm lined, wide crosspath, cutting diagonally toward the great diamond. We walked deeper into the palms that under normal circumstances would have created a peacefulness, a regal ancientness.

Looking anxiously for Norton, Bill seemed to ignore my protests of losing sight of the guards as we entered another path lined by 200 year old hardwoods that opened onto a fountain with thick, lime-green mulberry vines forming arches over a multitude of walkways down which I could imagine Norton lurking, ready for us to walk by. "God, we'll never find him in here, and I hope we don't," I cried, taking a sweeping look out over the bay at the sun, setting behind Mt.

Pellegrino, its shadow jutting ghostlike far into the blue Tyrrian Sea.

Yet Bill felt compelled to push on down path after path. Finally, I could take it no more. Just the thought of Norton grabbing me from behind a tree made me start shaking. Fighting my fears and trying to stay calm, I collapsed on a park bench and told Bill that I had to get control of myself; I then forced myself to think of clues that could lead us to Dr. Aliamo. Goethe had helped me once, and he'd visited here, so I concentrated with all my might and tried to ignore Bill who raced toward the next crosspath. I scanned the area for the mouth of the Oreto River which Goethe described as the home of the famous Phoenician, King Alcinoos. Maybe this was his Garden, I thought. I felt spurred on by the old familiar odor of ancient civilizations, oozing out of the black soil.

I recalled Dr. Aliamo's letter and his mention of the tapestries' Tyrrian purple color, a dye that the Lydians had gotten from the Phoenicians who extracted it from snails off their coast, an area that the Greeks called Phoinix - "Land of Purple." Then I recalled the research and tried to piece it all together. After the Lydians migrated to Italy, they kept in touch with their former friends who had moved here to the mouth of the Oreto. And when the Lydians, later called the Etruscans, were threatened with extinction, who else but the Phoenicians would they have entrusted with their precious tapestries, I reasoned. When

Bill came running back by, I grabbed his hand, pulled him down on the bench, and forced him to listen, reminding him that our most important mission was finding the tapestries not Norton.

"Where? Here? In Sicily?" He asked, peering down a path that apparently led to the other side of the Gardens. I had his attention momentarily even though his eyes never stopped darting in every direction.

"Exactly, Bill, with the tried and true Phoenicians." I said, as he stood up impatiently, pulling me toward another small square where vandals had bashed in a fountain and crashed the archways. The decaying smell increased. The deep pink streaks of the sunset darkened to purple. "But where would they have hidden them? Certainly not here in Palermo, I agree," I said, adding, "Besides, even if we had a clue, Bill, it's getting dark, and let's not forget Soderno's warning.

"Okay," he somewhat acquiesced, "but let's at least walk down the other side before we head back." He stopped, sniffing the air; it was a strong musty odor, ranked with heavy muskiness. "I told you I smelled a rat!" And he broke into a run toward a clearing where a high wall was laden with cages of first goats and chickens and then a huge purple-black bird.

"Damn, this is unbelievable!" I exclaimed, forgetting all about Norton and my quest. "It's a Raven!" And I ran over to its dingy cage. My eyes opened wide in amazement; I'd never seen a Raven in captivity.

"A what?!" He gasped, also momentarily distracted from finding Norton. "Come on, Charla...Holy shit. I'd have called it a Phoenix if I didn't know better!" We stood staring, our mouths gaping, our eyes wanting to bulge at the sight of the huge, proud bird.

"You know what they symbolize, don't you? They're messengers from the other side, Mephistopheles' mythic birds. Do you think Goethe is helping us again? Why else would this Raven have been placed squarely in our path? And why here, in this Garden?" I emotionally questioned, getting more upset by the moment.

"A holy bird?!" Bill questioned when it came hopping over toward us. "And in such a wretched cage? Wonder what it did to deserve this?"

Up close its Roman beak appeared even more dignified, and its muscular body even larger. "Shit!" Bill exclaimed. "I bet the wingspan alone could send this mighty bird soaring over the highest mountains." Then he stopped, seemingly having forgotten all about Norton, for he couldn't believe the timing of the bird as it flew from its ax handle perch in the thorny bougainvillea. As though answering Bill's question, it aimed its body upward against the triple wired cyclone mesh roof and proudly displayed its wingspread of at least four feet. At that moment, the sun struck its breast and created a brilliant white diamond pattern.

"Wow! Charla, did you catch that?" Bill asked in amazement.

"How could I have missed it?" I exclaimed. "It _is_ holy!"

"Even more amazing is the fact that it speaks our language!"

I turned to look at Bill to see if he were teasing. "Well, let's test it out. Does it have any water?" To which the bird responded by hopping over to the neighboring cage where the chickens had a trough of water. He poked his head through the wire and sipped. "Amazing," I gasped.

"Sure enough! This bird understands English!" Bill exclaimed.

"This is really upsetting. Do you realize, Bill, that this bird must have a direct subconscious link?" I blurted. It stared at me, its black eye shone with ferocity and fervor and lured me into a wild primitivism. Out of the black pools shot a dart of light, intense with powerful energy. At the same moment, the sun's last light struck its feathers at such an angle that they looked on fire.

"Now I'm convinced of it. This _is_ the Garden of King Alcinoos. This bird proves it, Bill." I emphatically said; but rather than get excited, I found myself getting more upset by the minute. Tears flowed down my cheeks. "Oh, I feel so sorry for it; nothing deserves being treated like this. Besides, Ravens don't belong in cages. They're free. They belong to the spirit of the air. This cruelty goes against everything I believe in!" I cried, the tears now streaking my mascara into my eyes and causing them to burn.

"Charla, I've never seen you this upset over an animal!" Bill said, as the Raven hopped back and forth in front of us, staring at us and cocking his head from side to side as though catching every word.

At that moment, some children with an old man came by. The old man taunted and jabbed the Raven with a stick, tantalizing with "crow, crow, crow," while the children laughed. Bill and I reached to help, when to all our amazement, the bird attacked the stick, snatching it with its powerful beak and wrenching it from the man who quickly dropped it, looked at the bird surprisedly, and hurried away.

"And to top it off, it's tortured!" I moaned, the tears flowing again. Hopping at great speed, the Raven maneuvered its way into the corner and forced its strong beak in the thick wire. Back and forth it twisted its large head with a wrenching rhythm. Our eyes riveted on the hole in the inner two layers of mesh which the bird had ripped away." Bill, look! A way out. That's its escape. It's showing us. Oh, Bill, we've got to help it!" I cried, my tears gone, my eyes shining with purpose.

Bill looked at me as though I had lost my mind. He nervously looked around to see if anyone had overheard us. His eyes again became intent in their search for Norton. "That wire is too thick. It would take wire cutters, Charla, which we don't have and couldn't find. Plus, we've got to find Norton."

I refused to listen to him and stepped back; I was surveying the cage for another way it could get out, when my foot struck a metal object that clinked up against the outside of the cage and caught my attention. We both looked down when a chilling shriek escaped my lips, for directly under my shoe was a bloody file, just like the one I'd seen in my dreams. I lost my balance and stumbled backwards.

"Oh, no, not again! Now I'm convinced it's real. See, Bill, I told you," I cried, as he caught me; he simultaneously reached down, picked up the foreboding object, and forced me to confront it.

"Look, Charla, you must open your eyes and look at this. Yes, it's real, but it's not what you think. Well...It's a file all right, but it's covered with rust...rust, Charla. Look!"

I slowly opened one eye, my face hidden in his shoulder, and to my shock, he was right. It was a long, skinny, sharply pointed, but rusty file. A big smile crossed my lips as I sheepishly admitted my error, but I also realized that Jane was wrong. This wasn't about being filed alive; it was a tool which we could use to free the bird. "Oh, Bill! We can rescue the Raven. We can."

"Wait a minute, Charla. Do you realize what the Sicilian authorities would do to us if we got caught? And let's not forget this high, spiked fence. Besides, I've got to locate Norton and stop him once and for all," Bill muttered as he pulled me away from the cage. I resisted, for I wanted to communicate to the Raven that we'd be back - at midnight, I decided. Leading me by my arm, he headed around the other side of the Gardens where I forced him to stop and look up at the scaffolding covering the original entrance. I lowered my voice. "Look where the spiked iron meets the pillar; see the slight ledge that could serve as a footstep and check out the niches for our hands. You could go first, then pull me up."

"You're getting us off the track, Charla. Sure it sounds workable, but I don't like it. I've got more important business to take care of right now," he insisted as he literally hauled me back through the Gardens.

But Bill couldn't stop me; I felt driven. Not even my fear of Norton could prevent me from freeing the Raven. "You must understand. I have to do this. Can't you just see the Raven perched up in that tall sycamore in the morning?" I asked excitedly. "Or would it head south as fast and as straight as the crow flies?"

"Come on, Charla. I know how you feel about the..." He stopped when we encountered the guards, waiting to lock the gates. "Let's head back to the hotel and see if we can't order a car. You're right, we need wheels to find Dr. Aliamo before Norton does," he concluded, heading down the winding streets and back to the hotel. *Signor* Soderno's deep voice on the intercom sounded welcoming as he buzzed the wrought iron gate. He smiled as the elevator reached the third floor.

"*Buenos noches*!" He greeted us. "You have had several important telephone calls. Please use the sitting room, and I will handle our operators. The first call is from *Signor* Don Meldon. The second is from Jane who left no number." He pointed to the lounge where we sat waiting until I picked up the phone and heard the warm, familiar voice.

"Thank God I've located you. Why haven't you called? Oh, never mind. Are you all right? I mean really all right? And how is Bill?"

"Fine, Don, we're really fine. I'm sorry for not calling. It's been so crazy. How are you? And where the hell is Jane?" I asked.

"She's had a delay, and, yes, I've been damned concerned. But I won't scold you." He said fatherly. "I'm too excited to find out what you've discovered."

I needed to figure out how I could secretly tell him about our intent to free the Raven. I paused, grasping for words and looking around to see if anyone were listening. "Of course, the Public Gardens. We just got back from the Gardens, you know, where Goethe had his vision about the Phoenicians?"

"Ah, yes, Charla. You're on to something. Arachne's tapestry depicted the most famous Phoenician princess, Europa, daughter of King Phoinix, being abducted by Zeus as the great white bull who carried her across the waves to Crete where she gave birth to the Minotaur," he excitedly told me. "And, of course, Daedalus was employed to design a labyrinth so intricate that not even he

could escape. But, Charla, you do know
where he headed when he escaped?"

Doing my best to understand his
symbolic message by using my intuition, I
blurted, "Yes, south, as straight as the
crow flies."

"W-e-l-l, no-o, you're on the right
track, but, he headed west - to Sicily,
where a Sican King, Cocolus,
conditionally took him in."

I was catching on fast. "On the
condition that he build him a labyrinth?"
I put the clues together, a cave, for I
knew about Daedalus' underground
fortress.

Bill, who had listened quietly,
nudged me. He had been looking at the
map, and apparently on hearing my
suggestion pointed to Agrigento, located
directly south. Then my eyes opened wide,
for I remembered Goethe's great,
memorable love for Agrigento, ancient
Acragas, Daedalus' legendary city. Bill
beamed when I shook my head yes, then
jumped up and checked with Signor Soderno
about a car.

"Yes, Charla," Don was saying, his
voice lower and sounding closer. "Now, my
dear, you must proceed very cautiously.
Do not miss a detail. You will see the
guideposts marked at every turn. Promise
me you'll be extremely careful."

"I promise. I'll call you as soon as
possible, Don. Please don't worry and
tell Jane to hurry and get the hell over
here," I said, hanging up and joining
Bill, anxious to find out about the car.
But *Signor* Soderno was leaving, shaking
his head in apology and repeating,

"*Domani*, Bill, *domani*." He turned over the front desk to a young night clerk. I was so relieved that we couldn't depart until morning, for I was more determined than ever to free the Raven.

Arm in arm we walked back down the hall to the room. Once the lock clicked behind us, we pulled out our maps, guidebooks, and notes from Goethe's experiences at Agrigento. We packed in order to leave first thing in the morning.

I finally convinced Bill to forget about Norton for the time being and to help me since releasing the Raven was the most important thing imaginable to me. He finally acquiesced; and after having something to eat in the dining room, we dressed in black clothes and tennis shoes, and walked out into the lobby as the clock struck midnight.

The night clerk looked at us questioningly as we got into the small elevator. Concern for our safety was written all over his face.

Hurriedly, we made our way to the water - then over to the Gardens.

"Damn, wouldn't you know it! Those old street lamps work," Bill lamented when we were in sight of the well lit Garden. "And look at that moon; I've never seen it so full nor so bright. This ain't gonna be easy, Charla. We're really off the track of the tapestries, and we're placing ourselves in a vulnerable position with Norton. Sure you want to go through with it?"

"Absolutely positive, even though I'm scared shitless," I replied stopping at the old gate and looking up at the dangerous fence, then at the busy traffic. "Damn, we'll be seen. I have it - let's pretend we're making out. When the traffic breaks, you go over first, so you can help me down on the other side."

"Oh-h," Bill groaned, his bulge evident as he pulled me close and began kissing me. "I'm liking this chore," he said as our kisses became passionate. The fire between us flamed as we pressed tighter against each other, forgetting all about the setting or our purpose.

When I opened my eyes, I snapped back to reality and noticed that the traffic had thinned. "Quick, Bill, go!" I yelled.

"My voice might be much higher if I don't straddle this fence carefully," he said as he climbed up on the pillar, crossed delicately over the spikes, and extended his hand to me which I grasped, stepped onto the ledge, then used the niches to hoist myself to the top as Bill jumped safely to the ground. I crossed over the spikes, saw Bill's hands extended, then leaped into his arms. With his hands tight around my waist, he lowered me to the ground. I knew that we had crossed over more than just a fence. We had entered another realm. "Run to that first hedge," he whispered. "Quick!!" The traffic poured down Umberto Street, streaking lights on the water as though from another world.

We crouched down and ran like bats out of hell for the first hedge row.

"Stay in the shadows," I called to Bill who was already out from the first hedge and heading for the second. The shadows eerily danced like apparitions as the balmy breeze blew across the still Garden. "And run serpentine," I called again, but Bill had already disappeared in the shadows of the second hedge. "Wait for me!" I yelled, crouching down and running as fast as I could into the moon drenched shapes.

Bill's extended hand grabbed mine as we stealthily skirted in the phantasmal reflections of the tall magnolias and the white sycamores with their bark, resembling sentinels watching over the Underworld. Within minutes, we were deep into the Garden. The haunting shadows stretched from every corner and danced off the hedges and the trees when the moon struck its fullest position overhead. Bill continued to grasp my hand as we bent our backs and raced for the final line-up of trees, skirting in front of the animals' cages.

The sleeping animals did not stir as we raced from behind the last protective shadows. Not even the chickens made a sound.

"Shit!" Bill huskily lamented. "All the cages look alike."

"Look for its ax handle perch," I recalled, "under the purple bougainvillea."

"It's gone. Damn!"

"No, it's not, Bill! There it is - on the ground. Isn't that terrible. Now it doesn't even have a perch."

"Sh-h-h! Charla, don't worry. It's next perch will be that tall sycamore." Bill whispered as he stuck his fingers in the wire mesh and bent it back. "Found it!" he said, picking up the file and getting to work. As he pressed against the wire, leaning on it with all his weight, a loud grating of the file reverberated across the strangely quiet Garden, sounding like chaulk scraping a blackboard. The chickens stirred. I cringed, remembering the dream.

"Shit! This wire is damn tough to file. This ain't gonna be easy."

"Or quiet," I whispered, pressing my palms over my ears. The grating, grinding noise was followed by the loud snap of a broken wire. After a few more tense moments and what felt like shattering sounds to my ears, I complained. "That's too loud. Somebody's going to hear us." Bill ignoring me, pushed and grunted, working steadily as I grew more and more nervous by the second.

"Please hurry!...Oh! Bill, did you hear that?" I jumpily asked when a loud bang came from behind the wall. "Oh, I just know somebody is over there, and they're going to come and catch us! Can't you hurry?" I asked, waited skittishly, asked again, walked back and forth in front of the cage; but by the time I asked the third time, it was Bill who was getting short with me.

"Do you still want to do this?" He asked curtly. "Oh, shit! I cut myself on this damned, sharp wire."

"I'm sorry, Bill," I apologized. "I just can't stand waiting here like sitting ducks. Are you bleeding? How deep is the cut? Now I feel bad for thinking of myself when you're the one doing all the work and getting hurt. Are you sure you're okay?"

"It's okay!" He whispered, his tone in between calmness and agitation. "Just a bad scratch from trying to bend this damned wire back." And he started filing again, the loud grinding and grating sounding like bombs exploding in my ears.

"How much longer, Bill? Is the hole big enough for the Raven to crawl out? Oh, Bill, did you hear that?" I asked, looking around to see where the loud noise came from. Nothing stirred except the wind.

"Be calm, Charla!" Bill said reassuringly. "I'm almost through."

"Oh, thank God! I can't wait to get out of here. Are your sure that hole is big enough?" After a few more grinding screeches, more snapping pops, a few more scratches, and some forceful bending of the tough wire, I couldn't stand it anymore. "Hurry, oh, hurry, Bill, please hurry." I whispered urgently as the noises echoed in the quiet garden. I never anticipated that it would take this long. I tried distracting myself. The animals never stirred. I wondered if the Raven even knew we were there, for I never saw its black head peak out from the stockade.

Finally, Bill announced proudly. "And that'll do it...at least it'd better do it. I've spilled my blood on this damned tough wire! Now to bend it back."

"How do you know? What if it doesn't see it?"

"Are you kidding? That bird is super intelligent, and I know that the first sign of any change in its environment would be immediately detected. It'll hop right over to its hole, find it big enough to get its body through, and then fly....Shit, I cut myself again!" He groaned.

"Here - let me help," I said as he shook the blood off his hand. But I couldn't bend the stiff wire at all, not even when I pushed with all my strength. I noticed blood all over the file, mingling with the rust and turning it deep red.

After a few more grunts and some heavy exertion, Bill was satisfied with the wire tunnel. "Thank God, it's done. The Raven can crawl through the hole and get the hell outta here. Let's do the same." Bill said, staring at the bloody file.

"Not so fast," growled a voice from behind the dark shrubs, skirting in front of the cages. It was Norton with the taxi driver and a dark haired, dark skinned thug. The blood drained out of my face as my mouth dropped and my knees shook so violently I could hardly stand.

"You bitch. I'll deal with you in a moment," he snarled, glaring at me. But before Bill could securely grasp my hand to flee, Norton reached out and grabbed him, jerking my hand loose and throwing me to the ground with such force that it knocked the breath out of me. He held Bill while the taxi driver pounded him in the stomach. A scream stuck in my throat, and my eyes hazed over with panic. I fought to control myself when I saw the blood pouring from Bill's lips. But when

Norton shoved the taxi driver out of the way to take a turn at Bill, I could take it no more, diving head first at Norton's knees. He didn't feel a thing, just threw me to the ground again and pointed for the thug to take care of me.

But my interference gave Bill a split second to recover; and when Norton turned back around, Bill clasped the file like a mighty weapon, gleaming red in the moonlight. With a flash, his hand struck Norton in the cheek with such force from the pointed instrument that he groaned as though he'd been bludgeoned, grabbed his face with both hands, and fell back against the cage. Bill struck again, this time jamming the file in the taxi driver's stomach. He doubled over, reeling forward before regaining control of his legs and running toward the darkened trees. The thug jumped off me and grabbed Bill from behind, locking his arms so that Bill couldn't move.

"You'll pay for this, you fucking asshole," Norton venomously swore, reeling his fist back, but he struck the cage. Suddenly, with a shriek and a gutteral cry, the Raven squeezed through the opening, spread its gigantic wings and swooped down maliciously on top of Norton's head, its craggy, sharp talons clawing at his eyes.

"Whoooa, help!" Norton screamed, completely caught off guard and scared out of his wits. So was the thug, who dropped Bill's arms and ran with all his might into the night.

Norton grabbed his face again as the Raven swooped up then descended once more with its black feet, aimed at Norton's eyes as though it would claw them out.

"Come on, Charla," Bill yelled as I stood there mesmerized and in shock at the spectacle. He grabbed my hand, and my feet literally left the ground as he ran at full speed, heading for the shadows of the sycamores. We didn't look back as we darted across the Garden. I thought my heart would burst it beat so rapidly, but I didn't dare slow down. Crouching over, sneaking low, and avoiding the moonlight, we crossed the inner sanction. The hedges havened our bodies as we skirted toward the ancient entrance.

Across from the iron fence, I came to such a sudden stop and pulled on Bill's hand so abruptly that we almost fell forward. "Wait!" I huskily demanded, not even sure myself what halted me.

"What is it, Charla?" Bill asked expectantly.

"I don't know...Shit! Look at that - it's that taxi driver! Damn!" I exclaimed, watching in horror as he pulled up in the empty lot, followed by a police car that shined its spotlight directly into the Garden at us, eerily lighting up the magnolias and sycamores.

"Duck!" Bill yelled as he placed his hand on the back of my neck and forced me to the ground. "Bastard is trying to get us arrested," he cursed, spitting up blood and shaking off the pain. "Lurking out here and getting caught by that Sicilian cop is not my idea of having fun. Look! They're both pulling out. Let's get the hell outta here," he exclaimed, standing us on our feet

simultaneously and bolting us forward
with great strength and speed. He barely
slowed when we reached the fence, and in
one felled swoop he was straddling it,
extending his hand to me, and commanding,
"Quick, give me your hand!"

For one brief moment as I
precariously held onto the pillar and
readied to jump, I took one long, last
look at the ancient Gardens, bathing in
the moonlight and soaking in the looming
shadows. And in that instant, I
envisioned the Raven, living in the
sycamore, calling out its gutteral cry,
and watching over the sacred area like
the sentinel of darkness.

"Charla, Jump! You're gonna get us
caught!" Bill shouted as the traffic
again started to pour down the street. I
leaped into his arms; in one motion, he
had placed my feet on the ground, grabbed
my hand, and was calmy yet firmly pulling
me forward, away from the ancient
entrance.

Around the Garden, past the auto
shops and the long rows of empty vendors'
tables, and up toward the hotel, Bill
flew, dragging me behind. I took two
steps for his one.

We were running so fast that we
hardly noticed the whistles nor the slow
build up of cars that crept along beside
us.

At least I didn't notice them. Bill
did, and I could feel a cold nervousness
run up his spine. It was contagious; and
a build up of pressure, like a hand
pressing on my back, suddenly flared at
the base of my skull. I cast an askant

glance at the carloads of hoodlums who were now creeping along beside us with their windows down; then I saw the taxi driver trailing very slowly behind them, his lights off.

Bill's grasp tightened, and I saw his neck veins bulge.

I heard grinding brakes and smelled the carbon monoxide fumes. But when we heard the crack of car doors opening and peripherally saw the men getting out of the cars and heading for us, Bill lurched forward with such force and speed that my feet barely touched the sidewalk.

"Run, Charla! Run for your life!" He commanded loudly, dragging me along with him. I could hear their stamping on the pavement behind us, and I squelched the scream that rose in my throat. Panic swelled in my chest. "Let's lose 'em," Bill shouted, as he took a sharp right down a dark street. I didn't object, but held onto Bill for dear life as we turned our next left, travelling rapidly in front of the chasers.

I never looked back, but the feel of the hand, reaching out to grab me never left, not even when we neared the hotel. We made for the gate and laid on the buzzer. There was no answer. The night clerk had apparently fallen asleep. Frantically, I pressed the button with all my might, just as Bill spun around and confronted the handful of men who came racing around the corner so fast that they almost went past us. Sneeringly, they turned to face us.

"Help!!" I screamed into the innercom. "Wake up!!" I cried in absolute terror, my heart pounding ferociously as the black, vacant area piercingly echoed my panic stricken words.

"Get back!" Bill yelled at the top of his lungs, throwing me up against the iron gates and thrashingly searching for the file in his back pocket.

"HELP!!" A blood curdling scream burst agonizingly within and escaped from my lips like a fierce siren. The gang of dark eyed, greasy, slicked haired punks hesitated only momentarily, casting a murderously evil glance in my direction before leaping for Bill.

Quicker than I'd ever seen him, he was one step ahead of them, displaying the file and thrusting it with such severe and swift motion into the chest of one of the attackers that it stunned and stopped the rest of them. The small, slick head bent over, groaning and grasping himself before doubling over. The others reached to support him.

Bill jerked the file back, the bloody cuts and scratches covering his arms, but the file was no longer covered with Bill's blood alone. Even in the dark, I could see the deep red, fresh color covering it and dripping into the dirt all over the debris strewn entrance.

Screaming again at the top of my lungs, I closed my eyes for a flashing second and saw the dwarf in the dream, wallowing in the bloody pool; but this time, Bill appeared with blood all over him. "No!!" It didn't even sound like my voice. But it was overpowered by the loud buzzing of the gate which opened just as the dark men lunged forward, their dirty hands grasping and ripping at my clothes. Falling and simultaneously being hauled by Bill, we crashed through the gate which miraculously clicked behind us. Without looking back, we flew for the elevator.

As we ascended, Bill dropped the bloody file through the bars of the elevator. As it fell, something in me got tossed away with it, something dark and heavy. It clinked with firm, yet ghoulish finality as it struck the debris strewn floor far below, and I hoped I never saw it again as long as I lived. Bill had taken quite a beating; I wondered if he were okay even though he acted fine, saying, "Long drinks!" as we creakily made our way to safety. My heart still pounded so loud I couldn't hear myself think; I steadied my wobbly knees and pressed my shaking hands against the top of my hips. Bill took the deepest breath possible and blew it out gustfully. I followed suit, trying to calm myself.

Bill was right; we needed stiff drinks, shots of cognac, I decided. The door opened and the sleepy desk clerk rose to greet us.

"*Buenos noches,*" he blurted, suddenly wide awake. He stared in shock at Bill's bloody arms and mouth, then shiftedly averted his glance when Bill just as quickly placed one arm around me and the other behind his back. Then he looked me up and down, checking out my scuffed elbows and torn clothing.

"Long drinks," Bill said again, as I pointed to the tall glasses, then to the dark, crystal-filled container of cognac which the clerk hurriedly took down, as though wanting riddance of any problem we might present. He filled two tall glasses completely full. Retrieving them with somewhat steady hands, I thanked him, wished him good night, and rushed across the oriental rugs to the hall door.

The fumes from the strong liquor were already taking some of the tension away as we reached the room and locked the door securely behind us. The bitter, sharp taste of the brandy cut like fire down our throats and warmed our bodies with its heat. We laughed nervously as our black sleuthing clothes hit the floor and as we plopped on the bed, the fiery liquid meeting no resistance as our glasses clinked again and again. "Mine's all gone," Bill proudly announced, gulping down one more toast to the Raven. His lopsided grin made me giggle like a schoolgirl.

"So's mine," I giddily agreed, holding up my empty glass. "He'll be asleep, Bill; just reach over there and fill 'er up!"

He needed no convincing and was off. The strong drink went to my head - and my feet - I noticed when I stumbled getting into the shower, wanting to wash off the nervous perspiration.

"Incredible!" I heard the lock click in the other room and Bill's voice: "We could sneak in the bar and drink all night. That clerk is out like a light!" In a flash, he was in the shower with me, holding the glasses away from the water. I washed off his arm and examined his

lip, making sure he was all right. I felt
better knowing that the scratches and
cuts were not too deep, and that Bill was
in no pain. We sipped as we soaped each
other down, giggling and rubbing our
slippery bodies together as we finished
the second drink, leaving us partially
numb.

Bill's huge erection caught my
attention as I kneeled. Pelting my head
like a heavy rainstorm, the shower
drenched and drowned all sensations
except the sliding, slipping motion of
Bill's smooth skin against my wet lips.
His urgent thrusts intensified down my
hot throat, feeling electrified by his
lightning strokes. Faster and faster like
wet satin, he moved until he arched
forward, swaying under such pounding
water that it seemed to drench him with
liquid fire.

"Oh, Baby," He moaned, slowly opening
his hazed, slit eyes; tiny, spasmodic
quivers raced up his arms. He lifted me
high up on his hips where I sat cradled,
my breasts smothered with his kisses.
When he walked me toward the bed without
even toweling, I complained, "But I'm all
wet," as he lay me athwart the bed.

"All the better to kiss you with my
dear," he teased as his head disappeared.
But I didn't hear him. I was lost in
ecstasy, lost in the shadows of the
Garden, lost in the depths of the mystery
of the ritual that pulses to the ancient
rhythms emanating from the earth. And my
moaning sounded like someone else's,
someone experiencing the rites of
fecundity, experiencing the release and

the entry into the infinite purity of vibratic, Dionysian ecstasy.

Then he pulled me to the edge of the bed and tilted my hips high in the air, swaying and lifting me from the bed as we danced to the ritual like the stick figures deep within Mt. Pellegrino's dark cave walls. A throbbing as though currents sweeping against the mountain's watery base rose and rushed through us, tingling with eruptive force.

The release was so powerful that Bill went over backwards onto the bed. "Hold on, Baby," he said as I landed on top of him; he wrapped his arms lovingly around me, and in utter exhaustion we fell sound asleep.

I slept restlessly, dreaming that I was underneath a skyscraper. When I finally found the way out, I was nude and being photographed by a dark male who ordered me to change my posture, to try a new attitude.

Dawn's bright light cut through my eyes as it streamed in the open shuttered window. I blinked and rolled off Bill. He groaned, trying to catch me, his hand glazing off my hips and lightly grabbing my buttocks. The moon still brightened the sky with its whiteness; its beauty caught in my throat. "Bill! It's dawn. Wake up," I nudged him, imagining the Raven sitting at the top of the tallest sycamore. "Thank God, it's free. It's finally free," I cried, tears flowing down my face.

"The Raven. Right," he groggily agreed, his eyes firmly closing.

For some time after he fell asleep, I watched the swollen moon and imagined the Raven overlooking the bespeckled bay. Then I slept like a rock.

The second time we woke up, the sun was blaring through the open window and burning us. "Hell, Charla, it's late and we've got to get a car and head for the other side."

"I can't get out of this bed," I groaned, feeling slightly hung over.

"I feel like shit too, but if we stay in Palermo one more night, we might not be able to get out of town," I vaguely remember him saying, or hearing him leave. What seemed like hours later, he woke me out of a strange sleep. He coaxed me out of bed and into the shower, telling me that he'd gotten the only car left, "A damn shoebox! And you won't believe this map!" I heard him muttering.

"Getting across this labyrinth of a town is going to take a Daedalus to figure out," he complained, studying the map's maze of crisscrossing streets that overlapped one another, gathered around fountains and splintered off with new names, then, a little farther down, repeated their loops around new fountains and changed their names again.

With the water pounding my head, I suddenly recalled Goethe's warning not to go through Palermo's "inner labyrinth" without a guide. Dripping wet, I rushed out to tell Bill, but he argued that Mr. Soderno would pencil in a route on the map for us to follow.

"Come on, Honey," he bruskly folded the map, "we just don't know how long before Norton and his asshole punks come back for us. You're right. Norton's dangerous, and all we've done is slow him down. Since we're now positive of his whereabouts, the race is on to get to Dr. Aliamo. So let's go!" He said.

Checking out, we told *Signor* Soderno that we'd call and get our messages later; then after he'd carefully drawn our route on the map, I questioned him so many times that he soon grew impatient and short. "It's really quite simple," he emphatically repeated for the last time. "After you have turned left on Via Roma and have reached the express, you follow the signs to Tripani and Mazara. You can't get lost!" He stressed as we thanked him again.

As the iron caged elevator slowly descended upon the debris strewn entrance, I shuttered, recalling the clinking of the file and searching for it in all the dark corners. I was relieved. It was nowhere to be found. Gone forever, I thought.

In front of the iron gate sat the tiniest car imaginable. "We're supposed to make a quick getaway in that?!" I asked as we made a mad dash and jumped in with Bill speeding off, clouding the area with dust, and scattering debris. To our amazement, no one followed us.

"You just leave everything up to me," he told me confidently as he traced his finger along the map's meandering, penciled route and ran headlong into a fountain with a maddening circle of streets. He swerved to miss cars converging on all sides, and after a few loops around, veered off on the first available street which sharply twisted and seemed to turn back upon itself. When I questioned him, he insisted. "No, I know exactly where we're going." After about thirty more minutes of the same narrow, contorting streets opening onto hopelessly confusing loops around fountains, Bill started sweating. He cursed and swore, but he remained adamant about knowing the way.

My head flew left and right, searching for Norton, but the cars whizzed by so rapidly, they were a blur. "Bill, this is not working," I complained, my head starting to ache from the fast, jerky ride and the rising heat. I got so upset over our awful predicament that I started crying and expecting Norton at any moment to try and stop us once and for all. I fought to gain control, for I realized that Bill wasn't - even though he refused to admit it.

"Come on, Honey, let's stop and ask for directions?" I complained again, but there were no gas stations, no one we'd trust to ask, and no more restaurants, previously lining the streets. My spirits sank lower by the moment. I could take it no more when I spotted an elegant, outdoor restaurant. "There, over there, Bill. STOP!" I demanded when he hedged, still adamant about knowing the way. He didn't argue with me, just pulled under the terraced bursts of bougainvillea and parked close to an ultra long, white limo with dark tinted windows and a foreign tag which I couldn't decipher.

"Pretty snazzy," Bill observed as he crawled out of the car and instructed me to wait while he got the directions.

"No way!" I refused, grabbed the map tightly and decided to be the co-pilot.

"Looks like the Mafia's getaway car to me," Bill said as I rounded behind the sleek limo and caught up with him in the restaurant.

"Way out here?" I questioned, grabbing the first seat at a tiny, side table and summoning up images in my mind of being mowed down, Al Capone style. I glanced around suspiciously at the table after table of huge families and at a more private section of the restaurant which was covered with a curtain of bright blooming bougainvillea. Deep, melodic, husky laughter drifted from behind the vines, and I could make out the outline of an apparently beautiful woman with long, exquisite, platinum blond hair. Also, I could hear her male companion's low voice whose sophistocated tones floated out sonorously, yet sounding very foreign and intriguing. I didn't recognize his language, but it was not Italian.

Before we could figure out how to ask directions in our pocket dictionary or even get the map open, the tuxedoed waiters appeared, spoke no English, and after a few moments of frustrating communication, began bringing food - ripe red watermelon, cafe latte, pastries, eggs with tomatoes, etc. Not having eaten, we didn't resist. In between entrees, the polite waiters kept motioning that someone would be there, and for us to wait. Finally, a dignified man in a suit arrived who spoke very broken English, but upon seeing the map's penciled route, he understood our needs, pointing a mere two streets over to the express.

"See, I told you I knew where we were going," Bill teased as he finished eating and paid the check. Just as he got up to leave, the tall blond also rose behind the curtained vines, and I could have sworn, watched us as we walked out. I recalled the blond in Rome, racing around the corner with my briefcase, but dismissed it as too farfetched; however, I could hear Jane telling me there was no such thing as coincidence. I quickly glanced back, but she was out of sight. Only her husky laughter lingered in the air.

Outside, leaning up against the white limo, a handsome, very muscular man waited. He looked Mediterranean, but not Italian. His bright blue eyes observed us closely as we left. Bill and I exchanged glances.

"Yea!" We both shouted when the Trapani sign appeared overhead. I was proud, for I now sat in the co-pilot's seat with the map tightly gripped in my hands.

"We're on a mission from God. We will rescue the tapestries!" Bill affirmed as we passed the beaches of Mondello. "Goodbye, Palermo."

I teased Bill about his bullish determination when we were lost. "Next time we'll listen when Goethe warns us. Like you said earlier, no one but a

Daedalus could have followed us. And then we wind up in a restaurant for the wealthiest Mafia...Oh, I just saw the connection to my dream. Remember, the publishers who skinned the dwarf were Mafia. The ones with the file."

"Hold on now," Bill interrupted as he drove over the expansive terrain, down the backside of Pellegrino, then up and around the wide gulf. "You've got to have some resolution on that dream after what we've been through. I saw you take control back there."

"You're right!" I blurted excitedly. "And I didn't even tell you my dream this morning." I showed him my new posture.

"Wow, Honey, that looks good," he congratulated me. "A new posture, huh, same as a new attitude? There's a clue here. Maybe the buildings of Agrigento are what we're looking under to find this new view...Wow, Charla, look at that!" He gasped, staring in the rear view mirror; his face completely changed as his jaw fell and he yelled, "Damn! That car's coming up on us fast; it must be moving at least 100m.p.h. No wait. I'm wrong. Don't look now, but they just dropped back and are moving at a snail's pace in the left lane."

"That's the same limo, Bill!" I blurted, recalling the big muscular man leaning against its door and not being able to stop myself from turning around; I stared at its dark tinted windows and its long, sleek whiteness and imagined the blond in the luxurious back seat beside the deep voiced, sophistocated man.

"It's tinted to keep us from seeing the Mafia Don and his blond bombshell in the back seat. I saw them in the restaurant, but thought nothing of it...Now, I wonder!" I decided, not believing that Norton might have such wealthy connections. I watched as it crawled forward at such a slow speed that it was getting farther behind us and growing smaller and smaller by the minute.

"That's mighty strange, mighty strange," Bill repeated with a foreboding tone as we turned and headed south for Mazara, gradually losing sight of the limo. We descended the tall limestone mountains, stretching their long lengths like steep, barren watchers across the dried out, broad valleys and causing the limo to completely disappear. After many miles we saw the southern ridge of limestone peaks stretching alongside the blue Mediterranean. I tried to forget about the limo as the road began to climb high up in the cliffs. By afternoon, we could see our destination - a long, green valley, abounding with olive orchards and rivers and sloping down to the sea. Up ahead, where the road wound up and around Agrigento, we saw our turn off. Something told me to look back, and I jerked my head around in time to catch a glimpse of the limo, travelling at top speed and veering sharply in and out of the cliffs on the high road behind us. They were gaining on us rapidly. "Turn!" I screamed to Bill. "Here they come!"

The car veered far to the right as Bill sped off the highway onto the narrow road, trailing steeply down. Taking another sharp right, we pulled out of sight where we could still see the white limo ascending the main road. "Yea!" We both exclaimed when it disappeared from sight. Bill jerked the tiny car into reverse and headed into the valley where we came to a four way stop.

"Turn, turn," I again directed, finding on the map the road leading into the archeological area. "Wow, look at this. We're on Vei Templi!" I gasped. "This is the Valley of the Temples! I didn't think it'd be this easy to find. And would you look at those temples! They're so beautiful - golden. Look! There's the Temple of Concord. Oh, it's still so perfect - and regal. There's Via Sacra. And down there by the river is the Sacred Area with its round altars. It's so special. And check out way up there - Rupe Atenea, Athena's rock, guarding everything. How...."

"Charla, pay attention. Which way?" Bill asked as we passed the crowds of tourists starting up the sloping ledge of the ancient street.

"Looks like the only way is up there," I said pointing to the town perched up above the temples; but as Bill began the ascent, a sign off to the right caught my attention. "Turn here, turn," I yelled at Bill as he veered onto the narrow road, hidden by a purple cove of bougainvillea.

CHAPTER IV: "DR. ALIAMO'S SECRET"

"VILLA ATHENA!" I screamed as though I'd lost my mind. I stared in amazement at the quaint, luxurious hotel, tucked like a shining gem amongst the olive grove. Things were going just too good to be true. My confidence in handling this mission grew stronger by the moment.

"And, look beyond." Bill said, excitedly pointing to a turqoise pool that sparkled like an oasis and reflected the temple's wavy columns. "How about a place to check in? A base of operations? Is this a sign or what? And we aren't even being followed. Get ready Dr. Aliamo, cause we're here to find you." He hugged me. "Complete with sheeps' bells," he added, pointing at the sheep all heading down to the river. "Now we're getting hot." He parked out of sight behind the vines.

"Really," I agreed. "Athena's rock, hotel...tapestry. You're right. That's hot." I grabbed all my gear and headed for the wide doors, flanked by bright pink petunias. Deep wood tones and oriental runners welcomed us inside the lobby. The blond desk clerk spoke perfect English, telling us that he had two rooms open for only one night. "We'll take both." And I quickly called and left a message for Jane to join us. While I realized we needed her help, just the thought of her showing up, finding Dr.

Aliamo before I did, then getting all the credit like she usually did, caused my excitement and my newly found confidence to vanish.

We headed up to the end rooms. Even the perfect view of the temples, the pool, the roses, or the lavishly set outdoor restaurant didn't revive my waning enthusiasm. And I didn't want to talk about it, not even with Bill's prodding. I just insisted on getting right to work on finding Dr. Aliamo as soon as possible. "Let's start up there," I said, pointing to Via Sacra.

We grabbed the cameras and were off. As Bill sped down the narrow lane, I pulled out the map and drew a quick plan of our attack. "Three strikes and we're out," I mumbled as we reached Vei Templi. Unable to turn left because of the traffic, Bill headed up toward the city. Finally, we found a a flat, rocky place in the mountain to turn around and headed back down. "Sure the brakes are good?" I asked, concerned about the steepness of the winding road.

"Of course," Bill responded, passing another tour bus, then pulling into the *Piazza* where tourists mingled in and out of the small restaurant and souvenir stands; we parked by the high fence of the Sacred Area, grabbed the water bottle, and joined the pedestrians walking up Via Sacra. "Let's act like tourists. I'll take a few shots of the Temple of Concord," Bill said, setting up his tripod.

"I don't feel good all of a sudden. Must be this heat; I've got to sit down for a second," I told Bill who clicked away. I sat down on the crumbling wall in the shade of a fig tree. At that moment, an ugly, deeply wrinkled woman appeared out of nowhere, smelling vile and stretching out her dirty hand for money. She pushed closer, her ragged, filthy skirt brushing my leg. "No *grazie*!" I repeated several times. Before I could get up and leave, she returned with her daughter, shoved the pathetic girl toward me, and held up her grotesque, deformed hand.

I jumped to my feet, anxious to escape, and questioning why I had attracted them. The mother's cruelty really upset me. I hurried away, climbing up along the side of the temple where bees buzzed my head and chased me up the hill.

Bill stood out of sight on a precipice with his tripod aimed at the temple; but when he saw me heading up the ridge, he stopped shooting and strategically aimed straight down the sloping road - never lifting his eye from the camera.

I swirled to see what he shot, and to my shock and surprise, the white limo sat parked in the middle of Via Sacra, blocking our path. I couldn't believe they'd gotten that close without our detecting them. Then I saw why. The mother daughter duet stood at the back window, extending their hands when a long, slender arm reached out, placing something in them. It was the blond, apparently paying them off. I could hear Jane telling me how often my emotions distracted me and prevented me from paying attention. But I had no time for a scolding.

The limo's dark window zipped up. I knew I was in trouble, even though no one got out and pursued me. Frightened, I turned and ran back down the hill, when some deep ruts leading up to a well beside the Temple of Juno caught my attention. Wanting to flee but reminding myself of my mission, I stayed close to the wall.

"Let's get the hell out of here. Where are you going?" Bill yelled.

"No," I yelled back. "First, come see this...Hurry." I realized that our time to find Dr. Aliamo was growing shorter by the moment.

"Charla, let's go!" Bill exclaimed again as he climbed the hill. Then he noticed what I was pointing at. "Chariot ruts...but to what?"

"Grain!" I concluded as he reached the well. "No water, nor caves. Protected by the Temple of Juno," I said, pointing inside the crumbling columns at the sacrificial altar, still reddened by blood. "I'm confused. So if Juno's protecting the grain, and Demeter's the grain mother, what's Demeter protecting? The water? That's it, Bill, the secret source of underground water. It would've been sacred to anyone who had to live in this hot, dry place. That's where the tapestries are hidden, not out here on this ridge, exposed to the elements. And God knows what else," I added, a chill running up my spine.

"I agree, Charla, this ain't it. And we're exposed too. I'd hate to see my blood added to that altar. Come on, we've still got the Sacred Area to check out." Bill said, cautiously observing the limo. "Looks like our Mafia Don's in our way. No coincidence that the limo showed up here."

"No it's not, and whoever it is, is closing in on us. But I'm not sure about our next move. I have a hunch about another area - up where we turned around. It's the Sanctuary of Demeter, and it's the oldest spot on the island. But first, we've got to get past them. But how, Bill?"

"I don't know, but it's time to lose them. Let's climb along the old wall out of sight of any nosy observers." He said, as we hiked behind the temples.

After some distance, I pulled out the map. "Not passable," I said, pointing to the old chariot entrance and staring straight down the steep cliff. "We're blocked. What will we do?" I asked when, from behind, a figure lunged forward, its head aimed at my hand. I screamed, terror shooting through me.

"Hey, Charla," Bill said. "Calm down. It's only a dog, and it's trying to lick the water bottle." He jumped off the wall and rubbed its honey colored head.

Relieved, I laughed nervously, its tongue licking my hand. Its round, bony chest displayed every rib. Its huge, brown eyes pleaded. "Ah..." I lamented over its pitiful condition and dug through a trash can for a cup, filling it

again and again with water; we became
instant friends.

"Who've we got here? A guide?" Bill
questioned.

"What a great idea, Bill! This is a
temple dog; he knows this area solid.
He'll lead us around the limo. Come on,
boy," I said, running alongside him, but
I stopped when he headed down Via Sacra
and climbed over a worn place in the
wall; he loyally waited on the dusty
trail that bordered the olive orchard.

"Come on, Bill. We've got to make a
break. We'll be hidden on the path," I
yelled, running in front of a large group
of tourists, disappearing behind the
trees and following the loping dog. The
path led down to Vei Templi, just before
the Piazza. We crossed the road by hiding
behind another crowd of tourists. The
dog stopped at the trash can, found a
pizza crust, and plopped down to savor
it.

"Charla, I still say leave no stone
unturned. Let's run down past those
temple giants and check out the Sacred
Area. Come on," Bill said, grabbing my
hand and leading me through the gate and
down the steep hill. "We know where the
grain was kept - high and dry! But
where's the source of the water?" Bill
asked as we scanned the area, making sure
we weren't being followed and checking
out the round altar with its two
concentric stone circles.

At the next altar were tear vessels.
"If the secret water source had been
known, the virgins would have had no
cause to cry for rain. I told you

before, Bill. This isn't it; we've got to look underground, and the last and most likely place is the Rock Sanctuary of Demeter, the oldest of all the temples."

"Right! This island has always been historically short on water. The ancients would have known its location. Let's head for it," Bill readily agreed, pulling me back up the hill. "Uh oh! Our friendly limo's still there!"

We hugged the fence until we could mingle among the crowd in the parking lot. The temple dog had retrieved another piece of crust and didn't notice us as we jumped in the little car and filtered into the busy traffic. We hid behind a tour bus, heading straight up Vei Temple. In no time, we were out of sight of the white limo, which, for as far as I could see, remained parked at the end of Via Sacra. The steeply angled road curved in and out, until, to the right, we saw the turn off onto the narrow, rocky road which tucked in tight alongside the mountain.

I scanned the map. "Look," I nudged Bill. "Rupe Atenea is straight up there!" I said, feeling we were getting real close. "And Demeter's Sanctuary is carved into <u>her</u> mountain!" I paused as we passed a very small guard house with a little, old man sitting in the window.

He was staring at us with an unusual gleam in his eye - a look that commanded both mine and Bill's attention. I turned and we locked glances. It lasted only a second but seemed to last much longer; a strange piercing in his eyes bound me to him. And just as quickly, it was over. My eyes shifted to the road ahead, which made a circle on the small, round plateau and came to a dead end.

"Wow! What kind of strange look was that? Was he scoping us out or what?" Bill asked, coming to a stop in the dusty circle.

"Think we were supposed to stop? I didn't see any signs; nothing was marked, Bill, and, yeah, what a strange glance! It's almost as if he were waiting for us." I said, stepping out of the car. "This really is remote! Does anybody ever come here?" Off to the right was the old crumbling wall. I scanned the steep cliff.

"It's down there where we want to go," Bill said pointing to the small, locked wrought iron gate which led through an opening in the wall and down to the sanctuary. "Odd that the Sacred Area had a huge gate, with several guards protecting it, and this place which is supposedly just as sacred has a tiny gate that anyone could easily jump over."

"And one strange little guard who doesn't look too fierce."

"Maybe not, but one who keeps quite a vigilance. Look, here he comes down the road." Bill confirmed. "We just lost our chance to sneak in."

I knew we had to deal with him, so I turned to observe him from afar. His age was impossible to guess. But there was something about the quickness in his step, an intensity in his forward motion that belied his years. Dust flew from his tattered and torn khakis. He didn't even look in our direction, but walked with the same quick gait over to the gate. The jingling of the keys, fastened to his scuffed belt, filled the late afternoon quiet with a sudden spurt of activity.

"All right! Let's go, Charla, that old codger is opening it for us. And he's moving fast. Quick, grab a couple of those cameras."

"Look! He's already out of sight. Hurry, lock the car." I said, looking back to make sure we weren't being followed and having to rush to follow the old guard's rapid steps, too rapid for his age, down the stairs. These were the steepest we'd encountered, but they didn't slow our guide for a second. The stairs jutted onto a narrow path before sharply angling straight down at a sharp, steep angle to the cliff. Bill and I were forced to pause as we reached the second set of steps. But not our guide. He moved even faster, with each step placed in the time worn grooves so perfectly that he could probably climb them in his sleep. I was almost panting by the time we were halfway down. I could see the bottom and our guide patiently waiting for us. The setting sun's light from behind his head caused his upturned face to appear even younger. Then I realized that part of the glow was his bright eyes that lit up his wrinkled face with the stirrings of an alert energy, dwelling beneath the intense gaze.

Over his shoulder, I saw it. It was an extremely crude, archaic structure which had so completely entrenched itself amongst the trees, that they appeared as one. The guide turned to see what held me

spellbound. Securely tucked up against
the cliff sat a structure with megalithic
stone blocks. Atop it, tufa stones formed
a tiered terrace. The perfect slant
allowed the once present water to flow
freely from small basins into huge tubs.
I couldn't hide my surprise. I knew
instantly it was Demeter's initiation
site, a never divulged secret ritual. Not
wanting the guide to become suspicious of
my obvious shock of discovery, I turned
quickly around, but he had already
crossed under the trees.

Stepping back into the light, he
motioned me forward. Again, the setting
sun's rays made his silver streaked hair,
growing low to a widow's peak, appear
reddish and his face even more
captivating and handsome. I stared from
him to the ruins as he quickly walked
back and extended his hand to assist me
down the step.

I accepted; however, to my surprise,
he didn't drop it, but held onto it
tenaciously and pulled me forward, saying
something to me in Italian.

"Wow!" I heard Bill exclaim from
behind as he viewed the structure. I
turned to get his help in freeing me from
the guide and to tell him about the
water, but with persistence, the old man
led me around the trees and toward the
squat, crude structure. I questioned if
his tight grip was his form of a pass.
Not noticing my discomfort, he directed
me to run my hand along the inside of the
smooth tubs. I tried to get away and see
if I could find the source of the water.

I knew it was near, and I wondered where Dr. Aliamo was.

The guard pulled my hand again and spoke to me in rapid Italian. I kept shaking my head to indicate that I didn't understand and nervously looking around for Bill. But the guide demanded my attention, leading me around the structure toward a high, rear wall. I followed, and as I walked back, time stood still. I could feel the peaceful people who once lived in this protected place. I wondered if these were the ones who hid the tapestries. Overwhelmed by the thought, my eyes stung as I fought back the tears.

To my surprise, the little guard sensed my emotionalism, and I felt him gently tug me into the darkness of the wall which I welcomed to hide my tears. However, his tightening grip concerned me as I entered the narrow, musky walkway.

Aiming his long bony finger at the fossils embedded in the thick, wall, his eyes brightened, even in the dark, as he excitedly told me in slightly broken Italian, yet at the same time almost perfect English, "Paleolithic!"

The word seemed to resound off the wall as I tried to detect some unusual tone to his accent. Then I realized what he'd said. My enthusiasm caused his eyes to sparkle with delight. "Paleolithic?!" I repeated excitedly.

"*Si*," he responded, holding up 7 fingers and making 3 zeros with his thumb and forefinger. In the darkness, I could see the multitude of odd and assorted white fossils which brightened the

crumbling structure. It was certainly old
enough to have been the Lydians, I
thought, forgetting all about his
tenacious hold on my hand. I wrenched my
hand loose, anxious to share the
discovery with Bill. Running around the
wall, I yelled,

"Bill, it's Paleolithic! It's
Paleolithic!" But I was moving so fast, I
didn't see him. Head over heels, we fell
backwards into the tub, and I landed on
top of him. But he could have cared less.
"Seven thousand B.C., Bill! It's old
enough to be the spot," I whispered,
glancing back at the wall to make sure
the guide couldn't hear us; then I saw
him, standing close beside us with his
hand extended to help me out. Without
thinking, I accepted, and, to my regret,
he again tightened his grasp and pulled
me back behind the wall where he kept
walking and pointing for me to look at
something carved in the mountain. "Come
on, Bill!" I yelled as he rounded the
rear wall.

Then I stopped dead in my tracks, and
I was glad the old guide had been so
persistent in hurrying me along. My eyes
rounded wide. Caves! Two of them, natural
openings that widened into two large
galleries.

"Get a load of that!" Bill said,
smiling over our discovery. "And check
that out, a place where the inhabitants
could climb through without ever leaving
their entire suite, complete with living
room and bedroom." Then he leaned over
and tried whispered in my ear, "But
where's the source of the water?" Bill

just couldn't whisper; he was so loud that it seemed like his words echoed.

Whether or not the guard understood him or not, I wasn't sure. However, he tugged at my hand, leading me outside the wall and alongside the cliff. In the far corner, he kneeled down in the dust and pointed inside to a third cave. It was much shorter in height than the other two and quite a bit narrower. As I kneeled down, he said, "*Agua! Agua.*" Then he repeated it in low Italian tones, like an omen as he continued excitedly pointing into the almost four by four foot opening.

Bill and I stared at each other, our eyes opened wide with absolute amazement, for we both knew this was it. This was the secret source of our search.

However, as I peered far back into the dank, dark cave, I cringed; spiders covered the opening, their draping, bug strewn webs crisscrossed with thousands of sticky threads. Then behind the locked gate I saw the pipeline, stretching its pink-toned length along the right wall and disappearing from sight deep within the cave. It was a water channel made of the smoothest terra-cotta I'd ever seen, and to me it had the most exquisite color in the world, its original brownish-orange fading to a light, yellow-cream and pale pink hue.

"I never thought terra-cotta pipes could look so beautiful!" I exclaimed to Bill as he kneeled alongside us. I could barely control my excitement. I wanted to jump up and down with joy.

"Nor so well made!" Bill calmly said, but neither could he conceal his wide-eyed wonder. But where the hell is Dr. Aliamo?" He whispered in my ear. "And why is this old geyser holding your hand?"

The guide suddenly released it, stood up, and from behind a nearby tree, he pulled out a piece of the original pipe, smiled, and handed it to Bill.

"Look at its oval opening! It has a removable lid, big enough for my arm to reach through. What an incredible seal!" He said. "I could fit my arm in this pipe. Nope. These perfectly carved lids would never leak. No siree, this pipeline was designed to last. No plumber needed." He grinned with pleasure over our find.

Yes, I thought, a seal tight enough to protect the tapestries, even under water. "After experiencing such a dry place, I can see why they wouldn't let a precious drop of this magic fluid ever get wasted. For sure, this is it. Look," I said as the old guide began to draw in the dirt, creating 7 perfectly round circles, from the largest at the top to the smallest nearest my knee, and then interconnecting them with parallel lines, representing the water channel.

He turned his hand, palm side down, over his drawing of the largest pool which was apparently the inception, to indicate the water flowing from the deepest down to the shallowest pool near the entrance. He held up one finger, pointed back into the cave, and said in Italian, "*Chilometro.*"

"I know what that means. That's less than a mile!" Bill exclaimed, then added,

"Do you realize that these master engineers have created a route to this ancient water source, and one that I bet anything is still accessible"; he pointed to the large top circle, looked at the old guard and made a diving motion with his hands. Then he reached over and rattled the lock, questioning him for entrance.

I thought Bill was crazy, for there was no way that I would ever crawl one mile back into that web covered cave with spiders crawling all over me.

However, my reaction was nothing in comparison to the guard's. He grabbed the pipe from Bill, opened its oval shaped lid and slammed it shut as though to show that the flow of the water had been stopped, for he simultaneously pointed in the dust to his drawing. Then he grabbed both his upper arms with his opposite hands and shook his body, to communicate the frigidness of the water. He again lowered his palm, waving it from side to side, as he shook his head no.

When Bill insisted, the old guide jumped up, squared his jaw firmly and pointed to his watch. His manner was abrupt, and his answer was unequivocally, no. Without further word, he left us kneeling in the dust. Surprised by his change in behavior, we turned to watch him quickly cross to the edge of the great ravine.

"What do you think got into him?" Bill asked.

"Really, what a strange little man. And what a strong reaction. Do you suppose Dr. Aliamo would have told him about the tapestries?"

"I seriously doubt it. This place is all this old codger has in his life."

"Then where the hell is Dr. Aliamo? You wouldn't think he'd be far from here. What are we going to do? It's sunset, long past closing." I asked.

"Come back later. But knowing this guy, he probably sleeps here." Bill said.

"Are you kidding! He has eyes in the back of his head. We'll never be able to sneak in here without him catching us. And forget crawling back in that cave. Look, he's coming back to throw us out. But at least he looks pleasant again."

"I'll stall. Maybe Dr. Aliamo will show up. Come on, hop up on the structure, and I'll capture some powerful images." Bill suggested, grinning with pleasure. At first, the guard waited patiently, but after a few shots, he insisted we leave.

I didn't resist when he pointed to his watch again. Dr. Aliamo was nowhere in sight as the sun set, casting its lingering corals on the valley and darkening the ancient structure with hazy purple. I followed the guard past the tubs and up to the stairs. He paused, glanced back at the ancient site, and with love shining in his eyes, placed his hand over his heart. His gesture was so genuine that it brought tears to my eyes. It was such a precious spot and I knew he felt responsible for guarding it. Then he turned on his heels and sped up the steep stairs. I couldn't keep up with him, and Bill scrambled behind us. He waited patiently beside the open gate as we raced across the path and up the final steps.

"*Grazie*," I said, and feeling the need to leave, added, "*Chiao*." Curt and anxious, he shooed us out, locked the gate, and disappeared down the dark stairs.

Reality struck when we almost couldn't see the car parked in the dusty drive. Nor could we see if anyone else were parked there. We bolted for the doors, jumped in, and scattered the dust as we tore out of the circle and headed back down the rocky road past the dark guardhouse.

"Put the brights on," I complained, not able to see in the dusky twilight.

"They are on," Bill said. "Any sign of the limo? We were down there some time. I'm surprised they're not waiting for us," he said, peering into the windshield at the barely visible stop sign ahead.

"Bill, slow down," I nervously cautioned him as we sped closer and closer to the sign. "You're gonna get us killed."

"Charla, I'm pumping the brakes. My foot's on the floorboard. Shit, Charla, get down. I've gotta make a run through this traffic." He yelled at me, jerking the steering wheel left and right. We swerved violently back and forth until Bill somehow got past all the charging cars, but we were heading downhill instead of up. He cursed and fought the wheel as he passed one car after another. We literally flew down the steep, curving road. After almost plowing into a tour bus and narrowly missing some tourists, we spotted the bougainvillea drive to the hotel. However, another tour bus pulled out from Via Sacra and blocked our way.

I hid my eyes with my arms, but it wouldn't have mattered. I was crying so hard I couldn't see. I wasn't ready to die. "Oh, please, God, don't let us crash," I screamed as Bill fought for control, swerving around the wide curve and into the parking lot of the Piazza. He veered on two wheels alongside the edge of the cliff, sideswiped the wire fence, and flew back across the road to Via Sacra where he turned and headed back down onto the main road. The runaway car slowed just enough for him to turn into the boungainvillea drive to the hotel.

Sweat poured from Bill's forehead, and his knuckles whitened from his death grip on the wheel as we neared the wide glass doors of the pinkened entrance. I covered my eyes again when I heard vines scratching and scraping against the car. Trying to stop my wildly beating heart and catch my breath, I shook all over, muttering the entire time, "Oh, my God. Oh, my God!"

Bill clenched his teeth and bit his lip as he fought to bring the car to a stop against the thick bougainvillea. With a thud, we rammed into a final burst of purple vines which clawed then completely covered us. For a few moments, we sat in silence among the grasping vines.

"Well, we certainly don't need to worry about a hiding spot," Bill said, sounding strained. "And no one could possibly have followed us." Without another word, he located a flashlight in the backpack, groped through the mass of thorny vines, and began checking out the car; he swore revenge with each scratch. After a few moments, he yelled from under the car, "Shit! Come check this out."

But I couldn't move. My knees were far too shaky, and my heart still pounded so loudly in my ears that I couldn't hear him.

"Charla," he repeated. "Someone has filed a pinpoint hole in the brake line. Those bastards did mean to kill us."

I didn't miss that word. "Filed?!" I screamed. "No!" That was the last straw. I could just imagine the bloody file being picked up from the lower level of Mr. Soderno's hotel. And once again, I could see it against my nose, filing it to a bloody stump. I fought to stop shaking and crying.

Determined to win mastery once and for all over the fearful image, I forced myself to gain control and decided that I would go call and get another car. I tried opening the door, but it was too entangled. I started feeling claustrophobic and slammed out of the car, the vines tearing at my arms and legs; freeing myself, I smoothed down my shirt and walked past the pink pots as Bill lay dumbfounded under the car, shining a flashlight up into the darkness.

"No problem. It will be here in five minutes," the blond clerk responded when I asked him to call the car rental company. Nor did he mind my asking him to deliver a message to Jane when she arrived that we'd be taking a drive up Rupe Atenea. I figured it was the very last place to look for Dr. Aliamo; and if we didn't find him there, I was at a loss. The thought of Jane coming in and finding Dr. Aliamo instead of me made me hurry back to the car where Bill was still underneath, swearing revenge.

Continuing to think about Jane's arrival and getting more upset by the moment, I hardly heard the approaching car until it stopped behind us and a uniformed young man got out and began examining the car squished inside the hedge.

"Oh, Bill, I forgot to tell you. I ordered another car," I exclaimed, apologizing and getting out to take care of the transfer.

Covered with grease and grime, Bill crawled out, unloaded the tiny car, and packed up the new one which was the same size.

After we took care of the papers, thanked the driver for the delivery, and drove off, Bill said, "It was the white limo. They distracted us long enough to file our brake lines while we ran around the temples. But I don't believe it followed us to the sanctuary. Whoever is trying to kill us probably thinks we're already dead." We turned onto Vei Templi with no one in sight.

"Regardless of our setback, I believe that we should explore Rupe Atenea before we take another step. We've got to find Dr. Aliamo pronto," I said.

"Okay! I agree. Just don't let us step off any precipice." Bill said, as we drove up to the top, the very top of the city, past the hospital and straight up Via Minerva until we came to a deadend.

Some lovers were sitting on the old wall with their motorcycle parked next to them. They were kissing with their bodies pressed together as our headlights beamed on them; they didn't even notice.

"Now that's what we ought to be doing," Bill joked, pulling the little car into a hidden niche at the top of the steep mountainous rock. "Look, there's a path off to the right. It probably leads out to the pinnacle." As we got out and started hiking down the path, waist high weeds tore at our legs.

"Private." The sign directly in front of us read. We deliberated whether we should keep going, but upon seeing the path winding around past the private garden and residence, we continued walking out atop the steep rock until we came to a crumbling foundation. There was nothing else around. We sat down on the ancient step, trying to figure out what to do next.

"Athena's former temple?" I questioned. "But where's Dr. Aliamo?"

"We can't see a thing in the dark!" Bill complained, looking out over the river valley. Nothing stirred as the crickets continued their song. The moon was just coming up, so swollen and heavy that it didn't look like it would make it.

"How romantic, Darling!" Bill whispered in my ear and pulled me up into his lap. "Can't we forget work for a minute?" We kissed tenderly and lovingly. But within seconds our kiss had become passionate, urgent, and so filled with desire that we pressed our bodies hard against each other.

From behind us came a piercing scream, and I saw the shadow of a woman standing closeby. She turned to flee, but when I called out, "Who's there?" she turned back again, yelling out in a loud voice, "Charla? Charla? Is that you?"

I jumped up so fast that Bill and I fell forward. I got up again, yelling, "Jane?! Jane? Oh, thank God," and ran toward her at full speed.

"Charla?" She excitedly repeated, and then we were hugging and giggling. Bill came running up behind us and wrapped his large arms around both of us. We all laughed, relieved that we'd found each other.

"God, am I happy to see you!" I said as I continued hugging her, forgetting all about my concerns over her arrival and feeling so wonderful to see her again.

"Paulo dropped me off at Villa Athena and drove over to Taormina. I took a taxi. Oh! We saw Norton in Palermo..."

"Oh, my God," I gasped, feeling sick over the mention of Norton, but also shocked by the sound of Paulo's name and the fact that they had been together.

Concealing my disappointment, I asked, "Did Norton follow you?"

"That's why Paulo went to Taormina - to fake him out while I came looking for you. I told him we'd meet him there. I sure am glad I found you. Who would ever guess you'd be out on this godforsaken rock. Lucky it was a full moon; I'd never have attempted it otherwise. But, thank God you're all right. There's much more involved than you ever imagined." She said in a serious tone.

"Damn, Jane. There's much more going on than <u>you</u> could imagine. I can't believe I let you talk me into taking this assignment," I responded, all the discontent and pain I'd suffered rushing to the surface and overflowing.

"Me? You're responsible. No one can talk you into anything you don't want to do. Lighten up. I told you it was for your growth; now I'm not so sure how much you've grown, especially if you're going to try and blame me for your actions," Jane snipped, apparently having gone through quite a bit herself.

"Growth?!" My voice rose, "You call getting shot at, almost raped, wrecked, sabotaged...growth?" My voice rose higher, the last word echoing against the rock.

"Uh, girls...Maybe you could discuss this later. We do have some rather important business at hand," and Bill reminded us of the urgency of getting to Dr. Aliamo as quickly as possible. He soon won our cooperation, telling Jane all about the sanctuary and the need to

crawl back in the tunnel to retrieve the
tapestries.

"Crawl back in a narrow, mile long
tunnel? Are you guys crazy?" She gasped
as though we'd given her horrible news.
"That's impossible."

"I couldn't agree more, Jane." My
voice had calmed. "But that's only half
of it. I already told Bill that getting
past this weird, ferocious little guard
would be..."

"What little guard? Wait a minute.
You do know that Don Meldon found a
picture of Dr. Aliamo?"

"A what?" I asked in shock, feeling
sick that Jane was going to present
evidence for finding Dr. Aliamo. Now
she'd get the credit instead of me.

"Anyone have a light?" Jane
interrupted my thoughts. "It's an old
Oxford picture of him, and you wouldn't
believe the eyes." She hunted in her
purse.

"What kind of eyes?" I asked,
suddenly wanting to know, as I recalled
the intensity of the old guide's bright,
blue eyes.

"The kind you never forget once
you've seen them. Oh, I can't see in this
moonlight. Let's go back to your
car...You do have a car don't you?" She
asked, stepping down from the foundation.

"This way," Bill replied, taking
Jane's arm with one hand and mine with
the other as we made our way like goats
along the rocky path with its sheer drop-
off.

"Keep your footing!" Jane warned. "We
don't want to be sacrifices, and I have a

strong feeling that quite a few have met this rock's maker." The high grasses tore at her skirt and scratched my bare legs. We passed the little house, the radio tower and the private sign. The lovers were gone.

"That's your car?!" Jane exclaimed upon seeing the tennis shoe car.

"*Si, Senorina*, but we do a havva light." Bill spoke in broken English, turning on the dim, tiny light.

The entire walk back to the car, I'd had a hard time controlling the lump in my throat and the sinking feeling in my stomach. I realized that something about the guard just hadn't added up. And now, even in the dimness, I recognized the eyes. "It's him! Oh, my God. That little man is Dr. Aliamo. I can't believe it. He doesn't look like the person I imagined; he doesn't act like the person I imagined; in fact, nothing about him fits! You should see his ragged clothes, his unkempt appearance. It's crazy," I blurted defensively, heart broken that Jane had indeed presented the most important piece of evidence in discovering Dr. Aliamo and beaten me to the punch one more time. I couldn't stand the defeat.

"There's one thing," Bill said confidently.

"What?" I asked plaintively, continuing to stare at the picture of a perfectly groomed, young man who looked as sophistocated as any professor I'd known and more handsome than most of them. I berated myself for my oversight.

"The eyes have it. That's the same discerning look that we saw when we passed him in the guardhouse. And just wait until we tell him who we are."

"How about right now?" Jane asked, taking control and crawling into the back seat.

Straight down the sheared cliff-like road we drove down and around the sharp curves with Bill continually checking the brakes.

"And, Sis, I know you've been put through the mill. However, it _is_ all for your growth," she said as I prepared to defend myself. "But...Can't we put this on hold until later?"

I reluctantly agreed, wanting to spill out all the emotional trauma for which I did feel she had some partial responsibility, even though she denied it, wanting to tell her how upset I was that she'd been the one to identify Dr. Aliamo, and trying to figure out how I'd handle her with Paulo. "Oh, all right," I murmured as Bill swerved onto the bumpy road to the sanctuary.

"I just don't understand why that old man didn't identify himself to us. He must have suspected something," Bill said, rubbing my knee as though to soothe me. He could tell I was upset. He turned off the lights as we passed the guardhouse. "Since he didn't recognize us earlier, let's just hope he doesn't have a gun."

The crickets were silent as he parked in the dusty circle.

As quietly as possible, we opened the doors. He was nowhere in sight.

Over the ancient wall we climbed, or I should say Bill and I climbed. Jane struggled with her white skirt, pulling it high as she took Bill's hand to hoist herself upon the wall. We said nothing as we headed straight down the sheer steps.

I raced ahead, determined to at least be the first to reach him. At the bottom, I stopped abruptly, searching left and right; my eye caught a quick movement behind the basins, brightly lit by the moon. Trying to calm my jittery nerves, I peered into the darkness of the rear wall's shadow; then I saw him. It didn't look like the old guard, but whoever it was headed directly for me. I swirled around so fast and bumped into Jane so hard that both of us went tumbling.

"Watch out!" I heard Jane scream, then with a thud we hit the ground. It happened so fast that Bill, who was taking his last step, fell head first over us.

"Wha-a-a!" He yelled into the night as he maneuvered his body into a roll and tumbled forward; but before he stopped rolling, he had run into the swiftly moving shadow of the man who now staggered and fell forward, landing close to my head.

"What is going on?" The deep, authoritative voice called out. "And I demand that you identify yourselves!" It was Dr. Aliamo, speaking perfect Oxford English and fighting to get to his feet to take control of the startling situation.

"Dr. Aliamo?" The three of us called out simultaneously.

"How do you know my name. Tell me who you are at once, or I demand that you leave these premises." He gruffly responded.

"We were here earlier at sunset...Don't you remember us?" I asked. "I'm Charla Morrow with the SILC Foundation...Don Meldon..."

"Oh, my. You're Dr. Morrow?" He gasped, his eyes relaxing and his hand grasping mine with warmth and vigor. "Why...why I expected someone older, like Don, and certainly not...forgive me, so beautiful. One does not normally find such rareness in the dusty experts of mythology. You have simply caught me off guard."

I too was overwhelmed that I hadn't recognized him earlier. Now, he transformed in front of my eyes. Not only did his outward appearance change so that he seemed even more handsome and sophistocated, but in that moment of recognition, I saw his tenacious will to go to any length, even death itself, in order to secure the tapestries that he loved so dearly. Staring into his eyes, I made a pact with him, one that needed no words. I became his partner, committing myself to the same task, even if it cost me my life as well. Perhaps Jane was right; maybe I had grown, for I'd never felt such determination. I hardly heard Jane and Bill as they tried introducing themselves. Nor had he. A bit reluctantly, he released his warm grip and reached out to shake Jane's outstretched hand.

"The second Dr. Morrow, I presume? The famous dream psychiatrist, taking up where Jung has left off? As with Charla, I would never have recognized you."

"Bill Balfour," Bill introduced himself as he shook his hand vigorously. "Hell, I should have known it was you."

"Well, I should hope not. That would mean that my disguise wasn't working, and it's held good for many many years." He whispered, pausing and listening to the wind and the crickets before continuing. "But why are you here at this hour?"

"Jane just arrived with a picture of you. Plus, Dr. Aliamo, we must move very quickly. Someone in a white limo followed us, even going so far as to try to kill us. Jane, too, was followed, by your former student, Norton. Did you know what a true villain he is? Why did you ever include him?" I confronted him.

"Oh, I'm sorry. I had no idea. The smell of money must have corrupted him to the core. His abilities as an archaeologist shouldn't have blinded my judgment; but I can assure you, he doesn't know my whereabouts. No one does. You must not give it away at this crucial time. Please leave, return at dawn, so that we can retrieve the tapestries as soon as possible." He said, giving us a list of items that he wanted us to bring and making sure that we were experienced divers. No sooner had Bill and I convinced him that we were than he told us again to leave.

We left without question, but at the top of the steep steps, I lingered for a moment, glancing back at the moon bathed basins. Again, the emotions swelled around my heart, and I felt an intense attachment to this core place.

"Thank God, you've come," he said, his voice cracking with feeling and relief. He turned and vanished into the shadows.

"Come on," Bill called from the gate. "Let's go before someone sees us."

All the way to the hotel, I was quiet, caught up in thought. Jane was so exhausted from jet lag that she went to sleep in the back seat. Even when Bill stopped to get us a pizza, no one spoke. The white limo was still nowhere in sight; apparently we had been left for dead. Nor did anyone else follow us.

We woke up Jane when we reached the hotel. Once in the room, she could barely keep her eyes open to eat the delicious pizza and passed out in the chair. Bill had to lift her into bed.

I slept restlessly, tossing and turning in anticipation of the morning's dangerous challenge. At dawn, Bill's inner alarm woke us up; wide-eyed with excitement and fear, we grabbed our gear and suitcases, just in case there was a problem in not being able to get back to the hotel, and headed up the hill to the sanctuary. Dr. Aliamo was nowhere in sight. A nervousness rippled in the morning air as we jumped over the gate and climbed down the stairs. I paused halfway down and saw Dr. Aliamo appear from behind the rear wall.

CHAPTER V: "OH, FATHER, FATHER, OH,
            HUSBAND, HUSBAND."

A beige safari jacket, with four stuffed pockets, covered Dr. Aliamo's tattered clothes. Even from afar, his blue eyes glowed with intensity. He saw me, waving his hand frantically for us to hurry. We cleared the steps two by two and sped around the foundation. He reached for my hand, grasped it warmly in his familiar grip, and pulled me behind the wall, saying in a low voice, "Someone was here last night, deep, unrecognizable male voices. Two of them came after you left. Quickly, Bill, Jane, please hurry. We may be in danger."

"But who? Norton's trailing Paulo to Taormina and we lost the limo." I asked.

"I don't know, but that isn't our most pressing concern," he said. "Preparation is," and he handed us wet suits, vests loaded with supplies, thick gloves and chaps, kneepads, and spelunkers' hats with lights mounted on the brims. By the time we were dressed and loaded down with pony tanks and packs for the tapestries, we didn't look like we could move, much less crawl through a mile long tunnel. None of us complained, though the look on Jane's face was priceless to me, as though asking, "How the hell did I get involved in this?"

"No one can talk you into doing anything you don't want to," I mimicked

her, feeling some satisfaction in the
fact that maybe now she'd understand what
I meant about this trip when she got a
taste of what I'd been through. She just
stared back at me with her blue piercing
eyes as though she saw right through me,
putting it all back on my shoulders; and,
as usual, I fell for it and began
doubting whether even I could handle such
an arduous journey, much less her. If she
wanted to challege me, I felt it. My
pockets bulged with pads and recording
gear, and my back already ached from the
pony tank, however light, that I rested
against the cliff as Dr. Aliamo locked
the cave where the supplies had been
hidden.

I thought I was loaded down until I
saw Bill. His large camera bag was
stuffed with every kind of photographic
equipment possible. He lumbered along the
wall behind Dr. Aliamo who pulled out a
small broom, and I just knew he was going
to brush away the spider webs. Jane was
behind me and couldn't see what he was
doing. I almost laughed, just imagining
her reaction when she saw them swarming
at the mouth of the tunnel. Since
childhood, she had detested spiders.

Turning, he said, "I must warn you.
Having to rush on such a rough journey
will take its toll. If at any point you
feel you cannot make it, we'll turn back
at once. Our lives must come first.
Agreed?" We all shook our heads. "Thanks
to the protection of the wall, no one can
see us enter the tunnel. Yet our absence
may be monitored by whoever was here;
they may come looking for us. Promptness

and accuracy are everything. But I will
not rush so much that I neglect telling
you the importance of this most famous
discovery. Charla, I want you right
behind me, recording as best you can. I
know it will be hard taking notes, but it
may be the only time we have. And Jane,
Bill will need assistance with the
photographic documentation. Ready, team?"
He looked into each of our eyes. "Then
God speed us."

Hugging the wall, we waited for him
to unlock the gate; the musty dankness
seeped into our nostrils as the gate
creaked open. Hundreds of spiders
scampered out into the sunlight as he
brushed away their webs. They were huge.
Backing up frantically, I bumped into
Jane who had stopped dead in her tracks.

"Come on," he yelled, and forcing
myself on all fours, I scrambled in
behind him. My eyes skimmed every
surface, searching for spiders. The pony
tank and pack leaned to one side and
almost toppled me over into the dirt.
That was the least of my worries, for
just past the entrance there was total
darkness. Trying to adjust my eyes, I saw
Jane crawling in hurriedly, doing her
best to dodge the scampering spiders.
Behind her, Bill was having a problem
forcing his tall body into the tunnel
much like he had crammed himself in the
tiny taxi in Palermo. Now it wasn't
funny, especially when Dr. Aliamo's
serious voice cut through the tense air.

"Here, take this key and brush, lock
the gate, and sweep the opening clean of
our footprints. Keep your lights off

until we are far out of sight in the cave."

"Holy shit!" Jane exclaimed, just a short distance past the entrance, "I can't see my hand, and it's right in front of my face. And what if someone follows us in here? There's only one way out. Plus, I'm cold already," she complained.

As much as I wanted some satisfaction that she was finally getting a taste of her own medicine, I was too scared to think and very glad she was so close behind me. A chill ran up then down my spine, and the air was so heavy with dankness and so thick that it made me gasp for breath. And we weren't even 20 feet in yet. "Oh, God," I moaned, running my hand over the smooth pipe that ran along the wall like a guiding arm. "Please get me out of this alive."

"Charla, there is no reason to fear for your life," Dr. Aliamo reminded me. "We're safe in here, and no one saw us enter. We can turn on our lights now."

Jane and I screamed when we saw the hundreds of spiders scampering all over the roughly hewn walls and all around our knees. I closed my eyes and scrambled behind Dr. Aliamo who'd taken off crawling as rapidly down the dark tunnel as he'd climbed the steep steps. When I opened my eyes, the tunnel walls were free of spiders, and I could see the chippings of some ancient tool. Somewhat relieved and trying to somehow accept the grim reality of what lay ahead, I kept quickly trudging onward, unable to keep up with Dr. Aliamo who was almost out of sight. "Hold up," I yelled into the strange silence as he nervously hurried forward.

"Of course, I'll wait for you, Charla," he said, stopping and extending me his hand to catch up. "I especially want you to hear what I have to say. As we make our way through this sacred tunnel," he spoke low as though addressing me personally, his voice echoing off the dank walls, "we will have some intellectual stimulation to keep your mind off the physical. I want to share with you what I know about the Ugaritic tablets, miraculously recovered in 1929, which shine light on the messages in the tapestries, lying just beyond our reach at the end of this long trek. After a fairly short distance - bear with the discomfort - we will reach the first pool where the tunnel opens up." He said, quickening his pace even more as cold blackness engulfed us. "Ever since the discovery, I have been drawn to one myth in particular, "Oh, Husband, Husband, Oh, Father, Father," drawn from a collection, forming the foundation of thought for the Canaanites, those ancient people who included primarily the Phoenicians and Hebrews."

I was all ears and excited about what he had to say, but I froze in my tracks when Jane, speeding up behind me, came crashing into me, just to tell him that she'd been working on the same myth for years. She proceeded explaining her theory when her words garbled and she gasped for breath. "What's that putrid odor," she asked, pressing her hand over her mouth and giving me some smug satisfaction that the horrible smell had shut her up.

"Guano," Dr. Aliamo said in a muffled voice and pointed at the opening.

"What?" I screamed. "Bats?" I screamed louder; my annoyance with Jane vanished, and I was filled with terror. "Not bats." I yelled again, almost knocking Dr. Aliamo over as I raced forward, slipped, and scratched my forehead as I tumbled into the opening of the low cavern. Plunk. Plunk. I was aware of the sound of water dripping into the shallow pool in front of me. Dumbfounded, I sat there staring at the small goblets of water, dropping from the stalactites.

"Charla, Charla, my dear, are you all right?" Dr. Aliamo asked with real concern as he rushed to my side, examined my forehead carefully, and helped me over to splash some water on my face. He cautioned me about moving too quickly in the narrow tunnel and assured me that he would prevent anything from hurting me. His tone and demeanor were so paternal that he made me feel as though he really did care about my well being. Not being used to so much attention, I pulled out my pad and began taking notes on the wide cavern lit up my Bill's flashing camera.

When we took off crawling again, I was anxious to tell Dr. Aliamo about the clues on the Phoenicians I'd discovered in the Public Gardens in Palermo that had led me to him. He hung onto every word, and, amazingly, never let Jane interrupt.

He paused in the tunnel, turned, and looked at me admiringly, saying, "Why,

Charla, I'm very impressed with your insights, for they are very similar to mine. I can see you know how important the Phoenicians were in forming the base for Judeo-Christian ideas recorded in the Bible yet how their myths were incredibly misrepresented, especially those relating to the view of the feminine; I intend to correct the injustices done to the women as a result of these distortions. I also know that you have thoroughly researched and are very well versed on Genesis' blatant example of Lot's incestuous relationship with his two daughters."

"How did you know that about me? I've never published anything on my research!" I asked in amazement. He didn't respond, but regardless of how he got hold of that information, I was impressed. It really made me feel good that such an expert admired me. "Well, thank you very much, Dr. Aliamo," I said with sincere appreciation. I no sooner got the words out of my mouth than Jane nudged me again with her foot which I'd been trying to ignore. I could read her mind; she had telling him all about her theories up her sleeve and couldn't wait to cut in.

SQUEAK. SQUEAK. The bats' shrill, piercing sound bouncing off the walls made me panic and hit the dusty floor face first, long before Dr. Aliamo commanded, "Lie flat," as the bats burst in flight over our heads. Jane landed on top of me, shoving my face even farther in the dust. "Ohhh!" I groaned, when Dr. Aliamo's legs trapped me from moving. The narrow tunnel closed in and claustrophobia struck. A gigantic spider crawled up my neck. That did it. I lost control, writhing, twisting, and yelling for Dr. Aliamo to move forward into the next cavern. Clawing at my neck, I bolted over him, tripped, and once more rolled into the opening of the next cavern.

"Charla?! Are you all right? Are you hurt?" Bill asked in alarm and rushed to my side to support me.

My embarrassment hurt me more than the bruises. I felt ashamed.

"Really, Sis, I know we're in a hurry, but you're going to get us out of here in no time," Jane said, attempting to make me smile.

Forcing my heart to stop pounding and my hands to cease shaking, I crawled over to the edge of the completely stilled, black pool. My smudged reflection scared me; wild, fear filled eyes looked back at me. I didn't recognize myself. Dr. Aliamo's wavy image appeared in the dark water as he crawled up behind me and sat down. His bleary eyes filled with concern as he said, "We must go back."

"What?" I asked in alarm, threatened over the loss of the story and my chance at success. "You can't do that. You can't put me before the tapestries. They're just as important to me. I'm ready to go the whole nine yards."

"Why...I never realized you were so dedicated," he said, his eyes beaming with admiration. "But you must come first. If you get injured, we'll turn around." I thought he was going to put his arms around me when he continued. "But if you're sure you're all right, we'll go forward." After I assured him several times, he added, "I'm pleased, my dear, really pleased that we agree so thoroughly. We'll work together quite well."

I was glad when he crawled over and helped Bill set up the lights which eerily lit up the long, low cavern, reflecting the chiselled ceiling and terra-cotta pipe in the black pool. I felt so grateful to him that it choked me up a little. I'd never had such a brilliant, enlightened man, such an authority like him think that highly of me. I was so grateful I wanted to cry. Out of the corner of my eye, I thought I say something moving in the dark water. I scurried back so fast that I knocked over one of the lights. It crashed on the ground. Dr. Aliamo set it back up, crawled over beside me, and looked me directly in the eye.

"There's nothing living in the pool, Charla. But hopefully you're releasing that reservoir of fear so we can continue." It seemed like he could read my mind. "You're too special to be holding onto something so negative; have you released it?" He asked in such a sweet voice.

I took one last look in the still water. Not a ripple moved on its dead surface. I relaxed, suddenly feeling free of a heavy weight. Dr. Aliamo was right.

"See, I told you this was for your growth," Jane said, leaning over and hugging me. "Just look at this dark water. Reminds me of Narcissus. Now we know what reached up, grabbed him and pulled him in the pool. Himself."

"Wait for me," I yelled at Dr. Aliamo, wanting nothing to do with her ideas.

"Tell the others to hurry. We've already wasted far too much time. The rest of this journey must be completed in record time. Please, hurry," he yelled at us as I crawled like crazy over the dusty tunnel floor and caught up with him.

"I want to continue my theory. Are you able to record?" He asked, and I eagerly shook my head. After Bill and Jane reached us, we climbed upward by the slanted pipe. Conserving his energy, Dr. Aliamo stopped talking. He wasn't the only one getting fatigued. I could hear Jane's breathing, and my own, getting heavier. No one said a word.

Finally, he looked around at me and started talking again, his breath short. "As I said, the Bible has Lot blame his two daughters for their incestuous union, saying they forced him to have sex with them. Lot is never held responsible. Bill, as you and I know, this would have been impossible." He chuckled at his insight.

"Exactly," Bill said. "Men can force women, but the reverse? Impossible."

Dr. Aliamo raised his hand as we reached the wide, far reaching pool. The vaulted ceiling was higher, the walls much broader. By our heads, the water moved headlong into the pipe that led down the incline. The rushing, gurgling sound filled the large area with the swoosh of a current. We cautiously crawled in.

At the other end of this active pool, a celestial quietness pervaded over the stillness. No movement rippled its surface; no sound came from its depths, yet it obviously created the swirl of the current at the other end by somehow forming a slow moving circle which completely mesmerized me. I couldn't quit thinking about how lucky I was to have met Dr. Aliamo, a true guide, and not at all like those abusive men who haunted me from the past.

Dr. Aliamo was impatient for Bill to finish. He again peered back down the tunnel to see if anyone had followed us in. Anxious to leave, he took off rapidly crawling. We slipped and slid on our knees on the wet, sloping rock. It had been cold and dark since we left the opening, some half a mile back. Now the damp cold was pervasive, chilling me to the bone right through the thick wet suit. Water drained from a higher source, not the pipes, for these didn't leak. This was the toughest part so far. We remained quiet, conserving our energy and measuring our breaths. Again, I could hear Jane's heavy breathing, and my own, getting more congested. But Dr. Aliamo was determined to continue his theories.

"As I said, it is at this period of change over in time when we first see the view of the feminine change from the nuturing Mother Goddess of the Old Stone Age people to Genesis' dark portrayal. Lot's daughters and Eve, for that matter, are viewed as the seductress who used sex, succulent fruits, or wine, to manipulate and undermine the masculine.

Hence, she is not to be trusted, even though Lot's daughters' motive for getting their father drunk and having sex with him was for propagation. See the problem with misinterpretation?"

I couldn't believe he and I thought just alike. But I couldn't answer him and didn't know how he could continue to talk, much less move as rapidly as he did. His breath was short. "This is perfectly shown in the "Oh Father" myth. El, the Prime Mover, has sex with his daughters; if they conceived, they produced Dawn and Dusk, and barrenness in nature if they did not. In Genesis, this symbolism is lost when Lot's daughters literally get pregnant."

"Alexander," this is great. I've worked on similar theories involving the feminine for years. However, I don't quite see what's happened to the matriarchal worship at the time of the writing of Genesis." I cringed at Jane's words. She was more interested than ever, and now I knew she definitely had something in mind.

I was so preoccupied with Jane's interest in a story that I was recording that I hardly saw Dr. Aliamo disappear into the next cavern, for a fine mist appeared from water, spurting from the opening. "Oh, my God," I heard him groan from the foggy cavern. "It's caved in. There's water everywhere."

I hurriedly crawled in beside him. The mouth of the tunnel opened onto the collapsed cavern. A fine, delicate, spray infused the air with a magical world of shapes and shadows, dancing atop the spewing water. Only one piece of the original ceiling stayed intact; the remainder angled across the terra-cotta at an incline, forced the water straight up before plummeting into the dark, round pool.

Bill was having a hard time packing his cameras in the wet, slick environment of the falls. Dr. Aliamo assisted him, and in no time, said, "Ready troupe? We must proceed with caution. This collapse greatly concerns me."

The tunnel dried out gradually as we crawled farther past the falls. The sound of splashing, falling water gradually decreased, and silence once more filled the tunnel. The mist slowly disappeared, and my breathing relaxed. Also, my tiredness decreased. This amazed me, given the laboriousness of the excursion.

"The fifth pool is some distance ahead!" Dr. Aliamo called out. "But you won't mind the extra work. Let's keep our minds busy. To respond to your question, Jane, this time in history was the change over from the worship of the Mother Goddess to that of the Father God, El, who became Yahweh in the Old Testament. But her worshipers did not give up easiy. They fought back in nonviolent ways, yet were finally forced to stand by and watch as their temples became brothels, their priestesses prostitutes, their virgins sacrificed, and their animals trained for heinous acts upon the women - all for sport. As a result, suppression of the powerful energy of the Great Mother, and thus the feminine occurred. Since it is impossible to destroy energy, only shove it into the depths of the subconscious, it has caused a sexual conflict and consequently sexual disorders, some deadly like sodomy as Arachne portrays which is the major cause of A.I.D.S. Now, we must reincorporate this energy or face disease and possible extinction. Let's hope we've learned from history and can reconcile the patriarchal with the matriarchal as we face this critical period when we must change our religious views."

"I see. Just like you described in your letter. You won't believe this, Alexander, but this theory is so close to the one I've been working on," Jane spoke up boldly, "that I'd like to use it in my new theory in psychology and...."

"What?" I couldn't believe my ears. She knew the only reason I took the assignment was to get the story, so I could become an authority - just like she'd already attained. In fact, she'd recommended it. My knees ground into the dirt as I turned around and stared at her in complete shock and anger. She just looked at me, as though she read my mind, and said under her breath so Dr. Aliamo couldn't hear, "Well, they don't have to conflict, Charla."

"I'll answer that a little later." Dr. Aliamo said, slowing down and lowering his voice as he turned around for the hundreth time to see if anyone were following us. He stopped at the mouth of the next cavern and held up his hand as though to silence us. "Thank God. It's not collapsed." And we crawled into the wide opening of the fifth cavern, or more specifically the fifth island.

I gasped. Somehow, the terra-cotta pipe's rapidly flowing water from the sixth pool had carved and molded the soft sandstone floor into a sculptured island of stalagmites that resembled the foundation of the ancient city of Acragas, the original Agrigento. As Jane and Bill crawled in behind me, they also gasped over nature's perfect mirror.

"So would this have been carved around the time that the tapestries were hidden here?" I asked, glaring at Jane as though I dared her to interrupt. "And if so, wouldn't this have been the perfect place? The island of women? And protected by Athena's Rock! It all fits together. This marks the place - a stamp of truth."

"Yes. Cecilia," Dr. Aliamo responded to my enthusiasm. "You're right on target, Charla. Like ancient Lydia, the inhabitants of Acragas were matriarchal; but unlike elsewhere, they harmoniously incorporated patriarchy into their Mother Goddess worship. He stared at me approvingly for a few seconds, helped Bill pack the camera gear, then asked, "Ready troupe?" And took off crawling.

Still hanging onto every glowing word of praise, I didn't budge until Jane, it seemed, intentionally nudged me to get going. But I refused to let her get me upset and took off crawling in good spirits even though it got steeper and the floor muddier and more slippery. Finally, we caught up with Dr. Aliamo.

"Now, let me respond to your request, Jane, to use my theory. It would be an honor. I'd like you to refer to it as the Arachnean Line since Arachne was an example of a Mother Goddess worshipper who rebelled nonviolently. But I'd like for Charla and only Charla to publish the story first. Will you both promise me this wish, and not let anyone, do you understand me, anyone, publish it before you, Charla?" He asked in dead seriousness. I couldn't believe it. What a surprise. I shook my head eagerly, a haughty grin spreading across my face. No one had ever taken up for me like this. Not wanting to gloat, I didn't even ask Jane what she muttered under her breath as she raced to keep up, so she could hear Dr. Aliamo.

Despite the worsening conditions, Dr. Aliamo wasn't even breathing hard when he continued, "Good! Now I'd like to address a second part of my theory that deals with Athena's tapestry. During this time, the people retained the belief from matriarchy that divinity was inherited through the feminine. However, with the figurehead now as male rather than female, this wasn't possible. So, a hereditary princess was appointed who was forced to have sex with her father, the king, in order to propagate offspring with divine bloodlines. Here again, the problem lies with interpretation. Like the "Oh Father" myth, the original belief was symbolic, not physical. We all know how detrimental and irrepairable incest is."

"You certainly proved that in your theory on the Julian Line." I excitedly added. "I couldn't believe you found proof through the name Julia in Caesar's family. How awful that his daughter, his aunt, Augustus' daughter and then granddaughter, not to mention all the other Julias, were designated the hereditary princess and had to have sex with their fathers and grandfathers. That makes...."

"....That as a result of so much inbreeding, seizures, named after Caesar, were common in the family." Jane interrupted. "That's why this is so perfect for psychology. This was what Ovid had discovered about Augustus and his Julias and was consequently banished." She just as excitedly added.

I glared at her again. I had done all the research on Dr. Aliamo's theory, even if it had been stolen; besides, if it weren't for me, she wouldn't have known any of it. However, I knew that regardless of what she said, Dr. Aliamo had promised the story to me and only me, and there was no way she could take it away.

"And this practice was again disrespect of the feminine? So you think that solving this sexual conflict is as easy as restoring the worship of the Mother Goddess? I believe you, of course, but it just seems so simple," Bill said.

"Yes, it is. The worship of Mother Nature as God's feminine is just that simple, but most importantly, it will simultaneously restore the feminine aspect in all of us to its former respected and revered position. You see, there is a form of incest that is good. It is again symbolic, and it is the inner marriage of the masculine and feminine selves."

"That's Jung's theory; he considers the union a necessity for resolving our sexual conflicts," Jane blurted, already sorry the theory wasn't hers. "Whew!" She gasped, quickly covering her nose and mouth just as Dr. Aliamo held up his hand to halt. Even though the horrible stench made it painful to breathe, I was glad, for it once again shut Jane up. "What the hell is that?" She cried.

Dr. Aliamo crawled into the cavern. "Stagnation! And guano mixed," he mumbled, his voice muffled by his hand over his nose. "And another collapse."

"It's freezing in here," I exclaimed as I entered the cavern. The cold, wet air cut me to the bone. Water poured in, soaking us thoroughly. Spiders crawled frantically all over us in an attempt to get away from the rushing water. The sharp, squealing squeak of the bats deafened us.

Jane crawled up beside me and whispered in my ear, "Pleease, Charla, you don't think I'm trying to steal your story, do you? You think I'd stoop that low?"

I didn't answer her, just kept my hand pressed firmly over my mouth. I wanted to say that it didn't matter since Dr. Aliamo wouldn't permit it.

"Let's get the hell out of here," Bill yelled as we all frantically scooted around the cavern, almost crawling over Dr. Aliamo who headed for the last pool. Although the incline was even steeper, the floor was dusty dry. Once past the sixth cavern, the horrific smell vanished and was replaced by the freshest scent of rain, smelling like dusty leaves falling into soft dirt. We inhaled deeply. The anticipation of reaching our destination silenced us as we conserved each breath in order to crawl faster. In no time, Dr. Aliamo cried, "Up ahead." If it were possible to run on bended knee, we did.

"It's safe, it's safe. Oh, my God, it's safe," Dr. Aliamo moaned, crawling into the seventh cavern. We rushed in behind him.

A pastel light emanated from an ancient, exquisitely beautiful shrine and cast a flitting halo of shimmering baby blue around the misty cavern. Smooth scallops of precious stones curved upward on both sides toward a rounded pinnacle, some eight feet high with a blue stone seat, a truly royal throne.

"Oh-h!" Jane and I simultaneously moaned, forgetting all about our being at odds with each other. A light lilted over a sacred turquoise pool as though rising from a pure, deep source. We fell to our knees beside Dr. Aliamo.

"Oh, my God!" Bill gasped. "Or I should say, Goddess. For the first time, I understand what you mean, Alexander, by worshiping God's feminine. Now I believe your theory. This shrine's existence is proof. My camera will never do it justice." He joined us, listening to the bubbling spring and watching me run my fingers over the shrine's inlaid gems. "Look at that! It'd take millions of sandings by expert craftsmen to get something that smooth." He quietly followed my fingers as they skimmed over the stones and scallops of the shrine. "But only water could carve stone so perfectly. Right? The spring actually carved it and then receded?" He asked Dr. Aliamo who nodded and crawled over to the spring.

Dr. Aliamo began acting very strangely, his previous joy dampened. He gazed into the mysterious water as though some power pulled him into the depths. When he looked up, the usual intensity of his blue gaze had darkened as though something deep inside him had broken. He blinked his weary eyes and rounded his shoulders.

I crawled over beside him, peered into the mystical pool, and searched the turquoise water for what he'd seen. There was nothing there, just exquisite beauty causing me to catch my breath. I couldn't resist reaching over and splashing its velvety moisture like a libation on my face; I felt completely refreshed.

"And what is this stone," Bill asked, "tourmaline, aquamarine, turquoise?"

When Dr. Aliamo finally looked up, his eyes still showed some deep ache. Something was wrong. Why wouldn't he feel great about finally realizing his dream. I did. Quite a few minutes passed before he responded. "No, Bill, there's no stone to equal it. The closest would be something like hemetite or other sparkling varieties of volcanic rock that are blown up from the very deepest core of our planet," he explained, his voice almost a whisper.

"So the shrine's curving line at the top is the oldest part of this entire cavern?" Jane asked, pointing up to the shrine's rounded pinnacle. "Bill's right?"

Again, he was slow to respond; however, when he did, his words came fast. I quickly took out the pad and rushed to keep up with him. "Yes, Jane. Bill's observations about the spring carving this miraculous shrine are accurate. And yes, Bill, it was the source of water for the entire Acragas Valley. No wonder they worshiped it; it sustained their lives." His voice rose and grew more emotional. "Long will our lives survive if we protect this pure libation given to us by the Mother Goddess. But now we have lost regard for Her entire realm. Hopefully, the tapestrys' precious code will help us survive. Ready to retrieve Her most precious works?" He seemed to have snapped back a little bit.

This change in him, even though slight, undermined my confidence in jumping in the spring. I depended on him maintaining his authority as he'd shown us earlier. I could barely say "Ready," along with Jane and Bill.

"Good," he said, his voice again low and serious. He took out our buoyancy compensators, helped us with the regulators, and checked the pony tanks.

Bill was too busy to help me alleviate my fears that grew out of control by the moment. He directed Jane on the video camera, strategically

positioned the floodlights on the water,
grabbed his underwater camera, and jumped
in.

Jane saw me hedging on the edge of
the pool. She quickly crawled over to me,
real concern etched in her face. Rarely
had I ever seen Jane show emotion. This
really unnerved me, for I figured she
wanted to make sure and not leave
anything unsaid between us - just in case
I didn't come back. "Don't doubt yourself
for a moment, Sis. You are the authority
here. Forget all that stuff between us.
It was just a misunderstanding. This is
your story, and you must be the one to
retrieve the tapestries." She paused as
though wanting to make sure she hadn't
forgotten any other unfinished business.
Now I was convinced that she thought
she'd never see me again. I fought to get
a grip on myself.

"You'll never know how horrible it's
been growing up in your shadow..."

"Charla! Stay in the moment. This
isn't about all that stuff from the past.
This is about you overcoming your fears
so you can retrieve these tapestries.
Come on, be brave in the face of fear.
That's real courage." She said, the
concern gone, and her old intimidating
self returned. I stiffened. Next, she'd
probably tell me to lighten up and not
take myself so seriously. I just glared
at her.

"Hey, this is freezing. Come on,
Charla," Bill yelled, "You can do it.
Come on," he encouraged me again. "Jump."

I took one last look at Dr. Aliamo
who still looked burdened by the world's

weight. A lot of help he was. I swallowed hard, got a reassuring tug from Bill, and slid into the frigid turquoise water, determined to show something to Jane.

I cleared my mask, exchanged glances with Bill, and tried to adjust to the strange glare of the floodlight, creating a swirling, strange environment. Fighting my panic and trembling uncontrollably, I scanned the smooth, round wall, running my hand along its silty softness as we monitored the depth finder. Down, down we descended to the 30 foot line where Dr. Aliamo had explained the huge urns would be hidden. The other hand tightly gripped Bill's. I couldn't have felt more grateful for his supportive presence.

The lights dimmed, the water churned, bubbling and gurgling as we searched for the well concealed ledge, running our hands along the smooth wall. Then I felt its opening; Bill and I exchanged wide-eyed glances through our masks and shook our heads in agreement. It was a narrow slit just like the rear wall of the sanctuary. I reluctantly released my tight clench on Bill's hand and slipped behind it with him photographing my entry. My entire body shook like a leaf.

Step by step I edged along the pitch black ledge. The energy in the narrow space was so intense that a nervousness rushed through me. Bill crawled in behind me, shining his underwater floodlight on the wall. I jumped. The glare was so intense on the ancient amphorae that it made them appear larger and stranger than I would ever have imagined. Even though they were only 3 or 4 feet high, the water monstrously magnified them. I inched over to the one nearest us, the smaller of the two, reminding myself the entire time to remain calm, though my heart raced wildly. Seagreens and clay-oranges shimmered through dark patches atop raised ridges that encircled the amphora from its neck to its rounded base.

Bill clicked away as I placed my hands on the urn, holding its round neck. I could feel the ribbed lines of the heavy clay which looked as though it might weigh fifty or more pounds. Concentrating on it helped me forget my fear. It was solid, resembling the amphora used for shipping wine or olive oil. I hooked my hands cautiously through the rounded handles on either side of the neck and prepared to lift it from its ancient resting spot. Leaning it against my body to position it, I could feel deep, sponge encrusted deposits covered by tenacious barnacles, indicating that the urns had at one time been in the sea. Odd, I thought, that these precious tapestries would have been placed on some common shipping vessel. Then I realized that this would have been the least suspicious way to ship them. I felt so protective that I almost rocked it back in its protective spot; but Bill, finishing his work for the moment, took hold of the other side, and together we inched it along the ledge to the opening.

I looked back at the larger urn, sitting alone in the darkness. Once in the upwelling water, we quickly ascended as though propelled upward by the bubbling current. The floodlight from above grew brighter and brighter. We grabbed the base of the amphora and lifted it high over our heads until we felt Dr. Aliamo and Jane grab it from above. Scurrying to get out of the water to help lift the heavy jar onto the floor, I hardly heard Jane moaning thanks that we were all right. I glanced at her, gloating over the fact that I'd done it. But I knew that it wasn't even close to being over. My hands shook so hard that I almost dropped the urn.

As soon as the amphora was secure and had stopped rocking, we quickly jumped in again. The second entry was a little easier. Our air was holding out, but it was limited. We wasted no time, quickly descending to the ledge. I moved rapidly behind the secret entrance. Upon reaching the second urn and tilting it onto its side, I noticed the difference in its size and weight. Bill worked fast, secured his cameras, grabbed the other side and helped me inch it along the ledge to the opening. Our ascent was even faster, especially since our air supply was dwindling and we still had to replace the urns in their secret space.

Jane and Dr. Aliamo's hands were on the amphora before it ever surfaced. We could feel its weight being lifted out of the water over our heads. I surfaced, ripping out the regulator and taking deep gasps of air before jumping up on the side and helping place the ultra heavy jar on the dusty floor. But I was so weak and my body shook so violently from the cold that I almost couldn't budge it.

I didn't think I could dive back in, and I thought about asking Jane to take my place; but when I saw her hands shaking and her pallid complexion, I knew I had to be the one. My love for her aside, I didn't want her taking any of the credit.

"Are you okay?" Dr. Aliamo asked with concern when he saw my uncontrollable shaking. I nodded my head yes. "Good, then we must hurry," he said, moving around the pool and the amphorae. With the same bent shoulders and weary eyes, he picked up the two large backpacks. Then he took out a chisel and hammer to open the lid on the smaller, lighter urn. My excitement made me forget the cold. I couldn't believe that Dr. Aliamo wasn't ecstatic about finally retrieving the tapestries.

"Look, they're the same lids as the terra-cotta pipe! Guaranteed not to leak," Bill observed excitedly as we all watched Dr. Aliamo gently chisel away at the odd looking mortar, lightly lining the lid. Like a sculptor, he opened the first and then chiselled away at the lid on the heavier, larger amphora that stored Athena's tapestry. Carefully, he removed its lid which clunked with an echo on the ground.

A spiral of white, dancing smoke shot high into the cavern from the urn, then gently descended like a vaporous protection around the mouth. In awe, our jaws dropped as we witnessed, in slow motion, the miraculous moment of Dr. Aliamo reaching in and removing the large, thick, yet perfectly rolled woven cloth. As the corner of her tapestry emerged, we could see the glowing, blinding brilliance of gold, the shining sparkle of silver, the shimmering sheen of purple silk, and the dazzling colors of precious gems. As he fully pulled out the heavy cloth from the mouth, again the pure opaque white vapor, spiralled out into the air. We caught our breaths at the phenomena, not knowing how to react to this strange smokiness which enveloped the huge fabric like a protective cloud layer.

"Oh, my God!" I gasped, overcome by this divine moment; my heart stuck in my throat, my mouth hung open, and my eyes filled with tears as he lay it ever so tenderly atop the throned shrine.

Bill handed Jane the camera as he and Dr. Aliamo replaced the lid. A specially prepared silicone sealant protected the jar. They inched the large amphora to the edge of the pool. Then Dr. Aliamo walked over to the smaller urn. As Jane handed the camera back to Bill, her hands shook so violently that she almost dropped the camera. Dr. Aliamo watched her with concern, knowing that the cold was getting too intense and that we must hurry with all possible speed.

He reached very gently into the jar and carefully removed the sparkling, shining cloth. The same white phenomena did not occur as he pulled out the smaller tapestry, but the same brilliance of colors and dazzling sparkles brightened the cavern. He lay it down on the pack, and again, helped Bill scoot the lighter urn over to the edge of the pool.

Wanting to linger, to touch them, feel their preciousness, yet being able to waste no time because of the danger of hypothermia, I forget my fears and jumped in with Bill; we grabbed the large amphora first, quickly descended to the 30 foot mark, found the ledge, and sat it back in its ancient resting spot. We repeated the process with the smaller jar, but when we sat it in its spot, it rocked against the larger jar and caused a hollow echo in the pool. It was so eerie sounding, that Bill and I raced to get off the ledge and ascend.

Dr. Aliamo had already packed Arachne's tapestry in the bulging pack when we surfaced. Jane was holding the larger pack as he began fitting Athena's tapestry inside, with just its edge protruding.

"Wait," I yelled, shaking uncontrollably and sensing the numbness in my body, but completely resolved that no way was I going to miss viewing at least one of these precious treasures that I'd just risked my life retrieving. "At least let us see Athena's tapestry before you store it, Alexander; you owe us that much."

"Really," Bill joined in. "We deserve at least one glimpse."

"I couldn't agree more," Jane added even though her skin turned ashen white.

I knew mine was as well. Even the dizziness and nauseau didn't deter me.

"There's no time," he nervously stammered, his own hands shaking violently. However, when he saw the look on our faces, he knew he had to at least unfold this one and let us have some reward. "Charla, I'm concerned that you may suffer acute hypothermia. Are you sure we can take this time? And Jane, I'm afraid that you may go into shock. Please assure me." We both shook our heads that we were fine. Reluctantly, he removed the cloth, and with Bill's help transported it back over to the shrine's seat. With each corner that he unfolded of the four foot square cloth, tiny spirals of the vapor drifted upward. Before he had even finished laying it out, the sight was so blinding that we had to shield our eyes.

Thousands of colors invaded my eyes with the richness of the rainbow. Distant fading hues of every color imaginable streamed from the gold, silver, and silk threads, weaving in and out with sparkling light. The gems' deep brilliance, sewn in and amongst the threads, gleamed like the cast of the shining earth at sunset.

"Oh-h-h! Ah-h-h!" We moaned, catching our breaths and inhaling the whitish vapor, rising from the tapestry. It smelled of ancientness with a distinct odor resembling formaldehyde or some agent which had miraculously preserved it.

Even the blood red, Tyrian purples appeared as bright as when the Phoenicians first extracted the dye from the snails thousands and thousands of years ago. As my eyes adjusted to the brilliance, the colors, threads, and gems began to weave a story. Pure, rushing water plummeted a wall of great white waterfalls of waves rushing into the Middle Earth with such force and strength that it gushed into the lowered, fertile plain and began filling the basin with its constantly erupting wall after wall of deep blue-purple wonder. Countless diamonds created the white walls of water, bringing to life the beginning of the great flood.

Like the Mound of Amun rising out of the site of the ancient wellspring of the Nile, Cecrops, the Mount of Mars, created by thousands of rubies, rose above the Mediterranean as though it were bearing on its red, rocky back the first land to emerge from the newly formed emerald sea. The green, sparkling water spread the continents, forcing Europe from Africa, Turkey and the Middle East, and splintering islands, glimmering with opals and sapphires.

Higher than all, rose the Mount, as formidable as any acropolis and bearing on its rocky red ledge the temples of the 13 gods and goddesses who presided over the creation. Athena sat to the East, erect and tall, standing next to her father Zeus, god of gods, whose image she bound in the purest of gold and the deep shine of silver to cast him, with his lightning bolt glowing, in the position of power over the ancient council of deified dignitaries. Neptune stood tall, shimmering blue-green all around his raised silver studded trident that directed the rushing water into the deep shelf and filled it to the brim, burying forever all traces of the fertile garden.

As all the deities watched this ancient division of the land, Athena raised high her lightning spear and pierced the earth's rocky red mount. Up sprang the silver, shimmering leaves of the olive tree. Silver threads bound black olives, cut from the deepest shining onyx. The regal tree bore the mark of Athena, the tree of life, food from the gods, balms of precious oil.

My eye was pulled from the bountiful tree to the four corners of the tapestry. Like a heavy hand, the energy darkened, and in dark, deep-red rubies lurked the thought of "DANGER!", communicated by the swirling mass of threads. My eye quickly fled from one corner to the other. All bore the same message, not just a forbidden warning sign, but a pictoral enactment of the most disastrous tragedies. Human forms emerged, contorted and twisting, writhing in horror and intolerable pain from their detestable incestuous acts. The cursed and suffering House of Oedipus was represented by Antigone, his beautiful, devoted daughter, forever silenced, continuing to pay for her father's unforgiveable sin. Pitifully, her dark stained beauty lurked in the rubied corner opposite the tragic figure of Haemon, her adoring lover and cousin whose suffering frozen face remained to remind all of the pain. It has spread throughout the family like a cancerous memory fraught with mortifying consequence. The once youthful faces attested to the unrelieved torture accompanying this family's dangerous act. Tragedy and waste were woven in dark silk threads, all communicating the suffering of the children.

In another corner, Cinyras, the King of Cilicia, who married Pygmalion's beautiful daughter, but whose incestuous intercourse with his own daughter, the hereditary princess, had caused him to desperately embrace the temple steps as he lay on the hard, cold stone and begged for mercy. The king's intense emotions flooded the shining, black eyes which welled with piteous, glossy tears. All around these scenes of suffering souls, Athena wove her peace bearing olive branch, its emeralds and onyx intertwined around their heads and represented the consoling, nurturing energy of nature.

Had the cold not been so pervasive, I would have remained transfixed for countless hours just staring at this incredible, precious treasure. But Dr. Aliamo could wait no longer. I saw why he rushed so in refolding the priceless cloth. Jane's face now turned sickly white, and she looked as though she would faint.

It alarmed me so that I forgot all about my own discomfort, not even realizing that my joints grew stiffer by the moment. However, the look on Dr. Aliamo and Bill's faces told me that we were in great danger. Their hands flew, stuffing the tapestry in the pack, hoisting them on their backs, and speaking quietly yet with grave seriousness; grabbing the gear, they nudged Jane and I toward the tunnel. I was so dizzy that I hardly remember leaving the divine blue shrine and spring.

Bill rubbed my arms to stimulate them while Dr. Aliamo did the same to Jane's. They coaxed us into the tunnel, and somehow I forced my legs to bend so I could crawl. Jane wearily followed me. Dr. Aliamo pressed something very warm in my hands; it was some sort of battery run heater which he also handed Jane. My body racked with pain as we rushed down the steeply inclined slope, not even slowing nor noticing the stench from the sixth cavern. As though in a strange dream, we slid silently down the muddy floor past the fifth cavern. Not even the roughness of the floor nor the drenching spray of the misty fountain in the fourth cavern averted my dazed eyes. The trip down was incredibly faster and easier. I was shocked when Dr. Aliamo forced us to stop in the third cavern. Then he commanded us to stand up and try and walk the remaining distance. I didn't even feel the continual banging on my head, nor the scraping of the jagged walls on my arms, tearing the wet suit's thick material. I vaguely saw the long stalactites in the pools; but, from afar, as the sun struck its rays through the mouth of the tunnel, I pushed forward, aiming at the warm light with every ounce of strength.

Dr. Aliamo scanned the outside. There was no one around as he unlocked the wrought iron gate, reached back for me with his groping, freezing hands, lifted me into his arms, and carried me into the brightly shining sun. My eyes flinched. I heard Jane groaning as Bill brought her collapsed body into the light.

"Hurry, Bill, let's take them over to the altar behind the wall. The sun shines directly onto it, and they won't be seen," I barely heard him whisper. Then I felt the hot rock under my back and Dr. Aliamo's body covering mine as he vigorously rubbed my arms and legs. Jane lay beside me as Bill pressed his weight atop her. After a few minutes, Dr. Aliamo moved and Bill stretched across us both until I felt heavy blankets covering me, then again Dr. Aliamo's weight pressing down. Some time passed before I finally felt heat returning to my body. My eyes fluttered and I looked over at Jane who stared at me wide-eyed, saying,

"Now I see what you mean, Charla. This is tough stuff." And she grinned at me; for the first time ever she had admitted she was wrong. I put my dispute aside, figuring I'd indeed proven something to her. In fact, it all seemed rather funny. We both burst out laughing, feeling very slap happy. We sat up, massaging our legs and watching as Dr. Aliamo, rushed to store the gear in the cave. With Bill's help, I shimmied out of the wet suit and pulled on a warm jacket. Bill loaded both packs containing the tapestries on his back and braced me with both hands. The entire time that we maneuvered behind the wall, groping toward the exit, Dr. Aliamo spoke rapidly, his old authority regained.

"Please, listen very carefully to my instructions. Your greatest task lies ahead. With these tapestries in your possession, your lives are threatened. With all haste possible, you must leave Agrigento, drive straight across the island without stopping for anything or anyone, take the car ferry from Messina, continue your drive to Rome without any delay, and place these tapestries safely in the hands of Signor Morano. If at any time on your journey off the island you need a place to hide, go to Aci Trezza, just south of Taormina. I have a dear friend there, *Signora* Costello, who owns a hotel, Eden on the Riviera. You can trust her. Promise me, that you will take no chances, or you will pay with your lives."

"We promise," we agreed as we reached the exit.

"Good, now you must leave here as quickly as possible." His face fell. In the overhead noon sun, he looked so old, worn out and sad. My heart went out to him; I hugged him with all the strength I could muster. His eyes reddened, and mine filled with tears. "You will promise to tell the story, won't you, Charla? You'll record the truth about the tapestries and their importance?" He asked, his eyes begging and commanding simultaneously, his love for the tapestries obvious.

"I promise," I whispered as I hugged him one last time. I couldn't bear watching as Jane and Bill said goodbye to him. Tears streamed my face.

"Now run, with all your might, run for your car and leave here with all possible speed. May God be with you," he moaned. "Leave. There's no one in sight."

My legs didn't work. Jane and I held onto Bill's arms. He literally hauled us around the basins and up to the steps. Staggering and stumbling, we climbed up the steep incline, reached the path at the top, and for one last moment, looked down on the sanctuary. I stored it in my heart forever. Again, lifting us both, Bill raced to the last few steps, carried us over the gate, and to the car which sat in the dusty circle just as we had left it many hours before.

Jane groaned as she climbed in the back. Bill handed her one of the tapestries to place under her feet before she collapsed in a heap. Then he helped me into the front seat, also storing the larger pack bearing Athena's tapestry under my legs. I too collapsed, falling over on the pack and curling into a ball. Bill stomped on the accellerator with such force that the car leaped forward in the circle and headed down past the empty, dark guardhouse.

"Good," I heard him mumble as we turned onto Vei Templi and headed down the steep hill. "No white limo. No Norton. The coast is clear, and the brakes are working." His voice rose. "Hot damn. We're making the break. We did it. We rescued the greatest treasures on earth," he yelled out the window. My lips barely curved into a smile before I fell into a deathlike sleep.

CHAPTER VI: "EDEN ON THE RIVIERA"

An intense headache bolted me out of the endless, long sleep. I opened one eye to see Bill staring at me with loving concern even though the red welts on his head, which he had been rubbing, should have concerned him more.

I groaned, feeling the knots that swelled on my forehead. My entire body ached. "Where are we?" I asked, snapping back to reality and glancing around at the strange terrain. Jane actually snored in the back seat. Scrapes and bruises covered her body. I didn't dare wake her up. Then I saw the incredible volcano.

"Yep. That's her all right. Mt. Aetna. We just passed Catania without even one incident. Paulo must have done a great job diverting Norton."

"Paulo?" Jane sat straight up in the back seat and looked around to make sure no one was following us. "Did you say Paulo?" She asked again, rubbing her eyes and moaning as she stretched her back. "Where are we? Did we pass Taormina?"

"No. Why?" Bill asking, continuing to stare at the monster of a volcano.

"Why do you think. Paulo's there. He's waiting for me to..."

"Jane, you don't think we could possibly risk stopping in Taormina? Don't be crazy. You remember what Dr. Aliamo made us promise about this trip. He said that we shouldn't stop 'till we got to

Rome." Bill said, staring at her in disbelief.

"You don't think for a minute that I'm just going to take off and leave him waiting there for me, do you?" She asked, amazed at Bill's reaction. "Besides, he has my pullman. I just brought along this overnight bag until I could see him again. I can't stay in these clothes; they're filthy and torn. Just look at them."

"Jane, we should get the hell off this island," Bill said.

"No way. I insist that we at least pick up my suitcase and thank him for all the trouble he's gone through. No one is following us," she argued.

"Well Paulo must mean a hell of a lot to you, Jane, if you're willing to take such a risk," I accused her, the old jealousy creeping in at just the mention of Paulo's name. I again savored the memory of his kiss and shut out any possibility that he might be more attracted to Jane than me. I felt a pang of guilt when Bill caught my eye, so I quickly dismissed the thought.

"I wouldn't go that far! Don't forget I need my clothes," she retorted. "Plus I don't think it's such a risk. Check it out, you guys; I repeat, no one's following us. But the least we could do would be to thank Paulo for all the help he's given us." That was it. Now I knew she liked him. But he'd met me first.

"You can wear my clothes," I said, trying to make her admit how she felt.

"I totally disagree. You'd just be asking for trouble." Bill said. "I'd..."

He stopped, did a double take in his rear view miror, and widened his eyes before blurting out, "Shit, I could have sworn I just saw that white limo turn off at the last exit, the one to Aci Trezza. I've been keeping real close watch. It must have been speeding like hell for me to have missed it." Jane and I jerked our heads around, searching for the long, white car. The color drained from her face.

"What will they do to us? And what if they've done something to Paulo? I'm to blame for having gotten him involved in the first place. Now, I'm convinced. We must stop in Taormina and make sure he's okay," she said, biting her lower lip.

I agreed with her. Just the thought of Norton hurting Paulo really concerned me. Frantically, I searched everywhere, but the limo had completely disappeared. All that was visible ahead was the black smoking conical giant, rising from the bright green vegetation.

Bill's eyes darted from the highway to his rear view mirror and back to the busy lanes of traffic as he sped up. Above, the smoke poured out of the volcano in a steady spiral as though warning us of the danger we now faced. "Well, shit," he lamented. "If they were following us, why did they turn off? It doesn't make sense. Something strange is going on here."

No it didn't, and this fact made me so nervous I couldn't stand it. I tried distracting myself from the fact that it was getting late and that we might lose our way in the dark. The sun lowering behind the smoking cone appeared ominous.

A long span of tense time passed with no one saying a word. Traffic became very congested as the many turn offs to Taormina appeared and confused us totally.

"Come on," Jane insisted urgently. "It will only take a few minutes to pick up my suitcase from Paulo. Please. We at least owe him the courtesy of making sure his life is not endangered. It's just too wierd that the limo turned off. Please."

Bill wouldn't give in, even when all the signs announcing Taormina appeared ahead, saying, "It's against my better judgment."

I grew more and more concerned about Paulo. Plus I wanted to see him again. "I vote with Jane. Bill it's two against one." I said.

"Well, I certainly believe in democracy, but I think this is a terrible mistake," he said, grimacing and turning off under the sign, "Sud Taormina."

However, instead of finding Taormina, we wound up in a small resort by the water where crowds of tourists packed the streets. Bill could barely maneuver around them in the bumper to bumper traffic. Inching along, we made our way beside the water where a short black lava wall lined the narrow one-way street.

Bill grew fidgety, constantly watching in his rear view mirror and swerving to miss the tourists. "I hope you're both happy. Now we're lost!" He complained as we came to the end of the street along the bay and had to make a

decision as to which way to turn. There
were no signs to Taormina; the road to
the right went straight up a cliff, so we
took a left and headed back south.
Again, we wound up on the same street
along the bay, looped back south again
and discovered that we were going in
circles. The heavy traffic and jaywalkers
began to get to Bill.

"Shit!" He cursed. "We're sitting
ducks, just making loops!"

"Want me to drive?" I asked, feeling
partially responsible for having gotten
us lost.

"No!" He snapped, then added. "I'm
sorry, Charla, but this busy little damn
town is getting on my nerves. And I think
we're taking unnecessary risks that could
get us in a helluva lot of trouble. We
could be walking into a trap. Jane,
afterall, you did send Paulo ahead to
distract Norton, so why should we...?"

"LOOK!" I screamed, when we came to
the same stop sign for the third time.
"There's Norton," Across the street at
the service station, Norton was stopped
in a red car as an attendant pumped his
gas. He twisted his neck around, leering
at us out of the corner of his eyes. Then
he sped off from the pump after us so
fast that he jerked the nozzle out of his
tank.

But Bill had already taken off with
such speed that we were looping back
south again and heading for the highway.
Dust and rocks flew at the tourists who
headed for cover. "It was a trap. I knew
it was a trap." He yelled.

I glanced back to see the attendant running after Norton with his fist in the air. I felt sick seeing Norton's blond hair swept back over his ears and the sharp profile of his British nose and chin. I could feel his hands again, groping and probing my body and his wet, drooling mouth. I felt faint, the blood draining from my face. I wanted to bury my face, to forget all the horrid images that flooded my thoughts, but I couldn't. Bill needed me more than ever to be the navigator if we were going to get out of this one alive. I knew how dangerous and revengeful Norton was, especially after the beating he'd taken in the park.

A barrage of signs appeared overhead. A confusing line up of toll booths appeared with even more signs above each one. "That one's empty," I screamed, pointing to the end booth. We swooshed past it. Norton was right behind us; but by the time he reached the booth, the toll keeper was stepping out, determined not to let another one through for free.

"Great, he's been detained," I yelled, as Bill floored the accelerator and we entered the busy lanes of traffic on the highway. By the time, Norton flew off the ramp, we were some distance ahead. "Whew," I blew out after about a mile. Looking far off to my right, to my shock and dismay, was the smoking volcano, lit up by the setting sun. It should have been on my left. We were heading south. "Oh, shit! We're going the wrong way," I screamed. "Quick, take the next turn off."

Bill swerved off the interchange's narrow ramp on two wheels. However, he was going so fast that he lost control of the car. Fighting with the steering wheel, he missed the entry ramp, and we headed down to the bay instead. There was no place to turn around.

Even Jane got emotional, crying, swearing that we were going to die and sinking low into the back seat, saying, "What if Norton opens fire on us?"

"Turn here," I yelled at Bill as we entered a tiny little town sitting atop the cliffs. Dodging in and out of the narrow streets, we descended farther and farther to the sea until we came to a main road that skirted the bay. We turned and headed back north. I looked back; and though Norton was not in sight, I knew he wasn't far behind. Then, far up ahead, tucked in the cliffs, I saw the sign, "Eden on the Riviera." It was *Signora* Costella's place. Relief flooded through me. "I vote that we hide out up there until we lose Norton for good," I said.

"Until the heat is off?" Bill asked, then quickly answered. "I agree. These back roads are hell in this light and at this speed. Norton's not giving up. He's hot on our trail. Faking him out's the best way to go."

"Count me in," Jane readily agreed, "I've had enough for one day." She got thrown against the car as Bill veered onto the steeply inclined, twisting road leading up the cliff to the hotel. She slowly raised her head. "Did we lose him?"

"Far as I can tell," Bill said. "But I don't feel good about this. I'm sure Norton still has a gash in his cheek where I jabbed him with the file. He's probably looking for a piece of my hide now."

"We can hide out with *Signora* Costello," I added, feeling the furrows forming in my forehead.

"No, he's not in sight, but that's as close to death as I want to come," Jane affirmed, taking a deep breath and trying to relax. She gazed out the back window and caught sight of the shimmering bay far below. "O-o-h! What a view! I feel better already."

"There's the hotel up there, with that wide porch extending over the cliff," I said, directing Bill to turn. Up ahead, we could see the parking lot.

"Look, over there...we'll be hidden by the vines," I said, grabbing the pack and my things. However, I could hardly run for it. My legs never felt so sore.

"Oh," Jane moaned as she maneuvered out of the small back seat with the pack.

"Really," Bill groaned. "Every bone in my body aches." He grabbed the suitcases and hauled them up the steps with Jane and I right behind him.

Out of sight behind the bougainvillea vines arching out over the wooden porch, our bodies forced us to slow down and catch our breaths.

"Whew!" Bill blew out, pausing to catch the last deep purple hues spreading out over the sea. "Get a load of that!" He pointed to the Cyclops' Islands sparkling like diamonds with a grand array of lights from some approaching ship.

"No Norton," I said, pointing down to the bay road and peering as far as I could in both directions. "But I just feel queasy about him." I added, grabbing the pack more tightly. "Cause I know he'd do anything for this."

"Or this," Jane said, hugging Arachne's tapestry to her chest and taking off under the trellises where tables were elegantly set with gold rimmed china, fine crystal, roses, and candles.

"Come on, Charla. I know we lost him," Bill said, leading me around the tables. "As a matter of fact, I feel it so strongly that I'm coming back down here for dinner. Want to join me, ladies? And we can keep an eye on things from our rooms up there." He said, pointing up to the high balconies.

He didn't have to coax me. We crossed the porch to the cool tiled lobby.

There was no one in the office. High above the counter, keys hung from small boxed compartments. A ledger sat out front with a registrar for guests. Behind the desk was a very large safe and assorted guests' needs. Off to the left was an empty lounge with brightly covered wicker chairs and a dark wooden bar.

There was no one around, and we were anxious to get to the rooms. Over in the far corner, we saw the activity. Tuxedoed men gathered around a poised, statuesque woman who resembled a queen. "*Signora* Costello," we all said simultaneously, relieved that we somehow recognized her full white hair, fashionably curled around her ageless face. She saw us watching her and immediately came over. As she crossed through the lounge, she stopped and observed our unkempt appearances.

"Dr. Aliamo," I said, and no sooner than the words were out of my mouth than she was grasping our hands, dropping any suspicious looks, smiling and speaking to us in rapid Italian in her deep commanding voice. In fact, everything about her seemed commanding, including her white linen jacket that was pushed up at the elbow as though ready for business. Her very presence was soothing and seemed to say that not even the likes of Norton could harm us in her hotel. She led us over to the desk, reached into the small boxes, and pulled out two room keys, handing one to Jane and one to Bill who a bit too eagerly extended their hands. Then she pointed to the registrar which we signed. Once accomplished, she nodded her head, smiled, walked back to the group of men who awaited her, and left us feeling as secure as possible.

We ran up the broad, beautiful marble staircase from floor to floor until we found our rooms located next to each other. Excitedly, we opened the doors to discover a tremendous treat. The large balconies, which we headed for, opened the room up entirely so that we could see a complete view of the bay.

"Hello over there," Jane called from the adjacent balcony. "We must have done something right to have earned this.

Isn't this incredible," she said, leaning far out over the rail. "And aren't the rooms exquisite!" She rushed back inside.

Far out into the bay, my eyes scanned the horizon which was now a narrow gray line. From the far northern curve, I again saw the huge shadow, moving toward the Cyclops. It was one of the biggest yachts I'd even seen. For some reason, a chill ran up my spine. "Oh, oh, it's time for the one eyed giants to throw their rocks at Odysseus' ship again. Look at what's pulling in!" I exclaimed, observing the gigantic hull cut through the water as though it were glass.

"Wow!" Bill gasped. "That must be over 200 feet long. Look at that - a Scarab on davits and a helicopter! What's that on the other side, a super sized car? If Onassis weren't dead, I'd swear it was his. But what do you think a megayacht like that is doing here?"

"Who do you think owns something like that? Jane? Jane, come out here," I called with urgency to her, pointing out the multi-million dollar ship. "Isn't that fit for royalty!" I asked, as it circled the Cyclops.

"Check that out," Bill observed. "It's dropping anchor off the islands."

"I don't know why, but that gives me an eerie feeling," Jane said. "But I'm too hungry to think straight." She paused. "Hey, I'm not going to complain about my lost suitcase again. That was really wrong of me. I'm sorry," she apologized.

"That's all right," I told her as Bill shook his head in agreement.

"Good, got something I can wear?" she added.

Reluctantly, I grabbed some dresses and walked over to her room. I really didn't mind sharing my clothes with Jane, especially in a case like this. But they always looked so much better on her that I never wanted to wear them again. So I'd give her the ones she wanted, then go shopping in Rome and replace them.

Just as I figured, she chose my turquoise silk dress, one of my favorites, that I knew would light up her hair and face brilliantly. A tinge of jealousy rose, but I didn't want that old stuff relating to Jane from childhood surfacing again. I fought it down and went to get ready.

"How about you wearing that hot pink magenta gauze?" She called after me, probably sensing my old insecurity. "That's a great color on you." I took her suggestion, showered and dressed as fast as I could.

Bill came out of the shower. "O-o-h, la! la!" He complimented me.

"And you are my handsome man!" I said, hugging him but not feeling any better about my appearance. However, Bill really looked good, and I questioned how I could ever have had an interest in Paulo. The soft coral shirt displayed his dark chest hairs and made a sharp contrast to the white slacks and shoes.

"Ready, ladies?" He asked, when Jane walked in, appearing exquisite in my turquoise dress. Suddenly, I didn't feel so hungry anymore. Bill picked up the tapestries. I took the smaller pack from

Jane containing Arachne's tapestry, and Bill shouldered the larger pack. At least, I felt confident about having rescued them. He held out both his arms which Jane and I accepted, and we walked three abreast down the marble stairs.

Signora Costello saw us, glanced briefly at the packs before giving an order to her maitre d'e, then headed toward us with outstretched hands. She smiled regally as she showed us to our table overlooking the bay.

"*Gracie*!" We said in unison.

"*Prego*!" She said, "*Bon Appetite*!" and left to give orders to our waiter.

The candle lit table created a glowing presence in the dimly lighted dining area. Brightly colored bougainvillea vaulted over us. Bill carefully placed Athena's tapestry under the table and reached for the other one, but I insisted that the other pack stay under my chair. I felt so protective of it.

We sipped the effervescent champagne that our tuxedo clad waiter had poured for us and made a toast to getting away from Norton. Next appeared a large tray of steamed clams with butter dishes, then some type of finger sized, rolled pasta with anchovies wrapped inside. Delicious soup came next, then an incredible salad with a bottle of local wine. We were getting filled quickly, so we decided to take a break. One toast followed another.

"Here's to saving the tapestries! Here's to Eden!"

Suddenly, Jane's eyes widened as big as saucers as she stared out into the parking lot. A sleek, European car slowly pulled in, its lights aiming our direction. Jane leaped to her feet, exclaiming, "Oh, my, God, it's Paulo. What's he doing here? How did he find out where we were? Wait here while I check it out."

"Wait, don't go, Jane," I called after her, but she moved across the porch so fast that she reached Paulo's door as it opened.

Bill rose, alert and ready to defend her, but she waved him back. Paulo stepped out, kissed Jane's hand, then looked our way. As much as I thought I'd gotten over him, my face fell when I caught sight of his large brown eyes brighten upon seeing me. I waved, my heart racing as I recalled the feel of his lips pressing on mine. He smiled warmly. I forced myself to keep my composure and reminded myself that Jane was with Paulo and that I loved Bill.

His head disappeared as he crawled into the back seat and emerged again, carrying Jane's suitcase. However, Jane wasn't acting pleased. In fact, she looked like she'd seen a ghost. Her steps were measured as they crossed the porch, hand in hand. To our surprise, Signora Costello rushed out to greet Paulo, calling him by name and embracing him warmly as though she'd known him for a long time.

I hardly noticed Jane dart around them and cross the porch; in fact, she kept blocking my view of Paulo who now turned and walked slowly toward me. As he neared, Jane stepped in front of him,

still trying to get my attention which
was locked on Paulo as his broad white
smile lit up his gorgeous, tanned face.
He kissed my hand, again tingling me to
my toes.

"Charlotta, my friend, how wonderful
to see you again. How are you?" He smiled
so sweetly and was so happy to see me
that my heart softened. Then he turned to
Bill, shaking his hand vigorously. "Bill,
finally, we meet. I told Charlotta, you
are a most fortunate man." He continued
staring at me admiringly. I felt a new
confidence; for once in my life a
gorgeous man was going to be more
attracted to me than Jane.

Signora Costello came over with a
waiter, bringing a chair and an extra
place setting. They spoke in rapid
Italian, then Paulo translated, telling
us that this was his favorite place, one
he had stayed in many times before. He
couldn't believe that we had discovered
it. He said he'd finally given up waiting
for us in Taormina and had decided to
come here instead. When we questioned him
about Norton, his face puzzled ever so
briefly, and then he assured us that
Norton had indeed followed him but that
he'd lost him in Taormina. He asked Jane
very innocently if he had done as she
requested.

"Perfectly, and I want to thank you
very much," she told him in a formal
tone. "I apologize for getting you
involved in such a silly situation.
Aren't some men so cavelike when they see
a woman they admire?" And she dismissed
the entire thing. Paulo seemed relieved

to let it drop. The subject made him
nervous. Nor was Jane acting like
herself. I was surprised at her reaction
to Paulo. Even though she had almost
admitted her feelings towards him, in his
presence, she appeared uncomfortable. I
wondered if she sensed the sexual tension
between me and Paulo.

She just kept staring at me, trying
to get my attention, until finally she
kicked me and pointed under the table as
though she wanted something. Her eyes
darted wildly, and I wondered if she were
all right. When I didn't respond, she
took her feet and forcefully pried the
tapestry from under my chair. I froze,
not knowing what she was up to and
getting very upset at her aggressiveness.
My eyes filled with indignation. The
nerve of her to force the tapestry from
under me, I thought. Her jaw set firmly,
and I could tell that no matter how I
tried to retrieve it with my feet, there
was no way she was giving it up. I
swelled with old, painful memories from
childhood when Jane always got what she
wanted. I shot her a negative glance, and
she stared right back at me as though
telling me to lighten up. This made me
even madder.

Plus, now Paulo changed; he couldn't
keep his eyes off Jane. And there she sat
in my turquoise dress. In fact, he was
pouring attention on her and ignoring me.
His eyes glowed with admiration as they
traced her face and her brilliant red
hair. Then he made a toast to her, and
it was all I could do to raise my glass.

"And here is to Jane, the most beautiful woman in the world, whom I am so very, very happy to have seen once again," then added, "and here is to my new friends." He looked totally enamored with Jane. He scooted his chair as close to hers as possible. Now his eyes shined. He reached over and selected one of the roses on the table, saying, "They smell sweet, but not nearly as sweet as Jane!"

I couldn't bear it. He was only too obvious about his choice. I wasn't sad; I was furious at her for causing me to suffer through the same old role that I'd always experienced when she was in the picture. I saw red, but when Bill reached over and grabbed my hand, I decided I'd better cool it. Besides, when I looked from Bill to Paulo, I saw how truly handsome Bill was. Even with red welts on his forehead, he outshined Paulo. I took a deep breath, coming to terms with the fact that I really did love him and that it was time to drop my feelings for Paulo.

And the more Paulo doted on Jane, the stranger her behavior became. Her hand actually shook when he handed her the rose, and her face was overly pale. At first she played up to him, but he became more and more nervous. Then he suddenly stood up, dropping Jane's hand and announcing that he wanted us to go down to the bay with him.

"Well, of course, we'll join you," Jane said unhesitatingly, pulling him back down and talking to him soothingly as his brow furrowed and his smile disappeared.

I couldn't believe my ears. There was no way that we could venture out without falling into Norton's hands. But I didn't even get a chance to resist. She pushed her chair back, grasped the tapestry under the full folds of my turquoise dress, and started crossing the porch to his car with Paulo explaining to her that he'd been out on a diving trip around the Cyclops and finished at dusk. He said he wanted to go get his gear, and he spoke in glowing remarks of the large fish he had caught which was being cleaned on the dock by a young boy and his father. *Signora* Costello called out and asked them to wait a minute as Bill and I scrambled to our feet. When we caught up with them, Paulo had again changed, his nervousness returned.

"Don't worry about a thing, Paulo," Jane boldly told him and waved to *Signora* Costello to hurry and come over. "Let's go get your catch," she said, guiding him to the car.

"Oh, *grazie*, Jane," he said, sounding relieved. "The magical view of the *Isole dei Ciclopi* from the bay is the best in all Sicilia," he further persuaded.

Leaning up against the car, he put his arms around her, pulling her close. Neither of them heard Bill and I cross the parking lot, nor did Jane hear our protesting that we didn't want to go. I could have killed her when she seductively said, "Don't listen to them; we'd love to go with you, Paulo, just to show you our gratefuless, wouldn't we Bill and Charla? Be good sports. Plus, it will release all the stress we have from traveling," she added in her most intimidating voice.

Bill, typically not wanting to cause a scene, went along with her.

Words were stuck in my throat. I was furious with the way she just took over, and I was ready to tell her off when Signora Costello showed up at the top of the steps. Jane, taking full control, almost shoved Paulo in the front seat, opened the back door for us and insisted we climb in.

"*Signora* Costello, just a second," she called in her most polite voice, her tone completely changed. After almost pushing us in, she swiftly climbed the stairs and spoke to her for a second. Bill and I sat stiffly on the edge of the back seat and wondered what the hell she was up to.

Spinning on her heels and causing my turquoise dress to whirl in the air, she almost floated down the stairs and got in. I watched her every move, but the dress spread around her so fully that I couldn't see if she had the tapestry or not.

I nudged her in the back and said in my most demanding voice, "Jane?!" as Paulo took off speeding down the hill, but she refused to turn around. Bill leaned way over the front seat, sticking his head between them and trying to see the tapestry, then turned back to me and whispered. "*Nada*," his eyes questioning.

I took a deep breath and tried to calm my nerves and squelch my anger. As I inhaled, I noticed a definite odor in the car, one that wasn't Paulo's musky smell.

I couldn't identify it, but it was so repugnant I plugged my nose; fuming over Jane's behavior, my suspicious mind zipped from one thing to another, trying to figure out what she had done with the tapestry and why. I flashed back to the tunnel and remembered Jane asking Dr. Aliamo for permission to record the tapestry's message as her theory. Was that it? I questioned. Was that why she ripped it away from me? Now I was so mad that I had to fight the stinging tears that flooded my eyes. How could she do this to me? I questioned bitterly, not even concerned about Paulo's fast turns around the sharp, steep curves. And why I ever let her convince me to take this trip, I'd never know. Some growth, I thought.

"Where's the tapestry?" Bill whispered, but I was so furious I couldn't talk, just shrugged my shoulders. "I don't like this. What's going on?" He asked more persistently. "Jane?" But she pretended not to hear him.

Not once did she glance in our direction. She conversed with Paulo as calmly as possible, laughing and acting as though things were fine.

In no time, we were past the bay road and heading down into the narrow streets of Aci Trezza where the area around the bay was packed with people. Bill and I immediately started looking for Norton. We peered into the outdoor cafes lining both sides of the street where men sat sipping drinks. Mothers watched their children who laughed and squealled around the steps of the cathedral. Norton was nowhere in sight. I slumped down in the back seat when we turned onto the busy, narrow street along the bay. Bill kept looking at me and asking what the hell was going on as the children stopped to admire Paulo's car and Jane reached over and blew his horn. Why doesn't she just announce to Norton that we're in town, I thought, while Bill just stared at me in disbelief. I continued taking deep breaths and trying to think more clearly. Jane was just acting too strangely.

I scanned the bay where the colorful shipping fleet lined the dock; just beyond, a shipyard displayed the same boats being built. My eyes searched farther around the bay where the dark shapes of the Cyclops loomed above the water, twinkling with the small lights of the nightly fishing boats. Then, finally, I saw it again, my eyes widening in disbelief at the huge yacht anchored behind the big island. I nudged Bill, discretely pointing at the dark colored flag with some kind of circle and star shape on it, visible in the ship's bright lights.

Bill and I peered out into the dark bay, searching the area for any sign of Norton. But Paulo asked us so many questions that it were as though he was trying to distract us. He pointed at the small restaurants that lined the bay and described the delicious food and the beautiful view. He asked if we were still hungry since we hadn't finished eating, and if we'd like to dine at any of them. Refusing to take no for an answer, he

asked if we'd like to take a stroll by
the water, pick up his catch, and have it
prepared in one of the quaint
restaurants.

"No," Bill and I kept repeating,
distracted by all the activity and the
constant stream of couples, walking arm
in arm along the path circling the bay.
They made me feel somewhat protected.
Hopefully, Norton wouldn't strike with
all the people around, I thought, still
trying to get over my seething anger at
Jane.

"Can we get out and walk?" Paulo
asked much more persistently and
nervously. "My gear is right up there,"
he said, pointing to the end of the walk.
"Also, it's the perfect spot to watch the
moon come up."

Jane gave Paulo a long look before
she agreed, saying, "Sure! Great idea - a
spot overlooking the bay sounds perfect.
You lead the way, Paulo."

"Wait," I protested vehemently, but
Paulo had already pulled into the first
available parking space, right next to
one of the outdoor restaurants, where the
elegantly dressed people in evening
attire could hear everything we said.
Before I could say another word, Jane
opened the door and crawled out, ordering
us to come with them. She didn't have the
tapestry. Bill eyes were as wide as mine,
but I knew he wouldn't make a scene. In
shock and disbelief, I followed.

"This is so-o romantic," Jane sighed.
But it didn't sound like her. She linked
her hand in Paulo's and crossed the
narrow street to the sidewalk which

encircled the harbor, leading out to a narrow point on the far end of the bay. Reluctantly and very fearfully, I followed, staying as close to Bill as possible. We strolled along with the other couples until we reached the point where the sidewalk curved out by the dock and the small fishing boats. Paulo suddenly stopped, instructed us to turn right out to the point overlooking the water, and announced that he had to made a quick telephone call. But he told us to go on alone, look for his diving gear about midway down the dock, walk out to the end of the jetty to enjoy the view, and to wait for him there. Then he left abruptly.

"What's going on, Jane?" Bill demanded. "What did you do with the tapestry?"

"Just keep walking, Bill," she ordered again, in her most authoritative voice, one that dared us not to disobey her. I couldn't believe she was acting like such a bitch. I was ready to get into a real fight with her, but I couldn't catch up with her. She was almost running down the long dock. Bill and I sped up, catching up with her as we passed the fishing boats where fathers and sons worked on the decks organizing nets and ropes in preparation for the next morning's work.

"Jane, I'm never going to speak to you again if you don't stop and explain why you're acting like this," I demanded in no uncertain terms. "And just where is the tapestry? What have you done with it? I said stop. Now!" But she hurried on.

"Charla, please, go along with me just this one time, please, I beg you," she pleaded with me, promising to tell me everything in just a minute. She grew quiet as we passed the people gathered on the dock and the boats. Then she ran on.

Finally, we were close to the end of the wooden dock, and we could see the jetty, extending far out into the dark bay. Paulo was not in sight, nor was any diving gear. My heart began to race. Bill and I grew anxious and more demanding of what was happening. Again, she told us to please just follow her and trust her. She climbed out onto the jetty. "No, Jane, come back," I screamed, but she only motioned more frantically for us to come with her. To our left, waves splashed against the breakwall and threatened to get us wet. Bill hoisted the heavy pack containing Athena's tapestry high above his head to protect it from the open water's continual wash against the wall as the sea violently swirled and smashed around us. It was so loud that we could hear nothing.

"Jane, I've had enough," Bill said, but he was silenced by the loud roar of a fast boat that approached at great speed behind us. Startled, we all turned and looked down from the jetty at a cigar shaped boat that came alongside so fast that it caught us off guard. We just stood there, looking down and trying to decipher the dark shapes in the black water.

In a flash, men were jumping out of the boat and running up toward us. The shiny, black barrel of a gun appeared in

view in the harbor lights. Then two more
pointed directly at each of us. We
couldn't see their faces, but as soon as
the deep male voice spoke, demanding the
tapestry, we recognized it immediately.
It was Norton, cursing, waving his gun,
and threatening to kill us if we moved.
Chills ran all over me at just the sound
of his voice. I froze. As my eyes
adjusted, I could see the huge scrape
down his cheek where Bill had stabbed him
with the file. I cringed with loathing,
shifting my glance to the two other men
accompanying him. They were the most evil
looking, pernicious people possible.
Never had I seen such expressionless,
cold, and deadly eyes. Their mouths
smirked of violence, and their attitudes
said that they'd cut and slice us to
slivers and never flinch. With
reluctance, I looked back at Norton's
hateful face. Gone was his handsomeness.
Instead, I saw an insolent, aggressive,
belligerent man who'd do anything to get
the tapestry out of Bill's hands which
grasped it tightly.

In no time, the two thugs had leaped
forward, grabbing the pack from Bill's
unyielding hold, smashing his head with
their guns, and punching him violently.
"Hold him for me," Norton spat out the
words. "Now it's my turn to get even."
And he pounded Bill's stomach with such
force that I thought he'd kill him.

I lurched forward, yelling, "Give it
to them, Bill. Don't resist."

He couldn't. In seconds, they had it,
pushing Bill backwards onto me and Jane
as he collasped, unable to breathe.

Unlike the encounter with Norton in the park in Rome, I didn't care if I got the authorities involved. Bill's life was at stake. I screamed at the top of my lungs, and even when Norton slapped me down and commanded me to stop, I continued to yell bloody murder. Norton looked at me with such contempt that I halted momentarily, then started screaming again. I saw him realize that he'd have to kill me before I'd cease. Bill needed help, and that was the only thought in my mind; I screamed even louder.

Grabbing the tapestry from the thugs, Norton tore off in a fast gallop down the top of the breakwall with his hired killers close behind him. They raced to the large motor boat and jumped in. Within seconds, they had cleared the wall and were out in the open water.

In the reflection of the lights, we recognized the boat - it was the same one we had seen hoisted by davits on the giant yacht. And it was in that direction that they headed as they rounded the Cyclops' big island. All I could see was Norton's blond hair plastered against his face in the wind.

"Oh-h-h!" I screamed in anger and indignation. "What a dirty, rotten, lowdown, shitty thing to do! The nerve of him to steal the tapestry after we worked so hard!" I couldn't keep the tears from swelling in my eyes and overflowing onto my cheeks as I tried to squelch my ire. "And you, Jane, what have you done? Did you know you were leading us into this trap?" I cried out. Then I came to my senses and fell to my knees beside Bill who lay crumpled over.

"Oh, Bill, Bill, speak to me. Are you all right? Oh, no. Be okay. Do we need an ambulance? Are you hurt? Oh, Darling, I love you. Please say you're okay." I wrapped my arms around him, crying and feeling his pain as though it were my own.

"No, no," he barely said, unable to talk. "I'm okay, just got the breath knocked outta me. Paybacks are hell. Don't worry, Charla," he said, pushing my hand away from the knot on his head where blood oozed out, "You know I'm too hard headed to be hurt," and he forced a grin.

"How can you have a sense of humor at a time like this?" I asked in amazement, making him lie back and placing his head in my lap. I swabbed his wound with my pink skirt, not even caring that it got bloody.

"They just arrived at the yacht!" Jane announced, watching the water. "Thank God, you acted so quickly, Charla, and saved Bill's life. I'm really impressed."

Making sure that Bill was not hurt too badly and comfortable, I stood up and confronted her. "Well, I'm not, Jane. In fact, I've never been so disappointed in anyone in all my life. You let us risk our lives. I'm surprised Norton didn't kill all of us. And you let him steal the tapestry. And God knows what you've done with the other one. I just can't believe this is the same person that I grew up with. The same person who always stressed impeccability. What a hypocrite! I..."

"Oh, Charla, stop. Don't say such angry things that you'll regret. Didn't you figure out what was happening? Didn't you smell Norton's cologne in Paulo's car? Come on now, you couldn't miss that odor anywhere in the world. Why did you? It's unmistakable. Apparently, he met Paulo down here at the bay and ordered him to come up to *Signora* Costello's and get us. I didn't want Paulo to have to force us or hold us at gunpoint, which he would have done if we'd resisted. Don't you see? There was no place for us to run. That car on the yacht was the white limo. We were surrounded by some of the wealthiest, most powerful people imaginable. There's much more involved than we realize. We're lucky we're not dead right now."

"Oh-h-h," I gasped, understanding what she'd done and realizing immediately what a terrible mistake I'd made; I wanted to take all those hateful words back. I couldn't have felt like a greater heel. It all fell in place.

"I hear you, Jane," Bill tried to speak. "But I need more of an explanation than that. Surely there was something else we could have done to save Athena's tapestry. We just handed it to them, but I won't say without a fight," he added.

"I don't blame you, Bill. I'm sure you may have thought that I was part of the set up. I had to take that chance and hope you wouldn't stop me. I'm not sure how Norton got poor Paulo involved, but I was convinced of the necessity to hand the tapestry over to Norton. There was no way of stopping him since he'd gotten such support behind him. So, I figured, that, number one, he still might not know that there are two tapestries; and second that without Arachne's tapestry, who'd ever believe that a goddess actually created the work. He's going to have a hard time proving that, especially without the documentation."

"Oh, Jane, please forgive me," I moaned, feeling so remorseful that I could die. I couldn't believe that I would have thought such awful things about a sister whom I loved so dearly. "Oh, please forgive me," I begged her again.

"As I always say, Charla, realizations are personal. And you've just experienced a big one. Of course, I forgive you. That goes without question. I love you regardless of your actions. But, I hope this whole thing proves something to you, Sis. All that stuff that you're telling yourself is preventing you from being in the moment. Your emotions are interfering with your observation, proven by the fact that you missed the smell of Norton's cologne." She said in her kindest words, her love for me shining through.

I started crying so hard that my whole body shook. She was right. This was one of my greatest realizations. She hugged me so warmly that it made me sob even harder. I released so much in that moment. All the times I'd been jealous. All the envy and negative thoughts I'd had toward her came pouring out in the salty tears that streamed my face.

"It's okay. It's okay," she kept repeating in a soft voice. Then, when I got control, she said, "Now, Bill needs our full attention."

"Hey, don't mind me," he said. "I love miracles; they cure me in a hurry. Charla, I've never seen you get it so fast. That's great."

I smiled, knowing he understood fully, and kneeled back down beside him. I swabbed his bloody head again with my dress. "Shouldn't we go to the hospital?"

"No way," Bill said with stern conviction. "It's amazing your screaming didn't already get the authorities over here. Besides they'd never believe us. We can't take anymore chances, especially with the other tapestry. Which reminds me, Jane, just where is Arachne's tapestry? I assume you took good care of it since you planned all this out so well."

He tried sitting up, but I made him lay back down, telling him, "In *Signora* Costello's safe, where else? Don't you see how perfectly Jane had it all planned? I can't believe I missed the most important clue of all - Norton's cologne."

"Wow," Jane congratulated me. "That's <u>exactly</u> right. What else do you know?"

"That Paulo's innocent. He wouldn't be hooked up with Norton," I said, realizing that I'd placed all my personal feelings about Paulo aside. "In fact, what probably happened is that Norton has done something with Paulo's mother. You wouldn't believe how attached Paulo is to her. She'd be the perfect person to take

as hostage in order to force Paulo to go
along with this scheme. I know Norton too
well. Jane, are you sure you're not mad
at me?"

"Lighten up, Sis. I know you better
than you know yourself and am a lot
easier on you than you'll ever be. Don't
take this to heart," she said, pointing
out into the bay as the yacht pulled out,
bound for the open sea. We sat in silence
for some time with only the waves
breaking through the quiet.

"I'm sure you're right," Bill quickly
agreed. "Paulo is too good a guy to have
turned on us. I'm sure Norton assured him
that we wouldn't be hurt. And with the
kind of big money that's involved, they
could easily have killed us. Considering
a priceless treasure and the kind of
money it takes for a yacht like that,
they could buy this whole village never
mind the local police. No wonder Paulo
was so nervous."

"What makes me so mad is that they
had us scoped out the entire time - set
up! Norton was connected with them all
along. They were just waiting for us to
get the tapestries out of the cave and
deliver them into their hands," I
complained.

Again, we were all quiet as we
thought back on the trip and knew they
had just been waiting for this minute for
us to arrive at the dock. For a long
time, we just sat there, swinging our
feet over the side of the seawall and
watching the last light of the yacht
disappear into the dark Ionian Sea. I
thought about Odysseus' ship and the

Cyclops' throwing the big rocks down from Mt. Aetna, and I wished we had some to throw. I'd be the first to toss the biggest one I could find at Norton. But there were no rocks, no giants, and nothing any of us could do except sit there and stare into the empty blackness.

"I know this sounds ridiculous," Jane broke the silence, "But I just can't get that old song about "Sitting on the Dock of the Bay" out my mind."

She couldn't, and neither could Bill and I. The power of suggestion was incredible, and for a long time we sat on the dock humming the old, familiar tune.

PART II: <u>ATHENA'S TAPESTRY</u>

Chapter I: "Arachne's Return"

A strange, low gurgle rose from the turquoise spring, and I quickly glanced below me into its dark depths, wondering if the sacred water were sending some message about returning Arachne's tapestry to the amphora. I shivered. Except for my bubbles, bursting over my head and racing for the surface, no movement followed me down. Again, it gurgled, and I blinked as Bill's flashing camera caused the cavern's shadows to eerily dance.

Trying to pay attention, to dismiss my fears over retrieving the empty amphora by myself, and to not think about my being so upset over this turn of events, I surveyed the green limestone walls, running my hands over the smooth surface until I discovered the open niche which hauntingly welcomed me onto the ledge. In slow motion, I struggled with the smaller jar which seemed to resist my budging it from its ancient resting place. Using my entire weight which helped me release some of my frustration, I wedged my body between the two and pushed with all my strength until it rocked free; I grasped the barnacled handles, inched it to the opening, and, directed by Bill's light, shot upward in the current.

"Thank God you're all right!" He said, grabbing the amphora from my hands.

"Charla, what are you trying to prove by taking such risks?" Dr. Aliamo asked, pulling me up on the side of the spring.

"I'd say it's you, Dr. Aliamo, who has a lot to prove - to me. I want to respect your decision," I said, yanking the regulator from my mouth and staring at him as he began removing the tapestry from the pack, "but I'm having a very hard time accepting all this. Maybe you can help me from having this sinking feeling that we've been set up in some way."

"Really now, Charla! You know that's not the case at all. This is the <u>only</u> place we can store the tapestry safely." He said paternally, unrolling the corner of the tapestry as he pulled it out. Its brilliant sheen of blinding diamonds, deep red rubies, and elegant emeralds lit up the cavern with sparkling lights shimmering on the gold, silver, and purple silk threads. He hurried to stuff the jeweled cloth into the amphora.

"Hey, hold on," I yelled, scampering over to the shrine. "You owe it to us to unroll it so we can see it at least <u>once</u> before its buried forever."

He looked at me long and hard before he said, "Don't say I didn't warn you." But I didn't have a chance to react to his strange remark before he unfurled the heavy cloth in front of me on the shrine's pale throne.

"Oh-h-h," the three of us gasped, spellbound over the incredible sight.

"Oh, my God!" I moaned, transfixed by the shimmering purple threads outlining majestic, mythic animals mating with maidens. Zeus, as the great white swan, hovered over the pale thighs of the raven haired Leda; her opal eyes opened wide in shock as he beat his broad feathered wings and clasped her at the nape by his large, black beak. My pupils dilated. I darted my eyes to another corner where Europa's slender legs straddled the white broad back of the bull, abducting her and heading for Crete. Her shiny, golden locks spread over her bare breasts as she fearfully held onto its sharp horns. With its powerful muscles, it sprang atop the blue green waves, dampening her curls and spraying her delicate feet as she cried for help and longingly looked back at her home on the distant shore which disappeared in the mist.

"Trrruuly pornographic!" Jane stammered, "But exquisite!" She nervously laughed.

"U-h-h, I'm speechless," Bill said. "But I might dream about this."

"Regardless of my reluctance to show you this, I guess it had to be exposed at some time in history, so this is a rare moment. Now do you mind if I shield your eyes from any further viewing?" And without waiting for a response, Dr. Aliamo rerolled the heavy jeweled cloth - even amidst my strong protests.

As it rolled, I raced my eyes to another corner where a shaggy coated, cloven footed satyr's ruby hoofs pressed frenzically, like vices clutching the petite waist of the beautiful, innocent

Antiope who frantically emerged from the emerald forest. And just before the final corner got stuffed into the amphora, I caught sight of a jungle, woven from jades, where a mottled brown, diamond studded snake slithered around the thighs of the unsuspecting maiden, Deo, who was unable to escape its seductive thrust.

I quickly looked away, wondering if I should have seen such a sight.

"I warned you. It's cursed," Dr. Aliamo repeated. "Now let's quickly get this safely out of the reach of any interested parties." With great haste, he replaced the lid, turned it several additional notches for extra protection, and applied a silicone sealant to the edge of the amphora's lid and then to its lip.

Bill's camera clicked away, recording the event that felt like a funeral. Such a masterpiece to be buried forever, I thought, unable to snap out of the spell it had cast on me. My spirits sank as Bill handed Jane the camera and jumped into the spring.

"Hold on," I complained about the moment being over so soon. My moment, I considered sadly, but I also realized that Dr. Aliamo's real hurry was because of the invasive cold that threated us all with hypothermia. I jumped in the icy water and grabbed the amphora as Jane and Dr. Aliamo lowered it on its side.

With each foot we descended, my spirits sank lower. Jane's words that, "Without Arachne's tapestry, which was actually woven by a mortal and, therefore, proof that the historic moment

really happened, who'd ever believe a
goddess created a work of art?" She's
right, I thought as the bubbles streamed
past. And I knew my story was lost.
Stolen from me. So even if I did attempt
the impossible and rescue Athena's
tapestry, who'd ever believe me? No,
without Arachne's tapestry, all was lost.
Running my hand along the smooth
limestone wall and locating the opening
to the ledge, I fought the tears as we
carefully slid the amphora back into its
ancient resting place. The jars clinked
ominously. Bill and I stared at each
other through our masks, our eyes wide.
Thumbs up, he gestured, pulling me by the
hand and hurrying me off the ledge. We
quickly emerged, the cold seeping into
our bodies, shivering uncontrollably
despite the thick wet suits.

Dr. Aliamo almost hauled us out of
the water and pushed us in front of him,
hardly giving us time to tear off the
flippers and shove them in the pack.
Jane, close to being overcome by the
cold, had crawled far ahead. We scurried
to catch up with her. I hardly noticed
the painful crawl. Inside, I felt so dead
and defeated that I was surprised when,
almost an hour later, the light shone
ahead at the tunnel's opening.

"Damn it, I just don't see why we had
to do that," I complained as soon as I
could catch my breath. Dr. Aliamo had put
me on hold all the way through the long
tunnel, and I could wait no longer for an
explanation. I crawled over to the wall

and leaned up against it as I wrestled out of the wet suit.

He rushed to lock the gate. "Please, Charla, stop repeating that. This is not the right time. We've got to get out of here as quickly as possible before someone sees us." He grabbed our gear from our hands and stuffed it in the cave.

"And just who is supposed to protect it if someone does see us?" I asked sarcastically, upset with him for ignoring me and demanding to know.

"You know I'll protect the tapestry with my life - before I'll let it fall into the wrong hands. Trust me. This is the <u>only</u> thing we could have done." He argued with me, rushing to lock the caves.

"Over your dead body, you mean?" I bluntly asked, beginning to doubt if our lives were worth anything to him since he was so willing to sacrifice his own.

"Come on, Charla, now isn't the time to talk about this. Please cooperate," he pleaded with me. "Please. If not for yourself, at least for your sister."

I turned for the first time and looked at Jane, who was bruised and blue. So was Bill, and I knew I appeared the same. "All right, I'll drop it." I said.

"And agree to hurry?" He asked, prodding me along behind the rear wall.

"I'm hurrying, Dr. Aliamo, but you must promise to tell us everything and explain why you don't even seem to care that you almost got us killed and...."

"And may still if you don't keep quiet," Jane hissed from her perch atop the shrine where she kept watch.

"Sh-h, both of you," Dr. Aliamo ordered, then spoke softly as we neared the opening in the wall. "Of course, I care, how can you even doubt that, Charla? And you know I'll tell you everything, so you'll be able to protect yourselves better. But you also must be patient. For now, Jane, jump down. Bill, lead the way."

"Coast is clear," Bill signalled, already out from behind the wall and running alongside the basins. I scampered behind him, stepped into the sunlight, and for one brief moment before I neared the end of the basins, I looked back and made a solemn wish to, "Please, please, keep it safe." Then I ran as fast as I could under the trees and caught up with Bill who helped me leap the steps two at a time. The last thing I want to do is die in this spot, I thought, ducking as Bill caught the gate keys that Dr. Aliamo tossed high into the air. In a few steps, we reached the gate and the road where our tiny car sat in the early morning dust. I climbed in the back seat, holding the door open for Jane.

"Thank God, there's no one in sight," Dr. Aliamo said as we took off down the rocky road. "We're almost out of this. Let's head to Villa Athena, so you can get some sleep before taking off across the island again. I can't imagine how you're still functioning." He paused for a second, his voice lowering. "You must believe me. There was no other way, or I would have spared you all the trouble. This is a much more serious situation than I could have relayed to you when you left here with such valuable artifacts. You probably wouldn't have risked it, and then...."

"Hold on," Bill cut in as we sped past the rocky cliffs. "I love adventure, but not kamikazi missions which...."

"Wait a minute, Alexander, did you say spared us all the trouble?" Jane interrupted. "You mean all the danger you exposed us to, don't you?"

"Really!" I yelled. "How could you possibly have selected someone like Norton in the first place. Don't even tell me that you don't know who that billionaire yacht owner is. And did you even care that they tried to beat Bill to death?"

"Please, Charla, please." He pleaded again. "We will discuss this later. But for now," he paused, looking both ways as we reached Vei Templi. "Good, no one's in sight," and we sped down the steep road. "For right now, I'll say this, Bill. I'm truly sorry you were hurt, but I assure you it could've been much worse...."

"Exactly," Jane abruptly cut in. "It could've been bullets in the back of our heads. And if you didn't level with us when we left here the first time, what makes us think you're going to be different now? As for me, if any further involvement with this assignment is going to be this dangerous, this exhausting, this nerve racking, this...this..." She stopped, unable to go on. Jane had obviously reached her limits. She sat up straight, flicked her red hair over her shoulders and discounted any further attention to the matter by gazing out over the Valley of Temples, shining golden in the rising sun.

"Cool out, Jane," Bill said. "You're not out of this yet."

Not out of this alive, I thought, realizing I was in the same boat. Jane's strong words raced through my mind as fast as the car zoomed around the curves. I recalled the tapestry's images of the animals and maidens mating and wondered if this were one of the reasons Jane resisted so. Its sensational message might have offended her. Usually, I agreed with her about such matters, but this time I couldn't discount its exquisitely perfect beauty. Regardless, I couldn't see burying it for countless more millennia.

"Very simply, it's not worth our lives. No worldly possession is," she added.

"I disagree, Jane." I couldn't believe my words. Since we were kids, I'd gone along with her decisions when it came to real serious matters like this one. But this time was different. As much as I thought all was lost, I wasn't sure I wanted to pull out on recovering Athena's tapestry, though I had grave doubts about getting it back from someone with such wealth and power.

"But I do agree with you about one thing. Norton or that billionaire's bodyguards could've killed us hundreds of times if they'd wanted to." I leaned against her as Bill veered the car into the hotel's parking lot. "But there's one very important thing that you've overlooked. We may have started an international crisis."

"An international crisis?" Jane raised her voice at me as Bill came to a screeching stop under the vines.

"Sh-h," Dr. Aliamo again hushed us then commanded us quietly to grab our bags. He raced ahead of us on the pink stoned walkway, held the door open, and told us to wait as he secured our rooms.

We could barely walk down the long hallways to the two rooms on the end before we flung open the doors and collapsed on the familiar, soft bed.

"What did you mean, Charla, about us having caused an international crisis?" Jane asked as soon as Dr. Aliamo locked the door. She sat stiffly in the chair.

"Wait. Before I explain everything to you, I want to first congratulate the person responsible for having saved Arachne's tapestry." Dr. Aliamo said.

That was it. No way could I stand for this mission to end with Jane getting the credit.

"U-m-m," she cleared her throat. "But it means nothing if you turn around and tell me that I've caused a crisis."

"What you've unwittingly done, Jane, is hand over the Greek's most revered and treasured artifact, created by none other than their namesake. Let's hope the Greeks don't find out that their precious work has been snatched by the Turks."

"Turks!!" We all shouted in unison.

"The flag! Oh, I should've recognized the ship's Turkish flag," Jane gasped.

"Talk about repressed violence! This conflict goes all the way back to Troy."

"Yes, Jane, you're right, and this theft is a serious enough offense to renew the bloodbath between these two warring countries, especially given the tense conditions in Cyprus," Dr. Aliamo said.

"Now I know I'll not get further involved," Jane resolved, standing up and walking over to the glass doors. "International tension is out of my league. If something's that old, forget it."

As Bill and I sat in shocked silence, Dr. Aliamo furrowed his brow, causing his bushy eyebrows to meet. "It goes even farther back, much farther than...."

"Back to the myth? To the contest?" I interrupted excitedly, suddenly seeing history fall into place. "To the creation of the tapestries?"

"Exactly, Charla, back to the original, unforgiveable insult when...."

"Insults, you mean," I interrupted him again. "Let's not forget that Arachne met Athena's charge of incest by accusing the Greek gods of sodomy, plus she attacked Athena's own father."

"Which was met by incredibly cruel punishment," Bill added. "Being turned into a spider is not what I'd call a favor. Why I'd...."

"Nor is it considered a favor by those who claim descent from Arachne," Dr. Aliamo cut in reluctantly.

"Kinship with arachnids?" Bill asked, sitting straight up on the bed and coming to complete attention.

"Who claims kinship? The Turkish billionaire?" I blurted upon seeing Dr. Aliamo suddenly look old and worn out, and I knew I'd struck a raw nerve. His shoulders rounded and his bright eyes glazed with dimness and exhaustion. "You know him, don't you?" I flatly asked.

"Yes," he stammered, even more reluctant to admit the truth. He took a deep breath and slowly exhaled as we sat on pins and needles waiting for his reply. "I've known him for some time. I realize I owe you quite an explanation and a sincerely felt apology for not telling you the entire story in the first place. His name is Idmon Ilkent, and he has a family seal that...."

"Idmon?" I gasped, "As in the myth? Arachne's father from Colophon, Turkey? That Idmon? He's a descendant of Arachne's father?" I asked again in shock.

"You can actually trace a family tree back thousands of years?" Bill asked, his eyes opened wide in utter disbelief.

"Yes, Colophon, south of Izmir, and just outside Kusadasi, the very port where Idmon is headed at precisely this moment. Don't you understand? There's just enough time for you to rest for a few hours, then drive to Catania and catch the train." Dr. Aliamo spoke urgently, his eyes bright again with persistence. "It leaves for Rome this evening at 9:00. I'm sorry for the inconvenience, but you must travel as inconspicuously as possible, taking the first morning flight out of Rome to Istanbul."

"Hold on a damn moment. Just what will Idmon do when he discovers he has the wrong tapestry? Come looking for us?" Jane asked.

"He doesn't know he has the wrong tapestry," Dr. Aliamo flatly replied.

"What?" Jane asked in shock. "Even if I were to get involved - which I'm not, you understand, right or wrong tapestry - I won't agree until we hear the <u>entire</u> story," Jane decided, her intense eyes fixed on him like pins.

"Really," I interjected. "We've had no sleep, no food, and now you want us to race across this huge island, catch an all night train to Rome, then immediately take a plane? Impossible!" My shoulders slumped. While I realized that all was not lost as I'd previously throught, and even if Jane might get the credit for having rescued the tapestry, I was shocked at the challenge I now faced. And I was very disappointed in Dr. Aliamo. He had kept quite a bit from us.

"By train, by plane, hey, you left out by boat," Bill said excitedly. "Count me in. I love adventure, plus I have a big debt to settle with Norton."

Dr. Aliamo looked at Bill, smiled, and said, "I knew Don Meldon sent the right ones on this mission. Come on Charla and Jane. He wasn't wrong about you."

"I still can't believe you chose someone like Norton," I told Dr. Aliamo.

"It had to be the money. I had no idea he would go to such lenths to...."

"Alexander?" Jane interrupted. "Sure you haven't found jobs for any other former students?" She asked leadingly.

He arched his eyebrows in surprise. Apparently, she had hit another raw nerve, and I wondered why he was still hiding things from us. There was a long pause before he continued. "You are most intuitive, Jane. Yes, I agreed to tell you everything. There is a woman involved." He waited, his face falling. "Her name is Suhvanna Nudir, a Turkish graduate student of mine who assisted me with my research - she helped me with everything."

"Everything?" Jane prodded when he again hesitated.

"Yes, she knows everything. I shared all my findings with her - except the exact location of the tunnel. That I shared with no one." He said.

"And the number of tapestries?" I asked. "Does she know there are two?" The words didn't sound like mine. Inside, I felt hurt, almost betrayed. Plus, I couldn't believe Dr. Aliamo would have been intimately involved with one of his students. Even though I recognized his obvious good looks, I simply had never considered such a possibility. In the tunnel, he'd sounded so enlightened - a man who wanted to help women, even me. This news didn't fit in with my image of him. I wondered just how well I knew him.

"She's aware of only one. You're the only people who know there are two tapestries still in existence," he said.

"What was your relationship with her, and where is she?" Jane asked, her eyebrows arched high. She was determined to get to the truth.

"Oh, she's half my age. Plus, she's extraordinarily beautiful - an ideal, aristocratic beauty - the flowering of the old European Lydians." His eyes brightened. "Indeed, she's a rare find - long platinum strands of the silkiest hair you can imagine and eyes the color of the Aegean. She was my top student, mysteriously intriguing, fiercely independent, and...," he stopped, as though it were painful for him to go on.

"Y-e-s," Jane pried.

"She disappeared one day," he spoke quietly, unable to admit it.

"Like you did?" I asked impatiently, feeling threatened by someone I'd never met, but wanting to get to the bottom of his involvement.

"Yes, I went looking for her and traced her to Rome where I discovered her...with Idmon who must have seduced her with his wealth."

"Did she know Idmon?" I asked.

"Yes. He came to Oxford, asking to hire our team for the very job I'd been working on for years. Uncanny! Both of us simultaneously searching for the same treasures, but he only wanted Arachne's tapestry. Of course, I refused. Then he met Suhvanna, and I...I lost my research assistant." Pain distorted his face.

"Are you sure that was all you lost?" Jane leadingly inquired.

"No, no, it's not what you think. She was like a daughter to me. But I don't believe it was she who led Idmon to Sicily. I agree with you about Norton

being suspect here." He again hesitated.
"I never thought he'd go this far. I just
hope to God that she will help us when
she realizes the worthiness of this
cause."

"Tell me again, Dr. Aliamo, what
cause?" I questioned, amazed and
overwhelmed by the added complexities of
this assignment. My old insecurities
resurfaced upon discovering I'd be
dealing with a woman even more
challenging than Jane.

He rose, walked over to me, grasped
my hand, and gazed deeply into my eyes,
his smiling face showing his former
kindness and consideration of me. "For
the cause, Charla, of resolving the age
old conflict between Greece and Turkey
once and for all. Oh, if you hadn't lost
the tapestry! It was an ingenuous plan of
unveiling them both at the Temple of
Minerva in Rome. And with your story,
Charla, I'd hoped to have you host the
occasion. But all is not lost. Please
assist me."

"What? Host what?" I asked. I perked
up, realizing I might still somehow
succeed in getting this story after all.

"I've told you all along, Charla.
This is your story. And if you promise me
again that you'll let no one else publish
it, you'll be internationally recognized.
Won't you agree?" He almost pleaded.

"Wel-l-l..." I faltered, not knowing
how I'd ever be able to say no. "I guess
I'm already involved." I couldn't bear
looking at him. I felt like jumping up
and running away as fast as I could - and

simultaneously I felt like accepting. Torn by indecision, I stammered, "But how?"

"If Idmon is coerced by Suhvanna to hand over Athena's tapestry, you can pass it right along to Greece; then Turkey can be offered Arachne's tapestry, both as promises for peace in Cyprus. That is if Suhvanna will help you. In fact, I'm not sure what she will do," he said, his excitement fading. "She's unpredictable, cunning, and complex."

"What a brilliant solution, but not for me," Jane spoke right up. "This has gone far beyond our original commitment to this assignment. And, Sis, I really think you should reconsider. Suhvanna sounds too manipulative. I know you've experienced some growth on this journey, but this could ruin all that. I know I originally suggested that you take this trip, but now I'm asking you not to pursue some unknown fate in Turkey. Plus, I wouldn't trust Idmon with my eyes closed, much less with my back turned. And you already know what a murderer Norton is."

I blocked out her warning. "Jane, I disagree. This is still part of the original agreement. Aren't you committed?" Her face shut down, and I knew not to argue with her further. "Well, would you at least stay in Rome?" I couldn't believe my words, actually suggesting she spend time with Paulo. But her staying close by was more important. "This mission terrifies me," I confessed, suddenly not feeling very adventurous.

"With good reason you fear. Can't I talk you out of it?" She asked again, but I shook my head no. "All right, but please don't ask me to have to come to Turkey and rescue you? Please?" I agreed. "Okay, I'm sure Paulo will show me around. I'd rather be charmed and dined than dead." She added, giving up the job.

"Idmon can't run the risk of scandal, much less murder. Please rest assured. Your lives are not in danger." Dr. Aliamo affirmed.

"But Athena's tapestry is at risk. I can't let Norton get away with this. Plus, I feel so responsible for these precious tapestries. I don't think I could live with myself if I didn't at least try to get Athena's tapestry back," I said, wondering just what in the hell I was getting myself into, but reassuring myself that it would all be worth it.

"And I'm not ready to live without you, Charla! As I said before, I'm in, and now, we'll be a team again, Honey, on the greatest quest of our lives." Bill said, reaching across the bed and squeezing me tightly.

"Excellent!" Dr. Aliamo said. "But first food and sleep." And he rose to order a pizza.

CHAPTER II: "TREK TO TURKEY"

I groggily awoke to Bill singing in my ear, "Oh, it's Istanbul, not Constantinople! Oh, it's Istanbul, not Constantinople.' Wake up, Darling, we're in Asia." And he planted a big, wet kiss on my dry lips. I groaned, refusing to open my eyes. I hardly heard him continue, "You know, something's been bugging me this entire trip. How did Dr. Aliamo find out that Idmon's ship was bound for Kusadasi is what I want to know?"

My eyes burned, my head ached, feeling as heavy as lead, and my brain and body were numb. In over 48 hours, I'd only gotten a few hours of sleep, for I'd been unable to sleep at all on the overnight train we'd taken from Catania, Sicily to Rome. Jane's unceasing pleading for me not to go had left me in turmoil. She'd even resorted to scaring me by reminding me how horribly women in Turkey had always been treated. Her words haunted me - "And let's not forget history's recordings of how dark mother worship got when its followers were forced underground - by the patriarchs, of course, who continue firm control over the women. Get out of this, Sis, you might die in God forsaken Turkey." I could also hear Dr. Aliamo's echoing words in the tunnel when he told me the same thing. I cringed, trying to force out their frightening warnings as I numbly made my way off the plane.

"One thing I do know is that we've got to get to Izmir, rent a car, and head for Kusadasi as fast and as straight as the crow flies," Bill said.

"Forget it, Bill," I snapped, feeling irritable and testy. "If you think for a second that I'm making a connection from Istanbul to Izmir without stopping and sleeping a few hours in a bed, then you'd better think twice. I'm exhausted."

He knew better than to argue with me; instead he pulled me close as we pushed with the crowd through customs. His sharp gaze penetrated the placard bearing crowd welcoming arriving passengers. Then, taking charge he directed us down to arrivals. While he took off to exchange our money into lira and check Turkish Airlines for flights, he directed me into a hotel reservations' booth. In a daze, I thumbed through the pictures of the rooms and selected one that looked inconspicuous and hopefully safe.

As much as I could pay attention, given the stupor I was in, I kept a watchful eye on the crowd of men who had gathered around me, even before Bill was out of sight. They stared at my blond hair. Eying me up and down, they edged closer. I scanned the area, searching for Bill to come to my rescue. I tried not to notice the men's dark eyes undressing me and studying my bare knees. I tolerated the obvious novelty of their interest until one of the men reached out to touch me. "Bill! Help!" I yelled when I saw him running down the corridor. He grabbed my hand and pulled me outside.

"Let's get out of here," he said, hailing a taxi. "Darling, are you okay?" I shook my head. "I'm sorry I left you. I won't do that again."

"Hotel Emmge, near Aksaray Square," I told the young taxi driver, checking him out and making sure he wasn't another one on Norton's payroll. He didn't seem to be the type, looking at me helplessly and politely opening the door.

"Emmge?" He repeated, unable to speak English and still displaying confusion, but loading our suitcases then taking off into the busy lanes of traffic.

"Talk about saving you from the wolves. I've got to keep my baby right by my side," Bill comforted me, pulling me close to him; I collapsed on his shoulder. We drove along beside the blue Maramara Sea which stretched up north to the Black Sea. And cold, wintry darkness, I thought as a cool breeze blew in the window.

"You were right about the layover. Sorry I wasn't considering what you've been through, Honey. The next flight is not until 10:00p.m., so you should at least get a nap," Bill said. Relieved, I took a deep breath and closed my eyes. Something about the mistiness made me think of Ovid, recalling how he'd saved Arachne's myth from extinction and how he'd been exiled to die on the Black Sea. And here I was, I thought, also involved with the myth. I didn't like the connection, and without warning, a terrible heaviness overcame me, caving in what was left of my energy.

"Yes, the Emmge," Bill repeated to the taxi driver who stopped again in the humid, crowded streets and asked directions. Immediately, a group of men crowded around the taxi. They spat on the street and stared at us. "Don't worry, Darling. He'll find it," Bill reassured, asking if I were okay.

"I - I'm not sure," I admitted as a chill racked my body.

"Real chill bumps?" Bill asked in amazement as we sped down a cramped, narrow street and came to a stop in front of the small hotel.

I was cheered somewhat by a lovely, eight or nine years old girl who greeted us as we walked into a very Turkish looking lobby. She spoke good English and took over after we'd registered, guiding us into a suffocatingly small, old styled elevator, with an outer door and an inner one that, as I pushed it open, caused the chill bumps to return. She pressed the third floor button, and we rode up in silence. As soon as she'd shown us the room and left, I hit the bed.

Bill landed beside me, rubbing my back and telling me that while I rested he was going down to the Maramara to try and find some information on Idmon's ship.

I tried protesting, telling him how wierd I was feeling and how I didn't want to be left alone. When he insisted, I even reminded him he'd promised not to leave me. But he sat with me, rubbing my shoulders and reassuring that he'd be

back before I woke up. It worked. I was
so drowsy that I hardly heard him leave.
I slept strangely, dreaming that I was
one of a group of pregnant women
surrounding a table; all of us were
dressed in grey robes and assisted by
doctors and nurses in the same attire.
Suddenly, I was next on the table; as I
watched, my large pregnant abdomen began
to contract. After the delivery, I stood
up, and the nurse handed me a bundle. I
walked toward the elevator which
mysteriously opened. I entered, pulled
back the blanket, and, in utter shock,
discovered a plant. Alarmed and
frightened, I glanced up and noticed that
a nice looking, yet strange, black suited
businessman was in the elevator with me.
Without warning, he sexually aggressed
upon me than raped me.

I awoke with such fear, horror, and
repulsion that I jumped straight out of
bed; looking around for Bill, I hesitated
slightly before running out the door, and
in a daze, racing down the dark hall; I
couldn't tell if it were night or day.

As though still in the dream, I
reached the elevator, for some reason
waiting at the third floor. Ignoring
whatever tugged at me, I flung open the
elevator's outer door, pushed in the
inner door, and stepped in. With a loud
bang, someone behind the door slammed it
solidly shut. Struck with panic, I tried
to scream, but a forceful hand wrapped
around my mouth so tightly I couldn't
breathe. Something exploded inside of me,
and sweat broke out all over my body. I
was trapped. His other hand pinned my

arms, but I wrestled my hands free and tried to jerk his hand off my mouth. Nausea swelled in my throat.

I looked up in the elevator's lurid light and saw the distorted stockinged face as he spun me forcefully around, crashing me into his large chest. He was a good head taller than me and easily able to hold my face crushed into his black T- shirt. I panicked from the suffocation. My eyes darted like an animal then fixed on his scarred arms that bound me like ropes against the wall. He jerked down my shorts and jammed his fingers in me - just as Norton had done. Oh my God, I gasped in pain, realizing what he too was going to do. He rammed me up against the door, pressed his sweaty body against me, breathed hot and heavy down my neck, and tried to partially release my arms so he could finish unzipping his black jeans.

Refusing to go through such horrible torture and seizing the opportunity, I wrenched his hand off my mouth and let out a blood curdling screech. He roughly slapped me and clamped his hand again over my lips like a vice, but I bit right through his skin, blood trickling in my mouth as he thrashed me about and ripped my shirt into shreds, exposing my breasts. All the horror of my encounter with Norton flooded over me when he forced his huge penis inside me. Almost fainting, I forced myself to fight to the death; I wasn't going to submit, and recalling how I'd foiled Norton's attempt, I somehow squeezed my knee in between his large thighs and brought it straight up with every inch of strength within me. He heaved, hunched forward, and grabbed his crotch.

"Charla! Charla!" I heard Bill yelling into the elevator shaft like a madman.

In a flash, the dark clothed assailant recovered, spitting on me and slamming me up against the wall with such force that it knocked the breath out of me. Growling like a wild animal, he grabbed open the door and crushed me behind it. I screamed again so loudly that it felt like I injured my throat. After he almost ripped off the outer door, I watched as he ran with all his might, fleeing down the dark hallway.

Shaking out of control, yet using every inch of strength in me, I jammed my finger on the down button. "Charla! Charla?" Bill again shouted into the elevator shaft, sounding as though he were on the second floor. My hand shook so hard that I almost couldn't stop the elevator on the second floor.

"Bill, Bill, here I am!" I frantically called back, as the door flew open and I collapsed in his arms. His breath caught when he saw my discheveled condition. His eyes flared red with anger, and his body shook with rage as he embraced me.

"I'm okay, really, Bill, I'm all right." I hardly got the words out of my mouth before he released me so fast that I fell back. "No, don't go," I called after him, but he'd already run the length of the dimly lit hall, slammed open the stairwell door and disappeared.

Scared out of my mind to be standing there by myself in the dark hallway, I jumped back into the elevator, pressing the first floor button with all my weight as if my finger supported my entire body.

Remain calm, I reminded myself, my fingers flying over my clothes, smoothing and straightening myself in a desperate attempt to gain composure. I reached the first floor and stepped out into the crowd of people gathered around the elevator with their mouths ajar. Suddenly, Bill burst through the stairwell door. "I've lost him. Where'd he go?" He yelled as the porters and desk clerk scampered for the front door to help him. I froze, gripped by the frightening moment. From the street, I could hear Bill angrily curse in a thoroughly disgusted tone, "Shit!"

I pulled my ripped shirt together when I caught the young girl staring at me in shock. Still uncontrollably shaking, I walked over to the door and looked out to see Bill turning the crowded corner at a fast speed with the desk clerk and porters close behind him. All the people on the street curiously gathered to watch. I turned back, heading for the empty lobby with the young girl sticking close behind me. Her small, wide open eyes continued carefully examining me.

Finally she spoke up, "My father said to tell you that in Turkey, men do not act like this," she almost apologetically added, "for they will be hung."

Bill burst back in, swearing and looking very defeated. His face flushed

with concern and love when he saw me, and
he rushed to my side, placing his arm
around me, and asking me again and again
if I were okay.

"Yes," I kept repeating, leaning on
his shoulder as he led me toward the
elevator. I caught the little girl
watching me with wide eyes. Not wanting
her to see how my body ached, I held back
my shoulders as Bill thanked her and the
others and helped me on the elevator. As
soon as the door closed, I panicked,
reliving the scene again. I was violently
shaking by the time it opened. I ran down
the dark hall, telling Bill, "We've got
to get out of this hotel right now."

He understood, rushing ahead to
unlock the door and helping me to the
bathroom. I quickly showered, trying to
wash off the awful, dirty feeling I felt
inside. I barely dried off, dressed, and
was out the door which Bill had guarded
the entire time. All the way down the
elevator, he held me close, telling me
everything was going to be fine. He
quickly checked us out, again thanked
everyone, and helped me into the taxi
which was waiting at the front door. "The
airport," he told the driver.

And only after we'd started the long
drive around the Maramara, was I able to
tell Bill about the awful incident. He
hugged me so tightly, asking again if I
were really all right. I told him about
the horrible dream and wanted him to help
me understand what it meant.

"A plant? Charla, don't you get it?
As in someone planted in an elevator just
to terrorize you. By Idmon, I'm sure. Our

dark clad businessman. Damn him. He'd <u>not</u> going to get away with this." Bill paused, looking at me lovingly, but I could sense something else was bothering him. "Okay. I admit it. You're right," he continued after my questioning. "I feel responsible for going off and leaving you. I promised you at the airport I wouldn't do that, and I'm sorry. I couldn't bear it if anything happened to you, and this is a much more dangerous mission than we might have realized. I...I..." And he couldn't go on.

"I know what you're going to say, but, Honey, I'm really okay. Please believe me. And even if you're right about his being a plant, it was just to scare us. Yes, it worked, but now that I understand it, I'm not so afraid." I couldn't believe my own words, nor did I know where the strength behind them came from. "Given the severe penalty for rape in Turkey, it's pretty obvious he is hired by Idmon. But remember what Dr. Alaimo told us about Idmon not running the risk of killing us?"

"If anyone comes at you again, I must warn you, I'll be the one doing the killing. But I wouldn't bank on Idmon one hundred percent," he said.

"It doesn't matter. I'm not running back with my tail between my legs. Besides, what if the plant is a symbol of the leaves of a book I'm supposed to write?" I asked, not taking long to make up my mind.

"You know I'm always with you, Darling. But if you get hurt, the adventure is ruined for me. So let's just agree to be super careful," he made me promise.

Then all the way around the sparkling, dark sea, he held me, stroking my hair. I was committed, but I was scared. Continuing to take deep breaths and blowing out the tension, I tried relaxing all the way to the airport.

With every step toward the gate, my eyes searched for the tall, black clad figure. But we boarded with no problems. During the short flight to Izmir, Bill carefully checked out the other passengers, but I refused to think about the danger, searching the vast, outer darkness for some sight that might make me more comfortable in such a strange, alien land. As we landed I told Bill, "In Istanbul, I made reservations at the Izmir Palace Hotel - it's near the NATO headquarters." I just hoped we didn't need any help from them.

We quickly made our way through the empty airport to the taxis and toward the hillside city that sparkled ominously in the large bay below. High up in the mountains, a castle lit up the velvet darkness. I took several deep breaths. Bill held me close as we reached the gulf, its waters splashing the broad stretching promenade where bright colored umbrellas at outdoor restaurants flapped in the wind. We pulled under the hotel's awning where a friendly, green eyed receptionist checked us in; her bright eyes and white smile lit up her face. "You're Americans?" She said delightfully, offered us one of the nicest suites overlooking the bay, and told us that she'd send up room service with dinner.

We climbed the wide, spiraling staircase to the second floor and carefully checked out the long hallway to the room where we quickly scooted inside.

I collapsed on the bed, resting only a short while before dinner arrived. It was exquisite - delicious red tomatoes in light oil and vinegar with olives and fresh cucumbers and some very sweet yet hot leaves that made our eyes water, wrapped vine leaves, rice, shish-ka-bobs, and white wine.

Before I was even through, Bill began rubbing my back with oil, whispering softly in my ear that he loved me more than anything and assuring me again that we were safe. As his large, sensual hands reached my lower back, I slowly began to relax. However, it took coaxing, more sweet murmurings, and a gradual ease into intimacy before I pushed away the painful memories; I finally gave in to Bill's quiet, gentle stroking. I moaned with pleasure as he applied more oil with his slipping, sliding fingers, creating friction and causing my body to eagerly respond. He rolled me over and spread the oil on my breasts. I pushed them together when he slipped atop me, moving sleekly from the enclosed velvet softness of my breasts to my mouth. Responding lovingly to my desire, he pulled me atop him. I slid so easily back and forth that I had to hold onto his shoulders. Finally, he released me gently, laying me on my back and pressing against me until I wanted to scream in ecstasy and grasp my legs higher and higher around his waist; in the embracing dance, we were entertwined forever it seemed, bound as one. Then all time stopped. And like falling leaves, my legs lost their grip and Bill slipped down beside me. Enwrapped, we fell into an exhausted sleep.

All night I slept fitfully, dreaming over and over again that a tall blond flirted with Bill who finally succumbed to her sexual overtones and even chose her company over mine. My anger was so intense that I attacked him, pinching him as hard as I could. When I awoke, Bill was already up and getting ready. "Coffee," he muttered, groping for the phone and ordering breakfast. Then he jumped back in bed and hugged me tightly, telling me how wonderful making love had been.

The awful dream flashed in my mind, and I confronted him as to whether he had an interest in another woman. He vehemently defended himself, telling me again that I was the only woman in his life and that he loved me with all his heart. As he showered, I thought of all the times I'd been jealous of Jane, but I'd never been jealous of Bill. I'd never really had cause to be. Finally, I rolled out of bed and made my way to the shower, climbing in with Bill. He soaped my back and nibbled my ear, making me forget all about the dream. The knock at the door interrupted his further attempt to recreate the previous evening.

"I'll get it - pretty quick for breakfast," I volunteered, grabbing a towel and suspiciously opening the chain latched door; sighing with relief, I discovered a smiling girl with our silver tray of food - incredibly pink watermelon, more sliced red tomatoes with feta cheese, salami, rolls, juice, coffee, and tea.

"U-m-m," I moaned, sinking my teeth into the scrumptuous watermelon and tucking some stray curls out of the way in the large, white towel.

"Reminds me of you," Bill teased, the sticky juice dripping down his chin as he took an enormous bite.

"So you have sex on the brain or something?" I grinned, ignoring him, pulling out the map and tracing our route south to Kusadasi.

"We'll be there in no time," he said, devouring the melon. "And with no problem." He gulped down his coffee, finished dressing and packing, grabbed the suitcases, and headed for the door as I sat there finishing my last sip of Turkish tea, pulling on my clothes, and shoving my clothes in the suitcase. I complained,

"Hey wait, I'm not completely ready." Suddenly, there was a shuffling in the hall when Bill jerked the door open so hard that it slammed against the wall. I snatched the towel off my head, grabbed my purse and bag, followed like Bill's shadow out into the dark hallway, and saw the tall figure, clad in the same black jeans and T-shirt, running for the stairs. He caused my skin to crawl as I screamed, "That's him! Bill, that's the guy." Bill dropped the suitcases and took off. Right behind him, I somehow pulled them to the elevator and descended.

"Quickly," I said to the receptionist who already had the bill ready, the car keys on the counter, and a porter to load the bags into the waiting Honda.

"He's not Turkish," she informed me with conviction as her round eyes widened with concern. "I saw him run out. He's Greek. Do you need help?"

"Greek!" I exclaimed. "Uh, no," I thanked her, jumped in the car and turned the corner of the outdoor restaurant just as Bill chased the fleeing assailant past the early morning crowd of tourists eating their breakfast.

Bill had sprinted to the end of the block by the time I caught him. I spotted the black clad figure racing for his car parked alongside the wide sidewalk stretching around the gulf. Just as he lunged for the door, a nut vendor pushed his cart off the sidewalk into his path. Nuts flew everywhere, almonds, pumpkin seeds, pistachios, and peanuts, causing him to trip and fall. As I got closer, I could see the horrible scars on his arms, and I recalled them pinning me to the elevator. I cringed, but felt some satisfaction watching the rolling nuts bring him to his knees. He actually groveled on the ground. I hardly heard Bill yell,

"Pull over, Charla," and before I could bring the car to a stop, he'd jumped in, swearing, "Cards have changed hands. His ass is ours. He's <u>not</u> getting away this time." And we zoomed down the wide bay road, raced by a horse mounted

statue of Ataturk rising triumphantly as
though rooting us on, and veered to miss
the tourists sitting under the colored
umbrellas and soldiers walking five
abreast.

"Watch out, Bill," I screamed as he
barely missed a car, swerved around a
large Moorish clock tower, and followed
the black car through the bazaar with its
maze of narrow alleys not suitable for
cars, much less ones traveling at such
high speeds. "He's Greek," I told Bill,
turning my head when he almost hit a
pedestrian, dodged the hanging racks of
Turkish rugs, and somehow avoided the
fruit vendors, scooting their carts of
peaches out of the way.

"Greek!" He gasped, following the
reckless driver left; then we were out in
the open again, climbing up through the
old hills. Mosques' spirals appeared and
disappeared as we wound through the
winding streets where strange signs
displaying Arabic lettering confused me
as I tried to locate a familiar street on
the map. Finally, we were back on a main
road, coming up to a roundabout where we
saw the sign to Kusadasi which caused us
both to yell, "All right!"

"He's going just our way," Bill said,
almost colliding with cars zooming around
the confusing circle as I frantically
directed him to the main highway's turn
off. "What do you mean he's Greek? Idmon
would never hire a Greek! Would he?" He
asked, riding the bumper of a huge truck,
darting out into the left lane, and
almost ploughing into another giant
truck.

I covered my face. "Dr. Aliamo said he hated the Greeks, so it makes no sense to me," I said, trying to keep my eyes off the dangerous road and distracting myself by gazing out over the mountains' low lying fertile lands, rich with cotton and tobacco fields. We passed Colophon, Idmon's home in the myth. I pointed it out to Bill. But he was far too busy for sightseeing. I continued watching the undulating green hills sloping down to a plain surrounding the vast ruins of the ancient Ephesus where the black car veered off past the crumbling temples and down the sloping road to the coast. The closer we got to Kusadasi, the more crowded it became from tourists streaming out of the motels lining the road. Finally, from quite a distance, I could see Idmon's gigantic yacht docked alongside the long pier. I pointed at the sleek, white ship with its glistening chrome, its decadent luxuriousness with its swimming pool, helicopter, and white limo gracing the upper deck. "Wow!" I gasped, my mouth ajar.

"Looks like Idmon's home," Bill said. "I can't believe this stupid jerk led us right to him. Nope, this doesn't add up," he concluded when the traffic came to a complete stop. Up ahead we saw why - the driver of the black car had come to a screeching halt, jumped out, and bolted off, leaving his car to block traffic.

"Meet me at that funny looking hotel," Bill yelled, pointing to a strange old round building as he leaped out and sprinted off behind him.

Fearing being left alone again, I jumped in the driver's seat and headed for the unusual looking building - the Caravanserai, I discovered as I illegally parked in front of the old fortress, locked the car, and split for the entrance. Inside, the immaculately restored, impressively vaulted building opened up into the most beautiful courtyard imaginable. The rounding, rustic sides skirted an open-aired middle section, while colorful art decorated the walls; within the flowering, bright green area, small tables surrounded a magically spewing fountain.

Scared to death that someone had followed me, I checked out every nook and cranny, then I riveted my eyes to the corner, drawn by one the most astonishingly beautiful women I'd ever seen. Her waist long, silky, platinum hair draped down over her curvacious shoulders as though protecting her voluptuous chest, tiny waist, and long, lean figure. The delicate strands created a brilliant glow around her perfectly carved face and chiseled nose and chin while her intensely bright eyes, heightened by a glowing tan, reflected the sparkling colors of the Aegean.

I knew instantly it was Suhvanna. She was the woman I'd seen fleeing around the corner in Rome with my briefcase. But I put that aside, trying to prevent it from interfering with what I was going to say to her. I was struck by her beauty, and as I got closer, I could see that she was exactly like Dr. Aliamo had described, only even more exquisite than his words, favoring, not the darker Turkish women in Istanbul, but as he'd said, the true flowering of the old European royalty. By her poise and statuesqueness and by her dazzling beauty, she resembled a queen.

From across the green trellised fountain, we exchanged glances, making quick contact. Her bright sea blue eyes, dilating as they traced me from head to toe, confirmed to me that she liked what she saw. I detected a wry, yet pleased smile form like a secret on her full, coral colored lips, delicately sipping white wine.

I walked right up to her, extended my hand in a friendly gesture and said, "Suhvanna, I'm Charla Morrow, with the SILC Foundation in Florida, a friend of Dr. Aliamo's who...."

The mention of his name made her quickly rise, her napkin falling to the floor. I kept my hand extended, detaining her. "Suhvanna, listen. A grave, dangerous mistake has been made. Idmon has stolen the wrong tapestry. If it's not returned, it will renew the violence between the Greeks and Turks, and then...."

Though her eyes flared wide in shock, she didn't miss a beat. "He'll never give it back," she huskily declared. "No matter what."

She looked me up and down before continuing. "You ask the impossible, Charla," she lisped, her pouty lips firmly set like a rosebud. "Idmon hates the Greeks!" Her tone hardened, and a glint appeared in her Aegean eyes.

After several moments of arguing back and forth, she finally listened when I said, "What is it you want? Money? Fame? You name it. The SILC Foundation is willing to work with you...as long as you're reasonable," I quickly added when she crossed her long, tanned legs and adjusted her pink mini skirt. Then her face shut down as she looked away, oblivious to my pleas.

Precisely at that moment, Bill came running around the fountain with one stride of his powerful legs. Anger, mingled with anticipation, was written all over his tanned face. His shirt, wet with perspiration, clung to his large arms and heaving chest. He glanced at Suhvanna questioningly, then quickly looked back at me. "No luck. No damn luck. He got away." He said, breathing heavily and trying to ignore her obvious interest.

With her eyes glued on Bill, she extended her hand, wrapping her long coral fingernails warmly around his. And with an alluring slither of a movement, edged a few inches closer to him, saying unwaveringly, "I want him," causing her rosebud pout to spread into a seductive smile.

"Uh...Bill, this is...Suhvanna," I stuttered with jealousy spreading over my face like an unwelcomed veil and lighting up my green eyes with such shining intensity that she teasingly acquiesced in a husky whisper,

"I'm kidding, of course." But she never released her grasp.

Bill stepped back, pulled his hand from her tenacious grip and nervously coughed, "Uh...Nice to meet you, too, Suhvanna."

I stood looking on in shock, not having witnessed such aggressiveness in a female before, especially not with Bill, causing my blood to boil and me to wonder if she were kidding, and if her real interest was Bill, me or the tapestries - and in that order.

CHAPTER III: INTO THE INTERIOR

"Where's Athena's tapestry," Bill immediately wanted to know.

"Why with Idmon, of course. Where else? And he's at Pamukkale getting the cure. You know - ancient Hierapolis...Turkey's famed thermal springs? You just missed him," she matter of factly informed us in her genteel British accent as she climbed gracefully into the Honda's small back seat, slinging her suitcase in the front seat.

"And he has left me in charge - of everything. So...now...you must answer my questions - where's Arachne's tapestry?" She demanded, her steel intellect again shining through her blue-green eyes as she settled herself comfortably.

I walked around to the other door, saying with just as much insistence, "Safe, with Dr. Aliamo. I told you once already, Suhvanna. But you must tell us the truth if you're going to work with us. Did Idmon send that asinine rapist, and if he didn't, who did? Anyway, where's Norton?" I impatiently questioned, opening the passenger door with vigor as she observed me, a calculating gleam in her eyes.

She pushed down my seat with her long, slender foot, looking me in the eye as she leaned forward, and saying without a hint of emotion, "Is this an interrogation? I only agreed to help -

not solve all the problems. Come on, Charla." She provocatively softened her husky voice.

"Sit back here with me, so we can talk. Bill can be our handsome chauffeur," she fluttered her thick, feathery black lashes in the rear view mirror at Bill who quickly looked away.

My eyes again darkened a shade greener as I clenched my teeth, wondering just how I was going to handle her flirtatiousness with Bill. And I hadn't even considered how I'd confront her about my stolen research.

"Come on, get in." She insisted when I hesitated, questioning if I shouldn't be the one deciding whether or not I agree to work with her regardless of my love and commitment to the tapestries. "I'll be the back seat driver and show you the way to Pumukkale where Idmon will answer all your questions. Come on." She again persisted.

The group of Turkish men who had been watching every move Suhvanna and I made, now riveted their dark brown eyes on me, undressing me from head to toe; and then, with slow progress, roving over every inch of my figure, they moved their beady eyes back up my body again.

Feeling somewhat forced, I reluctantly climbed in the back seat beside her. I wondered if I weren't going to experience more than just her control, not as the back seat driver, but as a real controlling force; she gave me further reason to question when she stretched her long coral fingernails through mine, sliding them against my

fingers. She then pressed our palms
together and pulled me close beside her
in the small seat.

"I'm sorry, Charla," she tried
sympathizing as Bill slowly pulled off
from the Caravanserai. The dark, lusty
eyes of the men followed us past the
gaudy souvenir shops. "Your rapist would
never have been Turkish, as you already
know, and there is no way that Idmon
would ever hire a Greek. Period. Plus,
he'd never hire anyone to hurt someone as
beautiful as you."

I couldn't tell if her compliments
were condescending, competitive, or truly
sincere. I was just unable to decipher
her real interest in me.

"I imagine though that whoever sent
him meant to scare you as much as
possible, so that you would be too afraid
to come into deepest, darkest Turkey
after the tapestry. Or isn't that still
the image that American women have about
my country?...But I can see," she paused,
again scrutinizing me, "I can see that
the attempt failed, and that you are
either very dedicated and brave, or very
naive and misled...or that you believe
Bill will protect you no matter what?"
She again fluttered her lashes at him.
"He _is_ so big and strong."

My indignation at her impertinence
and my jealousy must have shown, for she
added, "And I can readily see that it is
the former...As for Norton," she changed
the subject as my face relaxed for a
second; I didn't know how to take her.
"Idmon asked him to leave yesterday. How
shall I say...Norton's persistent

interest in me increased as did his boldness, until Idmon put a stop to it. He left angry and disappointed about Idmon's insistence on keeping the tapestry. Uh...You see, neither Norton nor I told him it was the wrong one...I didn't have the heart."

"Suhvanna, Dr. Aliamo said you didn't know there were two tapestries. He said...." I interrupted her.

"And you chose to believe him, I presume? Well, if I were you, I wouldn't. I'm sure you figured out that he was madly in love with me, so as you can see - he had ulterior motives. You know how these men are, Charla! Of course I knew about the two tapestries. I'm sure he told you all the gory details. I was his research assistant." She protested a little too much.

Now she really had me baffled, for there was no way I'd ever have questioned Dr. Aliamo's truthfulness. Why he would have any reason to lie I couldn't comprehend. No, until shown further, I'd believe him.

"So Norton tried to sexually lure you to help him get the tapestry back from Idmon? Right?" Bill asked, passing a souvenir shop where the superstitious blue eyed pins, that supposedly protected the wearer from evil, lined the window as though warding off all outside danger.

"He did," she admitted frankly and a bit too abruptly, crossing her long tanned legs and causing the same blue eyed pins to dangle from her pink mini skirt which now reached high up on her lean, taut thighs.

"Damn, so Idmon still doesn't know he has Athena's tapestry? That's amazing - given the differences in their messages. By the way, Suhvanna, what's wrong with Idmon? What's the cure at Pamukkale for?" Bill, struck by an idea, suddenly wanted to know as we headed out on the bay road away from the wide, blue gulf.

"A very bad illness - how do you say - congenital? He inherited it from his father, another Idmon who was killed when his son was very young. It is too bad, huh, Bill?" she asked, leaning forward and causing her already deep cleavage to rise and pour out of her striped pink top.

"You don't know its name?" Bill asked, trying not to look back at Suhvanna as he avoided the tourists milling around the motels that lined the road.

"Oh, I don't remember," she responded after a few moments of thought, "but he has uncontrollable attacks. It's horrible. He goes into spasms and forgets everything. Someone must be with him the entire time, or he will hurt himself. He won't admit it, and now he's gone off alone to Pamukkale."

"Seizures?" Bill gasped, turning around and looking headlong into Suhvanna's cleavage. He almost ran off the bay road.

"Seizures?" I gasped, shocked as well; the blue pins eerily eyed me as I continued staring at her in disbelief. "Are you absolutely certain?" And then cringing as she shook her head yes.

"Uh, Suhvanna, you are aware of the symbolic message inherent in Athena's tapestry?" I asked, my thoughts racing back to Dr. Aliamo's study linking seizures to the Caesars and, of course, their connection to the incestuous Julian Line that traced the preservation of the pure, royal blood lines through the matriarchal Julias. Incredulously enough, a warning against incest was the very subject of the tapestry - and Idmon had ironically snatched it in error. Or had he? I questioned. What if there were some kind of connection? Besides, I reasoned, she would know about this theory, for it was among the papers she'd stolen from me in Rome. "Damn!" I muttered, not feeling at all comfortable about this news and slipping my hand carefully from Suhvanna's light hold on it.

"Don't be too upset," she consoled. "I told you - you've just spent too much time being wrapped up in Alexander's theories. He hates Idmon as well for obvious reasons - and he'd love for you to think the worst of him."

She leaned forward, pressing against Bill's shoulder as she preened herself in the rear view mirror. He tried squeezing himself against the door.

A deep seething stirred. I wondered how much more I could take of her advances to him, but I also thought she was trying to distract me. Again, she protested too much, and I questioned if she too believed Dr. Aliamo and was trying to hide some kind of a similar Arachnean Line in Idmon's lineage.

"Regardless, he's getting the cure. So don't worry. At Pamukkale miracles happen," she almost sighed, as though concealing some secret.

"Uh, Suhvanna, would you mind moving your head? I want to make sure that the asshole we chased all the way to Kusadasi isn't following us." Bill requested, attempting to move her off his shoulder and looking into the rear view mirror for the dark car. "How do we know for sure that Idmon has the tapestry in Pamukkale?" Bill asked again with persistence as we neared Ephesus. "And if he does, can we be assured that we won't lose our lives trying to get it?"

"Look!" She exclaimed, obviously distracting Bill's attention and avoiding his questions. "A protector of one of the most ancient, revered shrines of the Mother Goddess who communicated oracles from that very site." She pointed at a stork perched atop the remaining marble ruins of the temple; in a flash, her delicate chin stiffened and her rosebud lips curled with contempt. "Of course, the Greeks stole and destroyed it, as they did all our sacred sites, built a monstrous temple atop it, and had the nerve to dedicate it to their bloodthirsty goddess, Artemis," she stated with a tinge of indignation. Then, realizing her exposure, she changed the subject.

"Bill! You ask too many questions. With me...you are perhaps physically safe," she teased, looking sidelong at him in the mirror. Catching me eying her suspiciously, she directed her attention to me, peering into my eyes. "Ah, but upon meeting Idmon, one never knows for sure if she is safe or not. He absolutely loves beautiful women."

She challengingly darted her glance from me to Bill. "But if you're most convincing, Charla," she gazed deep into my eyes, "especially if you persuade him, with, oh, I don't know, uh - build up his ego by showing him how he can outshine the Greeks in some fashion...Then, depending on your persuasiveness, of course, he just might cooperate. One never knows about Idmon, though I must warn you - he is hard headed, a most stubborn man, and even more important, very very powerful."

Her words seemed to fall like rocks dropping into the dry creek beds as we turned east on E24 bound for Pamukkale, and like a tourist guide she gave us all the facts on this upcoming ancient site.

But I barely heard what she said about Pamukkale being a mythic site where for centuries countless numbers of royal families and religious nobility made the long trek and soaked in its healing aqua waters.

I was still thinking of what Suhvanna had said about Idmon and wondered if he would be as flirtatious with me as Suhvanna was with Bill. It concerned me because Bill and I had never been challenged in our relationship by this kind of outside influence. And, in my mind, I discounted my attraction to Paulo. "Outshine the Greeks in what way?" I finally responded, interrupting Suhvanna who had completely captured

Bill's attention as we drove up through the low lying mountains and entered the Mendares River Valley spreading out its green, ripe fertileness on either side of the ancient trade road.

She ignored me, and I couldn't help but notice in her descriptions that she had discovered Bill's weak spot, his scientific love for the environment.

"And...uh...Just how much does he hate the Greeks?" I again, with more insistence, tried to interrupt her as she named for him all the types of crops, orchards, yellowed fields of sowed barley and wheat, then pointed out the occasional rows of poplars silhouetting the distant dark mountains.

"Yeah, Suhvanna, why don't you tell us about this hatred?" Bill, waiting for Suhvanna to finish her long winded description, got a word in edgewise when he noticed that I was getting a little exasperated.

"<u>Everyone</u> in Turkey hates the Greeks, only Idmon's filled with even more bitterness; during the massacre at Izmir they killed his father, his brothers, all his family except his mother and, and as far as I understand, his only sister."

"Whose name wouldn't just happen to be Arachne, would it?" A light went on in my head, which was still churning with thoughts of the Julian Line and all the Julias who where forced to have sex with their fathers and grandfathers just to maintain the blood lines. I wasn't even sure I wanted to know the answer.

She reluctantly shook her head yes, saying, "Of course, his mother and his

sister were both named Arachne, as well
they should - it's a family name that's
been passed down. Why're you interested?"
She asked suspiciously. "Because it was
originally a Greek name?"

"Greek? Oh shit! That's right,
Arachne in Greek means spider -
arachnid." I muttered, almost incoherent
with sudden realization, for I saw in a
flash Dr. Aliamo's theory. The belief in
the pure blood lines had been inherited
by the Romans from the Etruscans, the
same people as the Lydians, who brought
the tapestries with them when they
settled Italy. My mouth dropped in shock.

So did Bill's. He shook his head in
utter amazement, saying, "I think we just
found the missing link between the Romans
and the Greeks - the Lydians. Unreal!"

"The Turks you mean," Suhvanna
huskily denounced our conclusions; "Who
were raped by the barbaric Greeks, don't
forget. The women would never have given
in willingly." Her voice rose with
harshness and cold authority;
aggressiveness shone in her Aegean eyes.

I stared at her in disbelief, trying
to figure her out.

Realizing that she had exposed
herself to us, she abruptly changed the
subject, returning to her detailed
description of the interior that rolled
out beside us like some ancient unfolding
dream.

"Hold on." Bill interrupted, after
milling the subject over in his mind for
a few minutes. "If he's half Greek, like
probably most of the Turks, how can he
hate them so? Sure this isn't more like a

civil war or a feud - with the families
having forgotten what started it? Just
think, if Idmon will give us the
tapestry, maybe Dr. Aliamo's right - it
just might clear up all this enmity." He
added, but she shrugged her shoulders and
rolled her eyes as though dismissing his
suggestion as thoroughly impossible.

Outside Denizli, trucks, tractors,
and trailers congested the road and, she
reminded us, announced the hot, dusty,
but very important agricultural center.
We quickly drove through it, turning
north off the old highway and heading
down into the green river valley before
we began climbing into the mountain
range.

"So why didn't they kill off Idmon's
entire family? Why spare the mother, the
brother or even the sister?" I finally
asked, when from afar we could see the
spectacular, three hundred foot high
cleft in the mountain that truly looked
like a "cotton castle."

She didn't respond, instead pointing
out the cascading sheets of water rushing
over the sides of the cliffs and forming
white stalactites that clustered and
created a vast array of aqua pools.

Nor did I ask another question,
trying to forget my nervousness about
meeting Idmon and my insecurity with
Suhvanna.

"Wow!!" Bill and I gasped not
believing our eyes as we viewed the
natural wonder. We had never seen such a
staggering spectacle.

Oddly enough, it was Suhvanna who
returned to the subject.

"Kill off the matriarch of a family line dating back to mythic time? Who'd dare? You don't know who you're dealing with. Idmon's family is the oldest in Turkey, and very very wealthy. Thousands and thousands of years ago, the original Idmon, Arachne's father, used this same water to bleach the wool for her tapestry and set its phocis purple dye. This has always been a place of miracles." She said, again with an almost grating authority in her voice. I stared at her a second too long, for she quickly changed her tone. "At least this is what Idmon is hoping for." She directed Bill up the steep road, leading to the pools.

"I'm sure Idmon's at the Koru where he always stays. Keep going up, Bill, past the museum and the ruins."

"If they just wanted to save the matriarch, then why was Idmon spared? I don't get it." I asked, then got distracted, when, off to the left, bubbling water spilled over the sides of the white cliffs and created a long line of waterfalls.

"There's the Koru," she pointed out to Bill, then continued. "It was a miracle the Greeks didn't butcher them like they did everybody else. They escaped and fled to Manisa, Arachne's home, where their people hid them," she added, pointing down the road where we could see the Necropolis with its tombs and crypts lying open like ghosts upon the land, a constant reminder, she told us in an angry voice, of their having been robbed by the Greeks of all their burial treasures.

Finally, we pulled into the parking lot on the left. Suhvanna created a great amount of tension in the car, and I was glad to be stopping and getting out.

With a deep sigh and a shrug, as though she were truly fed up with us for such serious questioning, Suhvanna shoved the passenger seat forward with her long foot, then, leaned far up to open the door, causing her short skirt to rise even higher up on her curvaceous, perfectly tanned derriere and exposing her hot pink G-string. I thought I'd die. Bill's eyes were plastered on her rear end. She grinned and told us in the most mischievous voice, "Don't go away. Wait right here while I check on Idmon."

"Are you sure his bull dogs aren't with him?" Bill asked nervously, trying not to stare as she stepped out and shimmied the skirt back down. She didn't answer him, just turned, flashed her perfectly straight white teeth in a seductive smile, and flutteringly waved her long fingers at him.

I'd had it. "I really don't like this situation." I blurted in anger and total impatience as soon as she was out of sight. "I don't know if I trust Suhvanna - with you."

"Oh! Now, Charla, I'm not so sure I trust her either - with you."

"Whaaat!" I opened my eyes wide in shock, realizing that Bill could be right; the way she was acting toward me, she might be bisexual. I saw his dilemma as well. We sat there staring at each other in silence; my insecurities strengthened.

But before either of us could speak, Suhvanna had returned, jangling a room key high in front of her impishly grinning face and saying, "Idmon is on a tour of the ruins and will be back shortly. In the meantime, I have secured a room for us so that we can relax in the hotel's pool and perhaps even cure what might be ailing us." Her tone was so facetious that I didn't trust her at all. "Oh, don't worry, Charla, I'll join Idmon when he returns; I won't stay and pester the two of you...unless I'm invited." She smiled luringly.

"Come on, now, I won't take no for an answer. I am hot from this long, dusty trip and want to get to know my new friends better. Come...Come." She encouraged, opening Bill's door, taking his arm at the elbow and guiding him out of the car as he looked helplessly back at me. Then she came around to the passenger door, took my hand and pulled me from the back seat.

She placed her hand securely around my waist, inching me close to her swaying hips as we walked through the small lobby and out onto the walkways which led to the long row of rooms skirting the cliffs; they juxtaposed the natural aqua pools and overlooked the motel's multileveled swimming pools. The lush river valley lay far below.

Suddenly, as though blown from out of nowhere, a cool, low mountain wind rushed along the walkway and through a corridor that led past an enclosed, indoor pool. Suhvanna, her arm still around me, pressed me protectively closer. Surprised and unsure of her motives, I pulled sharply away, attempting to unwedge myself from her swinging hips.

A little farther down, she gently released me, having found our room, which she opened; a secret smile still played on her full lips. "I'll give you two some privacy," she said, disappearing into the large bathroom with her luggage as Bill and I stood staring at one another with blank expressions on our faces.

"I don't know if I'm ready for this," I blurted as we walked across the wide room to the expansive picture window, looking out over the pools and the valley.

"I'm not ready to get my ribs punched in again, that's for sure. I just hope to hell those goddamn musclemen aren't with Idmon. I'll never forget that beating."

"Yeah, Bill, but I don't know if I like her velvet claws any better...."

"Oh," Bill interrupted, opening his suitcase and pulling out his animal print bikini. "I don't know. She seems innocuous enough, don't you think?" He whispered, wiggling his body and adjusting his parts in the form fitting suit.

Trying not to take my eyes off Bill who I felt seemed a bit insensitive to my feelings, I traced my eyes up and down his gorgeous body; I wondered how Suhvanna would react to his perfect physique and experienced a little suspiciousness and uncertainty about his true feelings toward her. Furtively shifting my gaze from him to the suitcase, I searched for my red bikini,

Bill's favorite. However, he seemed not
to notice. Before I could even get the
suit pulled high up on my hips,
Suhvanna burst out of the bathroom,
wearing an iridescent, chartreuse thong
complimented by one of the smallest
bikini tops I'd ever seen. On anyone else
it would have been obscene, but on her,
the yellowish-green seemed to dance and
cause her lean, tanned figure to come
alive.

Bill couldn't stop his eyes from
looking her up and down. I could've
killed him, and she knew it.

She let out a long, low wolf whistle,
looking first me and then Bill from head
to toe as she luringly leaned against the
door frame.

"Ready, set, go," Bill nervously
responded, his eyes glued on me as though
making some attempt not to notice her
almost nude body.

In a flash we were all scampering out
the door when an even cooler mountain
wind brushed my face and instantly
lowered my body temperature. I felt a
chill.

We descended the stairs to the deep
aqua pool, shining in the afternoon sun.

Suhvanna broke into a run in front of
us, scrambling down the long flight of
stairs, and with a giggle, diving with
perfect form into the sparkling mineral
waters.

Bill, apparently promulgated by her
energy, grabbed my hand and almost
dragged me down the steps and into the
water.

As soon as we surfaced, Suhvanna was yelling, "Race you over there," pointing to a stone island rising out of the pool where the warm spring funneled up and bubbled over.

In a flash, Bill's hands reached high over his head as he raced her in a swift crawl to the island.

Feeling more threatened by the minute and trying to ignore them, I dove underwater, attempting to get out of the light wind.

Emerging, I kicked my legs and floated along very slowly, finally reaching where Bill and Suhvanna lay stretched out on the round slab, the sun beaming down on their darkly tanned bodies.

They were talking with Suhvanna's face up next to his, but because of the noisy pipes gushing forth the warm springs, I didn't hear what they said, something about Norton. I couldn't stand seeing her press closer and closer to him.

Wanting to join them and lie right between them, I hesitated. I was getting so jealous and threatened that my hands started shaking. Plus, the wind was picking up and making me even colder. Trying to ignore them, I watched the billowing black clouds that very slowly began to crawl into view over the distant eastern ridge, high up behind the theatre. For what seemed like an interminable time, I hovered, observing them and getting angrier and angrier as I hung onto the island and dangled in the warm, spewing water. As though in a mad daze, I continued shifting my gaze from the giant thunderstorm as it crept over the mountains to Bill and Suhvanna who had moved even closer together.

My eyes hazed with such intense emotions that I almost couldn't see the bright pink oleander on the cliffs that lined the white cascading pools and shook as the wind picked up.

"Hey, you guys," I finally yelled, unable to stand it any more. My voice harshly broke the silence and interrupted their intense concentration. "There's a pretty big thunderstorm on the way."

"Impossible," Suhvanna retorted. "In Turkey, it never rains in the summer. Never."

"Never say never," I corrected her, my voice edged with sarcasm and anger which caused her to lean her long neck over her slender shoulder and glance at the dark clouds. She lifted her chiseled chin, smiled sardonically, and said,

"It doesn't matter, I love storms!"

"That figures. I hope you mean it." I quickly added, trying to keep my shoulders under the warm spout. I also tried to keep my temper cool as jealous streaks shot up my back; "Because there's a monstrous storm approaching. Just look at that!" I said, as a lightening bolt struck through the dark clouds and caused the distant mountains to rumble with thunder. But they continued to ignore me. Finally, my patience ran out completely and I churned with anxiety. I had to do something. I interrupted them again. "Uh...Bill...I'm really uncomfortable being in the water when it's lightening."

"How absurd, Charla," Suhvanna cut in. "There's no danger whatsoever."

"I don't care. Bill, would you at least go with me to the indoor pool?" I asked him in a voice that he dared not refuse. The storm moved closer. A chill racked my body as he turned his head toward me and stared into my eyes which were probably dark green with jealousy.

"Well, I'd like to catch what few rays are left, Charla. Mind if I join you shortly?" He responded, innocently peering up at the sun to check the encroachment of the clouds.

I couldn't believe it. Now I was furious - and at Bill.

Wanting to strike out, I cupped my hands and in a violent splash, sprayed them with water.

Suhvanna squealed while Bill sat up on his elbows and looked me directly in the eyes. I couldn't decipher the communication in his glance, but I detected indignance and almost a reprimand for me to control myself. It was as if he were being authoritative with me. I was so mad my vision distorted. He cooly stared at me for another brief second; then, ignoring me, laid his head back down and continued a bit too calmly talking with Suhvanna.

My lower lip pouted farther and farther as my chin grew more defiant by the moment. I wanted to run away and make him feel guilty if anything happened to me.

Fuming and creating a loud splash, I pushed away from the gushing spouts, slid down the island's slimy step, then swam

as fast as I could to the side. The
entire time, I thought I'd show him.
Something awful would happen to me and
then he'd really be sorry. As I crawled
up on the underwater step, a bolt of
lightening struck just over the cliff,
which I felt like I was clinging to by
slippery fingers. For an instant, I
realized something terrible just might
happen to me, and I fearfully imagined
myself falling down into the valley far
below.

I decided I'd better get to safety
and ran up to the room where I
immediately turned on the water in the
shower as hot as I could stand it and
stood under it, trying to calm down. It
didn't work. I was so filled with
negative energy that I couldn't control
myself. My stomach gnawed, my body shook,
and my vision blurred. Climbing out, I
bundled up in a huge Turkish towel and
crossed the room to the window in a
stride.

With lightening flashing all around,
I looked down on the pool's stone island
and saw Bill bent over Suhvanna, the two
of them so close that a match could have
been lit between them. And his hand was
brushing her thigh!

He glanced up at the window and saw
me watching, obviously caught in the act.

I felt faint, the blood draining from
my face. Freezing cold and shaking
uncontrollably, I decided I'd better lay
down before I fell down. I jumped into
bed. Eerily dancing flashes of yellow
streaked the room. I covered my head with

the pillow and somehow forced myself to fall asleep. I dreamed I was on a plane.

Flight attendants served dinner, and I was one of them; however, I was distracted by all the activity, especially a woman passenger and her baby. Finally, I attired myself in the service uniform and was ready for work; but by the time I approached the in-flight attendants, they had finished working and were sitting down. Standing in front of them, I tried making excuses, but they wanted to hear nothing of it. Instead, they quickly told me off, sparing me none of their chiding words, reprimanding me for having gotten distracted. Unable to defend myself, I stood trying to ward off their sharp remarks.

Loud thunder followed a clap of lightening just outside the window, causing me to sit straight up in bed. Someone was in the bathroom, rummaging through Suhvanna's suitcase. The door creaked, and in the lurid light, I recognized the tall, dark stranger who had attacked me in Istanbul. He bolted out of the room.

A scream welled from within and caught in my throat just as Bill came speeding through the door, and yelling, "Charla? Charla?" In a stride, he reached the bed, gathered me in his arms, and told me he hoped I'd forgiven him for staying with Suhvanna but that he'd done so because he wanted to make sure we didn't miss Idmon.

"Bill!" I tried getting his attention. "Bill, listen! The rapist in

Istanbul was just here, searching for something among Suhvanna's things."

I didn't get to finish before he had bolted for the door and sped down the walkway. I jumped up and ran to the door, watching as he sprinted down past the indoor pool and through the small lobby.

Closing the door, I bolted it shut with the chain.

In a few minutes, he returned, his dark eyebrows set in a disappointed frown. Lightening struck all around as he sat down on the bed, breathing heavily and saying, "He's after the tapestry, Charla. Come on, Honey, don't get distracted. Maybe you're right. We may not be able to trust Suhvanna any farther than we can throw her, but then again what choice do we have but to go along with her. I can't believe you didn't know what I was up to. She gave me some valuable information. Didn't you realize that? It's too dangerous right now for you and me not to work as a team. Suhvanna shouldn't be left alone. Besides, what if Idmon had shown up?"

I ignored the flashes of the dream I'd just had which popped like a bolt into my consciousness. "Sure it's Idmon you're thinking of? And what about _me_ being left alone? You told me in Istanbul that you'd never do that again." I informed him, then curtly added, "Besides, I saw you."

"It wasn't what you thought. She dropped her key, and I picked it up for her. Then a bee landed on her, and I brushed it off. Maybe from a distance, it appeared different. But, Charla, come on, now, I could accuse you of the same thing. I saw you holding hands and walking very closely arm and arm. Look, Honey, don't forget, we're on a mission, and I found out something very important from Suhvanna. She told me who hired..."

"Norton? That asshole was hired by Norton to rape me? Is that what she confided in you?" I quipped. But a recognition flashed in my mind, telling me that the tactics were too similar; in fact, it was the same maneuver Norton had pulled on me in Rome. But I ignored it, still angry and wanting to strike out. "Probably Norton's way of getting even with me for my not having fallen head over heels for him like he believes every woman should. But as for Suhvanna - sounds to me like she met her match. Norton's just as self-serving as...."

"Yes, that's right, it was Norton, and I don't know whether to believe her or not. Regardless of Suhvanna's involvements, we must watch her like hawks. Let me repeat, this is no time to get distracted. You're right, she's very manipulative and seductive, let's not forget," he pleaded with me, adding whispers of apology and gently hugging me.

I gave in, realizing the danger we were in and knowing how much I needed him to protect me. Plus, I couldn't resist him. His large hands scooped under my buttocks as he lifted me onto his lap, tucked me tightly against his chest and lovingly kissed me. I melted, images of my dream slipping through my mind we fell backwards onto the bed.

Like typical lovers making up, we
were soon passionately entwined when we
heard a tapping. We rolled apart,
listening, again hearing a soft knocking
on the door. Suhvanna peered in, her face
brightened with a huge smile upon
thinking she had caught us in bed.

She darted across the room, leaving
puddles behind her, leaping headfirst
into the bed, and purposefully landing
right in between us.

I was aghast at the thought of what
she had in mind when she draped her long
lean leg over my hip and the other over
Bill's thigh. In shock, I watched as she,
dripping wet, quickly reached down,
pulled the cover high overhead and
snuggled closer to both of us. She rubbed
her smooth legs higher up around my
waist; then teasingly running her toes
back down my leg, she said, "It's so
intense to make love at the height of a
storm!"

"Now hold on there, Suhvanna," Bill
cautioned as I stiffly lay there, still
in shock. I was so happy he took control
and used such strong words.

"There's something more pressing that
you should know. Idmon's life may be
threatened right now," and he proceeded
to tell her the entire story of Norton's
hired hand going through her suitcase.

The sheets of rain that streaked our
large windows and the lightening that
flashed yellow white in the black sky
couldn't have been more dramatic than
Suhvanna's drastic change in expression.

Suddenly, she was all business.

"We must tell Idmon!" She exclaimed, rising and heading for the door with Bill and I close behind her; she bolted down the walkway and headed by the indoor pool. Then she stopped so short that Bill and I ploughed in behind her, with me caught in between.

"IDMON!" She screamed, causing us to twist our heads to the left and look through the glass into the depths of the deep green, indoor water.

Flashes of incandescent yellow light flooded the outer windows and funneled a stream of light on two people bathing in the dark pool.

I grasped the oversized Turkish towel that I had grabbed closer to me as we scampered behind Suhvanna down the slippery walkway; we entered the strange room with its pastel colored marine mural, looked more closely down into the deep green water, and saw the man and woman close together, her large breasts bobbing atop the wavy surface.

"IDMON!" Suhvanna screamed again at the top of her lungs, her voice echoing off the walls and water as lightening flashed and thunder crashed outside the window. She had come to a dead stop in her tracks, her body stiffening, her face flushing pinkish red, and her eyes bulging.

To which he responded with equal surprise, "SUHVANNA!?" Faster than the lightening, he got control and sternly demanded what she was doing there and not in Kusadasi where he'd left her in charge. "I thought I told you to wait for me." He said with firm reprimand. "And

what the hell is this all about?" His sky
blue eyes flared, first at Suhvanna; then
he turned his stark gaze on me. He looked
me up and down in a flash before
switching his quick estimating gaze on
Bill.

His silver hair lit up his tanned
face as he arched his pointed, dignified
eyebrows; I could see why Suhvanna was so
attracted to him - his very presence
commanded respect and his bold stance
bore a stamp of power in his undaunted
self assurance. His rugged masculine
appeal and his imperial handsomeness held
me spellbound. With a blink of his long,
dark lashes, he knew exactly who we were,
demanding of Suhvanna, "Why have you
brought them here?"

But for some strange reason, he
couldn't continue. His intense eyes
dimmed and clouded over as though
disturbed by some incredible energy while
a slight seizure travelled his body and
sent a shock up his spine. The illness
that Suhvanna told us about reared its
ugly head.

With her wet auburn hair floating in
the flashing lights and her large
breasts bobbing, the woman in the pool
turned all her attention on Idmon,
stroking, caressing, and almost nurturing
him to calmness.

Passing through him with the
intensity of the lightening flashing
through the wide windows, the driving
tremor left a stilled and detached
resoluteness in his cool, controlled
gaze.

"Suhvanna, this is my nurse, Delgan...Delgan...Suhvanna."

Suhvanna didn't acquiesce, angrily resisting Idmon's forced formality. She hadn't said a word, but her flushing, reddening face caused her tanned skin to darken to a deep rose and her blond hair to brighten whiter, creating an intense, electric glow around her face.

Clenching her fists so tightly that she drained the blood out of them, she fought back the tears and tried to hide the rush of jealousy and acute indignation that stormed out. "Your nurse!" She angrily shouted, unable to control herself. She swayed, almost falling into the water when Bill stepped up behind her and caught her.

He nervously whispered to me, "Here, help her, and I'll see what I can do. I just hope this isn't an old case of shoot the messenger, but here goes."

He turned to face Idmon in the pool and extended his hand to shake, "Idmon, I'm Bill Balfour and this is Charla Morrow. This may not be the most convenient time, but please speak with us. It's about the tapestry," Bill said as calmly as possible, continuing to extend his hand even when Idmon ignored his obvious gesture.

Instead, Idmon calmly and cooly stepped out of the water with each step measured with perfect exaction and masterful control over his every movement. Even though scantily clad, he was undaunted by our presence. He apparently told his nurse to meet him back in the room, for she swam over to the other side of the pool, stepped out, and left.

His tanned, muscular and fit body belied his years, and, except for his silver hair and his natural command as an established authority figure, usually hard earned from experience, nothing distracted from his youthful, yet distinguished good looks.

He emanated aristocratic charm and reeked of wealth; he wrapped himself in a red velour robe which brightened the silvery color of his hair and lit up his face.

Surefootedly, he walked over to Suhvanna and extended his bent arm as though he fully expected her to wrap her hand through it, which she did mechanically. He led her down the walkway, whispering commandingly in her ear the entire time and patting her hand paternally; he completely calmed her down by the time we reached the room, and, at the same time, he had successfully ignored us.

As soon as the door securely shut, Bill nor I wasted any time.

"Idmon, the tapestry is in danger, and perhaps even your life...."

"I don't know who you are, Bill Balfour, but let's get this straight - if anyone's life is endangered, it is yours, not mine...."

"Idmon, please listen!" I interrupted him this time as he completely dismissed Bill, causing him to again analyze me from head to toe. I sat down on the bed and pulled the bulky towel tighter.

"You have the wrong tapestry, and you must...."

"No! It is you who must." He put me down in a flash, with a sweep of his long, dark lashes, then turned to Suhvanna, saying, "I thought we got rid of these Americans. Now you have led them to me. I will quickly return to pick you up - without your..." he hesitated, "...acquaintances." He spoke with such cool, deliberate authority in every carefully chosen, chiding word that any thought of our detaining him was clearly overruled. Then he rose and walked to the door, with absolute assurance and power in every step.

"Idmon??? Wait, where's the tapestry??" I pleaded. "Suhvanna is in danger. Norton has hired a Greek mercenery who will...."

He walked out the door.

"Idmon?? Please listen. He was just here rummaging through Suhvanna's things, and...." Bill bolted for the door to stop him, but the door slammed in his face. Our pleas and arguments had fallen on deaf ears.

"I warned you about him," Suhvanna retorted in an emotion filled, shaky voice. Her deep eyes dimmed, their sparkle lost. Slowly and heavily, she walked into the bathroom.

However, within minutes, she had dressed and was amazingly re-energized, her old aggressiveness returned. She yelled back at us as she hurriedly walked to the door, "Stick to me like glue. Thanks to Idmon's keeping his cute nurse a secret, he has no bodyguards nor

chauffeur with him. He's driving a black
Rolls Royce. Whatever you do, don't let
me or him out of your sight."

"Suhvanna, don't leave. Dammit, Wait!
You may be in danger. Wait!" I yelled
after her, scrambling to dress and repack
and realizing that she was not aware of
just how much a terrorist Norton's hired
hand could be; afterall, he was looking
for something in _her_ luggage. I suddenly
felt sorry for her, laying aside my
former anger and jealousy.

"Hurry, Charla, let's get the hell
out of here," Bill excitedly ordered, as
he tore off his suit and jammed his legs
into his shorts.

"Just a minute, Bill!!" I screamed,
grabbing for his hand as he took off
running, dragging me and our suitcases
behind him down the slippery walkway.

He sped up as we passed the covered
walkway to the indoor pool. No one was
there. Not even slowing as we ran through
the small lobby, we got to the parking
lot just in time to see Suhvanna, a panic
stricken look in her widely opened eyes
as she glanced longingly back at us.

She sped away in a car with a tall,
blond driver.

"Goddamnit! It's Norton." I
disgustedly exclaimed. "And he's
abducting Suhvanna. I don't believe it."
Norton leered back at me as he slammed
Suhvanna up against the door. "Oh, he's
despicable!" I condemned him, remembering
the time he'd treated me like that. I
jumped in the car as Bill screeched out
of the parking lot with Suhvanna
helplessly gazing back at us. "And just

where the hell is Idmon when she needs him?" I asked, scanning the parking lot for his car. It wasn't there. We zoomed past the motels and came to a halting stop at the pools where busses loaded with hundreds of tourists blocked our way.

"That's what I want to know - where the hell is he?" Bill emphasized, zipping around the people who covered the area and jaywalked from behind the tour busses. Then we saw Norton's car with Suhvanna, still pitifully looking back at us. "And should we be chasing Idmon right now or her?" He asked as Norton's car passed the waterfalls.

Norton roughly grabbed her hand and shoved her up against the door when she tried signalling for us to turn around and look behind us. "Oh, shit!" Bill yelled as he glanced into the rear view mirror and saw the black car. Norton's hired hand was in close pursuit behind us, with a long barrelled gun concealed from the tourists but pointed directly at us. I could easily see him now - his beady eyes, bushy mustache, and scarred arms made me nauseous. Then, relieved, I saw Idmon's Rolls behind him and nudged Bill to look.

The nurse crouched down in the front seat as Idmon furiously dodged pedestrians, dotting the cliffs like flies and climbing in and out of the aqua pools. A gun rose and fell as he attempted to keep it down low in between him and his nurse. Passing like blurs in a dream, they followed us by the theatre and headed down behind us into the green valley; they continued alongside the white stalactic pools which spilled over and raced downhill into the peaceful river.

"Damn, shit, hell!" I cursed. "What is happening?   Everything is going wrong." I cried as we descended into the valley and rose on the other side with Idmon staying in close pursuit behind the black car and taking a shot at the driver who was firing at us. The bullets ominously ricochetted off the thin metal as we slowed to turn east on E24 at Denizli.

"I'm scared! What if we get killed? What if a bullet strikes the gas tank? What if..." Horror struck as I imagined the worst.

"Don't think it, Charla! We have enough of an explosive situation on our hands." He affirmed. "Now's the time to keep the faith and duck."

Suhvanna's long, glissening strands of blond hair trailed wildly out the window as she thrashed back and forth.

Driving at an incredible speed for an overcrowded agricultural center, Norton ran every red light, never slowing for the heavy farming equipment which pulled out in front of him, and barely dodging a large Mercedes farm truck whose bearded driver started to open the door just as we passed.

Ripping and snarling, the door tore free with an unbearably loud, grinding crunch just as the farmer stepped out, and in a panic stricken moment, was flattened against his truck by the pursuing black car.

I screamed as he slumped to the dusty road.

"Killers, Bill. We're dealing with killers. Hit and run. And I'm sure they'd love to kill us. I'm really scared," I started crying, unable to control the chills that racked my body with deathlike fears. At that moment, only my life mattered. Not even something as precious to me as the tapestry counted. Nor was my opportunity for success worth it. I fought the panic that swelled within like a cresting river ready to break its boundaries.

"You think you've got it bad, there's a gun wrestling match going on up ahead, and there's no doubt as to who will win. As big as Norton is, he's got her beat hands down," Bill commented with a cool calmness in his voice.

I peered up over the dashboard to see Norton twist the gun from Suhvanna's hand and brutally smash its black steel up against her fragile cheek. She slumped down as he aimed the long barrel back at Bill and fired.

I let out a blood curdling scream, suddenly realizing how much I loved Bill and how I could never live without him.

"Duck!" He yelled as the bullet zinged by the window. "What a bad shot that asshole woman beater is!" Bill sneered when Suhvanna raised up and Norton again struck her with the gun; then he shoved her up against the seat and nearly ran off the road into the yellowed fields of sowed barley. He barely missed a resting camel, kneeling under the poplars.

It agitatedly rose upon its tall back legs, and in a lunging motion forward, reared its front legs, opened its huge, mean mouth wide in warning, then snapped it shut just as we veered left, missing it in a hairsplitting swipe.

Out of control, Norton swerved, almost striking an old woman with a fig cart who stood suddenly. She jumped back out of the way of the maniacally driven car and knocked over the cart, heavily laden with her purplish yellow figs that rolled under our wheels, smashing their seedy, pink flesh. Hanging her scarved head, she watched the destruction of her day's harvest.

Without slowing and caring less about his slashing path, Norton ran right through the junction of Highway 585 to Salihli and continued heading west on E24.

"Holy shit!" Bill yelled, dodging a bullet from behind which zinged by the side mirror. "Idmon just took a right at the intersection."

"He's going off and leaving Suhvanna? Norton will kill her." I cried, watching in disbelief as the wild driver in the black car behind us stepped on his brakes with such force that his tires blackened the asphalt; he spun his steering wheel and whipped out of the whirl, stomping on the accelerator so hard that the car almost leaped forward and taking off behind Idmon.

Then I realized that we too were spinning and heading into the blue misted mountains. I jerked my head around. Norton dumbfoundedly turned, screeched on his brakes, and sat there for some time before he headed right behind us. Suhvanna, her face fallen with sadness and beginning to swell from Norton's brutal slappings, watched Idmon in shock as he disappeared down the road leading into the vast mountain range.

"I don't get it. Where're Idmon's priorities? How could he just go off and leave Suhvanna with someone like Norton?" Bill asked in amazement. "Could he really care more for the tapestry than her?"

"Poor Suhvanna?" I quipped, suddenly feeling very sorry for myself. "How can you think of Suhvanna right now. What about me? I want to turn around. This tapestry's not worth <u>that</u> much to me. Without you, my life would be miserable...and...and I'm <u>not</u> ready to die yet. I haven't thought through it all thoroughly enough," I blurted as the road worsened with the steepening terrain, and Bill fought to maintain control of the car.

"Let's turn back!" I cried out, with more forcefulness, but we had already entered the rugged mountains, and the road was too narrow to turn around. With my heart in my throat, I shook, attempting to breathe the thinning mountain air.

"Hang in there, Honey. It's not our time to die," he stoked my head. "Don't you believe that it's our destiny to save this tapestry? Don't say you don't care. I know you do, and we have a protecting hand watching over us just to make sure that our job is carried out - and that the tapestry is preserved. You've got to

believe that," he pleaded with me to let
go of my terror stricken fear. "Besides,
check out this drop off. I'm not so sure
if we tempt fate that we just might not
end up somewhere over the side of this
cliff."

"I don't see that it's much worse
than what we're facing." I resisted,
slowly rearing my tear stained face and
peering over the edge. Gasping and
swirling, I fought vertigo and realized
that Bill was right - death on the rocks
looked worse. There was no turning back.
For as far as I could see, the mountains'
pale blue mist mingled with the green
valley. No reasoning helped. Nausea
struck the pit of my stomach at the
thought of dying in such a desolate,
foreign place, or of Bill dying and me
being left to murderers and rapists like
Norton and his hired maniac. I became
filled with eerie forebodingness and sobs
racked through me.

"Charla, get control of yourself.
Just think of it as an opportunity to
confront these fears that have plagued
you all your life and left you paralyzed.
You can do it, Darling. Come on. We're on
a mission. We can't give up now."

"Yeah, as though we have a choice,"
I caught my breath, the irony coursing
through my veins. I knew Bill was right.
I knew I had to seize the opportunity as
best I could. Shaking, I pulled out the
map. Unable to see it through my tears, I
fought to recover the energy that drained
out of me like a swollen river at flood
stage. The map finally steadied in my
feeble hands as my eyes focused. I traced

the road over the high mountain range that led down to Salihli and the Gediz River Valley trough on the other side.

Desperately trying to calm down, I traced Highway E23 west out of Salihli, looking for a clue. Then I saw it. "Manisa! Shit, Bill, Idmon's heading for his old home town."

"Should've known. It saved his ass before. But it's not so good for us. He'll be on his turf then, so we must make double sure he never gets out of our sight. Where do you want to bet he's going - his old hiding spot, dating all the way back to his escape from Izmir. Only this time little does he know just how much more his life is on the line. By now, Norton's damn well realized that he's going to have to kill him to get that tapestry."

"Really, Bill," I recovered my voice, broken with an occasional sniffle.
"It's obvious that not even Suhvanna's worth that much to Idmon," I sadly replied, releasing some of the concern for myself and raising my head to look back at Suhvanna when another bullet struck the back window. "Shit!" I moaned, not truly believing that I could handle this. Deciding to not look and trying to get comfortable on the tiny floorboard, I scanned the map. I knew that our moments were counted. If any opportunity presented itself we'd have to act quickly, grab the tapestry and run like hell.

"We've got to figure out exactly where Idmon is going to hide, because that's where the tapestry is. I'm convinced of it, Bill. I just don't think he has it with him." My voice strengthened as I fought to gain control.

"I think we can take no chances right now." Bill declared, ducking a zinging bullet. "Nor can he. If he gets out of our sight, how'll we ever find him in this foreign terrain? I bet you nobody but nobody speaks English. And I wouldn't count on our getting Suhvanna out of that s.o.b.'s grips. He's brutalizing her to the max. You can bet on it. Just check it out. He's screaming right in her face."

"I can't bear to look," I mumbled, crouching back down, trying not to watch and continuing to scan the map.

"Come on, Charla. You can find it. Did you try going back to the myth?" He asked, veering the car to the left out of firing range.

"Great idea. Right, Bill, look at this," I excitedly pointed to the mountain peak just south of Manisa. "Mount Sipylos - Mount Spildagi. The map has the old name and the new one. Arachne was born under that peak."

"My brilliant babe!" Bill grinned, causing me to release even more of the terror that gnawed like a dull ache in the pit of my stomach.

"And just maybe there's some little place here with a name that's close to Hypaepa, the village where Ovid said Arachne lived. Look at this. It's a wild guess, Bill, but there is one - Halitpasa, in the same location too, right in the heart of the Gediz River Valley." The loud zinging of bullets drowned my voice.

"Mythic mountain here we come...Don't you worry, there must be a guiding hand to get us out of this one," Bill tried not to complain.

"With a long, pointed finger," I reaffirmed, "a long, wicked one that will take care of Norton." Another bullet struck through the back window and left a huge open gap that I could easily see through. The terror and shaking returned.

It was more and more difficult to remain calm as I looked up at the sharp, rugged cliffs of the pastel chiselled mountains that rose higher and higher. Like an aimed missile, we climbed the winding, rough road between the towns of Buldan and Sarigol, past potato farmers standing dangerously close to the side of the road with their tall, brown sacks spilling over with newly unearthed potatos.

However, as the swerving, high speed string of cars passed, the scarved women's faces flared in fear as they dropped the bags, lifted their long skirts, and ran back terrified into the safety of the high, mountain fields. The tanned, wrinkled farmer shook his fist while his potatoes smashed under the wheels.

For some reason, the terrorizing fear of the grasping hand of death reaching down to grab me struck again, but with even greater force. "Oh, God, what're we going to do, Bill? I'm not ready to die," I moaned as the primeval mountain range with its alien ruggedness challenged us to survive. Overhead, gigantic black walnut trees shook their leaves violently as we flew under their centuries old branches, their trunks some 25 feet in circumference. I raised my head to first see Norton aim once and blast out the rest of back window, then aim again right at me. To my amazement, at that instant a giant sycamore appeared alongside the road. Bill cut behind it, and the bullet buried in its thick trunk.

"You got your prayers answered. Looks like we've been given these huge trees, so we can play hide and seek from these murdering idiots." Bill said, maneuvering into a turn in the road out of firing range and passing in the shelter of the prehistoric sycamores lining the road. They were as big as large houses.

"I can't believe it." I wiped my tears, gasping in awe as we drove under the large branches of the chestnuts with their great prickly nuts shaking overhead.

Safe and hidden behind the great trees, I lifted my head to check out Suhvanna and turned to see a reversal in the interchange of energy between her and Norton. Her big breasts pressed hard against him; her long left arm stretched seductively around his neck; her coral fingernails on her right hand rose and fell out of sight, and from her luscious lips her tongue darted in and out of his ear.

With no rear window, I could see clearly. So could Norton, when we left the shelter of the trees. He again raised his gun and aimed it at me as another giant tree appeared. I ducked, saying in disbelief, "Can you believe it?

The cards are turned, now Suhvanna is seducing Norton."

"Just what he's wanted all along," Bill sneered.

But it didn't seem to matter. Although Norton continued to repeatedly fire, he began missing us by a wide range. "I think she's making a terrible mistake." I cringed, declaring, "God! I'd hate to be in her shoes." I peered out when one last line of sycamores appeared with their massive trunks meeting overhead and forming a tunnel. I saw Suhvanna's head disappear. With his gun clenched in his hand, he pressed the black barrel down on her blond head - and held it there as he nearly lost control of his car, almost running headlong into the great walnut tree.

"But then maybe she doesn't have any choice," I concluded trying not to look at his weaving car as we passed the damaged walls of Philadelphia, out of the protection of the primeval range. And when I looked back at the pastel mountains fading behind us, I saw her blond head still bobbing under his gun.

He never released his hand on the back of her head except to fire at us, which caused me to gasp, "Bill, I think I'm going to be sick."

"Just think of it as saving our lives, Charla. His bullets are not even coming close now. Plus, he might even wreck, the way he's weaving. I don't want to sound too macho, but what a way to go." Bill lamented, dodging the bullets from the maniac rapist in front. "But don't you worry, Honey. One way or another, we're going to escape this yet. And with the tapestry as our booty."

"Yeah, at Suhvanna's expense we will," I affirmed somewhat sadly, trying to put it out of my mind and continuing to scan the map to try and figure out what route Idmon would take when he reached the flanks of Mt. Spildagi. I thought for a moment about her awful predicament. "Regardless, I can't live with my conscience unless we somehow get Suhvanna away from Norton. I don't know if she can survive this." I tried not to look back as we raced from the primeval range.

"She's tough." Bill judged in an amazed tone as he watched in his rear view mirror, with Suhvanna's head still pressed down under the gun.

"Look, Bill," I gasped as Idmon took a left turn and headed west on E23 toward Salihli. "We figured right!" We trailed right behind him, making our way past the busy activity of Salihli. The highway stretched out again when Idmon swerved and barely missed hitting a carload of dusty looking scholars. I knew they were Americans just by looking at them. Their archaelogical tools rolled against the back window as they pulled out from the road marked, "Sardes" without even looking to see if there were traffic.

Making a sharp swipe, the closely trailing black car, driven by the hired Greek assailant just behind Idmon, turned at an incredible angle to avoid missing the Americans. The beady eyed driver was travelling at such a high speed that he lost control, and in slow motion zigzagged to the other side of the highway before he rolled like a deathtrap into the path of the on-coming car. With their eyes flared wide with ghostly panic, the scholars slammed head-on into the small car, ripping and tearing the metal into grotesque distortions.

"WATCH OUT!" A scream tore from my throat as Bill veered around the mangled metal of the black car caught under the wheels of the larger American made automobile. The trapped driver's blood spewed forth like a fountain on the pavement as his mangled and severed body dragged and tore on the pavement.

Even though I had wished the worst consequence on a man who had brutally attacked me, this went beyond my most contemptuous thoughts; I couldn't watch, shielding my eyes from the horror.

Norton screeched on his brakes, crossed into the dusty roadside to avoid the pile-up, and without a hesitation or a look at the mutilated body of a man that he had known, a man that had worked for him, he continued his chase.

"What a mercenery," I cursed, watching as the dust slowly settled over the body and the dried up river Pactolus. Depressed, I glanced out over the desolate and deserted valley - once the richest place on earth where gold flowed freely in its river. A few columns of the Temple of Artemis still stood like skeletons on the bleak, crumbling land.

"Don't think about it, Honey." Bill squeezed my knee. "Whatever hand is guiding us may have a wicked finger, but it also has a sure direction for us - and the tapestry to follow."

"It's going to be needed in dealing with that bastard, Norton," I vehemently uttered under my breath as we passed field after field of poppies.

"You just concentrate on Idmon and leave this asshole to me," Bill said as he turned to see if Suhvanna were visible. She wasn't.

I quit looking back, instead gazing out over the fields of future opium. We passed Turgutlu and headed down the Manisa road. Except fom an occasional bullet from Norton, we had little to distract us from checking out Idmon's every move. Up ahead we could see the long, low flank of Mt. Sipylos which Idmon began to study carefully. Red rock with slate gray streaks of water wear sloped higher and higher towards its peak. A maze of caves wove in and out of the long flank when an exceptionally large and blackened cave caught Idmon's attention.

Then the moment we had been waiting for happened. Idmon made his move. He drove off the road, spreading so much dust in his wake that we almost didn't see him come to a screeching halt at the last gate of a corral with a 10 foot high fence, laced at the top with rows and rows of barbed wire. He leaped out of his car, leaving his nurse behind, ran at an incredible speed up and around the barbed wire fence, and then disappeared into the bramble and thorny underbrush. Just as I had expected, he was empty handed.

"Shit! He doesn't have the tapestry." Bill cursed, slamming on the brakes and stopping so quickly that the dust again clouded the area. "And just where in the hell is he headed?" He asked in disbelief.

We both realized that this was no time for question or hesitation. We jumped out of the car and dashed after Idmon. As we ran by Idmon's Rolls, the fearful, stricken nurse crouched down on the front seat, looking deserted and destitute. There was no sign of the tapestry.

"Do you have the tapestry?" Bill screamed, jerking open the door and searching the car. He dumped the clothes in the suitcases, spilling them all over the car. There was no sign of the tapestry. "Key?" Bill demanded, but she apparently spoke no English, crying and cringing down low in her seat. "Key!" He screamed at her, spotting Norton rapidly approaching.

Slowly, very slowly, she opened her hand and exposed the keys which Bill grabbed and rushed around to the trunk. It was empty.

"Forget it, Bill." I shouted as I took off running when Norton's dust again covered the area with whiteness. "Idmon's going to lead us to it. Remember what you said? We can't let him out of our sight. If we lose him we've lost any hope of recovering the tapestry. Come on."

He threw the keys in the window and ran faster than I'd ever seen him as Norton stopped and opened fire, aiming directly at us and repeatedly pulling the trigger. As we dove for protection, we ended up on a sharp holly lined path.

I turned to see Suhvanna being dragged out of the car. Norton slapped her as she clung tenaciously to his right leg, holding on for dear life. Her face was bleeding and her body bruised as he brutally banged the door shut on her.

"Run!" I heard her scream. "Get out of here. Run!"

I felt awful just taking off and leaving her to suffer in his hands. But I really couldn't believe it when Norton pointed his gun at her head, jamming it right up against it, and mercilessly pulled the trigger.

Apparently out of bullets, he repeatedly struck her with the black barrel as we escaped into the tangled mass of thorny, thick underbrush.

CHAPTER IV: "ARACHNE'S HOME"

"Ouch! Damn!"
Cursing the purple thistle that pricked our ankles and the brightly polished holly that cut our calves, we tore like hell up the steep, bouldered lower boundary of the eastern edge of Mt. Sipylos, where dried up blue wildflowers clung to their dead stalks. Already high up, I paused to look down once more at the cars parked by the corral gate and saw Norton knock Suhvanna to her knees, crush her head between his legs, then force himself on her. I scrambled forward faster, feeling so sorry for Suhvanna but thinking I might be next if Norton caught up with us. Out of breath by the time we had to tackle the severely brambled path where the razor sharp holly grew head high, we halted when the mass of twisted, thorny undergrowth thickened and prevented our passing.
"Shit, this is going to be impossible," I moaned as Bill, squeezing my hand tightly, bravely took the lead. A scraggly limb, resisting his shoulder, released and ripped across my face. "Hey, watch it, Bill!" I cried in pain.
"I'm sorry, damn, you all right?" But in the next breath said, "Hurry," grabbing my hand again and hauling me up into a small clearing next to a tall fence, topped by three rows of the most wicked looking barbed wire I'd ever seen.

I had to stop and catch my breath, jerking my hand loose from his firm grip and peering in past the wire, figs and more thorny trees.

"Come on." Bill prodded agitatedly when I hesitated, glancing far up beyond the fenced area and seeing what edged him on - it was the Mother Goddess cave. Carefully carved in the cliff by a master sculptor whose obvious love poured into every crack, the powerful statue was niched into the top layer of pink and white, marble looking rock; streaked black and dark blue gray water lines, like fingers, motioned us forward. It dominated the entire area.

"Oh, God, look, Bill." Never had I felt such a strong energy pull.

"I know, I know...That's our target. And Idmon's headed directly for it." He paused. "Beats the hell out of me why he's leading us on this wild goose chase on this frigging mountain, but he can think again about me letting <u>him</u> out of my sight." His jaw jutted in determination. A low, muffled moan coming up from the brambled path caught Bill's attention. He froze. "Let's get away from here." he said, shoving through the gnarled brush covering the path.

Without him, I wouldn't have dared the treacherous climb or the fierce briar patch. I stayed as close to him as possible as we inched our way through the sharp holly. The high afternoon sun unmercifully baked then scorched our heads, causing dark specks to dart in my eyes and forcing me to catch my breath again; I sought shelter from its intensity in the shade of the smallest possible fig tree.

"Bill, I don't know if I can go on," I whined, feeling ready to faint as I peeked out from under the excuses for leaves, only partially protecting me from the blinding rays. I shouldn't have glanced down at the blood that oozed and trickled down my arms and legs. Then when I tasted the unmistakable saltiness seeping into my mouth, I was nauseous.

"You can't stop now." Bill opened his eyes wide in shock. "Look how far we've come. Besides, what are you going to do - turn back and face that asshole Norton's gun or God knows what else?...And would you really let Idmon escape? Hell, we'd never find him or the tapestry in this godforsaken place. Come on, Honey, look, the Mother Goddess cave where Idmon's heading is just over there, just beyond that rock slide area."

"I'm not attempting that!" I hovered under the fig, but not for long. Hearing Norton's mean, low voice behind us convinced me. "Okay, okay...but," I surveyed what was ahead, "but at least let's edge close to the fence."

"All right, but that barbed wire is a lot more deadly than these thorns. We must be super careful," he cautioned as I led the way around the top end of the corral where the mountain sharply angled upward.

Edging along the cliff with the barbed wire precariously below us, then parallel with our heads, we braced ourselves with every step. After a painfully short distance, the inevitable happened - I slipped on a steep slope where I couldn't get my footing, slid into the barbs and caused them to wrap around a thick strand of my hair so tenaciously that I stopped dead in my tracks.

"Oh, shit, Bill, Bill! Help!" My voice shrilled in panic. "Help!" I was completely pinned and not doing a very good job at staying calm; my footing slipped farther and farther downward, causing the barbs to tighten. I felt like I was being scalped.

"Hold on, Honey." Bill made his way on the steep incline towards me, concern written all over his face - which was only inches from the rusty barbs. Just as he released his hold and reached out, he too slipped, crashing into the fence. The sharp rows of barbed wire caught his cheek, gashing and ripping his skin.

"Shit!" He cursed in pain as I helplessly looked on, feeling the pain as much as he did. Then I couldn't look anymore at the gashes where blood bubbled up and trickled down his cheek. My eyes grew wide, my stomach queasy.

"Come on, now. Don't worry. If this is the worst of my injuries, I'm getting off easy." He squeezed my hand, examining the situation.

"Damn, Charla. Your hair's got to be ripped loose." He sighed, "Hold on," yanking and leaving a tangled wad of it wrapped in the fence. I bit my lip and grimaced. Neither of us complained, but pressed forward out across the sliding, rocky cliff. Unable to get any footing, we fell to our knees, the rocks imbedding

in our scraped skin. With every foot
forward, we slid back two. Muffled sounds
of Norton's rough, coarse voice kept us
going. Securing one step at a time on
some purple thistle clumps that somehow
eeked out their existence on the rocky
incline, we inch by inch climbed at a
creeping crawl up and across the
crumbling mountain.

Higher up, past a heavily thistled
and thorny area, the grand figure of the
seated statue created such an energy pull
that we hurried the remaining distance in
spite of our wounds and our slipping,
sliding steps. Once across the sharply
angled rockslide, I paused, irresistibly
drawn by this mighty, still Goddess,
towering to heights over 20 feet. Sitting
serenely regal on her throne, she gazed
down as protectively on the River Hermos
as Ramesses ever overlooked the Nile.

For some reason, uncontrollable tears
welled up as Bill grabbed my hand and
guided me across the mountain toward this
great, powerful source that had withstood
time itself. I'd seen many old, really
old, things, but none of them had ever
had such an impact on my emotions. I
simply couldn't stop crying. Through my
tears, I saw that only her missing arms
and deeply scarred face attested to any
temporal existence. Her great knees rose
authoritatively high, perfectly preserved
and rounded by water as though rubbed
affectionately since the Hittite sculptor
created the throned Goddess over 4000
years ago. Now, though once the revered
worship of entire civilizations, she sat
alone, forgotten and abandoned. Yet, her

primitively marred, ageless face actually seemed to smile down upon me.

Maybe it was because of her natural setting or the freedom of a gentle wind, rising from nowhere, that caressed my face and cooled my overheated body; whatever it was, I felt as though I were nearing Mother Nature herself. Mesmerized and blinded by tears, I climbed toward the stilled, seated figure, feeling as though she pulled me toward her broad, immortal lap.

A massive array of flowers surrounded the high figure - small, dried blue ones, purple blossoming thistle, and bright yellow effleuresence created a pastel flourishing fit to be at royal feet. I turned to look far below at the fertile river valley which flourished as through in tribute to its Queen, its bright green fields lining the ever flowing Hermos. Scanning the hot bramble and destitute, sheer cliffs, I noted that her brightly flowering shade and soft wind created a perfect oasis, protected and preserved forever.

Then we saw Idmon. He had been hidden out of sight inside the shielding barrier of the bright yellow brush, growing at her feet. He rose from bended knee behind the sun colored covering, a short distance away, where he'd apparently been praying. When he looked at me and realized that I'd been crying, the compassion in his eyes or something in his poignant gaze sealed a communication between us.

"He's praying, Bill. Idmon worships her. Oh, I should've known it.

Matriarchy. We <u>are</u> smack dab in the middle of matriarchy." And I started crying again, so moved was I that this most ancient Goddess of all goddesses was still worshipped and loved. For the first time, I understood Idmon somewhat better and could even identify with him a little; I realized that the intensity within causing me to cry stemmed from a love that I too felt for the image of this divine matriarch. Then Idmon mysteriously disappeared from view.

"Praying to save himself," Bill blurted and let go of my hand so quickly that I almost fell backwards down the thistled path as he dashed forward in an attempt to follow Idmon, who upon seeing us, raced down across the flower strewn incline in front of the seated figure.

Grabbing the moment of a lifetime, I rushed toward the statue, scooted up on the carved ledge, and leaned over to kiss her blessed feet. Bill disappeared in the bramble while I took my long, lingering second at the oldest, most revered spot I'd ever experienced.

Running back again, Bill yelled at me, "He's gone, Charla, gone, goddamnit, and I can't figure out where in the hell he's disappeared to, but we've plain out lost him." He paused, looking up at the serene figure, and then in an attempt to prod me, he insisted. "He must've headed back down. Come on. We've got to move fast to cut him off before he reaches his car and makes the break to his hideout."

Suhvanna's scream cut across the mountain. Down below, we could see Norton nearing the corner of the corral and dragging her through the sharp holly thicket.

My eyes met Bill's; I knew that if we didn't get to Suhvanna soon, she'd be dead. It really wasn't a tough decision - to save her life or potentially lose Idmon. Shrugging his shoulders and throwing up his hands, Bill quickly acquiesced, saying, "But first I've got a bone to pick with that bastard. Come on, Charla, let's cut him off at the corner of the corral. Before he gets the barbed wire around her neck, I intend to wrap it around his balls!"

I readily shook my head in agreement, realizing the inevitable choice; neither of us could live with ourselves if we let her die.

He helped me down from the high ledge, and my feet hit the ground running. Racing past the array of wildflowers, sliding and slipping over the steep rock slide, and rushing headlong down to the far end of the corral, we reached the corner of the treacherous wire. At the other end, Norton cautiously edged up the mountain past the top rows of barbed wire. He roughly dragged Suhvanna along, not caring if she were being cut and gouged.

Finding an area where the bottom wire had been lifted by goats who left their black deposits scattered around the small opening, we bellied under the fence and headed into the security of the olive trees. Then we made our way toward Norton and Suhvanna on the other side of the corral. Thick clumps of coarse hair, stuck on the olive branches and tall holly, caught my attention. Just what the hell was in this corral, I wanted to know as I surveyed behind every tree. I couldn't imagine an animal with such creme colored hair.

Suddenly from out of nowhere, a tall, spindly legged camel charged. With the ferocity of a bull, it came at me and Bill with a snort and a loping leap. "Whoa!" Bill yelled, grabbing my hand and shooing me to safety inside a small clump of thorny trees where it couldn't fit. We stayed for a second, attempting to judge the charging camel's next move, when we heard the soft, consistent buzz of bees approaching. Peering out around the olives, we saw them swarming and heading directly for us, causing us to maneuver out of the thicket.

Suhvanna's cries led us forward when a shot rang out, forebodingly echoing off the cliffs. Dead silence followed; then we heard a rolling, rock falling sound, followed by something tearing and ripping down the mountain, succeeded by a loud thud. Then again, silence.

"Oh, my God!" I screamed, "Norton's killed Suhvanna."

"Damn, I thought Norton was out of bullets." Bill cursed as we stared in disbelief at each other. Then both of us took off running as fast as we could toward the other side of the corral in the direction of the shot. Reaching the densely vegetated corner, Bill hoisted himself high up on a limb of a large fig, branched out over the rows of barbed wire. Peering through the fence from behind the thicket, I was the first to see Suhvanna, running as swiftly as she could through the holly. Overjoyed, I couldn't believe she was alive - and alone.

Her face bled profusely from all the cuts and scrapes; blood trickled down her arms and legs, and panic gripped her face and eyes which flared as wide and ghastly as if she'd seen a ghost.

"Suhvanna!" I hissed under my breath, smiling from ear to ear over her having escaped, but hoping that if Norton followed, he wouldn't hear me. "Over here," and I stuck my face closer to the barbed wire.

She blinked in amazement, then blurted, "I killed him. He's dead. Norton's dead. We struggled...I thought the gun was empty, but then, it went off. I shoved him down the mountain - over there." She pointed. "He rolled all the way down into the briar patch at the bottom."

I grimaced, imagining the cliff streaked with blood.

Then she began sobbing uncontrollably, on the brink of hysteria. "He deserved it. Oh, Charla, he did deserve it. But I never wanted to kill anyone." She slumped to her knees, bruises covering her body and her blackened eyes flooding with tears, causing her mascara to streak and darken them further. She didn't look like the same person.

Bill hopped out of the tree and scrambled over to the fence. "Good God,

Suhvanna. Did that bastard do that to you? Where is he?"

"Dead!" We both replied simultaneously.

"Dead? Oh, my God," Bill gasped, but as soon as he surveyed her battered body and crumpled state, he took control; in a kind but firm voice, he told her to stay put and that he'd be right there.

"No, no," she resisted. And to my amazement added, "I can make my way along the fence." She grabbed the barbed wire and pulled herself up.

Using a sympathetic tone and soothing words, he led her along the steep cliff to the hole in the fence. Upon reaching the low opening, she crawled over the goat droppings and collapsed in Bill's arms. Not for long, however, for within seconds, the camel charged at full speed, his spindley legs flying, his slobbery mouth drooling. Suhvanna's eyes widened to the size of saucers as she froze, panic stricken in her tracks and dead weight in Bill's arms. Bill lifted her off her feet, threw her over his shoulder, and ran as fast as he could toward the clump of thorny trees.

I reached the safety of the olive clump and tried holding back the branches for Bill and Suhvanna, but as they rushed inside one of them released and whapped Suhvanna with a loud spank on her rear. Thinking it was the camel, she screamed, leaping off Bill's shoulder and landing squarely on her feet. When she realized what had happened, she couldn't conceal the small grin which crept into the corners of her mouth, cracking the coagulated blood. Then, realizing she was all right and alive, she took a deep breath, braced herself against Bill, and took another deep breath.

"Suhvanna, you saved our lives," I thanked her from the bottom of my heart, hugging her with appreciation and feeling real affection for her. She clung to me like a sister, shaking with relief and exhaustion. Her blood smeared all over my arms and shoulders, but I didn't care, not even trying to wipe it off.

"It happened so quickly," she muttered defensively. "He tripped, and I jumped on top of him. Then the gun went off." She started crying, unable to go on.

"That's self defense," Bill protested, not wanting her to blame herself, when we heard the buzzing swarm of bees coming closer. "Let's get the hell away from here." Seeing that the coast was clear from the camel, Bill again carried Suhvanna over his shoulder, and we charged down the mountain toward the gate. We heard a car start and scratch out at a great speed. "That's Idmon leaving!" Bill yelled, halting and gazing at the gate far below in the dust. "Damn, how the hell will we ever follow....?"

"Don't worry, Bill," Suhvanna interrupted in quite a strong voice, given her weakened state. "I know for a fact that Idmon is headed to at least one of two places - either the Manisa Museum or his home." Then without another moment's hesitation, she added in an even stronger voice, her face taking on the steel eyed business expression I'd detected earlier, "No, without a doubt he's headed for the museum; I'm absolutely convinced of it."

Our eyes focused questioningly on Suhvanna. However, without any time to consider her decision or her condition, we felt compelled to rush along, down around the corner of the corral, down the steep paths with coarse clumps of hair hanging off the thorn trees and brushing in our faces. Down among the dried wildflowers and prickly purple thistle, we hurried, both of us supporting Suhvanna arm in arm. As Bill helped her over the gate, I straddled it, taking a lingering last look at the Mother Goddess statue and feeling her loving protective presence - who was in turn apparently protected by the camel, for it again charged and chased me off the gate.

With great speed to get away from the area - and Norton's body, before we got caught; we jumped in the car and took off, leaving the camel leaning over the fence in a trail of white dust. I turned and watched behind as the falling dust settled over the wildflowers and the bright shiny holly on the thorny path, daring anyone to tackle the bramble protecting the cave. I could imagine its siltiness covering Norton's body like a shroud and burying it from sight. I tried not thinking about a goat herder, probably the only one who ever used the path, discovering the bloated body after a few days.

Dismissing the gruesome thought, I turned my attention to Suhvanna, asking,

"To the museum, Suhvanna? Are you certain? My guess is that Idmon will head for his home," I argued, wondering why she was so adamant on this point. But when I examined her condition, I acquiesced.

She was shaking uncontrollably and looked as though she might go into shock. Her unfocused, stress filled eyes attested to her being in such an intense emotional state that she didn't even notice the blood seeping steadily from her face and limbs nor the large red welts rising on her face. I swabbed her wounds with a damp tissue then placed my arms around her. Forgetting all the doubt and jealousy I'd experienced earlier, I actually felt real concern for her well being.

Sensing my caring energy, she breathed deep, momentarily relaxing.

"Sure that isn't what the entrance to Idmon's home looks like?" Bill asked, attempting to lighten us up. He pointed at the armed guards high up in the towers who watched over a heavily barbed wire square area on the side of the road; it looked more like a prison or concentration camp than a military installation.

He succeeded, for she took another deep breath and somewhat smiled at his obviousness. She responded, "Manisa is well guarded. There's one at the other entrance...But Idmon's?" She almost warningly added, "Oh, no, it is impossible to get past its entrance without me." Despite her wretched condition, she began to sound stronger,

almost like her old informative self.
However, she was extremely edgy and
nervous. And when she too passionately
added, "We must hurry and get to the
museum," I wondered, for I noted a hint
of panic in her voice.

"But why is Manisa so well guarded?"
I asked, attempting to sound light and
alleviate her growing tension as we
entered the town and I noticed the heavy
banking center - with a bank on almost
every corner. "Because of its wealth?" I
asked, yet as we drove through the small,
quaint, and very quiet streets, little
attested to a rich culture. Nor did
Suhvanna even notice what I was saying.
In fact, she didn't even seem to hear me;
she was obsessed about giving Bill
directions left and right as though she
knew the area like the back of her hand.

I strongly questioned Suhvanna's
persistent resistance to any other
potential explanation of Idmon's next
move, wondering what she knew that we
didn't. I couldn't understand why she was
so adamant about going to the museum. I
studied her and noted a perceptible
change in her which, I reasoned, could
have easily been attributed to her
unbearable torture by Norton or by her
subsequent emotional upset over killing
him.

I couldn't quite put my finger on it,
but I couldn't let her just lead us
astray; I asked bluntly, "But why
wouldn't Idmon hide the tapestry in the
safety of his home? And why are you so
certain that he has taken it to the
museum?" I had to interrupt her rapid

fire of directions to Bill - to finally turn left and head up a narrow, winding road toward Mt. Sipylos whose blue shrouded, jagged peaks hovered over the city like a protective dragon.

Satisfied with her directions, she turned, saying, "I'm not sure of his motivation. You see, after he retrieved the tapestry from...."

"Retrieved? Suhvanna. Don't you mean stole...I spilled my guts trying to prevent Norton and Idmon's goddamn bruisers from ripping it out of my hands," Bill interrupted as she again ignored him, instructing him to pull up in front of two large doors where a group of young boys milled about. Their shy, smiling eyes surveyed us as though they were unaccustomed to foreign visitors.

"Wait here." Suhvanna commanded when a tall, dark man exited from the huge doors which bolted as tightly shut behind him as a moat being drawn on a castle.

As she quickly jumped out of the car, the large doors mysteriously opened and she disappeared behind them as a uniformed guard pulled them firmly shut.

Jarring us with surprise and shock over her erratic actions, Bill and I stared at each other, undecided about our next move.

The young boys crowded closer and closer. Admiringly, as the men had done in the airport in Istanbul, one of the young boy's hands reached through the window to touch my hair, fascination glowing in his eyes. But when the others extended their hands to stroke it as well, that was it. I was out of the car

and heading for the large doors with Bill
right beside me, saying, "I couldn't
agree more, Charla. We're not losing her
too 'cause she's all we've got." He
grabbed my hand. "No Suhvanna, no
tapestry. It's as clear as that." He
approached the mysteriously opening door.

A guide, stepping from a group of
uniformed men as though he had been
waiting for us, welcomed us inside a
courtyard, covered with stony fragments
of pillars, tubs, altars, and statues
propped indiscriminately against the
walls. He smiled at us and led us up some
steps leading into a larger area. On no
side of the walls did I see any obvious
hiding place for the tapestry.

"Suhvanna?" Bill questioned the
guide, who obviously spoke no English,
excused his inability to respond to us
and motioned us to climb the steps and
enter the central room. Sculptings from
ancient Lydia lined the large square. He
directed us past the many broken statues
of Cybele, Athena, then Artemis and
toward an important looking, small dark
room on the left side. There was no sign
of the tapestry nor Suhvanna who was
nowhere in sight in the spacious inner
area.

We peered into the dimly lit room as
the guide stood close by, monitoring us
carefully. Bill winked at me, nodded
toward the guide, and told me with his
look that we'd have to play this one
carefully. I read him clearly. This was
no time to assume that the guide didn't
understand English. I scanned the dark
room for Suhvanna or the tapestry,

finding neither; then I dramatized the typical tourist, saying in an absolutely amazed tone, "Just look at all the wealth here!"

"Enough established wealth to stock some of the oldest artifacts in existence. Do you realize that surrounding us are dusty, yet still breathing stone monuments, preserved for a glimpse into our most ancient past?" Bill said, smiling patronizingly at the guide.

"You bet it'd take wealth to protect these gems," I added. "I think congratulations are in order to the keepers of these irreplaceable links to a heritage, a regal heritage from our first generation." I eyed the observant guard who gave us no reaction.

"Check out these fossil footprints - talk about old and valuable!" Bill exclaimed, walking over to the display case with the protective guide right behind him. "Says on this plaque - '50,000 B.C., the oldest somantic examples of humanity...now protected under the earth.' Didn't we pass this place - the Demirkopru Dam?" I shook my head in agreement, recalling the turn off just past Salihli. "Say's here there're many more of these footprints buried under it." Then he questioned under his breath, "But where the hell's Suhvanna?" He checked out every available wallspace for the tapestry and politely smiled at the guide who led us from one case to another.

"And how about this one?" I blurted upon seeing the very famous, tiny Mother

Goddess figure of baked clay with its pregnant stomach and swollen breasts. I didn't have to overdo the acting, for it was difficult to unglue my eyes from one after another of the most revered objects which I'd formerly only seen in pictures. I blinked, coming back to attention and scoping around the room for Suhvanna. For some reason, a quick movement caused my eyes to dart to a side door leading into an even darker room. I sensed Suhvanna's presence. Then she emerged from the shadows of the dimly lit door, appearing even more battered looking than before and causing me to seriously question if she should have medical attention.

I wondered why the guide didn't act like he noticed her condition and her state of shock, clearly evidenced by her blank, unfocused stare.

Again, she seemed to sense my concern for her, for next, acting as if she were consumed or possessed by some energy that she apparently thought I'd understand, she grabbed my hand and urgently motioned me out of the museum. We passed by all the keepsakes from the subsequent generations that once lived in this most ancient area of the earth; we passed the group of guides who gathered at the giant doors, and we passed the car parked by the sidewalk.

Bill, running behind us to keep up, sharply questioned her about the tapestry, but she ignored him, adamantly insisting, "Charla, you <u>must</u> come with me. Bill, you <u>must</u>." She led us up a steep sidewalk running behind the museum.

"Suhvanna, we must come where?" Bill tried slowing her. "Come on, what is going on? Why'd we go to the museum? Where the hell is the tapestry? I've really had enough of these wild goose chases," he yelled after her as we cut through dark backdoors and sharply inclined alleyways.

"I can't explain. Just please trust me. When we get there, you'll see," she said, and she would neither take no for an answer nor slow down, forcing herself to climb up and up the crowded, narrow walkways of the city, located below Mt. Sipylos. The small paths led from one secret passageway to another, angling up and across the stacked housing.

"As I said," Bill began to shallowly breathe, "I've had enough of mountain climbing for one day. And so have you, Suhvanna, and so has Charla." He spoke for me as I struggled with all my might to keep up with Suhvanna, yelling at her, "Stop, Suhvanna, please stop. In your condition, this is not a good idea. Let's go back and get the car - it's so much easier."

She never even responded, just kept climbing, pulling on a reservoir of energy that I knew was empty. Finally, completely out of breath and wondering how Suhvanna could ever walk much less climb such a long distance after what had just happened to her, we reached a huge blackish, red and dark grey streaked rock. It was perfectly carved by nature into the smooth shape of a woman's face - the soft contour of her eyes, finely chiseled nose and mouth, and even swirls

of rocky formation that resembed hair.
But the most dominant feature of this
incredible rock was that out of her stone
eyes, surrounded by delicate moss and
tiny grasses, water trickled forth.

Stunned by the mysterious spectacle
of the weeping rock, Bill and I sat down
some distance from Suhvanna on the steps
of a theatre, being carved out of the
mountain; we gaped at this miraculous
stone, yet lifelike face. What surprised
us even more was Suhvanna's reaction to
this rock. It was as if every possible
stored stress, frustration and pain came
pouring out with such force that it
knocked her to her knees. Wiping the
tears that streamed down her face, she
finally spoke, her voice broken with
emotion;   yet   she   was   strangely
strengthened by the presence of the
formidable stone face. "This is Niobe's
Rock and every Friday since time began,
it weeps. Today, I think it cries for
me." A wind sweeping down Mt. Sipylos
wailed eerily around the rock.

"Niobe's myth?" I gasped, recalling
Ovid's recording and positioning of this
account in his Metamorphosis exactly next
to Arachne's myth; he'd explained that
the two women were childhood friends.

"Better fill me in, Charla," Bill
whispered.

"Niobe had 12 children, all heirs to
two thrones, Thebes, part of mainland
Greece, you know, Oedipus' home, and this
land. She was the only daughter of King
Tantalus and wife of King of Thebes. As
the myth goes, she boasted a bit too
proudly about her children and refused to

worship Leda, you remember - depicted on
Arachne's tapestry mating with Zeus who
took the form of the great, white swan.
Leda was the Greek mother of Apollo and
Artemis who, in revenge, sent her
children to kill off all Niobe's children
and husband. Devastated, Niobe
subsequently cried for so long that
finally Zeus took pity on her and turned
her into stone - and now, I find out,
this very rock that weeps."

As though infused with some strange
energy, Suhvanna rose from her knees.
Again, her eyes glinted and her
expression hardened as she spoke, "Not
just killed - slaughtered, and with the
Greeks bloodthirstily screaming genocide
and hoping that all traces of inheritance
through Niobe would be removed from the
face of the earth." Her voice rose, her
hands trembled. "So that through Niobe's
brother, Pelops, whom they ate whole as a
baby and spit back out a Greek, they
would have no competition in claiming the
throne - and our land, our rights, our
very lives. It was his grandsons,
Agamemnon and Menelaus, who brought the
regiments to viciously rape and sack
Troy. But you see, they didn't succeed,
for Niobe had one surviving son -
Ilionous, and his decendants defiantly
live on, determined to...."

"Determined to what, Suhvanna. What's
there to prove?" Bill interrupted as her
voice broke.

Her face reddened then went stark
white, and her swollen eyes filled with
rage. Judging from the violence of her
reaction, I knew she hated the Greeks as

much as Idmon did.

Regaining composure as the anger within her faded, she continued, "I can tell you no more, but as you can see, it was no myth. Niobe herself is interned beneath this rock. Since I was a child, it's been a healing place for me. And God knows I've never needed it this badly." She slumped to the ground, hugged her body tightly, shakingly pulled in her knees and lowered her head. In a very weak, small voice, she added, "I'm sorry. I'll be okay in a few minutes. Then we'll go to Idmon's. You were right, Charla, the tapestry's not in the museum. It's hidden in his home. I didn't know if you'd understand or be patient, and I just had to come here."

Her voice faded as the wind again wailed around the weeping rock.

Bill pointed his finger, indicating for us to give her some space. We quietly removed ourselves, heading down around the theatre to a sun dappled, lush ravine where an idyllic brook babbled noisily as it splashed over small waterfalls spilling down among deep woods and wildflowers.

"Can you believe it? Another story of atrocity. No wonder the Greeks and Turks have such deep seated enmity," I said as we crossed over the tiny bridge and entered the beguiling, ancient kingdom of Tantalus.

"Regardless of her self-prescribed form of royal repair, I think our Highness needs medical attention. That gash on her head is still bleeding, and we can't rule out internal injuries,"

Bill decided, never taking his eyes off Suhvanna's slumped form.

"I agree." I nodded, yet wanting to give her a few more minutes. "But do you suppose she knew all along that the tapestry was indeed securely hidden in Idmon's home? And why didn't she tell us? Why did she lead us on?"

"I have no earthly idea. Maybe we had to prove something to her." Bill relaxed for a moment, wrapping his arms tightly around me.

"Like saving her life?" I murmured in his shoulder.

"Let's just make sure we do," he added, as we linked arms, crossed back over the bridge and headed up toward Niobe's rock. "As I said, I'm not sure she doesn't need medical attention. And, after all, she _is_ our last chance at getting the tapestry back. Hopefully, she's cognizant enough to help us find our way back to the car? What a maze she led us through!" Bill declared.

As we reached Suhvanna, we found her even more hunched over and broken looking than when we left her. Bill lifted her gently, for she couldn't walk nor hold up her head. She didn't resist. It was as though her energy had completely drained out; but as we climbed up over the rock, with both of us supporting her, she seemed to recover long enough to direct us back down to the car.

The group of little boys, who had reappeared and grouped around the car, eyed us suspiciously as we lay her in the back seat. Again, even in her broken

state, she shooed them away, then weakly
directed Bill back through the town.

"Look. A hospital," I pointed out the
building on the long road stretching out
of town. Suhvanna immediately reared up,
her face aghast at the thought.

"Are you kidding, Charla. They'd ask
me all kinds of questions. No way. What
if they've found Norton? They might make
a connection." She protested violently,
pleading with us to drive on. "Idmon will
take care of me. I promise you." And she
lay pitifully back down as we reached the
low lying trough of the Gediz River
Valley where tall grasses, richly
vegetated fields, and pastures of grazing
animals greeted us.

I couldn't believe the change in
Suhvanna, and the change in my feelings
toward her. I no longer felt threatened
or jealous of her, nor did she show any
further interest in Bill - or me.
Norton's torture and the trip to Niobe's
Rock had quietened her, almost subdued
her spirit.

Outside of Halitpasa, we turned off
on a dusty road, hidden amidst the tall,
gently swooshing grasses. Bill winked at
me knowingly as though congratulating me
on my intuitive perception in knowing
that the tapestry was at Idmon's all
along and that I'd been right about
Arachne's ancient village. Then he
grimaced upon seeing the tall, stoned
wall with masses of barbed wire topped
three to four rows high, running for
miles alongside the road and announcing
the approach to Idmon's.

Far up ahead, we could see the giant iron spiked gate protected by a group of armed, uniformed guards. Off in the distance, other guards stood at high, turreted posts. It looked like the military installation on the outskirts of Manisa. It couldn't have been more the fortress. Suhvanna was right. No one could have penetrated this impregnable estate.

The armed guards, their guns ready, eyed us suspiciously as we pulled up in front of the great gate; but upon seeing Suhvanna slowly rise from the back seat, they smiled broadly, not even seeming to notice her condition. Speaking in rapid Turkish to her, one of the dark haired guards, leaning over in almost a bow, nodded subserviantly. He picked up the microphone from a complex communications panel, sent some kind of message, waited a moment, spoke to someone on the other end, then turned to the other guards, apparently ordering them to open the gate, for the great iron doors creaked slowly out.

On the other side of the gates, another world of beautifully manicured green gardens unfolded, with multiflowering blossoms beside colorfully laden fruit trees. The long lane, disappearing into dense greenery, led up and up into the inner sanctuary of the centuries old castle, set in the midst of the lush river valley. Off to the left, bent over with fruit, were long rows of orange and olive trees with perfectly matched flowers, directing the curving walkway out to a bright white gazebo, which was decorated with swaying wicker rockers and swings. Stretching as far as the eye could see, heavily laden vineyards covered the earth with their white, luscious grapes.

Bill and I looked at each other in absolute amazement as we drove down the winding road, never having seen such a lush environment.

Up ahead, the stately mansion rose out of the thick vegetation.

My breath caught in my throat as my mouth dropped. Its solid stone masonry stretched skyward; its vaulted roof impressively topped the heavy formidable structure, resembling, no, almost mirroring the famous Caravanserai in Kusadasi where we met Suhvanna. I wondered if Idmon owned the Caravanserai as well.

Brightly blooming vines covered the massive wrought iron door which suddenly slammed open as we neared, banging loudly against the thick stone walls. Idmon, an almost grieving emotionalism brimming in his eyes, rushed headlong out the clanging doors. His silver white hair intensified his face, set in a grimace of worried concern. Without even waiting for us to stop, he wrenched open the car door.

I moved forward, pulling the back of my seat up, just before he leaped into the back seat, stroking Suhvanna's hair, rubbing her legs, leaning over to kiss her swollen lips and bruised cheek, and whispering in her ear as he gathered her gently in his arms. He hardly noticed us as he pulled her limply from the car,

yelling loud and authoritative orders.
Through the doors, people came running
from everywhere as Idmon continued
shouting out directions. Delgan
appeared, oddly clad in a white nurse's
uniform, along with servants, also
dressed in crisp, white uniforms. They
gathered around Idmon, disappearing
through the doors with Suhvanna, a roar
of excited cummunication following behind
them.

Bill and I took a deep, deep breath,
blowing out with a gust of relief, then
collapsing back onto our seats. "Thank
God we delivered her in one piece - and
on time, let's not forget; I'm not sure
how much longer she would have lasted
without medical attention." Bill said, as
we recovered our energy. "Her time had
run out."

"And, as it appears, so had ours - at
least any chance at ever recovering the
tapestry. We'd never have gotten in this
place without her," I noted, realizing,
as I looked around the vast complex, that
we were still going to be challenged.

"Have you ever seen such a place?"
Bill gasped as he stepped out of the car
and entered the marble walkway
surrounding an inner courtyard with a
large mosaic fountain, bright tropical
plants and ancient sculptings.

I followed him inside when a servant
approached us from down the long marble
walkway. He smiled at us warmly, then led
us around the green and colorful
flowering courtyard, with the same
magically splashing fountain as the
Caravanserai, to a formal seating area.

Soft, fleecy white sheep skins and a throw of Turkish rugs covered the pastel mosaic floor. From the tall vaulted ceiling hung a massive, clinking crystal chandelier that cast pockets of silvery colored, darting lights on the low, glassed table and on a soft, creamy leather sectional and chairs, with brightly designed pillows scattered about.

Motioning with his hands, the dark eyed servant led us over to the sofa and stammered something in Turkish. Before we could respond, Idmon appeared, ordering his waiter, "Raki for our guests," then he sank into the large leather chair and rubbed his hands together, his face serious in thought as though choosing every word. His entire demeanor had changed. Arching his thick black eyebrows, he finally turned to us, his blue eyes still filled with worried concern.

"How is she?" I inquired before he could speak.

"She is resting. I have been assured that she will be fine - with time. I am aware and totally grateful to you for having saved her life. For reasons that I cannot explain to you, I had to leave her, hoping somehow that she would get help from you." He paused, waiting for some reaction, then continued. "You can't imagine what she means to me. Words cannot express her importance. Thank you both. I owe you a great deal. How can I ever repay you?" He asked.

I was glad he expressed so much concern for Suhvanna, for after the

incident with his nurse, I had wondered
if Idmon even cared for her. I was also
glad that he was being gracious to us,
not so rude and abrupt as he was at
Pamukkale.

"You can repay us by working with
us," Bill spoke up. "You don't know what
it means to the world to end this
conflict your country has with Greece.
And these tapestries are the key to a
resolution."

"You can never imagine what the
Greeks have done to us. I will never work
with them. Do you understand - never.
Please, do not bring up the subject
again. It is impossible," Idmon answered
abruptly, reminding us of his former
pigheaded stubbornness.

The servant returned with the drinks
on a silver tray. The ice clinked in the
crystal, sounding as loud to me as the
iceberg sinking the Titanic. I refused
to believe that we wasn't going to work
with us, especially after having come
this far and having risked our lives so
many times.

"Idmon, why?" I protested, my spirits
sinking. But he ignored me, picking up
his drink and proposing a toast to
Suhvanna's quick recovery. In an instant,
he had changed his ingratiating posture
to keen defensiveness. Damn, I thought,
my mouth puckering from the thick, smoky,
and I soon discovered, strong liquor,
tasting like the Greek's ouzo. It made my
spirits sink lower, especially when,
without a word, Idmon downed his drink,
clinked his glass down loudly on the
table, and rose to leave.

"Wait!" Bill protested, trying to detain him and flashing his friendliest grin. "Come on, Idmon, at least tell us why you led us on that wild goosechase up, down and then back around that mountain. What were you up to?"

"I'll discuss this at another time, Bill. For now, I must return to Suhvanna's bedside. We will dine at 9:00. The servants will show you to your quarters." He told us matter of factly as he dismissed himself.

"To hell you will!" Bill cursed under his breath. "We'll find it ourselves."

We rose to follow the white clad servant who led us down the mosaic hallway. I fought the fogginess as the smoky liquid went to my head. I realized that all our attention was needed. I didn't agree with Bill that we should take matters into our own hands. It was too dangerous. I tried to tell him; but he was so busy checking out every piece of antique artword covering the walls - Hittite, Lydian, Lycian, etc. that he didn't even hear me.

"Where do you suppose it's hidden?" Bill whispered as we crossed down one art filled hallway to another. "It has to be here somewhere."

Then the rounding walk opened up into an exquisite bedroom, sitting room, courtyard, and large bathing area. I threw up my hands and shrugged my shoulders, not feeling nearly as confident as Bill that we'd ever find the tapestry. The servant dusted off our suitcases, spread down the bed, and excused himself.

"Let's go find the tapestry," Bill said excidedly, heading for the door.

"Oh, come on, Bill, I haven't had a bath for ages. We have a few minutes. Do you realize we haven't stopped since dawn?" I argued, not at all ready to take off on another adventure, especially without a clue as to where we should begin. I walked over to the sunken marble tub, stepped down and turned on the faucets. I resisted Bill's pushing me, choosing some of the fragrant bath salts and liquids from the mosaic containers and pouring them into the splashing water.

"Charla? How can you think of a bath at a time like this? We should be looking for the tapestry. Besides, what if Idmon absolutely doesn't agree to swop?" Bill asked, marching around the huge four poster bed.

I resisted the thought, glancing through the stained glass windows to the green gardens and pulling the thick, purple velvet draperies over the tub closed.

"I need a break. Come on, Honey. This has been the longest day of my life." I pleaded, stripping off my dirty clothes. I didn't dare look in the long mirror.

"Oh, all right." Bill, seeing me naked, couldn't resist; unzipping his shorts and shaking off his shoes, he dipped his toes, popping the soft bubbles. In an instant, he was undressed and immersed. The tub was so large and deep that he dived underwater and emerged on the other side where I sat on a marble seat.

Bubbles burst between us as he lovingly took me in his arms and kissed my wet lips. "Sorry I was so pushy, Honey." He kissed me again. "And I'm sorry that you were so upset earlier about Suhvanna. Don't you know that you're the only woman in my life? I'm madly in love with you."

I hugged him lovingly, feeling sorry that I had mistrusted him so. I kissed him back, relaxing and feeling the old tingle creep up my toes and warm me with burning sensation. My body melted as I gazed into Bill's deep blue eyes, filled with love and affection.

Our loving kiss fired into a passionate one, and our tongues flickered as fleetingly as the disappearing rainbows in the bubbles. His wet chest hairs tickled my breasts as we pressed our chests closer, then harder together, his mouth covering my breasts with kisses. I rubbed my hands over his muscular buttocks, pulling him closer to me, closer, closer; the yearning to merge, to become one engulfed me with overwhelming throbbing desire. I wanted to crawl into his body, his mind, his being and feel his heart beat as mine. One together, one alone - forever intertwined as one.

I was not even aware that the water moved around us, caressing and rhythmically rocking us to and fro; gently at first it cradled us like twins within the watery womb. Then faster and faster it sloshed, dipped, and swayed our bodies with its churning intensity. With urgency and a drive toward the void, our merged bodies became one with the resounding water, until all that we could hear and feel became emulsified liquid. All around, like quicksilver, stillness in motion bound us. As the sounds of the water disappeared and the driving energy ripped through us like molten lava, time and space ceased.

Slowly, ever so slowly, after what seemed like an infinity, the churning water calmed around our bound bodies, solidifying the inner fire and binding us together.

And just as slowly, I opened my clenched eyes and took a deep breath as I came back to reality and stared into Bill's glowing, smiling eyes. "I love you." We said simultaneously, grinning and splashing each other.

"Wow!" Bill gasped.

"Double Wow! I love you, I love you!" I repeated, leaning my head back against the velvet curtains when something clinked against the marble.

"What the hell?" Bill exclaimed, reaching back to examine the round metal object secured within the folds of the purple drapes. "S-h-h!" He put his finger to his lips as he rolled out the small microphone.

"I love you, darling," I carried on, realizing that someone had just had an earful of lovely noises, but also realizing that "mum" had just become our favorite word. "Idmon?" I silently questioned, mouthing the words as my thoughts whirled. Bill was right, I decided. We had to act and act quickly.

Bill shrugged, saying a bit too loudly, "What a great idea to stop and relax. I'm exhausted. There's time for a nap?" He dried off on the huge, white Turkish towel, walked over and rustled the silky sheets, then quietly began dressing.

I wondered what we could discuss that would really bore someone listening, then recalled my earlier dream. "Remember that dream I had this morning at Pamukkale when I was fighting off being jealous over you and Suhvanna?" I noisily splashed out of the tub, dried off in the luxurious white towel, and quietly opened my suitcase.

"You mean your dream admonishing you about getting distracted?" He opened the door, peered down the hall, and motioned me to hurry.

Placed visibly atop my jeans was another small microphone. My eyes opened wide as saucers as I urgently signalled Bill to come back.

"Norton?" He silently mouthed the words, then continued loudly, "How could you ever have mistrusted me? I'm completely loyal to you - till <u>death</u>."

"Oh, darling, it's not a question of your loyalty; it's about me, and it could be anything that could cause me to lose focus of what I'm really supposed to be doing. That's death to me," I winked, forming Norton's name with my lips and sliding my finger across my throat to indicate that if he had hidden the microphones then indeed we would have nothing to worry about.

However, we both knew that this was

not the time for assumption. I quickly
dressed, checking my watch. It was 8:30,
only 30 minutes before dinner.

Both of us stuck our heads out the
door, then scooted down the mosaic hall.
Left, right, we searched the art display
on the rounding walls for any sign of
Athena's tapestry. Up ahead, we
discovered a widely arched doorway
leading into another incredibly huge
room, containing an apartment similar to
ours.

"No, Bill," I asserted, preventing
his going into the room. "There's another
one up there," I pointed around the hall.
He scanned the walls, four poster bed and
floors, then caught up with me just as I
reached the second widely arching doorway
leading into the next apartment. "It's
exactly the same, Bill, and there's
another one up ahead. Come on." I
continued moving around the hallway,
checking the art gallery with artifacts
that lined the walls from the floor to
the ceiling. Nothing. There was no sign
of the tapestry.

After a few more arched doorways, I
realized that they surrounded the
castle's inner courtyard. Barraged by the
vastness of the art that filled the
castle's walls, I halted, grabbing my
forehead in dismay and doubting whether
we'd ever find the tapestry hidden amidst
such a ceaseless collection.

"Check out the next arched doorway,
Charla," Bill whispered, grabbing my hand
and halting me as he caught up. Low,
feminine tones floated from the dimly lit
archway into the courtyard. It was

Suhvanna and Idmon in their apartment. On tiptoes, we inched forward a few feet. "A microphone?!" Suhvanna rather loudly blurted. Then we heard heavy footsteps, rapidly approaching the door.

Bill grabbed my hand so forcefully that my feet almost left the ground. He spun us around and headed down around the galleried hallway with such speed that we went past our apartment and up to the next arched doorway leading into a large library. Stunned, Bill stood under the archway and stared up in amazement.

"What is it? Come on, Bill. We've got to get back to our room." But I somewhat relaxed upon realizing that Idmon remained with Suhvanna.

"S-h-h, this is important. This archway is lower than the others." He reached up and rubbed his fingers across the surface. They were white with plaster. "Check this out." His voice rose in excitement as I stood there dumbfounded. "Given my height, maybe you can't see it from my angle, but it's damn well lower - and freshly plastered. Here, look!"

He lifted me off my feet. "I see what you mean, Bill." I looked around frantically, afraid someone would come. "But put me down. I don't want to get caught...Hurry," I yelled, upon hearing footsteps coming from the other end of the hall. We ran back to the room, quietly closed the giant doors, and collapsed against them as we caught our breaths.

"What do you want to bet - their room is bugged too." I said with hushed conviction. "Norton?" I mouthed the words. Bill quickly shook his head yes.

"I can't wait to experience the gardens around here." He said a bit too loudly, obviously speaking into the microphone again.

"Really! Did you notice that white gazebo? Wasn't that beautiful?" I just as loudly stated, making obvious faces at Bill who was about to destroy the clothes which I'd carefully folded in the suitcase.

He searched for his paisley bowtie and the cummerbund to his tuxedo. "After dinner, let's ask Idmon to take us there," he suggested, sadly displaying his wrinkled tux, then walking over to the intercom and ringing for the servant to press it.

"Oh, mine too," I complained, upon pulling my only black gown, more wrinkled than Bill's tux, out of the garment bag.

The servant tapped at the door, and Bill motioned his hand like an iron moving back and forth, pointing at the clothes. The servant smiled at his antics.

"Time to get back in that tub again?" Bill, waiting for the servant to disappear, whispered, then nibbled on my ear as I applied mascara.

"Got any paper?" I whispered, trying to squelch the pangs of desire that Bill stirred.

"Pronto," he congratulated himself, producing a yellow legal pad on which I wrote,

"We have to convince Idmon that the house is bugged."

"By whom?" Bill wrote back.

I shrugged my shoulders as I traced the curving line of my lips with a soft red lipliner. I peered at my face in the mirror for any sign of fatigue from the horrible rigor of the day, but found instead a glowing complexion; my cheekbones were quite rosy. I smiled realizing that I owed my glow to Bill. I had trouble paying attention to what he was writing.

He fondled my hair as I brushed through its tight curls. "Somebody connected with Norton - some Greeks connected with Norton?" Bill continued writing as I reached over and hugged him.

"Yes!" I grinned; while he kissed me on my neck, I wrote, "We've got to convince Idmon that Norton was connected with the Greeks...That he was going to sell Athena's tapestry to the Greeks. And now they're planning on snatching it out of his hands." I ended it with a huge exclamation point and "later" which I added with my red lipliner.

Bill grinned and indicated that he agreed by drawing a happy face; then he pulled up his black silk underwear with my eyes tracing his perfect body. We both jumped when the servant tapped on the door, handing us our pressed clothes and announcing dinner. He waited outside as we dressed. Bill and I must have made quite a transformation for when we emerged from the room, the servant's eyes grew wide over our striking, and apparently handsome, appearance. He led us down the hallway and past the lowered arched doorway leading into the library.

"What do you want to bet." Bill again announced, forming his lips into the word, "tapestry," deducing that it had been sealed into the dropped archway. He almost tripped on the servant who halted and with his hand motioned us through the next archway into the dining room.

Never had I seen such an long table, large enough to seat 25-30 people. Bill ran his hand along the smooth rosewood and atop the plushly cushioned tapestried armchairs. The Turkish rug's colors blended with the chairs, and the walls were again covered with every conceivable form of art.

My eyes darted past it all, down to the far end of the table, where Idmon sat regally waiting, dressed in a black silk tuxedo with a pink bowtie and cummerbund. Talk about a transformtion! The color completely lit up his intense sky blue eyes, framed by his glowing silver hair.

Describing him as handsome would have been an injustice. Gorgeous was more like it, exquisitely sophisticated, reserved and filthy rich. My mouth must have dropped upon seeing the change in him, for he smiled as I walked toward him.

Directly glancing in my eyes, then tracing my shoulders, breasts, waist, hips, legs, feet, and back up again with the same incredible stare, he completely assessed me and undressed me. Satisfied, he smiled knowingly again.

"Suhvanna won't be joining us?" I questioned, attempting to ignore his overattentiveness as he stood to pull out the chair for me on his right. I extended my hand, but instead of shaking it, he

kissed it, touching his lips ever so
softly and teasingly. I sat down slowly
as he pushed the chair back under me.

"Is Suhvanna all right?" Bill, also
attempting to ignore Idmon's obvious
reaction, asked with concern.

"She's resting, and yes, Bill..." he
said, finally shifting his attention on
him, "She's feeling better, but should
stay in bed, even though she made me
promise to let her know when we were
through dining. A most determined young
woman! Has to be in the middle of
everything. Oh, well. Perhaps she can
join us for an after dinner drink." He
told us.

I breathed a sigh of relief, thinking
that if Suhvanna joined us at the gazebo,
she could help us convince Idmon.

He looked at me sidelong, as though
knowing what I was thinking. He added,
"Besides she's having dinner in bed and
didn't feel like dressing...So, Charla,
you're looking quite lovely," he
complimented.

"Thank you," I responded as demurely
as I could, hoping he'd let up, but his
presence alone commanded my complete
attention. There was no denying that his
powerful control was being established
without a word said. I felt tongue-tied
and slightly intimidated. I wouldn't want
to be in Suhvanna's shoes, I thought, not
after having seen him with Delgan in
Pamukkale. I knew she must have a tough
time handling the presence of his
mistress. But how I wish she were
present. For without her, Idmon directed
his entire attention on me.

His charm, his wit, his boldness in
expressing exactly what he thought and
felt, and his mystique clothed around me
and made me realize why most women would
fall at his feet. I could see why
Suhvanna had stayed with him over the
last few years. By far, his eyes were his
most outstanding feature which
intensified when he spoke; his stark gaze
was directed so deeply within my eyes
that he made me more than slightly
uncomfortable, for it seemed as though he
could see right through me. Tension rose
within as I recalled Suhvanna's message
about his loving beautiful women, and
that he might work with us if I and only
I asked him. My mind rushed. I needed an
approach. But I questioned if he could
ever be manipulated by anyone. He exuded
control, over himself and others. And,
for sure, I certainly didn't want to lead
him on sexually, for there'd be no
turning back with this man.

The servants silently moved about us,
serving at least a seven course meal.
Even after the main entree, a polite
young man placed in the middle of the
table a large tray of delicately prepared
young birds - doves, Idmon informed us,
which I didn't have the heart to eat;
however, I had devoured the wonderful
salad plates, calamari, different types
of fish, shishkabob, rolled grape leaves,
every kind of vegetable, and finally
desserts I'd never heard of; and, of
course, aperitifs, one local wine after
another, and, last but not least, Idmon
ordered after dinner drinks.

I really did need a walk in the worst way, so, I reasoned, if I asked Idmon to go to the gazebo, he might think my motive believable.

As though reading my scheming mind, he stared at me, telling me in no uncertain terms, "We will not discuss the tapestry."

Then he smiled, stood up and walked around to pull out my chair.

"I had no intention." I tried defending myself, but knowing I was caught.

Bill interrupted, coming to my rescue, "Great meal, Idmon. Be sure and congratulate your chef." He stood up and stretched his long legs.

"By the way, got any camels that need walking?" He joked, trying to lighten Idmon up, who, at just the mention of the tapestry, had completely changed his expression.

"Yes, an absolutely beautiful dinner!" I chimed in, catching his eye as he pulled out my chair. Then, as honestly as I could express, I said, "But seriously, I'd love a walk through your gardens. Won't you escort us to the gazebo?"

He slowly pushed in the chair, his face relaxing slightly.

"Great idea, Charla. Got a wheelchair for Suhvanna, Idmon? Bet some fresh air would do her good. How about it?" Bill, plugged, again trying to lighten Idmon up.

"Yesss," Idmon just as slowly agreed. "That _is_ a marvelous idea, Charla, I'll go and see if Suhvanna won't accompany

us." He walked to the wide archway,
paused, briefly looked back and continued
in his formal voice, "On second thought,
I'll meet you there. It's a beautiful
night, and you can enjoy it while you
wait."

He directed a servant to escort us.

Down the mosaic hallway, past the
lowered library archway, which Bill and I
studied carefully, and around the inner
courtyard where the chandelier magically
sparkled with light, the servant led the
way. He opened the tall arched iron gate
and motioned us out into the night. The
sound of chirping crickets surrounded us
as we entered the deep gardens. Night
blooming jasmine perfumed the air, and a
light breeze feathered our faces with
softness. I relaxed, feeling the night
warmly welcome us. Lanterns and
groundlights directed our way.

The script with Idmon rolled over
and over in my mind, reeling out the
unfolding event - what I would say, how
he would respond, how we could convince
him. His inflexibility concerned me, for
a key was needed to break through his
wall. The last approach, in suggesting an
exchange between the two countries to
solve the age old conflict, hadn't
worked. Something new was needed. I
questioned just what it would take.

Bill's hand slipped into mine,
warming and reassuring me as the white
clad servant continued leading us down
the well lit breezeway which crossed
through orchards, vineyards, and
manicured gardens all encircling the

white gazebo, appearing in the center up ahead.

"Ready for this?" Bill asked, spotting Idmon and Suhvanna walking down the breezeway on the other side.

"Oh, God!" I cringed, slowing my gait for a second. Suhvanna's appearance shocked me, for her bruises were even darker. I couldn't believe she was out of bed and walking around.

"She refused to ride in the chair." Idmon defended himself as they got closer. His arm wrapped protectively around her waist; her long, flowing saffron robe draped around his black pantleg as they walked.

She and I exchanged glances from afar, greeting each other with smiles and then hugs, first on one side and then the other, as we reached each other. "I had to come. You need my help," she whispered in my ear, then, releasing me very slowly, captured my gaze and communicated something in her eye contact that I couldn't interpret. It was just a flicker, a slightly dark flicker of her blue- green eyes, but I caught it and felt its cold seriousness. She turned and hugged Bill almost brotherly, her former seduction of him having vanished.

Helping her up the steps of the quiet gazebo and into a white wicker rocker, Idmon motioned for us to sit in its center on the softly cushioned, wicker sofa.

"Idmon?" I didn't waste a minute, not wanting to lose my nerve. I looked around quickly to see if the servants had left.

"Bill and I believe your home is bugged and we know why...."

"Bugged?? In my home?" He suspiciously asked, obviously not understanding the term. "What do you mean bugged?"

"Yes," Suhvanna frankly admitted, explaining the term to him. "Idmon and I also found microphones in our room."

"This is horrible news! I can't believe the security of my home has been threatened. Nothing could have been more defensible, so I can't possibly understand how anyone could have planted microphones. This has <u>never</u> happened. All right. Do you have any idea what's going on?" Idmon flatly questioned.

I saw my opportunity. "Norton worked with the Greeks. Just because he's dead," I paused to see if he'd interrupt me, "doesn't mean a trap has not been set. They don't believe that you will ever willingly give up the tapestry. They know you are with us, and they believe that you will cooperate with us in order to safeguard the tapestry. But what they don't know, I'm quite certain, is that there is another tapestry."

"Yes, after discussing this with Suhvanna, I now believe that there are two tapestries, and I think you're accurate about Norton not knowing. But tell me, how badly is Arachne's tapestry torn?" Idmon inquired, the same look of worried concern in his eyes that he'd had earlier for Suhvanna. It amazed me how much he loved the tapestry.

I knew that I had his attention and that I'd have to choose my words carefully. "Where Athena slashed Arachne's tapestry with her shuttle only adds to its divine beauty and causes the animals to sway as though they are alive. And it doesn't interfere with its exquisite perfection, so perfect that not even the gods could believe it was created by human hands. That's why Athena slashed it; the marks prove that it's the original."

Suhvanna abruptly interrupted, "That's not why she slashed it. She was trying to destroy it - that was part of her punishment to Arachne."

This struck me as strange, but I didn't challenge her. I just kept trying to entice Idmon with the description. "You can't imagine it, Idmon. Its gold and silver threads outline the most majestic, Tyrrian hued animals; its diamonds, rubies, emeralds, and other precious jewels weave the images of the most beautiful women on earth and create, along with the shining thread, settings that rival nature and that...."

"I want to sell Athena's tapestry to the Greeks." Idmon urgently interrupted.

"So did Norton," Bill bluntly stated, "And look what happened to him!"

"I'm sorry, Idmon, but the SILC Foundation would not allow the sale of either tapestry - only an exchange." I unrelentingly responded.

Idmon's eyes flared. "You want the Greeks to have it for free? Never! Over my dead body," he vehemently protested, sounding exactly like Dr. Aliamo.

"Idmon, listen. You must realize the cutthroat quality of the mercenaries

Norton's hired. One almost raped me in Istanbul. Do you really want to jeopardize your life and especially Suhvanna's?" I equally protested. "They will do anything, Idmon, so why don't we set them up with a fake plan and a fake tapestry?" I added.

"Idmon? Please," Suhvanna interrupted again, her old, friendlier tone restored. "Bill and Charla are right. Norton <u>already</u> tried to kill me."

Scooting his wicker rocker closer to her, he wrapped his arms around her, looked deep into her eyes and said with emotional conviction. "There is one way, and only one way that I'll give up the tapestry." He paused, as though choosing every word.

"Yes-s?" Suhvanna, growing impatient, asked.

"If you will marry me, Suhvanna, I want you to be my wife."

"<u>What</u>?!" She blurted in amazement, looking at him as though he'd lost his mind. Her mouth dropped. He had obviously caught her very off guard. Her buises darkened and she looked faint. I wondered if she shouldn't be in bed.

"You are even more important to me than this tapestry which I have dedicated my life to recovering for Turkey." He said, almost swearing to her.

Suhvanna sat up straight and blurted out, "I won't have it." She tried to stand up but Idmon stopped her. "I simply won't have it, Idmon. I will never be more important to you than Turkey - or the tapestry. I will be honest with you." The look that I couldn't decipher earlier returned to her eyes. "You see, I too have dedicated my life to the same purpose. That is why I attended Oxford, even going so far as working on my doctorate in archaeology - just so I could work with, regardless of what you feel toward him, Dr. Aliamo, the foremost expert on the Etruscans, whom he believed to be the Lydians, the first Turks. I've always been convinced that the tapestries existed. But this is the wrong tapestry, Idmon, and in order for us to get Arachne's back, we must compromise with Bill, Charla, and the SILC Foundation." Her voice didn't quiver even though she began to shake.

"And you trust these individuals?" He interrupted.

"They saved my life," she flatly stated. I couldn't figure out what she was up to, but something was amiss. She was loading it on too thickly. "Yes, Bill and Charla are to be trusted. Their aims are altruistic." Her husky voice lowered. "But I too have my needs. Archaeology is not my chosen field - I'm a journalist. So you see, I not only want Arachne's tapestry for Turkey, I want it to be my story, written by me, a Turkish journalist." Her cold eyes and her set, pursed lips face made me realize that she couldn't have been more serious. My breath caught in my throat. A loud voice in me screamed, "NO!" I'd been through too much to let this story slip through my fingers now. What was Suhvanna up to? I started getting upset. Had she been using me all along just to get her way with Idmon? And to think - I'd dropped my jealousy towards her, even begun to like her, to almost feel sisterly towards her. On pins and needles, I hardly heard her go on.

"For many years, I have prepared for this breakthrough in my career." She stopped and stared right at me just like Jane used to do, but there was a hard glint in Suhvanna's eyes. Jane's words, that Suhvanna was much more manipulative than I realized, flashed in my mind. She was also much more competitive - I now was finding out. I cringed. "Charla, we share the same profession; and as one writer to another, you must promise me that the SILC Foundation will not publish any word on the tapestries."

I froze, gripping the arm of the sofa. She sounded just like Dr. Aliamo, insisting to me and Jane that no one publish the story but me. "In other words, Charla, you must agree to give the story exclusively to me." She stared me down as I grasped fully what Dr. Aliamo had warned me about her; somehow he'd known about her all along and had tried to prepare me for this moment.

I stammered, "Exclusively?! ...Well..." She'd caught me so off guard that I didn't know what to say. If I agreed, then I'd break the promise to Dr. Aliamo; plus I'd lose the story. And if I didn't agree, I knew that she'd never work with us; there'd be no chance of getting the tapestry back from Idmon. Cold clamminess spread through me. "Well..." I repeated, feeling put on the spot and pressured to respond. "Well, how about an exchange?" Thinking fast, I figured she needed the research she'd stolen from me to write the story. "You give me my research back and agree to not use its contents, and I'll give you the story."

"Charla, wait! Don't you think we need to check with the SILC Foundation before we give Suhvanna that answer?" Bill spoke up quickly, realizing the barrel she had us over. I shook my head no and nudged his leg. He looked at me long and hard, whispering under his breath, "Let's walk away from this, Charla and not strike up any Faustian bargain."

But there was no way I could give it up. Too attached to saving the tapestry and panic stricken that I'd lose the story forever, I made a snap decision. Figuring I could tell Suhvanna I'd go along with her, but all the time play her game and beat her at it, I never dropped my gaze from Suhvanna's unflinching, intense stare, the dark glint in her eyes sparkling like a black diamond. I shivered.

"Good, Charla!" She quickly answered me, then turned to Idmon. "And if you'll assure me that you'll exchange the tapestry and then guarantee me that nothing will interfere with my story, then I'll make the arrangements for our wedding."

"And have my child?" Idmon whispered in her ear. Dropping her eyes, she nodded her head yes. "Oh, Suhvanna!" Idmon burst out, wrapping both arms around her and smiling broadly. "You have just made me the happiest man in the world. My dream is finally coming true. Combining the ancient houses of Niobe and Arachne will pave the way for uniting Turkey's past with its present."

"Whaaat??" Bill gasped, seeming to forget what just happened. "Queen Niobe? Arachne's childhood friend from Maonia, uh Manisa? That Niobe? From mythic times?"

I tried to snap out of the mental fog and understand what was happening.

"Yes! You see, Bill and Charla, she has not told you, but Suhvanna's inheritance is linked through multiple, multiple generations to Ilionous, Niobe's only surviving son; she rightfully holds claim to the Kingdom of Tantalus."

"Unbelievable!" Bill gasped as I stared blankly, trying to see Suhavanna from a completely different perspective and attempting to recover from the shock of losing the story. Remorse instantly rushed through me, and I couldn't believe what I'd just done. Nor could I grasp this serious news.

"No, very believable," Idmon corrected Bill. "And the tapestry is a symbol of that union, and our children will be the future statement of Turkey's true recognition in the world as the first and most ancient civilization on earth. It's preserved in mythology and Arachne's tapestry will be living proof of that fact."

Bill's eyes opened so wide that I could see my own shocked expression reflected in them. We were both speechless.

Suhvanna covered Idmon's face with kisses, crying and softly whispering her love in his ear. With real tenderness, he lovingly embraced her.

"You must stay for our wedding," Idmon announced proudly, rubbing Suhvanna's shoulders. Bill congratulated them, and I somehow stammered something out.

"I'd love to, Idmon," Bill carefully choose his words. "And I hate being a spoilsport, but we've got to take care of this tapestry pronto before someone takes care of us. You soon to be proud parents are in one helluva danger. First things first. I figure if we announce on one of the microphones our plans to get the tapestry out of the country, that we could turn around and set them up..."

"...With a fake copy? I see," Idmon quickly interrupted, catching on. "What if, in the meantime, we alert the authorities when we'll be leaving and tip them off that someone is going to try and get an artifact out of the country on my ship? And you know the severity of that crime. Yes, they will arrest them immediately, with no questions asked." He grinned broadly as though he'd thought of the idea. "Yes, very smart! And I know exactly what ancient piece to include in the package that would put someone permanently in one of our most well guarded Turkish prisons." He beamed, repeating, "Yes, very clever. Now, Suhvanna and I will walk you back to your quarters, where we'll address the microphone. Then Suhvanna, you must go back as soon as possible to your bed. I'm afraid you will not be able to go with us tomorrow to Kusadasi."

She started to protest, but he pressed his finger against her lips to quiet her. "On this you will not win. You can meet us as soon as you are feeling better; I insist that you stay in bed at least a few more days. Besides, until the issue about Norton's death is resolved, it would not be safe for you to be seen in this condition," he told her.

"Then I shall work on the final part of my story," she acquiesced as he took her hand and helped her to stand. "But I must be informed of every detail just to make sure I have the perfect ending, and that nothing goes wrong." It was almost a threat, but I was so relieved she wasn't going that my shoulders slouched forward.

I stood and stretched out some of the tension as Idmon led us back down the breezeway, past the manicured gardens, vineyards and orchards. Suhvanna paused to rest on a bench nestled among the orange trees, bursting with summer fruit, and I lingered behind, pouring over and over in my mind the fact that Suhvanna had already written the entire story except for the ending. Just what story did she have, I wondered. "It's not over yet," I kept repeating to myself, straightening my shoulders and getting a grip on myself.

Bill sat down on the bench beside Suhvanna. He whisered to Idmon, "The tapestry is hidden in the lowered archway leading into the library, isn't it Idmon?" Bill caught him so off guard, that even in the dim lights of the breezeway, Idmon smiled so broadly that his white teeth gleamed.

"You are a very intuitive man, Bill. Yes, I have devised a wooden frame to hold the tapestry. Perhaps you will help me remove it in the morning? I have a similar way of storing it on the ship. By the way, when all this business is taken care of, I'd like to invite you and Charla to spend some time on board with Suhvanna and me. I think a cruise in the Mediterranean is in store."

Right, I thought to myself. Someplace in the Mediterranean to set up the exchange of the tapestries. Just the reminder, that I wouldn't be the emcee and get the recognition for all the hard work and suffering I'd experienced on this trip, made me feel ill.

We entered the tall arched iron gateway which the servants held open, passed the inner courtyard and made our way slowly down the mosaic hallway. No one spoke, not even after they followed us to our apartment where we staged the scene, holding the two microphones from my purse and suitcase close to our mouths as we discussed the trip to Kusadasi, the storing of the tapestry aboard the ship, and the securing of it in the ship's safe.

Still we had nothing to say to each other except formal nicities. Remaining especially quiet, I was glad when they said goodnight and responded stiffly when Suhvanna a bit too affectionately embraced me good night, saying, "Thank you again, Charla. I knew there wouldn't be a problem. Sleep well."

"Very good," Idmon chimed in, "We'll see you at breakfast in the inner courtyard by 9:00." He again kissed my hand and shook hands with Bill.

No sooner were they out the door, than Bill was running the water in the large sunken tub. "I sure hope to hell we can talk Suhvanna out of first rights on this story! My head's starting to hurt. Think we could put business aside?" He asked, taking the time to add the bath salts and bubbles before he stripped. He stepped into the tub, pausing to unzip my black gown before he immersed himself in the warm water. At first I resisted, my mind still on my bargain with Suhvanna; but the rustle of the black silk, as it slid over my shoulders then with a plop dropped on the floor, caught my attention. I snapped back in the moment, grinning at him and agreeing to let it go. Then I carefully stepped out of my black pumps so I wouldn't snag the gown. I waded into the warm water with bubbles bursting all around my thighs and crawled onto Bill's lap.

CHAPTER V: "RACE TO THE AEGEAN"

"By helicopter?" Bill gasped, grinning at the prospect. "Turkey by bird's-eye view? Definitely, Idmon, I'm game." He stood on a ladder and chiselled away at the plaster covering the tapestry that was encased above the library's archway. As I waited, I bit my nails and felt the tension rise. I'd slept restlessly, thinking about my bargain with Suhvanna all night.

But the excitement of seeing the tapestry again pushed away the painful thoughts. Dodging the falling pieces of debris, I decided to just forget about having lost the story and concentrate on saving Athena's tapestry. That's really the issue at hand, I told myself. "Can't you hurry, Bill?" I urgently asked, fighting the creeping suspicion that the tapestry was not safe. A thin bead of sweat on his forehead trickled down his face when he raised his eyebrow as though asking me not to interrupt him. I stepped up on a chair and tried to catch a glimpse of Athena's tapestry through the chipped out holes. It was spectacular.

The diamonds, rubies, and emeralds shone out of the encased darkness like stars. The shining glimmer entered my eyes like guiding lights and caused my heart to catch in my throat, its beauty overcoming me. "Wow!" I exclaimed, "This is a sacred moment." The words seemed to escape from my lips. "But why do I feel like this is history repeating itself?" I careened my neck to get a closer look and felt the excitement overwhelm me. Seeing it again shot nervous energy through me, causing me to peer down the wide hallway and scan the courtyard. I wanted to rush Bill, but resisted. The more I felt the tapestry's presence and its powerful energy coming out of the plaster, the more scared I got that someone would see it.

"Just as I have always said, myth is history. But you see, Charla," Idmon said flatly with no obvious reaction to the emerging treasure. "I now have proof - messages woven deep within the tapestry." He looked up at me as he paused from his chiselling on the bottom of the archway, his intense eyes seeing through me. I quickly glanced away, feeling the same discomfort that I'd experienced at dinner.

"Uh...say, Idmon, isn't Athena's message disturbing to you?" Bill, confronted him, forcing off a big hunk of plaster as I peered in. "After all, wasn't that the original insult? In so many words, didn't Athena accuse the Lydians of incest?"

"Yes, Bill, of course," he said with indignance. "But what else would you have expected of a <u>Greek</u> goddess? Regardless, to have made the Lydians an example of a practice that all the ancient royal families adapted - the hereditary princess - was completely unfair. And let's not forget, even the Greek's deities were products of incest. What a projection! To have accused us of that which they were most guilty is simply unforgivable. How can you not agree?"

"Wel-l-l, Idmon," I carefully chose my words as I got off the chair, met his gaze, and tried not to offend him. "Couldn't the Greeks make the same accusation? The message that Arachne, speaking for the Lydians, wove in her tapestry against the Greek gods is, after all, sodomy. Now, you've got to admit, that's pretty awful. Couldn't the Greeks in self defense, say that was a projection as well?"

His stern look reprimanded me. "Apparently, you don't understand, Charla. Regardless, Look at Athena's torturous treatment of Arachne. After trying to hack her to death, she cut her down and covered her with poisons that shrank and shrivelled her body until it was blackened, dismembered, and grotesquely deformed beyond human recognition. What kind of goddess would have committed such a heinous act? Such injustice?" His voice broke, his emotions obviously involved. Taking a deep breath, he continued, "Then to make matters worse, Athena placed a horrendous curse on her and all her generations. What other creature can you name that is more dreaded or loathed than the spider?"

I wondered if his generation was cursed. But as soon as I thought it, I saw anger streak through his blue eyes as though he had read my mind.

"And all Arachne did was tell the truth. Now you can see why this tapestry is so important to me - it is proof,

proof of the cruel and inhumane treatment to our people in the hands of the Greeks." Idmon quickly retorted.

"But, Idmon, that's just the literal interpreation, the same one that Arachne insisted on that got her killed. Those were divine animals she depicted with the maidens; that union is symbolic as well," I interrupted, but his intense stare made me back off. I jumped back on the chair as Bill began freeing up the frame. Dismissing Idmon's words, I grew more excited by the second. Once again, I was going to have the opportunity to witness the only surviving work of a goddess. In awe and anticipation, I waited.

"Come on, Arachne attacked the Greek's gods. Look at how many people have been brutally murdered in the name of religion?" Bill said sarcastically, rocking the tapestry from side to side in order to maneuver it from its hiding place.

I followed the tapestry's every movement with my eyes. "Careful, oh, careful, Bill," I cautioned, wanting no harm to come to something so precious.

"And do you know how many people have revolted when forced to bend down and obey some foreign deity? Arachne would never have worshipped Athena. She believed in the Mother Goddess just as she and all her generations have," Idmon bluntly informed us, gazing up into my eyes and communicating something to me. All three of us grasped the tapestry and began carefully pulling it out of the archway.

"Just as you do? Is that why you went to the cave?" I asked, already believing I knew the answer, but wanting to hear his exact response. I stepped down, running my hands lovingly along the frame.

"The Mother Goddess shrine has survived four millenium, Charla! It is not just _my_ source of strength and inspiration, but one for the world as well. She was our first form of worship on earth; out of her lap, we are born, we live, and we return when we die. She _is_ Mother Earth. How foolish to worship some invisible god in the heavens and ignore our reverent existence here. We owe her everything, for through her we are promised immortality," Idmon said, with shining eyes.

I couldn't believe he sounded so similar to Dr. Aliamo, but I was distracted from any further comparison by Bill who grabbed the top of the frame and balanced himself precariously on the ladder. Idmon paused as well, grasping the frame as
Bill climbed down the ladder and grabbed the bottom, lowering it to the floor.

"Oh, please, please be careful," I pleaded, excitement and anxiousness growing within. Seeing this rare masterpiece twice seemed impossible. I wanted to cry over being so fortunate. I held my breath as the tapestry settled noisily in the frame; and as Bill pulled it out, it released the same whitish vapor that we had first seen spiral from the amphora, creating the sheen of brilliance and grandeur like thousands of

colors with the richness of the rainbow.
The Tyrian purples, multicolored threads,
and gems again unfolded the story of the
blue, pure waters when they first rushed
rush into the Middle Earth. And the same
council of gods and goddesses presided
over the historic event.

"Oh, my God!" I gasped upon seeing
the regal tapestry and again feeling its
incredible wonder deeply touching me.
There was no doubting its divine truth.

"Unreal!" Bill exclaimed, "What a
miracle! Too beautiful to be real!"

Idmon, however, was very quiet,
studying all four corners where again the
dark, deep rubies and the gold, silver,
and purple threads imprinted the lurking,
dangerous warning of incest. His eyes
locked on pitiful Antigone who weeps and
waits for her death. His eyes darted to
Haemon, who is being killed by his own
father. Idmon looked away when he saw
King Cinyras pitifully crying on the
temple steps, having to pay for his
incestous relationship with his beautiful
daughter.

"Absolutely amazing. Simply divine."
I muttered, shaking my head and becoming
lost in its dazzling beauty and its
prophetic message. My heart poured out to
it.

Idmon, nervously shifting his weight
from one leg to the other, finally opened
his mouth to speak when Suhvanna walked
in behind us from the courtyard.

I wondered how she would react, for
Idmon had told us that she hadn't seen
the tapestry yet. At first, she appeared
to have no reaction to it. I didn't

understand how anyone could see this exquisite masterpiece, this wonder, and not be awed by it. In fact, she treated it like any common weaving.

"This may upset you, Charla, but I have proof that Athena's tapestry was not woven by Athena. Contrary to what you believe, it's not divine." She broke in before Idmon could say a word, just as Bill pried the wooden frame off the tapestry, which collapsed corner by corner into his hands.

I turned on my heels and gaped at Suhvanna, unable to believe my ears. The tension over her getting the story lingered like a coiled snake between us. I tried to ignore it as I responded carefully, "Not Athena's tapestry?! <u>Not</u> hers, Suhvanna? What on earth do you mean?"

She didn't respond, just stood there as Idmon and I stared at her with our eyes open wide. Even Bill, who had been folding the tapestry, stopped and looked at her as though she'd gone crazy.

After what seemed like an interminable time, she finally said, "I will tell you on the way to Kusadasi, but not now." Her hands began to shake as she dartingly looked around her, saying in an emotionally filled voice, "I feel an urgency, a real urgency to leave here as quickly as possible." An obvious change came over her. Her Aegean eyes clouded over.

"<u>We</u>? Suhvanna, you are not well enough to travel," Idmon said.

"Yes, we." She answered with such firm conviction that she silenced him. "I

<u>must</u> go with you. You can't leave me
here. I sense danger, and we must hurry.
Please believe me. We're not safe here."
Again, she jerked her head left and right
and wrung her hands, her eyes now filled
with fear and apprehension.

"I've never questioned your uncanny
ability to predict, Suhvanna, and you've
never said anything with so much
conviction," Idmon said, placing his
hands on her waist and gazing into her
eyes. "But are you sure, and can you
travel?"

Precisely at that moment, the
castle's alarm system went off, blaring
with high pitched intensity. Bill stuffed
the tapestry in the pack with tremendous
thrusts, tied it securely, and threw it
onto his back.

We grabbed our bags which we had
packed and brought to the library with
us, as all the servants came swarming
into the courtyard, shouting excitedly
over the shrill alarm. Several of the
tall, muscular servants came running over
to Idmon who in a calm but authoritative
manner gave orders in Turkish. His square
jaw clenched, causing the wrinkles around
his mouth to deepen; his thick eyebrows
set firmly as his eyes darkened. Then he
was off, and we were right in step behind
him, circling by the dining room and
around to another arched doorway which we
had never seen before, for it was
concealed by a large painting. He pressed
a hidden button, and sliding doors
opened, leading to a secret passageway -
a long, well lit tunnel with a moving
sidewalk. Three of the largest, most

muscular servants accompanied us, taking our bags and running ahead through another arched doorway and another until the last one opened, and they stepped outside. A helicopter was located approximately one hundred feet away from the passageway.

The servants sat down the bags and came back to assist Idmon; he had slowed down to help Suhvanna who was moving along very painfully. Supporting her on either side, they carried her to the outside door where she halted abruptly, the morning sun catching in her silky blond hair and lighting it on fire.

"No, Idmon!" She yelled at him, reached out, and grabbed his arm. "We can't take the helicopter. Please, we must go by car." Drowning out her voice, a loud explosive boom shook the earth as the helicopter burst into a ball of fire and torpedoed fragments of glass and shredded metal into the air.

I screamed as Bill knocked me to the ground and covered me with his body as metal shards, shrapnel, scraps and flying glass spears pelted and tore at our skin. I fell on top of Suhvanna who was crammed up against the outside wall and protected from the burst of debris. My arm wrapped around Idmon's neck, and I could feel warm trickles of blood under my fingers. I jerked my hand away, shaking violently and trying to maintain control. Somehow Bill had swung the pack with the tapestry to his chest, and it weighed solidly on my back as he pressed against me, breathing heavily and cursing. At least it's safe, I thought, then corrected myself, wondering how in the world I could ever consider placing the tapestry before our lives.

Like Bill, Idmon was even madder - vehemently spitting out words in Turkish as his neck stiffened like a bull and his body tightened with such suffocating rage that I thought he would explode next.

"Stay calm everybody," Bill warned, his voice muffled. "Think of the good part - at least we can thank our lucky stars we weren't up in the goddamn helicopter." He swore as Idmon very slowly stood up. "In fact I think we ought to kiss this sweet ground." He continued.

Suddenly Idmon crashed back down on top of us as gunfire opened up just above our heads. Bullets ricochetted off the walls, zinging dangerously close to our ears. I started crying, thinking any moment that I'd be dead and realizing on second thought that the tapestry wasn't really worth that much after all.

"Stay down!" Idmon ordered in his most authoritative voice as we heard another deafening exchange of gunfire. He raised his head and signalled his men; then, sounding like a commander in chief of the armed forces, he ordered us to, "Run for the garage. We'll take the Mercedes, it's already armed."

Hunching over with fear and staying as low as possible, we crawled alongside the castle toward the large multicar garage and scooted inside the dark building as his servants continued firing at someone on the other side of the blackened, smoking helicopter pad. One of

them ran ahead of us with our bags, drove
the Mercedes out of the back of the
garage, threw our luggage in the trunk,
and headed down to the next garage door,
following Idmon's Turkish commands and
breaking into a wide stride like a
commando on the front lines.

Sweat broke out all over me as icy
chills racked my body. I didn't see how
we were going to survive this one. I
looked long and hard at the tapestry,
seriously questioning again why in the
hell we kept risking our lives for it.
But the same reassuring answer came -
don't think, just act.

"What's your intuition on this one,
Suhvanna? Is she gonna blow?" Bill posed,
cautiously eying the idling black
Mercedes as we readied to jump in the
back seat.

Although Idmon was obviously in pain
from the cuts on his neck and back, and
even though his reddened face attested to
his angry preoccupation over losing his
helicopter and being fired at outside his
most private secret entrance, he mused
over Bill's concern, a half smile playing
on his lips as he said,

"Don't worry, Bill. Suhvanna's
intuition is not needed on this one. I've
kept it well locked and guarded since we
arrived. Get in now. My bodyguards will
act as scouts, escorting us through Izmir
and down to Kusadasi. And they will very
soon have dealt with our uninvited
nuisance," he added, glancing back at his
servants who opened fire on the lone
gunman who was trapped up against the
high, barbed wire, outside wall.

Within seconds, the tall assailant's body jerked violently as he held onto the fence and slowly slumped to the ground.

"Why'd you kill him?" Bill asked. "Now we'll never find out who he is or who sent him." He wrapped his arm around me as I hid my face and squelched the nausea in my stomach.

"He's a Greek! Come on now, <u>get</u> <u>in</u>. We'll discuss this in the car," Idmon said as I stood there cringing at the sight of the crumpled figure; I was unable to move or take my eyes off the bleeding body. But I clearly heard Idmon, when he commanded me again to get in the car.

Shaking off the cold shivers that ran up and down my spine, I crawled over the hand guns in the back seat, hoping to hell I wouldn't have to use any of them, but laying one of the smaller ones on the floor close to my foot just in case. Trying to wipe out the image of the dead man and holding my breath, I watched as the servants opened the juxtaposing garage door and started the sleek, black Porsche. The dark skinned, goodlooking driver caught Bill and I staring at him, grinned, and held up a small piece of plastique with a dangling detonator.

"Whew!" Bill blew out his breath as they sped by in front of us.

I didn't look as several servants, who came running out of the secret passageway, surrounded the body which clung to the fence with a death grip. I clamped my eyes shut as Idmon stomped on the accelerator and followed the black Porsche out through the fruit orchards, the vineyards and the manicured gardens where the breezeway cut through to the white gazebo.

The white wicker chairs rocked gently in the morning breeze as I reflected on the previous evening's conversation. I tried clearing out my head. Now I realized why Idmon had been so upset when the microphones were discovered in his home. He knew that security had already been breached and that his sacred hideout was no longer impregnable. His coolness and lack of nervousness in waiting until the next morning, then tediously chiselling out the tapestry amazed me, especially when he must have known that an attack could come at any moment. I was impressed.

Thoughts mulled over and over in my mind as we drove down the long green road to the great iron entrance gate. But Suhvanna puzzled me most. I looked over the seat where she had slumped over, broken looking, her eyes closed, her vibrant energy gone. I thought back to the first moment I met her in the Caravanserai, how her shining energy emanated through her incredible eyes and how she had tried to conceal her shock when I told her that Idmon had the wrong tapestry. She didn't know that. She had never seen it.

We sped out of the gardens.

Or maybe she did, I reasoned, and simply refused to admit the existence of Athena's tapestry. This puzzled me even more - why in the world an educated professional would want to argue whether or not Athena wove her tapestry. I knew

she must have a reason, and I hoped it
wasn't because of her hatred for the
Greeks, and her refusal to believe that
their goddess ever created anything so
important and so long lived.

"So, Idmon, who the hell ordered
this ambush?" Bill questioned, breaking
into my thoughts. "With Norton dead,
who's the head of this operation? Do you
know?" Idmon turned briefly. "One other
question - you seem pretty relaxed. Is
that your usual cool calmness, or are you
just convinced we're out of danger?"

A small smile formed in the corners
of Idmon's lips. "To answer your first
question, no, I don't know," he answered,
"unless, of course, it's the Greeks you
mentioned who were working with Norton.
You see," he paused for a second. "Norton
is the only one I suspect, for he has
been to my home via helicopter from the
ship. He accompanied me when I came here
to hide the tapestry. And, no, Bill, he
did not know it was aboard the
helicopter. No one did - not even
Suhvanna." He looked down at her, lying
on the front seat. Their eyes locked, but
I couldn't decipher their communication.
"As far as my servants go, they are
completely loyal, so to answer your
question honestly - I simply don't know."
He picked up a carphone and began
speaking in Turkish to his men in the
Porsche.

Now I was terribly confused. Suhvanna
had told us at Niobe's rock that she knew
all along that the tapestry was at
Idmon's home and that the wild trip she
took us on to the Manisa Museum was just

to get her to the rock. If Idmon hadn't told anyone, how would she know? Bill tightened his jaw, making it even more chiselled, and grew pensive, trying to put the facts together. I gazed past him, taking a long, lingering look back at the white gazebo and the rocking chairs still swaying in the wind. I thought of Dr. Aliamo and his love for Athena's tapestry. I knew that he'd <u>never</u> agree to Suhvanna's assertion that Athena didn't create the tapestry, and I wondered if this had become a problem between them. I wished I could talk over this troublesome issue with Bill, for I really didn't know what to think of Suhvanna or where she was coming from.

Just whose tapestry did she think it was? I questioned in frustration, not wanting to get involved in such an inane thought, but at the same time having it tantalize me and not understanding why. I nestled closer to Bill as he gazed out across the great estate.

Up ahead the great iron spiked gate rolled open as the armed guards aimed their guns and readied to protect us. Apparently, the attack was over; for we passed through without incident as Idmon slowed to give orders to the dark eyed guard who, in turn, conveyed his message on the microphone to the servants in the castle. Given Idmon's coolness, it seemed that he believed we were past any danger. The long dirt road stretched out ahead through the great river valley. The tall grasses swayed as we sped past the fertile fields and peacefully grazing cattle.

With the tapestry nestled at my feet, I sat back, finally feeling some degree of success and readying for the long trip. Mt. Spieldag's jagged, high peaks seemed to smile down protectively. Without further incident, we sped along in silence, the dust from the Porsche blanketing the fields with its whitish trail.

By the time we reached the main road, I could wait no longer to question Suhvanna. I leaned over the seat and felt a little guilty about disturbing her rest, but I had to know. "Suhvanna, before the alarm went off, you said that this wasn't Athena's tapestry; was it because you wanted to throw the Greeks off the trail? Did you know then that they had broken into the castle and were listening to us?" I asked, leaning back, pausing, waiting patiently for a response, and giving her plenty of time; I knew that this journey was my opportunity to convince her to give up her request for the story and to turn around my mistake that I made at the gazebo in having agreed to give it to her in the first place.

When she didn't respond right away, I pretended to be distracted, helping Idmon search left and right down the lone road before he turned towards Manisa.

As she slowly reared up from the front seat and spun around, I sat up on the edge of the seat; she looked at me as though she were sizing me up, her expression again displaying the strong intellect behind her beauty which could easily intimidate most people. I didn't back down, my face close to hers. Her left eye flinched ever so slightly, and again I detected the glint in her seablue gaze.

"No, Charla, I have very strong intuition. I knew we were unsafe, but I meant what I said about the tapestry not being created by a goddess." She looked at me as though she dared me to dispute her words, but I didn't bat an eyelash. She continued, "It doesn't make it any less valuable, but it simply wasn't created by divine hands," she concluded in the most authoritative voice I'd heard her use.

I knew not to meet her challenge immediately, for my mind churned. Suhvanna was wrong. The tapestry would be less valuable; if its message were not from Athena, then divine interference and, therefore, its forceful truth would be regarded as less important. This was most serious, and Bill, shuffling his knees and sensing what was happening, spoke up first.

"After what I witnessed back at the castle, I'm as convinced as Idmon about your being one psychic woman!" He congratulated her, but I was well aware that his subtle approach had an important question to follow, "Knowing that Athena didn't create this tapestry is not another example of your powers, is it?" Even without words, I knew Bill and I were on the same wavelength. I squeezed his hand.

"Absolutely not," she defended in an irreproachable tone.

"What kind of proof could you possibly have?" I confronted her again, my voice edged with irritation given my reluctance to even ask the question. For some reason, a flickering wave of resistance and frustration flashed through me, pulling up emotions that went far beyond the issue of the story; I fought the anger that rose from the depths and made a strong effort not to get defensive. If Suhvanna was going to make such outrageous statements, she'd have to prove it.

"First of all, Ovid, in borrowing the Lydian myth, never used Athena's name per se." She attempted, sitting up even straighter, but I cut in tersely,

"Of course not. He used Latin."

"That's obvious! Now, may I continue, Charla?" She asked, with a hint of condescendence. I stiffened, wondering if she knew just to whom she was talking. This was my field she was discussing - and I'd researched this myth extensively. I felt my lower lip jut out defensively and I braced myself, feeling offended at being spoken to in such a tone. She kept waiting as though I'd interrupt her. I didn't. "In the earliest surviving manuscripts, the name Pallas is recorded; this name is neither Latin nor Greek. It's Sanskrit, and it's a name for a tree, not a goddess." She looked at me long and hard with her unflinching eyes as though daring me to stop her. But I just glared at her, knowing she was grasping at straw.

"So what?!" I blurted dumbfoundedly, staring at her and not believing my ears.

If Suhvanna was the expert she claimed to be, she'd know that Athena was a collective goddess, with many different names and attributes. How dare she, I thought. How gutsy to try and reinterpret a myth, our oldest, our most revered artifacts, our first literature from our most ancient civilization, our, our...Oh! I felt like stomping my foot and shaking my finger at her. I knew what she was up to - she intended to change the myth for her own self-serving advantage.

Her pursed lips broke into a half sneer as though she knew she had the upper hand and could wield her power over me. "During the attack on Troy, the Greeks stole a sacred wooden statue which the Trojans believed protected their city, and, consequently, once removed, the Greeks were convinced that it brought them victory. It was the Trojan's 'palladium' which, of course, comes from the root word, 'Pallas.' That's as close as the Greeks got to an original meaning of Athena's name." She paused for a moment and took a deep breath, the steel glint persisting in her eyes as she tried nonchalantly looking away at the Hermos River, cutting its course through the fertile fields. Watching the flowing waters with her, it hit me - this was her story. My mouth involuntarily dropped open.

"Later, 'palladium' broadened in its meaing to 'palatine' which referred to anyone, usually of royalty, who was the safeguarder, the protector of order in the palace. So in Manisa, ancient Maeonia, at the time of the weaving contest, Pallas was that authoritative figure, not a goddess, but a young woman just like Arachne, except that Pallas was the daughter of the Greek military leader who had control of Maeonia and who dared to call himself and his daughter royalty." She turned to look at Idmon who returned her gaze with a long stare and a smile of agreement.

"My God, Suhvanna? Do you know what you're implying?" I asked, looking at her in absolute amazement. Something in her eyes gave her away. "What in the hell could possibly be your point?" I demanded, my voice rising as I leaned forward, our faces not inches apart. I refused to back down and so did she. I hardly noticed Bill pulling his hand away from my sweaty grip. "So?" I demanded again when she didn't answer, but just glared me down. "Is that it? Is that <u>all</u> the evidence you have to support such a hair brain idea? You can't publish that!" I yelled.

We crossed over the old river as the tall grasses swooshed, but Suhvanna didn't notice. "You're absolutely right I'm publishing this," she yelled back, not even hearing Idmon when he politely asked her to keep her voice down as he made one call after another on his car phone in an attempt to set up all the contacts and make sure the plan was carried out successfully.

"No, you can't!" I almost screamed, my mind racing along with the river which seemed to gain speed, as one thought led to another. I couldn't let her get away with this. "Listen to me. Do you realize that if you link Athena to Pallas' name, and, therefore, Sanskrit, you're talking pre-Greek? You must tread lightly. Certainly, you don't want to infer that Athena is older than the Greeks. You'd deny them the name of their first city – Athens. All this sensationalism will start the bloodbath between Greece and Turkey all over again. Besides, if you make her origins older, she might even be linked to the Trojans, and, if so, to the Turks. How ironic! But I know what you're up to. You just want another way to gouge the Greeks. This is all about your prejudice, your hatred for the Greeks, and you're manipulating our most ancient histroy, a 4000 year old myth, for your own self-serving ends. This doesn't have anything to do with the truth. This has to do with your ambitions," I confronted her, spewing out the words.

"I agree." Bill spoke up, getting more interested as the tension rose and sitting straight up in the back seat. "If Athena wasn't an original Greek goddess, then where's the claim that the Greeks, via Athena, began the original insult against your people? Get Charla's point?" He nudged the pack as he tried crossing his legs. "Fact or not, it's not as good a story. Then the Turks would have no reason for being involved in this bloody feud. Now would they?" He asked, playing devil's advocate.

"No _excuse_ you mean?" I sat back stiffly and abruptly, catching Idmon's condescending look in the rear view mirror as he paused from his busy phone work.

"And just where did you get that date?" Suhvanna haughtily demanded, "For it is most inaccurate."

"Where else?" I sat back up. "From the <u>real</u> authority - Dr. Aliamo who has <u>real</u> evidence that the contest was held before the earliest recorded volcanic eruption on the Greek island of Thera in 1550B.C.," I said the words with such force and conviction that tiny flecks of spit flew out of my mouth and missed Suhvanna by inches. I wondered if she were indeed going to be so bold and audacious to even think of discrediting such an expert.

"And you believed him?" She asked incredulously. "Even after you found out that he was in love with me?! How naive of you. You are dead wrong. As my advisor, Alexander plagerized my idea - not vice versa. He stole the whole...."

"Now wait a minute," Bill interrupted her, getting annoyed at her addressing Dr. Aliamo in such a disrespectful way. "Dr. Aliamo is not that kind of man."

"We won't discuss exactly what kind of man he truly is - nor will anyone bring up the man's name again in my presence," Idmon commanded us, his face contorted with rage at just the mention of Dr. Aliamo.

"Besides, his is an impossible date. It was after the Trojan War in 1250B.C. that the contest was held and the tapestries were created. You see," she spoke in her grating, authoritative tone. Her eyes flickered their steel flint and her face flushed. "There was a group of soldiers from Thessaly, northern Greece, who aided Agamemnon at Troy, and they wound up with the Trojans' sacred statue; for at the end of the war, these Greeks refused to return to their native country. They knew they'd be forced by Agamemnon to hand the prized statue over. So, they fled, choosing this place as their new home, the richest stronghold in the ancient world," she spouted off so vehemently that she had to take a breath.

"They forcefully took it over and protected their statue with their lives. You see the true character of the Greeks is to kill and die for a wooden statue. Because that's all it was - a wooden statue, not a goddess," she said, spitting out her words as we entered Manisa. "And typically, their most aggressive military leader became their king, and it was the king's daughter who was named the 'palatine' and who was designated as the protector of the palace. A military dictator's daughter, born in Asia Minor and claiming to be a princess."

Her face became even redder, her bruises deeper, and her former beauty dying within her as her hatred filled her face with distortion and darkness. And it tore right through me as though it were a poisoned arrow as she continued. "And when this power wielding, oppressive, and arrogant bitch, who credited herself with being divinely inspired, met Arachne, she killed her; and it was just because Arachne was by far the superior artist and because she refused to worship their stupid wooden statue. Arachne's masterpiece portrayed the real truth about the Greeks. You see, those were the Greek leaders portrayed in her tapestry, calling themselves kings and acting out the roles of the lustiest, most beastial rapists - sodomizers, carefully characterized after the Greeks' most revered gods!"

My mouth hung open as I stared at her with absolute amazement.

"And all Arachne did was weave the truth, for which she was tortured beyond recognition, then hung - not by a goddess but by a jealous, competitive, and spoiled young Greek woman - the daughter of the so called king, using the title 'pallas' to account for her malicious treatment of Arachne who dared to challenge and then create a perfect, flawless tapestry." Her voice rose higher and higher as she spoke, and I thought she was going to faint. But I was so mad at her that I didn't have much sympathy when her face became flushed and her eyes dialated.

Idmon hung up the phone and patted her knee. "Relax, relax. Maybe this should be discussed when you're feeling better, Suhvanna," he told her kindly as he made his way behind the Porsche through the busy streets of Manisa. Heavily scarved women carrying small children displayed broad smiles and waved at Idmon as he wove in and out of traffic.

"That's not the truth! You don't think the Greek men had any concession on rape and sodomy, now do you, Suhvanna?" I screamed at her when several men, shopkeepers with large Turkish rugs displayed on the outside racks and restaurant owners getting up from their sidewalk tables, walked up to the car to greet Idmon.

"Quiet," he insisted, forcing Suhvanna to lie back and rest and staring at me with the most intimidating look in his eyes. Then he addressed the men like a dignitary as they stared at him with wide eyed respect. As we drove away, heading through the narrow streets and down to the turnoff to the highway to Izmir, he demanded of me in a very stern voice, "Please, Charla, if you have no concern for Suhvanna's condition, at least think of the others whose ears you are hurting."

I was infuriated. He was blaming me for all the commotion. The nerve of him. I threw my shoulders against the back of the seat and sat there fuming. Bill reached out, grasped my hand gently, and tried to reassure me, but my palm was still so sweaty that it slipped out of his light hold.

"Never mind," I complained, trying to distract myself and calm down by observing the cliffs that rose higher and higher on either side as we cut through Mt. Spieldag's massive range. The Gediz River Valley rolled peacefully away behind us as we left Manisa and its strategic position at the mouth and narrowest point of the fertile valley where I could still visualize the Mother Goddess, carved out of the massive mountain, and forever its protectorate.

But none of it made me any calmer or happier with the awful situation.

Bill again reached over and grasped my damp hand firmly and securely.

"It <u>was</u> the king's daughter, Charla." Suhvanna said, unable to let go of the subject. She spinned around in a stiff, upright position in her seat again to confront me, her eyes red and bloodshot. "And you've already agreed to give me the story, so let's just drop it. It's mine, and I intend to publish it."

"You're just as bold and audacious as Arachne, and if you're not careful you might wind up the same way," I threatened her to the maximum, having enough of her pushing me around.

"I've had enough of this!" Idmon yelled at both of us, "And if it doesn't cease, it is I who will call off this entire deal. Now QUIET! Both of you." His eyes bulged and his face turned beet red.

"Oh-h!" I gasped as Suhvanna fell back on the seat with Idmon's arm holding her down. Bill stared at me and tightly grasped my hand. After a long time, I was able to let it go. And my breathing finally calmed down as I stared at the high cliffs and closed my eyes.

CHAPTER VI: "VOYAGE ABOARD ARACHNE"

"How much longer?" Bill asked, sounding like he couldn't wait to get out of such an intense, cramped space. We headed down E24 past the turnoff to Colophon. "Never mind," he added, "I see where we are. Your home town, Idmon. By the way, what caused your father's family to leave this area?"

Bill's words awoke me with a start, making me feel agitated; how shallow Bill's question sounded to me when such an important issue concerning the tapestries was still unresolved.

"Business, of course," Idmon answered, sounding equally tense and anxious to talk about something else. "Originally, the Murex snail was used by the original Idmon to make a purple dye called phocis. When the news traveled about ancient Maeonia being the richest valley in the world, he went there to earn his fortune, met Arachne's mother, and wound up dying threads for his daughter's weavings."

"Arachne's mother is not mentioned in the myth," I corrected him, leaning over the front seat to see if Suhvanna were still asleep. She was. I grabbed the opportunity, hoping I could get Idmon to help me force her not to publish such an awful story. "Whose name just wouldn't happen to be Arachne, would it?" I asked leadingly, recalling that on the way to

Pamukkale Suhvanna had told us that the females in Idmon's family were also named Arachne.

"Of course. Why?" He asked suspiciously.

"Idmon?! You already said that you're aware of the royal family's incestuous use of the hereditary princess to preserve the bloodlines. Surely, you...."

"My family is not royalty. Just what are you hinting at?" He curtly asked.

"Perhaps you are not aware of Dr. Aliamo's theory of the incestuous Julian Line in Caesar's family in which he links all the daughters and granddaughters named Julia in the family to the hereditary princess; nor do you seem to know he believes there is a similar Arachnean Line in your family with an hereditary princess always named Arachne. Is there? And if so, just where is your sister, Arachne? Suhvanna told us she escaped from Izmir during...."

The mention of her name caused Suhvanna to bolt upright in the front seat, turn around and glare at me the entire time Idmon spoke.

"I told you not to bring up that man's name again. And as for my family, that is my private business and will not be discussed. Let me make myself perfectly clear - that subject is closed," Idmon swore at me, his forehead wrinkling into a furrowed frown and his piercing eyes staring at me intimidatingly in the mirror.

But I wasn't going to back down this time. I'd had enough of his condescending attitude and his authoritativeness over me. I grew bolder by the moment. "It'll be all our business when Suhvanna's slanted story hits the headlines. Besides, you're getting married and plan to have a baby. Don't you realize that you could pass on the seizures to your children and then...."

"NO! Charla," Suhvanna yelled at me, her husky voice so low that it sounded coarse and grating. She got up on her knees and leaned over the front seat with the most warning, pernicious look in her eyes that now appeared dark and deadly with intent. "It is you who does not know nor want to know the real truth and who blindly chooses to follow the writings of an old, lonely man who cannot face his own failure. You will not throw another of Alexander's theories up in Idmon's face again. Or you will answer to me. The fact that Idmon has chosen to protect his sister and shield her from public viewing is his family's business – not yours. But I can see just how underhanded you truly are. And how ambitious and determined you are to get this story back at any cost."

"Those are all projections – about you. And I can see just how truly far I am from being impeccable or I wouldn't even be in competition with you. Yes, I admit that I assumed I was past competing since I thought I'd learned my lesson from Jane. But your story is sick and it will hurt many people if you publish it – and you don't care who you hurt. But you're wrong about me. And it will be my business and the world's when questions are asked as to whether Idmon stole Athena's tapestry in order to hide the fact that his family seems to have an hereditary princess still in place today. Then who's going to be hurt most? Idmon, that's who!" I yelled back at her, wanting to strangle her for stooping so low. But I was just as determined not to let her get away with it.

"Suhvanna?!" Idmon accusingly addressed her, never hearing a word I said. He stomped on his brakes, almost ramming the Porsche as it slowed for the traffic in Selcuk. "How dare you! You've told them that I've kept my poor, deformed sister from ever being seen by anyone but me and her servant? Did you? Because..."

"Whaat? Your sister's in the castle?" Bill tried to interrupt.

"Because if you have," Idmon paused to acknowledge Bill's question, "then you have also betrayed me and my family's most well guarded secret; I am terribly disappointed in you. How could you have?!" He spoke in a low, hurt tone, signaling his driver in the Porsche, already heading down the bay road to Kusadasi, to pull over. He stopped the car by the Mother Goddess shrine. Slowly he turned, every muscle in his body controlled, and confronted Suhvanna, looking her straight in the eyes.

We all held our breaths, especially me. As much as I wanted Suhvanna to be taught a good lesson, I wouldn't have traded and been in her shoes for anything.

She gulped, sitting back down, stiffening her shoulders, and facing him squarely. She didn't flinch for a second.

"All I told them was that you and your sister escaped Izmir. Nothing more. It's Charla who's made all the suppositions. She's the one to blame. She manipulated you so you'd divulge this information. You are wrong to attack me, Idmon. It is she who is guilty," she pleaded in her even deeper voice as she intertwined her long, coral fingernails around Idmon's silver curls at the nape of his neck. Then she very demurely lay her head on his shoulder, looking up at him with wide-eyed innocence.

I wanted to throw up. I disliked Suhvanna more by the moment and was determined more than ever not to let her get away with her scheme. She was moving in for the kill and was only looking out for number one. Not even Idmon mattered. She'd intentionally divulged his family secret - all for her own selfish ends.

"Well, Idmon?" Bill persisted. "Where is she in the castle? Off another of your hidden passageways?"

Suhvanna whirled around to yell something at Bill when Idmon reached over and firmly placed his hand over her mouth. "Why have you told them? You know that only her servant and I know of her secret chamber. We are the only ones who have laid eyes on her since she was a baby. She can <u>never</u> be exposed, <u>never</u>. Let me make this perfectly clear to all of you." He looked like he was about to have a stroke. Dark blue veins bulged in his forehead. Suhvanna leaned way down in her seat as he vehemently continued. "Let me remind all of you, you too, Suhvanna, that <u>I</u> am running this show. And if any

of you, you included, Suhvanna, do not do
what I say, then this whole escapade is
stopped right now, and the exchange of
the tapestries is off." We all shook our
heads in ready agreement as he started
the car and took off down the bay road.

"Idmon, you want to hide Arachne just
as incest has always been hidden?" I said
even more boldly, grabbing my
opportunity. Suhvanna struggled to get up
on her knees again so she could stop me.
"Don't you realize that for the first
time in thousands of years, people are
willing to discuss the subject of incest
openly? You could be an excellent
statesman for the cause and...."

Suhvanna perched far over the seat.
"You just don't get it, Charla. You won't
back off. Because you refuse to believe
the truth. You and your western world,
being so naive, have adopted the Greeks'
cultural inheritance as part of your own.
What you don't realize is that the Greeks
have always wanted the genocide of my
people. And it goes back thousands of
year. When my people fled their slaughter
in Lydia, settled ancient Italy, and
changed their names to the Etruscans so
they couldn't be traced, the Greeks
formed an alliance with the Romans and
finally did annihilate them. Nothing
remains except their burial chambers.
Then they tried to wipe out all the last
remains of my people in Lydia - in our
own homes on our own land. But they'll
never destroy us. And the world will know
just what true barbarians they really
are. Pallas, whom you call your precious
Athena, wove the message of incest in her

tapestry and then, being so stupid, portrayed Greek fathers raping their own daughters. Because that's just how low they will stoop."

"Suhvanna, those weren't just Greeks in Athena's tapestry. How about King Cinyras? Come on, he's from Cyprus. But what are you saying? That now the Greeks have a concession on incest as well as sodomy? Get off it, Suhvanna. You've gone too far. This is just another example of your poisonous hatred and racism," I shouted. I didn't even care if I got the story or not anymore; all I wanted to do was stop Suhvanna from publishing something so pernicious. "You're determined to gain your own self-serving ends by insisting on a strictly literal interpretation of these tapestries, just like Arachne did." I paused for a moment when she almost came over the front seat at me with fire brimming in her now darkened eyes. Her former beauty was now completely lost and replaced by a brooding, vicious hatred.

"For God's sake, Suhvanna," I yelled as Bill grabbed Suhvanna's hands just before her long nails were inches from my face. But I didn't back down.

"What is wrong with you. You don't think the Greek fathers were the only ones forcing sex on their daughters, do you?! And how can you say that the Greek men were the only leaders who forced sodomy on the women? Are you so blind and prejudiced that all you can think of is condemning just the Greek men? Are you kidding. That treatment of women was widespread all over Asia Minor, the entire Middle East, and the Mediterranean. What about the Turks? Are you honestly going to sit there and tell me that the Turkish men are innocent of the same charges?" I leaned back to avoid her swiping nails that wiggled out of Bill's grasp.

"You're only scratching out your own eyes to spite you own face. I really get it about you. You're so ambition and prejudiced that you consider yourself a Turk before you consider yourself a woman," I spouted at her, determined to make her see what she was doing. I'd had it with those women who wanted to put their nationality, their color, or whatever, above their own sex. "First and foremost, you're a woman - then you're a Turk. And if you don't get this important fact then you'll ruin it for the rest of the women in the world. Those were aggressive acts - the most barbaric. And the women didn't have the choice to say no. They were forced to have sex - in whatever form the men chose. And if you don't change your attitude, and if you publish that story, you'll put women back in those dark, deadly days again. And rape, incest, sodomy, you name it, will again be the lot of women. Don't do it, Suhvanna, stand up first as a woman."

For a moment, she didn't say anything. "Besides, where's your understanding of the figurative meaning of these tapestries. Incest is symbolically the woman's inner marriage to her masculine self which is her source of pure authority. And mating with divine animals symbolically means that women can intimately connect with the potent creative energy within themselves - for the animal is connected to the powerful energy of the subconscious world. Don't you understand symbolism?" But by the resistant, blank look on her face, I knew she didn't. I took a deep breath, ready to wash my hands of the matter.

Just for a moment she hesitated, and I thought she'd at least consider some of what I'd said, but she didn't. "It was the truth about the Greeks - and Arachne wove it in her tapestry. That is <u>all</u> I care about - the truth." She yelled at me, snatching her hand free from Bill's grasp and plopping back down in the front seat as though everything I'd said had gone in one ear and out the other.

"Well shit!" I lamented, determined to have the final word; I was fed up with Suhvanna and her pigheadedness. After the last outburst, a long silence ensued.

We entered the outskirts of Kusadasi where tourists rode bicycles and walked along the narrow bay road, lined by motel after motel.

Trying to ease the tension in the car, Bill made a friendly attempt to turn the energy around and re-establish some harmony between us. "Forget the literal and figurative. Look at it from the superstitious point of view - no one goes out of his way to kill a spider. It's bad luck. Maybe that's why the spider represents the weaver - to remind us to never get entangled in any of its intricate web of meanings. Come on, everybody, lighten up!" And he looked right at me as though reminding me of all the times Jane had said those same haunting words to me.

He struck a vein. "You're right," I said. "To hell with it," and let it go.

Idmon's tight grimace slipped from his drawn lips, and even Suhvanna raised up beside him and briefly, yet affectionately placed her head on his shoulder. She gazed distractedly at the dangling blue eyed pins, sparkling in the sunlight and staring glassily back at her from the gawdy display windows of the souvenir shops that now lined the narrow streets of the busy town.

"Hey, there's a bank, Idmon! Think it's safe enough to stop, so I can unload this pocketful of lira?" Bill asked. "No offense, but I understand foreign banks won't touch it."

Suhvanna sat up straight, exhaling her breath and turning up her nose. "It is <u>Greek</u> banks that refuse our lira. As I explained," she looked over her shoulder at me a little haughtily, "the Greeks want to destroy our country any way they can."

I tried to ignore her, but it was obvious that she wasn't going to let me do that. I figured I'd better just stick to business and not let her distract me. "Me too," I spoke up, sitting up on the edge of the seat and spotting a phone booth. "Do you also think it's safe enough to use the bank's phone over there to contact the SILC Foundation? Mr. Don Meldon, our president, is setting up the arrangements for the exchange of the tapestries, and I'd...."

"Preferably, the location is my choice," Idmon interrupted me, slowing down to pull into the busy bank's parking area. "Instruct your Mr. Meldon that I would like the tapestry exchange to occur in Akrotiri, Santorini in the archaeological excavations. And that I would like international media coverage, and finally -that Suhvanna will emcee the ceremonial occasion," he added authoritatively.

"Aye, aye, Sir!" I tried teasing him. "Got it," and I didn't let on for a second that there was no way in hell that I'd let Suhvanna get away with internationally broadcasting her lies. I jumped out as soon as the car stopped, anxious to get away from her and her tension, but leary of stepping away from the car until the bodyguards in the Porsche stood watching us. Bill grabbed my hand and quickly scooted us through the busy doors. "Here," I told him, unstuffing a huge wad of lira from my wallet.

"Keep your eye on me," I pleaded as I picked up the phone and lost sight of him disappearing in the crowd. As fast as I could, I dealt with the operators, telling them it was an emergency. Finally, I heard Don's deep, warm voice on the other end and almost couldn't talk. I was so choked up. He was so happy to hear from us and to know we were all right. After listening carefully to Idmon's demands, he readily agreed, telling me he'd see us in Santorini, and to be "Very, very, careful." I quickly hung up, looking frantically for Bill amongst the throng of people. Finally, I saw him, running toward me.

"Let's go Greek!" He excitedly told me, handing me a handful of Greek drachmas. "And on that queen of the high seas!" He pointed towards the bay. Even from some distance, we could see Idmon's yacht tied up to the long dock. My breath caught in my throat. Its size was that of an ocean liner, and it couldn't have looked more regal, surrounded by the bright blue Aegean Sea. Never had I seen a ship like this, so big, so sleek, and so unbelievable.

"Wow!" Bill and I both gasped, gawking as we quickly crossed the busy street with Idmon very anxiously urging us to get back in the car as he gave the go ahead to his bodyguards, waiting for us to get in then leading us through the busy streets where the people at the outdoor cafes turned to stare as though we were celebrities.

Bill patted the tapestry affectionately, saying, "I'm protecting this with my life. No one's getting this out of my hands again."

"Don't say that," I said. "Those were Dr. Aliamo's words and...."

"I said, don't bring up that man's name in my presence again," Idmon curtly interrupted me, weaving in and out of the busy, narrow streets leading down to the bay. "And I hope the next thing you will tell me is that all the arrangements are in order, and that your Mr. Meldon will have Arachne's tapestry ready for...."

"Idmon, you know that Dr. Aliamo is bringing the tapestry. He's...."

"He's what?! If he comes, then the
exchange is definitely off. I will not
tolerate that man's presence. I order you
to change those plans immediately."

"Idmon, I will not do so." I
blatantly responded. "Dr. Aliamo has
risked his life to protect these
tapestries, and he deserves to attend
this important meeting. How could you
possibly deny him that opportunity after
he's devoted most of his life to...."

"That is a lie. He was not protecting
them, he was only trying to prevent me
from getting that which was always
rightfully mine and my family's," he
stopped and stared at me for a long time,
apparently not ever having been
confronted so many times by a woman. He
wasn't any less shocked at my growing
boldness than me. Even Suhvanna leaned
over the front seat to observe me for a
second. "I will personally deal with your
precious Dr. Aliamo as soon as we get to
Santorini." He added authoritatively. I
took a deep breath, relieved when he
didn't turn around and go back to the
phone at the bank.

I looked past his clenched jaw and
again out the windshield saw the
incredible yacht that majestically loomed
over the docks and cast its grand shadow
over us as Idmon turned toward the water.
He pointed far out over the blue gulf to
a distant, green island, apparently
dropping the issue of Dr. Aliamo, "Over
there is our main problem. If everything
goes as planned, as it seems to be, and
if any of Norton's Greeks are left to
carry out his plan, then they'll never

make that mile long strait over there to Samos, another of our islands that Greece stole. But when the authorities get through with these thieving Greeks, they'll wish they never thought of trying to steal something from my ship - nor from my country. No one, but no one takes artifacts out of Turkey." He concluded with a calloused smirk.

"My God, what a ship!" Bill kept repeating as he gazed up at the giant yacht.

"Now you must listen very carefully to my instructions," Idmon told us in a very serious tone. "The Greeks are very dangerous - and they're heavily armed, so follow my orders precisely. Charla and Bill, you will first go into my apartment and immediately secure the tapestry in the frame. Then replace it in the archway just as it was in my castle. Quickly, come out into the living room and join us for our bon voyage party and act as though nothing were going on." He went on with several more details to Bill as I thought about the series of events that were about to take place. I realized that we were all going to get separated and that this was the last time I might have to talk with Suhvanna. I didn't want to leave our communication on such a sour note and decided to try and placate her in order to get her back on our side. Regardless of her horrible story, she was a needed ally in order to make sure nothing happened to the tapestry.

She sat up straight in the front seat and turned around and stared at me as though she knew I had something up my sleeve. "You'll never convince me that the Greeks weren't the first sodomizers - Arachne's tapestry proves it otherwise, so don't even think of trying to change my mind again."

"Suhvanna, what's with you and symbolism?" I asked, quickly losing my good intentions and my patience with her. "Are you so literal and attached to the physical world that you're blind? Why hold so tenaciously to one view? How about two? How about if both the literal and figurative meanings are true?" She disinterestingly looked away. "Okay, okay," I quickly added. "But come on, Suhvanna," I made one final plea. "Can't we put it on hold 'till later? And agree to work together right now, so we can all come out of this alive - and save the tapestry from being stolen?"

She lowered her eyelids briefly, then sprang them wide open again, fluttering her long lashes, and saying, "Why, of course, Charla. I've had enough talking about it. But as I said, don't think of changing my mind. It's made up." She looked back at me with a faint glimmer of reconciliation in her sea blue eyes.

I blew out my tense breath as Idmon came to a stop in his parking space some distance from the ship. "Come, the bodyguards will escort us," he instructed us; his voice filled with tension and his eyes darted around the empty lot. The Porsche's driver jumped out and headed for Suhvanna's door as she slid across the seat. As she stepped out, she momentarily lost her balance and was supported by the driver on one side and

Idmon on the other. Idmon instructed the other guard to stand beside me as Bill helped me out, securing the tapestry as tightly as possible to his chest and wrapping his other arm protectively around me. We walked as fast as we could behind Idmon who constantly called out instructions to everyone. White uniformed servants came running from the huge ship to gather our bags. It loomed high above us as we hurried toward its safe entrance.

Idmon waved to the armed, uniformed port authorities who smiled and waved back as we stood waiting to climb up the teak stairs to the ship.

Even though the tension created an abundance of stress, I couldn't resist observing the gigantic ship, its dizzying four levels and various sub-levels reached by sweeping stairways in two-story entrances. I couldn't believe all the guards standing at all the levels, watching our every move. Their tense forms seemed oddly placed among the opulent displays of crystal columns, glass elevators, and the shining presence of marble, lapis lazuli and gold.

"Holy cow!" Bill gasped, also gaping in utter awe at such luxury.

But I quickly riveted my eyes back on Idmon whose piercing eyes searched the huge ship from end to end while his bodyguards moved ahead of him, checking around every corner and making contact with the personnel who poured from every nook and cranny of the sleek ship. The captain came down the elevator and greeted him, then began giving orders in

Turkish to his crew. Then, in a flash, we all moved like a tight circle toward the elevator which we took up to the top deck; we hurriedly passed brightly varnished teak decks where guards watched our journey past the luxurious replicas from his castle – the main salon, the bar, the dining room and lounges, and finally Idmon's apartment.

I took a deep breath and tried to release some of the stress. It felt like a bomb ready to go off. I could just smell the tension as we stepped out into an even more posh environment, with Idmon directing us toward the archways of his living room and pointed down the hallway toward the archway to his bedroom suite.

"Quickly," Idmon broke the silence as we crossed through the plushly carpeted entryway, his voice edged with nervousness. "Bill, Charla. You'll find the frame inside the master closet which is aligned with the archway leading into the entertainment room. Inside the closet is a crate with the frame. Move as fast as you can to get the tapestry inserted, sealed and ready for plastering. Plaster it as perfectly as the archway over the library at the castle then hurry back to join us here." He paused, turned and looked carefully around the ship as we stood in anticipation, waiting for his next instruction. He stood very erectly, flexing his chest muscles under his blue blazer. "For the final part of this plan, I've decided, rather than lock this other pack in the safe," he removed the pack containing the artifact, "to instead strategically place it on the table for easy lift-off for our soon to be arrested predators." His eyes gleamed with a different sparkle which I'd never seen before. I wondered if it was his anticipation of revenge. "This is it," he proudly announced. "Charla, if you can assist Bill, and, Suhvanna, please lie down over here on the couch. Rest assured, my friends, this will succeed. Now come, let's proceed with haste." All his previous nervousness was gone and again he was as calm as when we left the castle. He again showed us the way down the streaked oak and teak hallway toward the entrance to his bedroom before he went back to assist Suhvanna over to the grand, white leather sectional, decked with brightly colored cushions, which all the rushing servants fluffed and placed around her.

"Come on, Charla," Bill said excitedly, grabbing my hand and heading for the archway to the master suite. "We've got a tapestry to save."

"How can you be so excited over something so scary. Those Greeks will blow us away in a flash for this tapestry," I glanced back to make sure the bodyguards stood at all the entrances. "This is horribly tense," I said, trying to stop my hands from shaking. "And how could Idmon be so calm? And why is this going so easy? Where are the Greeks? I don't get it. What's going on?"

"Don't question, just act," Bill said, hauling us toward the master closet next to the archway where the crate was stored. "We're on a mission! Come on,

Honey, don't doubt us now. Just help me with this," he told me, grunting as he picked up the heavy crate. "Keep your faith. Very shortly here, this swanky ship will be swarming with the port authorities and the military police just itching to fill up their Turkish prisons. Just as soon as we get this in the frame, that is."

"You're right," I quickly agreed, getting to work and trying to stay busy so I couldn't think about having my head blown off at any second. I pulled out the stepladder and grabbed the pack off Bill's back.

"Well, of course, I'm right," he teased. "Just don't think about it. Picture a shield around your body and believe that it will protect you," he spoke in a calm, yet hypnotic tone, instructing me to take deep breaths and blow them out quickly. Meanwhile, he roughly forced the frame out of the crate.

I did what he said, making a protective mental shield around the tapestry as I picked up the pack and held it in my arms lovingly, saying, "Oh, please keep this safe," unzipping the pack and carefully pulling out the tapestry.

The same whitish vapor of dust mingled with gold, silver and jeweled colored threads of light wisked out of the pack as it unfolded corner by corner into Bill's awaiting hands. It again made me catch my breath in reverence over its precious, brilliant beauty. Gently, we fit it into the frame. Trying not to put

fingerprints on the delicate material, we
gingerly maneuvered it as we sealed it in
the frame. Bill climbed the ladder as we
lifted it up, carefully placing it into
the niche in the archway. With both legs
in a firm stance, I braced the frame
above my head as Bill's hands swiftly
applied the plaster which spattered down
my khaki shorts and brown leather shoes.

"Hey, be careful," I said when a
slight tremor, lightly rocked the ship.
It started in my legs, ran up through my
body and caused my hands to shake. The
frame vibrated.

"Hold it steady," Bill said.

"I'm trying to. Didn't you feel that?
Something made my legs shake." No sooner
were the words out than there was another
jolt, as slight as the previous one.
"There - did you feel it that time?" I
asked as Bill kept going back over the
unleveled plaster and smoothing it out.

"Honey, pleease, hold it still," he
said when a third vibration ran through
the ship.

"There, you had to have felt that
one," I said, again trying to keep my
hands from shaking. "The water's very
calm. What could be causing that?" I
nervously asked, looking back down the
dark hallway, but I could see nothing,
only shadows that I kept swearing were
moving. My head swung left and right,
searching everywhere for someone to rush
out and point a gun directly at my head.

"There," Bill said after an endless,
unsettling silence. "No one will ever
know it's there." He beamed over his
success, hid the tools and supplies back

in the crate, stored it in the same spot in the closet, grabbed my hand, and pulled me forward with incredible speed and strength, adding, "Let's leave no evidence," and leading us full speed through the bedroom, around the huge kingsize water bed, and past the double closets and dual marble baths.

"Wait a minute," I said, tugging on Bill's hand and forcing him to come to a stop so suddenly that I ploughed into him. "Look at my shoes." And I turned back down the hallway toward the bath. I stepped into its lavishly decorated gold, marble, and crystal bathing area with a large sunken tub just like the one at the castle. I grabbed a hand towel and wiped off the chaulky plaster.

"Hurry," Bill hissed outside the door, impatient to get away from the tapestry. I was hardly out the door when he again grabbed my hand and ran down the long hallway and around the corner into the living room where Idmon, upon seeing us coming, rose and offered his hand to Suhvanna, saying more calmly than ever,

"Come, My Dear, you must be starving. Lunch is served."

Bill and I looked to the left. What should have been a romantic setting for two was ready for four with the finest china, silver, and crystal. A white clad steward stood behind each chair, appearing eager to serve us.

As soon as I smelled the delicious food, I felt the hunger pangs, but my stomach felt too nervous to even consider eating.

"Oh good, I'm starved," Bill said, ready to relax.

"Everything is going as planned," Idmon assured us as we crossed through the long living room. "Sorry I couldn't join you, so much to do, you know. And Suhvanna needed my attention. Everything is in order, I presume?" He asked as though he knew the answer.

Suhvanna smiled at me, as though she'd dropped all her former hostility. She also acted as calm as could be which again made me wonder what the hell was going on. Why had Suhvanna changed so? I questioned, the tension slicing through me. How could everyone be so at ease when a bomb was about to explode.

"What are the Greeks waiting for? And what the hell is going on?" I whispered in Bill's ear as we crossed the living room and neared the table.

"Keep your shield around you; nothing is supposed to happen to us," he whispered back, reaching for my chair; but the steward stopped him and pulled it out instead; then he pulled out the tapestried armchair next to me for Bill who reached over and squeezed my hand and looked at me as though reassuring me that everything was going to be just fine. It didn't help. The ball of nerves tightened in my stomach, not even dispersing when I sipped the cool dry wine or sampled the caviar. In fact, it didn't go away the entire meal, and I could hardly eat even small bites of the bright green salad, or the wrapped vine leaves, or the delicious shishkebobs. My eyes were constantly checking out what might be lurking behind the crystal columns or just on the other side of the colorfully splashed mural, running the length of the long dining room.

But, except for the stewards, coming and going from the galley, and the idle, forced chatter of stiff conversation, with our eyes saying much more than our words, we dined without incident.

However, my nervousness never subsided; and as I rose along with Bill, I caught my napkin and pulled a half glass of wine into my lap. "Oh, shit," I cursed, then whispered to Bill; "First plaster, now wine. I hope everything getting dumped on me isn't symbolic." The stewards rushed to assist me, leading me into the dining room head where I again wiped off my shorts with a towel. This is getting to be too much of a habit for comfort, I thought. Squelching a streak of fear that suddenly raced up my spine, I foced myself out the door. Everyone was gone from the dining table, even the servants. Something wasn't right, and I slowed almost to a stop as I turned the corner into the living room.

Then I knew why. As I rounded the corner, I bumped headlong into Bill, standing stiff as a board and waiting for me. I stopped dead in my tracks.

The blood drained from my face as though I'd seen a ghost, for there was no mistaking the tall, blond, well built figure, even from behind. It was Norton - come back from the dead.

His macho straddle gave him away as he stood facing Idmon and Suhvanna, who sat on the white, pillowed sectional. The deadly stranger reached forward with long, muscular outstretched arms and extended his gun's silencer to within a few feet of Idmon's head.

My body turned ice cold as my mouth dropped open. In the entryway, Idmon's bodyguards, the captain, the chef, and all the stewards were tied up and bound on the floor, their eyes filled with failure and remorse. Above them, thick necked and broad shouldered men with dark, curly hair stood at attention – their submachine guns pointed directly at me and Bill. A chill racked my body, and I froze like an icicle.

"Oops!" Bill muttered under his breath. "Impasse at O.K. Corral, is it?'

The Greek gunners' fingers itchily wrapped around the black triggers.

"This is no time for jokes, Bill." I said, my voice trembling. "Where in God's name did he come from?"

"To hell and back." Bill whispered. "There's no stopping him now."

"And just where are all those port authorites and military police like you said?" I asked, panic stricken and scared out of my mind as I lost all hope.

Suhvanna's face paled then drained and turned ashen white as she stared at Norton who spun his tall frame on his heels, locked his cold, murderous eyes on me, and sneered haughtily, "So-o. We meet again." Cuts and scrapes covered his body and bruises darkened his face which still had the mark where Bill jabbed him with the file. "Only this time, I'm taking what is mine. MINE! You really thought you'd get away with it, didn't you. But

I'm the one who wins here; and if you don't stay out of my way I'll finish the job on you, Charla, that I started in Rome and then..." A tremor crossed his thin lips as he boastfully held the pack, the fake pack that Idmon had brought for a decoy, high over his head. "Tie 'em up." He commanded.

"You bastard," Bill swore and lunged forward. But I stuck out my foot and tripped him, knowing that if I didn't stop Bill that Norton would kill him in a flash.

"Ugh!" Bill groaned, landing flat on his stomach and looking up at me as though I'd lost my mind. "Charla? What the hell did you do that for?"

"Bright as ever, I see." Norton sarcastically snarled. "I always said I loved an intelligent woman; and as I told you before, you're not the fish that got away. Not yet anyway," he threatened me as his armed guards surrounded Bill, their barrels provocatively tapping his head.

"Now sit down, Charla, over here – with your newly found slut friend and her old Midas sugar daddy," he scorned, grabbing me by the hair and swinging me across the room.

As though struggling against chains, Bill thrust and squirmed violently, reaching out and grabbing Norton's leg.

"You stupid jackass! First, you jab me with a file then leave me for dead." He maliciously yelled, pulling back his black boot and kicking Bill viciously over and over and over in the stomach until blood started coming out of his mouth. I thought Norton was going to kill him. Bill groaned in agony as he clutched his stomach and bent over in excruciating pain.

I wanted to strangle Norton with my bare hands. I jumped up, but Norton shoved me back down with all his strength. I landed on Suhvanna who grunted and tried moving out from under me.

"Yeah, you'd better stand in front of her. Fucking whore tried to kill me. You double crossing slut - guess you didn't tell them the whole story about our little planned car ride from Pamukkale, did you?" He yelled at her.

My mouth dropped open in disbelief over the horrible scene having been staged. I quickly looked at Idmon. He had no reaction, which shocked me further.

"You would've killed me - you almost did," she hatefully hissed at Norton which made me wonder if I should continue shielding her from him. I was in the line of fire; for by the murderous intent in his eyes, it was obvious he'd kill her in a flash. Against my better judgment, I didn't move.

Even with all the pain Bill was in, he waved his hand for me to get out of the way; however, it was too late. Fire almost brimmed out of Norton's eyes as he stepped closer, and he was cursing both me and Suhvanna with such venomous words and spewing such threats at us that his spit spattered on my face.

"No, Suhvanna. Shut up." I cupped my hands and whispered in her ear so Norton couldn't hear me. "You'll get us both killed."

"You haven't gotten what you deserve yet. Don't push me, you slut. You'll never have any better than me," he spouted off, lunging forward, knocking me out of the way but not before his black boots kicked me in the shins; then he grabbed Suhvanna, slapped her and roughly slung her at Idmon's feet.

She guiltily glanced up at Idmon whose face now turned blood red then ashen white as he questioned what she'd done; his eyes simultaneously filled with suffering, sadness and surprise over her betrayal.

In pain, I grabbed my leg, but somehow managed to awkwardly roll back over in between Norton and Suhvanna so that he couldn't get at her so easily; for now it was obvious that if she said anything else, he would indeed kill her. While I still had mixed emotions about her, I certainly didn't want her dead.

Her legs shook with rage - mine with fear as Norton glared at me confrontatively, his cold blue stare chilling me to my toes.

With a glint in his eyes and a sneer on his thin lips, he stepped back to his straddled position. "You're too worthless to kill," he screamed at her, grasping the pack securely under his arm as though he were getting ready to leave. "You double crossing whore." He spit at her, his spittle landing on my chin which I was sure turned my jaw a sick shade of yellow. I quickly rubbed it off on my shoulder.

"Why don't you tell them the truth,
you two-timing bitch," he cursed, trying
to come at her again. "Why don't you tell
them now how we had this whole thing
planned - how we were going to sell the
tapestry and retire on an Aegean island?
Tell your old sugar daddy how you really
feel about him, how he turns your stomach
and makes your skin crawl every time his
hands touch you. Now I wouldn't have you,
you slut," and he reached around me,
grabbed her face, shoved it into Idmon's
crotch and laughed heinously. "All the
money will be mine. All of it!"

My eyes must have resembled poisonous
darts and my hands daggers as I spread my
arms around Suhvanna and protected her
from Norton, but he just sneered at me,
furious that he'd been wrong about my
intelligence; he slapped me across the
face and scorned me for being so stupid,
snickered contemptuously, spun on his
heels and directed his men to head for
the elevator.

I saw red, his slap making me so
angry I could cry. I'd had enough of him
pushing his weight around and acting like
such a bully. It felt like steam came out
of my ears as I got up on my knees. My
face stung from his heavy hand and my
shins ached from his vicious kick, but I
could have cared less.

Despite the agony he was in, Bill had
somehow managed to crawl closer to me and
when I lunged forward, he grabbed me, put
his hand over my mouth, and held me back.
Mumbling curse words of rage, hatred, and
contempt, I struggled to get free, as
Norton and his men step by step backed

away, aimed their guns at our heads the entire time, got in the glass elevator, and started down. I finally struggled out of his grasp and bolted for the elevator.

"Go get him," I screamed at Idmon, who sat idly listless on the couch, his face still contorted in pain over what Suhvanna had done. Nor could I get a reaction from her. Doing everything she could to placate him, whispering continuous apologies and vows of her love for him, she soothed and stroked him.

"Idmon, DO SOMETHING!" I screamed at him again, totally annoyed that he could be so preoccupied while Norton was getting away.

"Charla, relax," he finally said to me when I got right up in his face. "Everything is taken care of; my plan is foolproof, well...almost everything is taken care of," he sadly informed me, still glancing pitiously into Suhvanna's pleading eyes, darkened from being slapped so many times by Norton.

I stared at him in amazement. He was placing his relationship with Suhvanna above everything, even catching such a villain. And I knew he was going to take her back - that wasn't the issue. I was furious with both of them.

I ran back over to the elevator, and in slow motion watched as Norton and his men poured out onto the next deck, just behind the captain's bridge.

"Stop them," I yelled at the top of my lungs as they took the winding stairs down to the main deck where a speedboat was tied just off the aft port deck. Then I realized that no one was chasing them -

no port authorities and no military
police. They were going to escape. I
whirled around, but Idmon was still
sitting there with Suhvanna begging him
for forgiveness. Deciding they were
hopeless, I crossed the room in one
stride over to the corner where I untied
the bodyguards and the captain who in
turn assisted the stewards; then he began
shouting commands in Turkish to them. I
ran back over to the glass doors as the
captain and a few stewards piled into the
elevator while the bodyguards broke and
ran down the winding staircase to the
main deck.

While I knew Bill needed attention,
I was so intent and excited that I barely
had time to kneel down to make sure he
was okay. Then I was on my feet again,
glancing aft and seeing one of Norton's
men jump in the boat and begin to untie
it from the back of the ship. I knew that
if the port authorities didn't appear in
seconds that Norton would indeed escape.
Nausea overwhelmed me at just the thought
that someone so contemptuous could get
away. Even the artifact that Idmon used
in place of the tapestry was extremely
valuable and would bring him hundreds of
thousands of dollars.

"Bang! Bang!" The shots rang out as
Idmon's bodyguards opened fire from
behind the captain's bridge, striking one
of Norton's men who grabbed his chest,
stumbled toward the back of the deck and
fell headlong, far down into the water.
Bullets ricochetted off the ship as the
crystal columns shattered. Submachine gun
fire deafened the area as it hit the

marble and blond walls. Blood covered the area as one of Idmon's bodyguards fell with a thud, after being struck in the head. I closed my eyes, knowing he was dead when the blood spurted everywhere. I was even angrier when I saw Norton's blond head bobbing in and out as I watched him flee across the teak decks. He was within five feet of the aft stairs.

All I could visualize was his escaping, getting to Samos, realizing we'd duped him, chasing us down on the high seas, and making off with Athena's tapestry, but not before he'd systematically murdered us one by one in cold blood. "IDMON!" I screamed out of my mind while he just sat there totally wrapped up with Suhvanna who rubbed his back and continued her cries for forgiveness. I was so upset that, when he didn't move, I decided to take action myself, running over to the middle of the living room and demanding a gun.

"No, Charla," Bill demanded in a low growl, barely able to speak. "Don't go out there. You'll be killed," and he struggled to stop me, but I was too fast. I grabbed a gun, darted around him and headed for the winding staircase.

"Stop her," Idmon yelled authoritatively, finally realizing that I meant business; but his men had all scattered down the stairs, even the stewards and other servants. Norton's men again opened fire on Idmon's bodyguards, then mowed down two of the white clad stewards who gawked from the captain's bridge. Glass shattered everywhere. The gunfire roared, droning out Idmon's protesting commands as I took off behind a couple of servants; I hugged the stairs and crawled down a few of them on my hands and knees as bullets flew over my head.

Finally, finding a safe vantage point on the next level, I peered expectantly from the main salon. I saw Norton jump in his boat with his men right behind him and Idmon's bodyguards right behind them; then Norton and his men unexpectantly stopped and fired on the bodyguards who were caught out in the open on the aft deck. I closed my eyes as one of them collapsed, puddles of blood spreading all around them. Flashing my eyes back open again, I raised the gun, pulled back the trigger, and fired directly at Norton. I missed, but it took him so off guard that he quickly looked up at the main salon and ordered his men to open fire. Crashing to the floor with a thud, I flattened my body as glass chards flew everywhere, the back panels bursting into thousands of fragments.

When I slowly reared my head, I saw Norton's speedboat pulling away from the end of the ship, then head out into the open waters for Samos. My heart fell, but I was so angry at his escaping that I again opened fire, unloading every bullet in the gun. And with every shot, I recalled every horrible thing he'd done to me and prayed that a bullet would stop him. It didn't. Completely distraught, I dragged myself over to the stairs, walked out to the aft deck, and watched despondently as Norton's blond hair began to blend with the sun's rays, farther and farther out in the blue Gulf. Angry tears welled in my eyes.

Then, suddenly from nowhere, armed guards in military boats at lightening speed raced behind them, aiming barrel after barrel of black submachine guns at Norton's head; using megaphones, they commanded him to halt or they'd open fire. Excited and feeling the satisfaction of revenge race through me, I watched as ten or more boats with more than fifty soldiers joined the race after Norton. They were going to catch him.

I fell to my knees and wept. Tears of joy, relief, revenge, every emotion both negative and positive came pouring out of me, for I realized that finally this long ordeal was almost over. And once Norton was taken care of, it was for sure over. Those Turkish port authorities might as well have been riding white stallions, for in my mind they were my knights in shining armor.

But none of it eased the horror in my mind as I looked over all the dead bodies lying all around Idmon's white ship, their blood streaming everywhere. Dozens of white clad servants rushed from all over the huge ship to take care of them and to mop up the blood. I clenched my eyes tightly shut, trying to remove all the horrible images, but realizing that I wasn't going to ever forget it. In that instant, I felt deep remorse that I'd ever gotten involved with the tapestries. With bitter sweet, mixed emotions, I continued to watch as Norton was moments from being caught. The port authorities' voices blared over the megaphones in Turkish, apparently ordering them to drop their weapons, for they overtook and surrounded Norton without a shot being exchanged.

"Coward!" I screamed at him when his hands reached for the sky. I peered into the blue haze, attempting to see the handcuffs clamp down securely. Then, for what seemed an eternity, I stared far off in the misty water as the Turkish boat hauled the long speedboat behind it into the harbor. Blowing out all the tension and trying to pull myself together, I finally rose and slowly, very slowly walked back up the winding staircase to the top deck.

Bill couldn't have been more relieved when he saw me. But he didn't scold me for long when I ran over and took his head in my hands, kissing him and asking if he was all right.

"Charla, I assured you it was a perfect plan," Idmon almost bragged. "I am just so sorry that it may cost me dearly; I have lost a few of my employees, but at least we are all alive," he added, sadly watching as the final men were removed on stretchers. "And I have been told that only a few are critical." He stood at the window and motioned for us to join him. The authorities had just reached the wharf and were disappearing with Norton and his hired hands. As Norton walked down the long dock, he never gave us the satisfaction of looking back – not even once.

"I've got to hand it to you, Idmon. As frustrated and angry as I was at you for not taking action, I still can't believe you could have been so calm. I guess you really believed in your plan," I said. "Congratulations." I turned toward Suhvanna, asking her, "But tell me, how the hell did Norton survive? I know you shot him out there on the mountain." I said more than asked as the three of us stood staring transfixed at the empty wharf. "It's as though he truly came back from the dead."

Idmon and Suhvanna exchanged a most unusual, yet telling look. They had obviously come to some kind of terms about her betrayal.

"Pretty damn deadly boot he's got," Bill swore, hugging me and making sure I was all right. He apparently wasn't even concerned about himself, but he rubbed his stomach the entire time. "Sure this charge will hold for this asshole?" He wanted to know. "Because if it doesn't, I've got a few punches signed, sealed and delivered for him."

"It's completely foolproof," Idmon responded. "Nobody, but nobody today tries to leave Turkey with an artifact. And, trust me, I chose a valuable treasure - one that will put Norton in a Turkish prison for the rest of his life."

"Where I hope he rots," Suhvanna swore. "I hope he...."

Idmon cut her off, staring at her as though he were waiting for her to tell us something. She couldn't even look at us, lowering her guilt ridden eyes and muttering under her breath, "Idmon is right. I have made the most serious error of my life. Idmon has agreed to forgive me; and I must ask with all sincerity that somehow you find it in your hearts to understand why I could have acted so selfishly and with so little regard for what's really important." She bent her head as Idmon patted her hand.

I couldn't believe this was Suhvanna speaking. Something was wrong. She couldn't have changed that fast. Somehow I knew that this was exactly where Idmon wanted her, that somehow he'd known about her betrayal all along, and that the reason he hadn't stopped her was because he knew he'd have her indebted to him – and in his control. But I couldn't see how Suhvanna could play that role for long.

"Well now that you know what's important, I'm certainly ready to forgive and forget," I told her, knowing that the threat of her publishing her awful story had just weakened significantly and hoping I could hold her to her new resolution.

Bill also readily accepted her apology.

"Okay, okay, I'll call my stewards to bring on the champagne, and as soon as I can find the captain, we'll be underway," Idmon announced. "Let's not forget," he added; "we too are in danger of absconding with the most valuable artifact in all of Turkey."

"In all the world," I elatedly agreed, trying to ignore Suhvanna's glum guiltiness. "Listen, Suhvanna, Norton's

first impression fooled a lot of people,
so don't take it too harshly. As Idmon
said, at least we're all alive," I said.

As the huge ship silently started
and pulled away from the Kusadasi dock, I
stood wrapped in Bill's arms and stared
back at Turkey blending with the blue
Aegean. Thoughts of the mysterious land
rolled through my mind like the
undulating waves washing upon the ancient
coast.

CHAPTER VII: "VISIT TO LOST ATLANTIS"

"See what I mean about getting involved with these tapestries? I got punched in the ribs, had the breath knocked out of me," Bill said, pausing to rub his stomach, "chased from one end of Turkey to the other, gunned down, and almost blown to bits by bombs, now that's what I call exciting...."

"And successful, don't forget," I reminded him of the most important part of the mission - saving the tapestries. I took a deep breath. I'd had enough adventure for a while, I thought, ready for some luxury as I leaned back in the lounge chair and sipped the very best tasting, most expensive champagne. Once out of the gulf and past Samos, the vast Aegean's blue wonder opened before us.

Bill scooted his chair closer and grasped my hand affectionately, love shining in his eyes. The champagne's effervescent bubbles burst lightly against his glass as he toasted, "You're absolutely right - to us and to our success!"

"But how about other losses? Invaded privacy...destroyed property; I could go on," Idmon offered a little defensively, walking over from the bar. As he and Suhvanna joined us in the adjacent lounges, I observed how handsome and relaxed he appeared. He wrapped his arm possessively around Suhvanna who in her

newly acquired subdued, humble way was so
subservient to Idmon's every wish that I
wondered if something were wrong with
her. Their relationship had really taken
a switch, and Idmon loved every minute of
it. "But let's not forget the most
important part of this whole ordeal - we
have all survived," Idmon said, proposing
another toast as our glasses all clinked.

"Some survival," Suhvanna quipped,
sitting up in her lounge chair and
wiggling out of Idmon's hold. "While I
realize that I brought it all on myself,
you can't imagine how it feels to have
been treated so contemptuously," she
said, her husky voice lower than ever.
Her dimmed eyes and her faded beauty made
me almost feel sorry for her. Even her
tanned complexion was discolored by all
the bruises which added a yellowish tint
to her skin. I questioned if somehow her
spirt were dampened by all that she'd
been through regardless if she brought it
on herself or not. She stared right back
at me as though reliving the horror of
her moments with Norton who had
apparently carried out his part a bit too
believably. However, there was a hardness
in her that still made me uneasy.

"Too much compromise?" I asked her in
real sincerity, noticing how the wind
stirred the colorful pots of petunias
surrounding us and lilted Suhvanna's
blond silky strands around her shoulders.

I must have struck a nerve, for she
coldly stared at me. "Let's not get
confused, Charla. I have compromised only
my ethics, not my determination to place
my country in its previous, prestigous

position as the birthplace of the earth's first civilization - and with Troy its capitol. Turkey is the most ancient culture and the richest, not only in your American dollars, but also a cultural wealth contained within the folds of the yet to be discovered earth mounds which have not been destroyed by your technology and so called progress. Just look at how your top archaeologists have flocked to my country - all to exploit it and say that they discovered what we Turks know has just been waiting to be uncovered." She paused, a low simmering light growing in her faded eyes.

"Doesn't the word impeccable mean anything to you, Suhvanna? Come on, if you compromise your ethics, what else is left? Let's not disguise ambition by putting on a new mask called nationalism," I quickly told her, realizing that perhaps she wasn't as beaten as I'd assumed. I detected in her gaze, no longer concealed, her old, still faint, yet fiery glow beginning to surface from the depths of her eyes. Oh, no, I thought, what was it going to take for her to finally get it? Would she ever back off? I decided to try reasoning with her.

"Besides, Suhvanna, you can't retake Troy - it is in complete ruins and has been for thousands of years. Can't you let it and all the great people who died there rest in peace? I know you realize that history is repeating itself with the reappearance of the tapestries, so why not use it to the good of all? End this old enmity with Greece. If you

publish that awful story, you'll start
the ancient war all over again. Can't you
see that?" I felt like sitting on her,
for I could tell by the way she just
stared me down that this was an old
rehashing of a worn out subject for her
and that there was no convincing her of
anything.   The   hard   glint   again
reappeared in her eyes along with her
stubbornness. "How can you justify that?"
I point-blank asked her.

She couldn't. She just turned toward
Idmon   and   Bill   who   were   patiently
listening to our conversation and waiting
for a moment to break in.

"Come on, you guys, the worst is
over," Bill said, clinking his glass to
mine. "Let's celebrate our success."

"No, the worst is not over and won't
be until we have traded the tapestries
and Arachne's tapestry is securely placed
in the Manisa Museum," Idmon added.

An unsettling quiet ensued, and I
could   feel   Suhvanna's   tense   energy
rekindling when she started staring at me
again. I braced myself. "You are wrong,
Charla," she finally spoke. "Troy has
been retaken nine times already and with
each devastating act of destruction, it
rekindled with greater fire. Now rebirth
comes to all of Turkey - with the
tapestries as proof of how the Greeks
have stolen everything from us. It is
time the world knows how they have raped
my country." She paused, only to gather
steam. A light shone in her eyes that
resembled that of the most fierce
fanatic.

"You can't publish that, Suhvanna!" I shouted at the top of my lungs. But I realized it was hopeless and just plugged my ears as she ranted on. It was hard to tune her out, but I finally had to come to terms with the fact that I'd have to turn her over to Dr. Aliamo. Maybe he could handle her. I couldn't, or, at least, I chose not to. Trying to completely ignore her when she paused to take another deep breath and apparently continue on, I excused myself, stood up, and sat down beside Bill in his plush lounge chair. It caught him so off guard that he opened his arms wide and gave me a big hug. It felt so good that I felt my whole body sigh with relief then almost wilt with exhaustion. I didn't even hear Suhvanna as she continued her fiery rampage, having completely captured Idmon's ear.

"You are so beautiful, my Darling - so much fire and energy. How you uplift me," Idmon announced, proposing another toast to, "My soon to be bride...my queen...and the soon to be mother of our own little Arachne." He beamed as Bill and I snuggled back in the chair and watched them, his doting making me feel ill.

"Arachne! Never! Idmon," Suhvanna retorted, distracted by his interruption. "How can you even consider naming our child Arachne? No, it must be Niobe. There's no taint whatsoever to her name!"

"No taint?" Idmon huffed, jutting out his jaw.

"Just think about it, Idmon. Then she'd be true royalty, named after a

queen and of royal blood. Plus, wouldn't
Arachne be pleased if she somehow knew
that we'd chosen the name of her
childhood friend? Also..."

Idmon interrupted her and continued
to resist her argument.

"Uh-h, you guys," Bill offered when
it was obvious they weren't giving it up.
"What if it's a boy?" He stared at them
as though reminding them of our presence.

They both stared back at him as
though he'd lost his mind.

"A boy?! Let's hope not. There's one
thing you Westerners just don't
understand. A matriarch is needed to
carry on the tradition and to...."

"Bill does have a point, Idmon,"
Suhvanna interrupted him, pulling her
lounge up close to his. "And if for any
reason that might be our fate, then I'd
certainly want him to be named Idmon and
to...."

"Why, Suhvanna! How loving of you!"
He exclaimed, gazing deep into her eyes
and pulling her over on his lap. He
hugged her tightly, and they kissed which
quickly turned passionate.

I didn't think we should be listening
when she, finally tearing herself from
Idmon's tightening arms, said a little
too formally, "Then it is done. And today
is a very special day. Since the night at
the gazebo, as I agreed, I have been
using the special thermometer that you
gave me, Idmon, to determine when I can
conceive. And tonight is the night." She
sounded like she was signing a contract.

Idmon got so excited that it made us
uncomfortable. He beamed like a light.

Bill felt forced to ask, "Like a little time alone, guys?" Not waiting for an answer since they were again even more passionately locked in each other's arms, Bill picked me up as he turned the chair toward the pool, overlooking the now darkening waters of the blue Aegean. We tried to ignore them.

I took another deep breath, let out all the tension, and collapsed on Bill's shoulder, nestled my head into its comfortable crook, and closed my eyes for a moment. "What a day!" I sighed, trying not to think about the next day, for the nagging suspicion that Dr. Aliamo might not be able to stop Suhvanna started to bother me. "Uh, how long do you think before we get there, Bill?"

"Now don't you worry your head about a thing," he stopped me, reading my mind. "This great big ship will get us there faster than you can blink those long lashes. But...uh...do blink those long lashes," he teased me as pulled me closer.

He felt so comfortable. And he wasn't even interested in Suhvanna's passionate display with Idmon. "I love you, Darling, I do, I really do," I whispered in his ear. "I mean it. That's what I've discovered on this trip."

"You can trust me now is what you mean, Darling. maybe the first time you've trusted anyone. And I love you, too." He murmured in my ear, squeezing me even tighter as I wrapped my leg around his. "But I don't want to burst your bubbles by telling you that...."

"That what?...That's it's not over, and that something else might happen?"

"Well hold on now." He interrupted me, taking my glass and sitting it down. "Before anything else crazy happens, why don't you and me go explore our compartment?" He kissed me, gathering me in his arms and lifting me to my feet. I felt a little wobbly, the champagne going to my head.

Idmon and Suhvanna didn't even notice us.

"Bye," Bill called to them, adding in a whisper, "You future parents," and we headed across the sundeck, around the rustling umbrellas and hot tub, past the bar and down the winding staircase with its ornate crystal columns. Choosing our steps carefully to make sure we didn't slip on the varnished teak, we passed the main salon where stewards busily set the long dining room table for dinner. The maitre d'e spotted us and asked us to wait.

"Uh-h, think we might call for room service later?" Bill asked him as we stopped on the stairs. "And you might want to check with Mr. Ildir about something similar." He pointed up to the top deck.

Good, I thought. As tired as I felt, a formal dinner sounded strenuous. We took off down the stairs. Finally, we made our way to our apartment. Bill swept me off my feet to carry me over the threshold and kissed me so sweetly that I melted. I kicked open the door with my foot. We were both surprised to see almost an identical apartment to the one we'd experienced at Idmon's castle.

"Oh, could I use a bath!" I complained as Bill carried me through the elegantly furnished living room and bedroom.

"Think there's the same tub?" He asked excitedly, heading for the marble bathroom. "Well, would you look at that. Isn't it wonderful to be blessed!" He said, kissing me again as he sat me down on the side of the shining, sunken tub, turned on the water, and began unzipping my shorts. I barely had the energy to kick them off, but when he unbuttoned my blouse and kissed my breasts, I tingled down to my toes. The tub filled as quickly as we shed the rest of our clothes.

Bill lowered me into the cool, bubbling water that soothed and comforted all the aches from the long, tortuous day. Like a fish, he slipped beside me in the tub, pulled me onto his lap, and kissed my wet lips long and lingeringly. It was such a loving, emotional kiss and made me feel so passionate that it caught me off guard. Grasping his face in my hands, we kissed again so tenderly that I felt the urge to merge with him, to share the beating of his heart, and to become as one intertwined being. I cradled his head against my breasts, and he covered them with kisses so wet and slippery that I slid off his lap beside him, locked my legs around him, and sloshed in the bubbling water that bound then swayed us to the gentle, rhythmic waves beneath us.

I could imagine somewhere out in the Aegean darkness where porpoises leaped toward us from the enchanted depths. Like the dancing mammals, Bill and I dipped up and down in the churning water, rocked by the ship and bound together by the liquid softness. To and fro we were gently tossed until, drunk with ecstasy, we felt something streak through us, some gyrating, primitive force sent up from the bottom of the sea.

My moans sounded far away and not mine. All else was lost except the loud pounding of our hearts as we gazed deeply into one another's eyes, ablaze as though some underwater fire burned and bound us in an eternal embrace. Like the porpoises, we were transported into the vastness of the deep sea where the resounding rhythm coursed through our veins and throbbed us with vibration.

"I love you. I love you. I really mean it. I love you," I cried through my laughter and tears. "Oh, God, I love you!"

"We're one, Darling. We're truly one," Bill gasped, opening his hazy eyes. They looked glazed over from what I imagined to be a transcendent journey that we'd taken on the backs of the sauciest mermaids of the Aegean. "Wow, you're such a wonderful lover!" He squeezed me so tightly that I almost couldn't catch my breath.

The tremendous release was accompanied by a tremendous tiredness. "I don't think I can even dry off," I complained to Bill as I continued sitting on his lap, unable to move. "Can you carry me to bed, please?" I asked, locking my legs around his waist as he grasped my buttocks; he stepped out dripping water all over the marble bath, patted my back with a fleecy white towel, and walked me over to the canopied bed. All I remember was my head hitting the soft pillow and Bill whispering in my ear, "Sweet dreams, Darling," as he covered me up.

Waves lightly slapped against the ship all night in the long crossing through the southeastern edge of the Cyclades as we headed for Santorini, and all night I dreamed over and over that I was taking a science test which had left out the classification of the crocus flower. Upset, I confronted the professor and told him that, "You can't leave out the crocus! That's where saffron comes from - the color symbolizing inner power." But he so fiercely argued with me that he had a heart attack, then keeled over and died. It woke me up, and after that, I slept restlessly. Waking up again and again during the night, I noticed that the waves were splashing harder, causing the boat to roll and slosh. Finally, the sun pierced through a heavy fog; I sat straight up in the rocking bed, then peered out the porthole to see what was causing all the commotion.

Bill opened his eyes, grabbed my shoulders and pulled me back down beside him. "Morning, Honey," he said with a huge smile. "Feel as good as I do?" And he hugged me affectionately against his chest. I hugged him back, trying to relax, but I couldn't. And then I

remembered the dream, telling it to Bill
in hopes of some kind of relief, but he
only blinked his eyes and said, "You
always tell me I'm too literal, but don't
you think it relates to what's about to
happen?"

"Oh-h!" I wiggled out of his grasp.
"Wel-l, yes, that's too literal." I sat
back up, noticing that the rocking was
more intense. "And that's absolutely no
help. It was definitely symbolic." I
snapped, beginning to feel a little
nauseous.

"Well nothing. We see things
differently. Take this island, for
instance. I'm interested in experiencing
what the world's earliest recorded
volcanic eruption felt like. You know -
how the Akrotirians all got wiped out,
yet it perfectly preserved their homes
with hundreds of feet of ash and debris;
or how it sent a mountain size tidal wave
for thousands of miles, created three
islands, and formed a powerful, colossal
cloud that traveled around the globe.
Now, you wouldn't see it that way
necessarily. That's why I don't want to
influence your dream. See what I mean?"
He asked, not even noticing or being
affected by the rocking ship.

"What? Uh, yeah, Bill, I see what you
mean. Never mind." I distractedly added,
getting even more sick when I noticed the
bed moving faster. I swung my feet over
the side and tried to stand up. "What is
going on?" I asked, stumbling across the
room.

Bill raced ahead of me to the door,
shoving his weight against it. When it

finally opened, the wind blew in so ferociously that it shoved him inside. "Gale force winds," he said, looking at me as though he wondered what that symbolized.

"Change," I said. "The winds of change. But I just wonder what kind of change. I have an uneasy feeling, and a lot of it is related to Suhvanna. I just hope Dr. Aliamo can handle her. It's also related to this rocking boat. What an anchorage!" I tried holding onto the bed in order to get to the suitcases.

"Yeah," Bill agreed, crossing the room in one stride, scrambling through the suitcase, and finding the suit he was wearing for the event. "We're sitting in the deep caldera." Then, for some reason, he pulled out a pair of jeans and T-shirt.

"Don't remind me," I almost snapped, irritated over my wrinkled suit.

"Now don't you be getting anxious," Bill told me, zipping his jeans. "This is our success story. Everything is going to go fine, but first," he slipped his shirt over his head, "I want to retrieve the tapestry from the archway and convince Idmon that it's safest in our hands."

"Oh-h, be careful. Tell them we must be the ambassadors," I instructed him as he forced the door open against the wind and stepped out. His auburn curls whipped about his face. "Surely they'll agree," I added, as the door slammed in my face. But some eating suspicion made me again feel uneasy about what was going to happen. I dismissed it, walked into the marble bath and splashed my face with cold water. I hadn't even finished brushing my teeth than he reappeared, saying in a distraught voice,

"Shit, they refused, Charla. Or I should say Suhvanna made Idmon refuse...."

"Whaat? Come on. She can't do that." And I started to get upset.

"Hey, none of that, now." He crossed the room, took me in his arms, and held me for a moment. "Visualize. See the setting. See the successful exchange of the tapestries. See how easy?"

"Okay," I gave in, determined to remove my uneasiness over the situation. I got dressed and met Bill at the door which he again forced open with all his weight. The strong wind whipped my face with my hair and shoved me up against the staircase, its crystal columns clinking in the high wind as we struggled to the top deck where the wind flapped the pink tablecloths, rattled the silver trays set out for breakfast, and rustled the tightly drawn umbrellas. White whisps of fog lingered over the pool and floated out over the blue Aegean like long steamy fingers stretching over the whitetops of high waves crashing into colorful red, black and brown cliffs that rose straight up to a dizzying height; a cluster of white buildings sat perched atop it like an eagle's nest swaying in the wind.

I felt dizzy. "Wow! That's where we have to go?" I gasped over the incredible sight. The wind caught me off guard, and I tettered backwards onto Bill as I leaned back a little too far to try and see the top of the steep mountain. "And just how are we going to get up there?" I asked as he sat me back on my feet.

"No, no. First, breakfast. Then business. Okay?" He asked, passing a platter of chopped red tomatoes, cucumbers, meat, feta, and other assorted cheeses as he popped a black olive in his mouth. But I opted for the tray of fruits, picked up a luscious piece of watermelon and bit off its pointed end just as Suhvanna appeared at the glass elevator, draped over Idmon's arm and looking like a million dollars. Her skin glowed, all her bruises vanished. Idmon appeared regal as well, attired in his white pants and blue blazer which brightened his tanned face. He carried the tapestry in his arms as though it were his crown jewels. I stared at the pack, wanting to argue with Suhvanna; but by that old hard look in her eye, I knew it was impossible. However, I couldn't resist trying.

"Well, good morning. Did you sleep well?" I asked politely, wanting to be nice to her since I was going to ask for something. "Say, wouldn't you rather we be the ones delivering the tapestry, Suhvanna? Bill and I would be happy to handle the exchange since you'll be dealing with Dr. Aliamo?" I glanced at Idmon, whose eyes dilated at just the mention of his name. "I just thought it would be easier, given the fact that he has the other tapestry, you know. And from what it sounds like, you all don't seem to be on the best of terms, especially...."

"And I supposed that he's already poisoned you about how I deceived him...."

"Deceived him?" Bill quickly asked. "It was all a set-up? You led Idmon to the tapestries?! I see. But then, Aliamo, the old fox, outwitted you and called in the Feds - got the SILC Foundation and the Italian curator involved - and now the three of you are going to have to confront each other? Pretty clever I'd say!"

My mouth dropped open in shock. A set-up? I questioned, wondering why Dr. Aliamo ever fell for that. That meant Suhvanna used him right from the beginning. Poor Dr. Aliamo, I thought, feeling very sorry for him.

"Suhvanna, don't respond," Idmon just as quickly stopped her and turned to me as though ignoring Bill. "I think I made it absolutely clear in our agreement that I'm not going to deal with that man in any way whatsoever. No doubt, your Don Meldon can handle this. That is why he's come, is it not?" He added sarcastically, smoothing his tossled hair and squaring his jaw.

The wind picked up, catching Suhvanna's short jacket and exposing her low cut bandeau. "Really!" she retorted, straightening her jacket and pouting her red lips. "Isn't that why you're here, Charla, to handle the likes of men like him?"

"And what do you mean by that? As I said before, Dr. Aliamo has just as much right to be at this important event as you do." I said calmly, feeling the tension growing thicker by the moment. "That's why I suggested that Bill and I handle the exchange. You are both aware of just how stubborn Dr. Aliamo can be." And how furious he's going to be, I thought, as I finished the piece of watermelon.

"Uh-h, tomato juice, anyone?" Bill asked, trying to lighten things up as he passed around the colorful tray. We all took a glass. "I thought so," he added, trying to get back on their good side by proposing a toast to, "You proud, soon to be parents!" They both relaxed a little. We all clinked our red glasses. "And to a successful exchange!" To which we all toasted a little harder, the crystal sounding like noisy chimes in the swishing wind.

But Idmon never gave over the tapestry; he set his glass down with a loud jar and began giving orders in Turkish to his servants and bodyguards who appeared from around the corner, the wind pressing their jackets against their chests so hard that it outlined their guns and holsters. His blazer flapped in the wind as he walked over to the elevator, motioning us to get in. The tray rattled as we set down our glasses with a clink and pushed against the wind to the elevator. I stepped in beside Suhvanna who held tightly to a valise tucked snugly under her arm. I knew it contained her story and her speech all prepared for the press; I just hoped to God that Dr. Aliamo would be able to stop her. She avoided my eyes.

We rode in strange silence down to where the boat waited to take us ashore. Wind whipped us back as we crossed the aft deck. Idmon informed us that the cable railroad had been closed because of the severe winds and that we'd have to ascend the cliffs on donkeys.

"Donkeys?" Suhvanna and I gasped, looking up at the steep, sheer cliffs and at the cablecar precariously swinging in the high winds; then we watched the helicopter taking off from the top deck. I wondered where it was going.

"Don't be alarmed," Idmon assured us as we climbed into the large speedboat. "The donkeys are very safe, and the winding brick passageway is not nearly as steep as the cablecar's route." He pointed high up the foggy, russet cliffs.

Salty spray blasted the boat as we dipped in and out of the whitecapped waves, churning up from the crystal blue water, shining with sparkling iridescence. I stared deep into its frothy, swirling depths and wondered what the violent weather symbolized. Behind us, sulphur mingled with the yellow mist rising over the blackened crust, suspicious reminders of the newly forming cone of the ancient volcano. I shivered. As we crossed the blue caldera, I could see cafe owners hurrying to secure their tables from the waves which splashed higher and higher on the drenched wharf. Finally, we docked and stepped onto solid land.

Above, Idmon's helicopter monitored our every move, its rotors chopping hard against the dangerously high winds that threatened to smash it into the cliffs. Up ahead, through a narrow alley, I could see the donkeys and their owners grouped around the corner.

After haggling in Greek, Idmon procured the donkeys, and we were off, up the hairpin curve, winding switchback across the steep cliffs of the caldera wall. Trying to forget the tense, impending confrontation, I got some satisfaction in watching Suhvanna trying to handle her stubborn donkey that adamantly refused to climb the steep mountain, even when its owner, running along beside it, thrashed and screamed at it. Finally, it took off, but right in the path of the descending, barebacked donkeys that raced down the winding path. Then it broke into a spasmic gallop and almost threw Suhvanna off its back. Idmon, so concerned over her "delicate condition," made every effort to stay beside her.

Finally, we reached the top. Taking a right as Don had instructed us, we quickly made our way on the narrow, brick walk to Hotel Kavalari where we descended the steep steps to the small office. The owner smiled at us knowingly, walked over to the window, and pointed far down the steep flights of winding steps to the outdoor tables where Don and Dr. Aliamo sat drinking coffee and looking out over the caldera far below. Idmon and Suhvanna stiffened, standing dead still as we gathered around the window. Idmon sent two of his bodyguards to precede Bill and me down the long flights of sharply angled steps; the other one waited expectantly to follow Idmon and Suhvanna.

Bill and I raced around them into the lead, jumping the narrow steps two at a time, for we realized that help had finally arrived and that this confusing, dangerous mission was near completion. "Don Meldon," I called out as we reached the last long flight of steep stairs. "Thank God, you're here," I said, leaning all my weight against his huge form and feeling like collapsing. "Tell me you're here to take over everything." He hugged me very warmly and reassuringly.

"Well, of course, Charla," he said, reaching around me to shake Bill's hand and then hug him as well. "The most important thing is that you're both fine."

I ran around him to Dr. Aliamo, who had been sitting at the table on the far side, some distance from Don. He watched like a hawk and protectively tapped his foot on the pack containing the tapestry. "I might have really messed up this time," I said, giving him a big hug and experiencing a rush of release. I couldn't tell him fast enough about my mistake in agreeing to give Suhvanna the story in exchange for the tapestry. "I just know you can correct it." I quickly added.

I thought he'd be very upset, but he wasn't. He just said, "Then you must keep your word. For it is your stamp on reality. However, Suhvanna cannot publish her story." He paused, and I took a deep breath of relief. But by the furrowing of his brow and the fierce intensity in his eyes, I knew something was amiss. He lowered his voice to a whisper, "I have not brought Arachne's tapestry." He glanced down at the ground, his foot continuing to nervously tap the pack. "This is a fake. The real tapestry is gone - buried forever. I just couldn't bear the risk of Idmon sending someone to steal it; so right after we replaced it in the spring, I blew up the tunnel. Now it's protected forever."

"You what?! You buried it? Protected it?! You mean destroyed it?" My voice broke and my heart sank when he looked at me so blankly that I knew it was the truth. At first, I was in shock, then I was devastated. "How could you have?" I asked, not believing he or anyone in his sane mind could have destroyed something so valuable, so irreplaceable. My eyes swelled with tears that at first trickled then poured down my cheeks. "How could you?" I kept asking over and over.

He didn't respond, only hung his head. "One day I know you'll understand. You must believe that I had to carry out Athena's wishes to never again have human eyes view such a work. There are and will be many more copies around, but the original is too much for the human eye to bear. You understand very well why it is forbidden." His voice quivered and he spoke even lower, his eyes darting up to the lobby for any sign of Suhvanna and Idmon. "And we both know that it is cursed."

Suddenly, Idmon's helicopter beat its chopping blades up the cliff and within minutes swirled into view. The strong

winds forced it overhead as the megaphone
blasted. "Hand over the tapestry, or
we'll open fire."

"See what I mean? Idmon would steal
both of them if he could. So let him
try." He threw up his hands. "Shoot! Go
ahead and shoot!" Dr. Aliamo wildly
shouted at the top of his lungs and
pointed to the top of the cliff where the
Greek military stood with their weapons
pointed and the reporters waited with
their cameras all aimed at the
helicopter. It didn't even sound like him
but like some madman screaming over and
over again - "Shoot, shoot." I stared at
him through my tears as though seeing him
for the first time.

Idmon stepped out at the top of the
stairs. I could see him haughtily stiffen
and deeply grimmace over the fact that
his hijacking hadn't worked. He
reluctantly waved his hand at the
helicopter to back off. Then he started
running down the stairs, glaring at Dr.
Aliamo and yelling at him in Turkish.
Suddenly, he froze, realizing that Dr.
Aliamo wasn't even noticing him - he was
staring piercingly at Suhvanna who
stepped out onto the landing. Idmon
rushed back to retrieve her.

I felt Dr. Aliamo flinch, his eyes
riveted on her as she slowly descended.
With each step she took, I felt his
sexual tension rise. I fought for
control.

"Come on, Dr. Aliamo. You can't just
blatantly lie. What are you going to tell
them?" I asked, suddenly aware that this
whole ordeal wasn't almost over and that

the worse was yet to come. The winds grew higher, whipping the tablecloths and potted flowers, but Dr. Aliamo didn't even notice. His eyes were fixed on her every move. I did my best to stop crying and pay attention.

"They'll never know it's a fake. It's as perfect as the original," he said abstractly, hardly able to pay attention or to notice my growing anguish.

"And just how did you have such a perfect copy made so quickly? There hasn't been enough time? How can you possibly expect to get away with this? If Idmon doesn't recognize the difference, Suhvanna will." I said, but he hardly heard me.

Dr. Aliamo couldn't take his eyes off Suhvanna, not even when he earnestly pleaded with me to tell no one. "I know I can trust you, Charla. You're the only one who will ever know. Don't fail me now. We both know the danger Arachne's tapestry will bring to humanity if it is ever brought out of hiding and...."

"Wait a minute. Are you telling me that you gave us a fake to begin with? That the tapestry Jane risked her life to save wasn't the original? That we could all have been killed for a reproduction? That...."

"Don't doubt me now. Everything I've done has been to save the tapestries, but when I saw what was happening, when I realized that Idmon knew the location of the sanctuary, I knew he'd be back. Don't you see, there was nothing else I could do. Idmon forced me. Everything I've done has been for the tapestries.

You know I'm telling the truth. You're the only one I can trust. I'm begging you. Please stand by me so that Athena's divine message can again be heard in this time of need," he pleaded, never once turning to look at me.

"Well, that's a helluva lot to ask of me," I finally spoke up, my voice shaking and filled with uncertainty, but he didn't even hear me. Suhvanna descended the final flight of steps and stood on the bottom landing. Nothing else seemed to exist for him except her. I couldn't have been more disappointed in him and peeved at Suhvanna. I'd never seen a man so mesmerized. What Suhvanna had that made these men melt in her hands, I couldn't figure out; but I stiffened at the thought that just maybe Suhvanna had been right all along. Maybe Dr. Aliamo was so madly in love with her that he was trying to get back at her with the tapestry. Now I was really confused and didn't know who to believe.

I was speechless, yet I knew by the way Dr. Aliamo continued to stare at her that he was as obsessed over her as Idmon - and as Norton had been. I felt relieved that she hadn't gotten her hands on Bill, but when I glanced over at him standing with Don, he was staring at her too. So was Don. I turned to look at what they all saw in her. I had to admit; she was glowing - radiant, her former beauty completely restored. Just because she got her story, I thought, watching as she swayed right up to Dr. Aliamo, stopped abruptly in front of him, and slapped him so hard that his cheek immediately turned pinkish-red.

His eyes lost their mystic blueness and flashed fiery specks of darkness that flew at Suhvanna. I couldn't believe the change in him. "Well, I see you're still the same, not a bit altered, Suhvanna. And I'm not surprised to discover that you're as ambitious as ever." He spit out the words, maliciously eying the valise tucked tightly under her arm. He sounded like a rejected, hostile lover, full of revenge. "You'll pay for this!" He yelled angrily, his voice crazed with emotion.

"Like hell she will!" Idmon yelled back, running to her side and snatching her back from him. "You're the pitiful one here. And I hope you rot in your grave and suffer forever. Now hand over Arachne's tapestry before I call this whole deal off." He looked like he could kill Dr. Aliamo with his bare hands.

"You'll never call the deal off, you coward. We all know that you care more about this tapestry and want it much more than you ever wanted Suhvanna. But you'll get it back only under my terms. Now let's get it straight. This exchange will be done properly and befitting the international attention it deserves." Dr. Aliamo said, each word measured and exact. He turned to Don, motioning him to ascend the stairs. Then he smugly turned to Idmon, telling him in a sarcastic tone, "Yes, of course you are aware, the exchange is taking place in the Akrotiri excavations on the other side of the island. Shall we proceed?"

"Yes," Don spoke up and started the steep climb with Bill following him. I took off behind them, anxious to get away from the tension, but Don turned back to me, saying, "Charla, ride in the limo with Alexander. You must follow this to its conclusion. It's very important," he insisted when I resisted.

My mind whirled along with the wind that threatened to loosen my footing up the narrow steps. I couldn't think straight; how could Dr. Aliamo have buried the tapestry? Something so precious? Tears burned my eyes as we crossed from the hotel to the cars parked on the side of the cliff.

Bill glanced back at me quizzically, asking, "What the hell is going on? Are they going to make the exchange or not?" He opened the door of the limo for me.

"Wh-what?" I answered, hardly hearing him. The wind slammed the door shut and he forced it open again as I crawled in, still in a daze. The other door opened and wind shot through the limo as Suhvanna climbed in beside me, eyeing me cautiously. Idmon sat beside her, and Dr. Aliamo sat facing us, along with Idmon's bodyguards who looked ready to attack Dr. Aliamo.

Bill glanced at him as though asking, "Sure this is safe?" when the wind blew the door shut with a loud slam. I would have gotten out if Dr. Aliamo hadn't pinned me to the seat with his eagle gaze. He glared at Suhvanna, his eyes alternating from sadness and rejection to hostility and rage. We drove off with the helicopter loudly chopping the air overhead.

"Wave them on! Wave them on!" Dr. Aliamo yelled at Idmon. "We have some unfinished business." He commanded him as we took a right on the main road and curved around the steep blue caldera with Idmon's boat appearing miniature in the deep water below. It sloshed in the high waves. So did my thoughts. I couldn't have been more confused, especially when Dr. Aliamo immediately confronted Suhvanna with, "I assume you've told Idmon all about your betrayal, how you used me purely for your own self-serving ends?" His words were full of poisonous sarcasm and his eyes darkened with the hostility of bitter rejection. "And all along you professed so much love for me and so much concern for the tapestries. Lies, all lies. Well, now you'll get what you deserve."

He looked away, trying to regain his composure, but a biting, thin lipped grimace strained and distorted his face. Suhvanna couldn't even look at him. She said absolutely nothing while Idmon stared him down, daggers darting from his eyes. Tension filled the car. The bodyguards kept their hands tucked inside their coats - on their guns. This was the worse yet, and I was convinced that we'd all perish in some horrible bloodbath. I cringed, sitting on pins and needles.

"Look at me!" Dr. Aliamo demanded of Suhvanna. His tone changed, however, when she feigned innocence by opening her eyes wide and pretending to pay attention. It worked. Dr. Aliamo's facial expressions flickered soft then hard again. "Is it true? Can it be that it was all for your story? Will you stop at nothing?" He emotionally continued. "Could I have been so wrong to have shared everything with you - all my information, my findings...my love?" His voice broke. "Have you no defense for yourself?"

She dropped her head, but I knew she was incapable of feeling guilt, much less shame.

"She's had enough," Idmon interrupted, staring him down, his words so terse they could kill and his blank, set gaze daring him to continue.

Dr. Aliamo sat straight up in his seat, his expression quickly altering. "Well, well, well," he sarcastically quipped, his words guttural and ugly edged, his softness for Suhvanna completely overshadowed by his contempt and obvious dislike for Idmon. "I see very clearly that you've been used to satisfy her and fulfill her ambitions as well. Perhaps there's more connection to Arachne's fate in your life than you realize, Idmon. After all, spiders do drain...."

"Unless you want my fist in your mouth, I'd suggest you say nothing more to Suhvanna." Idmon's jagged words cut through the air like a rusty knife. "Nothing. Do you understand? Nothing was done for herself. Everything she has done, she has done for Turkey - not me."

Dr. Aliamo didn't say a word. He just looked disgustedly at Suhvanna's valise which she held close to her breasts.

The tension seeped in the car as thick as the clouds that hung to the tops of the cliffs as we wound around the caldera, steeped in a white mist with only the burnt island cones protruding from the fog. Outside Fiera, we crossed the high mountainous range leading over to Akrotiri.

"We'll see about Suhvanna," Dr. Aliamo finally spoke after continuing to stare at the valise for some time. "And just what do you have to say for yourself? Do you really expect me to believe that you have any ability to be loyal to anything or anyone when you are only out for yourself?"

She finally raised her head and looked him squarely in the eye. "Back off, Alexander. Idmon and I are going to be married. I am pregnant with his...."

"You're what?!" Dr. Aliamo blurted. "How could you - knowing that..."

"The Arachnean Line has been broken." She tried to answer him.

"Then there's even more reason for me to stop you from publishing your story. Suhvanna, if you insist on printing these lies, then I will be forced to publish my findings on the Arachnean Line and expose Idmon's sister so that...."

"You what?!" Idmon screamed in shock and anger. "How did you find out about my sister?" He demanded, leaning far over to stare angrily at me.

"I've told no one," I defended myself, not wanting to get embroiled.

"Suhvanna told me long ago," Dr. Aliamo smirked. "And hear me out - this is no threat." And he held up a folder

with his article ready to be printed. He
smugly sat back comfortably in his seat
and glared at them.

Suhvanna stirred nervously, but the
dark glint in her eye never changed as
she stared back at him with the same
smugness. "Then go ahead."

"Wh-what?! Suhvanna, what are you
saying? You wouldn't dare make a pact
with such a devil," Idmon gasped, his
eyes almost bulging over Suhvanna's
betrayal. "What about my family? My
reputation? The ancient House of Arachne?
Our marriage? Your own child, Suhvanna?
Surely you wouldn't do such a thing to
me. To us."

But it was obvious from her folded
arms, her shut down expression, and the
whitened tightness in her lips that she
indeed had made up her mind. Idmon was
devastated. His face fell, causing him to
show his age. His eyes clouded over and
tears ran down his cheeks.

Dr. Alaimo couldn't have been more
pleased. He grinned evilly, and just sat
there basking in having exposed Suhvanna.

I couldn't believe what he was doing.
All along he knew that Arachne's tapestry
was a fake and that if she published her
story all he had to do was expose her
further, only publically. For the first
time, I saw the darkness rise from within
Dr. Aliamo and spread over his face like
a black veil, and I realized that he was
the same as Suhvanna, that he'd set this
whole thing up just so he could have his
moment of revenge. His darkness matched
hers. Any kind of admiration I'd had for
him vanished out the window and

disappeared into the fog that surrounded us as we turned on the road to Akrotiri.

Even worse, in that moment of eye opening awareness, I knew it was all a projection. All the darkness that he'd never faced in himself, he'd transferred to her. Oh, yes, I thought, it took two to know the steps of this dark dance. My heart fell. He'd set me up too, pretending to be my wise old man, my bright masculine, my ideal. What a front! And I'd fallen for it. He'd made me his ally only to use me in tracking down Suhvanna and bringing her back to him. I didn't know what to do or say. They were both liars. And I'd gotten caught in between them. My disappointment was complete, but no way was I going to blame Suhvanna as Dr. Aliamo had done. Oh no! Hopefully, I've grown a little on this trip, I thought, no, it was my own doing, and he'd baited me along because he knew how much I wanted the story. Pain flooded my body, and I fought to control myself. What a tough lesson. We got closer and closer to Akrotiri. I was at a loss.

Suhvanna and Dr. Aliamo continued staring at each other, locked in their darkness. And Idmon sat crumpled in a heap, unable to move or speak. However, I knew he'd take her back, even at the risk of ruining his life; and sure enough, after a few minutes, he reached over and grasped her hand in his, telling her he forgave her and that since he'd made an agreement about her story, he wouldn't back down now.

I stared at him in disbelief. Incredible, I thought, absolutely

incredible. But I had my own problems.
Was I to step in and tell the world the
tapestry was a fake? They'd believe Dr.
Aliamo, the utmost authority in the
field, not me. We pulled into the parking
space across from the gated area where a
tourist bus, loaded with miserably hot
passengers, waited for the gates to open.

"Come, we must hurry," Dr. Aliamo
said as Don and Bill pulled up beside us.

The guard opened the gate and locked
it behind us, directing us to the
spreading, tin roofed area ahead where
current excavation had been halted for
this special event. I spotted the camera
crews just inside the crumbling structure
where silt covered everything with a
white, ghost layer. The wind whirled the
ash into little funnels of activity as
though life somehow continued within the
vacant walls. A mixture of eeriness and
mystery could be felt. Trying to
concentrate and pay attention, I peered
in through empty doors and windows, where
small, rustic beds and chairs were
arranged as though its former inhabitants
still sat and slept in the tiny abodes.
Catwalks extended high up under the
broad, corrugated roof, leading up the to
huge storage bins of incredibly large
pots of every shape and size imaginable.
We urgently hurried around to the left
until we came to one of the largest
structures with a high wall which ran
along the small square, marking the
center of Akrotiri.

There were even more camera crews,
bearing insignias from CNN, CBS, UPI,
ABC, NBC, API, the Greek and Turkish

media, and others from all over the world that I didn't recognize. The reporters poured into the tiny streets and began questioning us about the tapestries.

I hardly noticed, and I couldn't answer them. All I could think about was what I was going to do about Arachne's tapestry. Bill kept asking me over and over again what was going on, but I never responded. I didn't know what to tell him. He pulled me back against the wall; and even after he continued questioning me, I was speechless.

I was further shocked by another change in Dr. Aliamo who appeared back to his old self; he stepped forward in all his dignity and authority and conducted the entire program, introducing Idmon and Suhvanna who had followed close behind him, not letting him or the tapestry get out of sight. Then he brought out Don and finally turned around to search for me and Bill. He jerked his hand to motion us to come forward. "And these are our heroes. These two are responsible for bringing to fruition this extensive investigation of the oldest, best preserved, and most valuable treasures on earth. And Charla, we'd like you to take charge of this special event.

How could he, I questioned. He must have known what I felt about the fake tapestry. Bill stood so straight and proud, and Don couldn't have beamed more. Dr. Aliamo looked at me long and hard before he handed me the microphone.

"Uh...uh," I stuttered, not knowing what to say when suddenly the wind caught the large corrugated roof, rose it high in the air, and slammed it down with such a crash that it startled everyone. But it brought me to attention. "Yes, thank you very much." The steady clarity in my voice surprised me. "Would the Greek Ambassador step forward and receive this gift, this revered artifact from the Goddess Athena." Don almost had to wrench the tapestry from Idmon's hands, but he finally handed it over. "This is offered as a token of peace, both from Athena and from Mr. Ildir and the Turkish government, in hopes that the old enmity will end and a permanent truce be declared in Cyprus. It seems certain that divine hands insured the survival of both these tapestries, for they communicate ancient laws governing our sexual conduct and forbidding the practice of incest and sodomy. Athena's tapestry will now be revealed," I said calmly as the cameras flashed; I helped the ambassador unroll the heavy weaving.

A catching of breaths could be heard when the same whitish vapor with the rainbow of colors whisked out into the silty square. The brilliant gems shone through the dust like some distant stars, and the gold threads glistened along with the phocis purple silk which shimmered and danced in the white ash. There was no mistaking its authenticity.

Not wanting to rush the moment, but feeling the urgency to hurry, I asked Dr. Aliamo next to hand over the pack containing Arachne's tapestry. In slow motion, as though resistance filled his every move, he handed Idmon the pack containing the fake. Even though my knees and hands shook violently, I fought to maintain control.

"Arachne's tapestry is the oldest surviving weaving created by a mortal. Its perfection and beauty attests to the height of human artisticness. Athena has rightfully preserved it as a permanent message which illustrates sexual conflict and warns against sodomy. While it may be difficult to understand her cruel treatment of Arachne, we can see that it has engrained the myth forever in our memories so that we will never forget her divine laws." And I helped Idmon unroll the tapestry.

When Dr. Aliamo tried to stop us, Bill grabbed his hands and pulled him back.

Everyone's breath caught as the sparkling cloth revealed its sensational scenes of the divine animals mating with maidens. The slash where Athena struck it couldn't have looked more authentic. I was pressed to imagine how a copy could be so perfect. The cameras flashed as everyone astonishingly looked on in shock; no one said a word. The silence was unbearable.

Finally, I could stand it no longer, and some inner voice forced me to speak out, "But I have some very terrible news." If Bill hadn't had a hold on Dr. Aliamo, he would have ripped the microphone from my hand which shook uncontrollably. "There has been a very terrible accident. The news couldn't be worse. This is a fake. Arachne's tapestry is buried forever in a tunnel in Agrigento where it...." I was

interrupted by Idmon, who shoved me
aside, even when I told him how sorry I
was and that I was no part of it. His
fiery eyes were so filled with hatred and
violence that I thought he'd have a heart
attack.

Then he pounced on Dr. Aliamo like a
raging lion, grabbed him by the throat,
and choked him so viciously that Dr.
Aliamo turned blood red, his eyes bulging
before Bill could grab Idmon and pull him
off. Idmon's bodyguards were instantly on
Bill, throwing him to the ground. The
Greek military rushed from their lookout
atop the wall, and the reporters
scrambled closer, their lights flashing.

Dr. Aliamo staggered back, reeling
and appearing very disoriented when
Suhvanna attacked him, clawing his face
and trying to scratch out his eyes with
her long, coral nails. Blood streamed
down his cheeks; he stumbled backward,
but instead of pursuing him, she turned,
and in the shuffle rushed at me, tearing
the mike out of my hands and shouting her
story to the reporters and camera crew.

She screamed into the mike, swearing
how Dr. Aliamo was a liar, how he'd
stolen Arachne's tapestry from Idmon whom
it rightfully belonged to, and on and on
condemning Dr. Aliamo with every damning
breath possible.

I hardly saw Idmon's bodyguards rush
to retrieve Athena's tapestry, nor the
Greek military step in and order them
back, nor the helicopters circling the
building - my entire attention was
focused on Dr. Aliamo who glared at
Suhvanna with blank, empty, eyes so

filled with anguish and pain over her words that they couldn't hide his broken heart. His body shook violently as he stood there in a broken heap. Then his eyes opened wide as though he'd seen a ghost; he cried out in pain, gasped for air, clutched his heart and collapsed backwards almost ten feet into an excavation pit. Dust flew everywhere as he fell, and I barely saw the blood rushing from his head or his body jerk violently. I climbed in beside him, screaming for someone to help him, but no one saw him fall into the freshly evacuated hole nor heard me call. He couldn't move, just stared blankly up at me, and begged me to come close to his lips which barely moved. He turned completely white, and by his breathing and agony I feared he was dying.

I placed my ear next to his dry, cracked lips and held his old head in my lap. In a whisper, he said, "I meant it about my theories on the feminine. They're the truth even if I've failed in living up to them. You will preserve them. Please, promise me." His voice broke, and I thought he was dead, when suddenly his eyes flared wide. "But I told a lie..." His chest gurgled. "It is the real tapestry. I only wanted Idmon to embarrass himself in front of Suhvanna and the world." And his old head rolled over in my lap. I'd never closed anyone's eyes before, but they looked at me so blank and hauntingly.

A scream rose deep within me, and I fought to get out of the pit just as the wind again caught the corrugated roof and slammed it down on the excavations site with such force that the white dust covered everything like a shroud. Pushing past all the people rushing to Dr. Aliamo's aid, I searched frantically for Bill. Tears streamed down my face and blurred my vision. I couldn't breathe. The dust settled and coated the eerily flashing cameras. I had to get outside. Suddenly, Bill had a tight grip on my hand, and I was yelling to him, "Hurry, Bill, let's get out of here." All the blood drained from my face, and I thought I'd faint as I collapsed against him; even though he limped along and half carried me, he somehow dodged the reporters crowding around us.

"I can't breathe," I gasped, my panic growing. "I need fresh air." He circled behind another group of reporters in hot pursuit and rushed us down the old street, past the empty houses where the white dust settled and created a strange feeling of movement inside the small windows. "Hurry," I almost screamed when I saw the beams of light from the entrance streaming through the ghost filled mist. My mind raced in wild confusion, my thoughts horribly jumbled. I was stunned, not knowing what to believe. Everything rushed through my mind - how I'd become so preoccupied with my filed alive dream that I'd missed its message about the set up, or how I now realized that the dream about the death of the science professor was Dr. Aliamo, or, or - and it felt like my head was cracking open. Finally, we rushed out the exit. Gasping and hyperventilating, I fought to catch my breath as I shook my hand free from Bill's grip and fled over the hill toward the black sandy beach below.

"Wait for me," Bill called. I hadn't even realized that I'd gone off and left him. I stopped, determined to get control of myself. I turned to watch Bill limping up the hill toward me when something caught my attention beside the roadside. I glanced down to see some small flowers sprouting from the black, ash strewn dirt. To my amazement, they were crocus. Tears burst from my eyes as I stared and stared at the delicate blossoms.

Bill wrapped his arms around me, and together we stood, for what seemed an eternity, and stared at the small flowers. Then, slowly, very slowly, we turned and headed down the hill toward the beach.

As the wind carried us down, Bill held me close, saying, "Our mission is accomplished. We've done it, Darling. We delivered the tapestries to their proper resting place," and telling me over and over that everything was going to be fine. We paused and took off our shoes. And, arm in arm, as we crossed the fine, black sand and waded into the cool, crystal blue water, he hummed softly in my ear, "'I'm just wild about Saffron, and she's just mad about me.'"

And all I could visualize were Akrotirian ladies gathering handfuls of crocus in the spring.